T

BOOK ONE

Auryn Hadley
Spotted Horse Productions

DEDICATION

When reality is a little too boring, think outside the box. Look at everything from a different perspective. Try on someone else's shoes – then walk a mile. There are always two sides to a story.

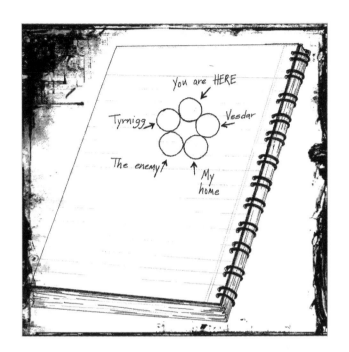

THEN

The Five Planes Of Existence

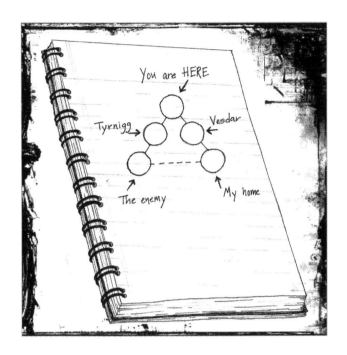

NOW

1

———————————————

I had just sold my first painting. For years, I'd dreamed of making it as an artist, but starving had never been on my list of things to do when I grew up. So needless to say, I was thrilled. Thrilled, and running late for work.

I put ten bucks of gas in my car – enough to make it across town – and jogged toward the store with my long, copper braid slapping against my back. The plan was to grab an iced coffee and something sweet to keep me awake all night. My big check should clear first thing in the morning, and I'd be set.

Under my shoes, the bodies of crickets crunched disgustingly. I tried to ignore it, but they were always drawn to the lights at the front of the store. It didn't matter what store. Summer nights meant crickets, tons of them, rubbing their legs just loud enough to turn the night into a cacophony of primitive pickup lines.

"Evening, Sienna," the man behind the counter said.

When the gas station attendant knew your name, it probably wasn't a good sign, but I adored Jamal. He'd told me once that he'd worked for ten years to save enough to buy the store. Ten years of hoarding every penny just to have a chance at a better life, and now he drove a BMW. It gave me hope that maybe, just maybe, I could do the same. Not that I wanted to own a gas station on the corner of the interstate, but I did want to show the world that I could make it on my own. That was why I was working nights, to save enough to pay my own way through college before I turned thirty, and hopefully come out debt free on the other side.

"You off soon, Jamal?" I asked as I pulled a bottle of iced mocha from the refrigeration unit at the back of the store.

"Two hours. That isn't all you're having for dinner, is it?"

"Yep, but I sold a painting. Soon as the check clears, I'll be able to eat like a real person."

He shook his head at me and pointed to the side. "Grab a sandwich, at least? It's on me."

I grinned. Who was I to say no to free dinner? He did things like that all the time. I tried my best not to take advantage of him, leaving a few bucks in his "give a penny, take a penny" tray when I could.

I picked up a bag of fruit-flavored candy and looked at the selection of sandwiches. When the chime rang, signaling someone else had entered, I didn't think much of it. After grabbing a turkey and bacon sandwich, plus a couple packages of mustard, I turned to the counter – and stopped in my tracks. Standing with his back to the door was a tall man in all black, but it was the ski mask in the heat of August that made my heart stop. Glaring between the two of us, he pumped the shotgun, making that distinctive sound.

"Both of y'all, give me your money."

My mind froze, stuck wondering what I was supposed to do. Walking up to him with the sixteen dollars in my pocket seemed like nothing short of insanity, but not doing it seemed worse. Over and over, the options spun in my head, keeping my feet glued to the ground.

"Did you turn stupid, bitch?" he snarled, tipping his head to the counter. "Money. Now!"

I gulped and nodded, shuffling to him quickly. Out of habit, I set my things on the counter and reached into my pocket, passing him the ten, five, and a bit of loose change. Jamal was pulling stacks of bills out of the till, but even I could see it wasn't exactly a fortune. The sign on the door did say there was only sixty dollars in the register after dark.

"That's it," Jamal said.

The robber snatched the cash from the counter and shoved it into his pocket. "Drop more, you piece of shit. I know how this works."

Jamal nodded nervously and fumbled out of my line of sight. There was a machine back there to help him make change for large bills. I heard something fall, sounding a bit like a coke machine, then he passed over a tube with a twenty in it.

"Ten minutes until I can pull another."

The robber grunted in disgust and pointed the gun at my head. A large barrel made of cold, smooth, beautifully shiny metal stared me straight in the face. Behind it, everything else faded. Chills ran down my spine, and I wondered if it would hurt. Maybe he'd be a good enough shot to kill me quickly. I didn't want to end up as one of those people with half a brain, unable to talk, barely able to move without assistance. Mainly because there was no one I could trust to be there. I was on my own. The man behind the counter was the closest thing I had to a family, and that was only because he bought me a coffee every week.

"Find more money real fast, or the bitch takes one in the face."

"I have credit cards," Jamal pleaded, pulling his wallet out to slap it on the counter. "That's it. I can't make the safe drop faster. It's made like this for a reason!"

"Then unmake it."

"I can't!"

It happened in slow motion, like most horrifying experiences. The thief's jaw clenched, his eyes hardened, and his muscles flexed before he turned, swinging the tip of the shotgun toward the sweet man behind the counter. His fingers simultaneously contracted on the trigger. The sound of the gun was deafening, but seeing Jamal's eyes was worse. Just as the shot went off, they went wide and focused on the end of the barrel, filled with complete and utter fear like I'd never seen before.

"No!" I screamed, reaching forward as the shotgun recoiled, not even thinking about what I was doing.

Crimson stains, the color not nearly as red as in the movies, splattered Jamal's white polo, growing larger as his body went limp. With a thud, he dropped out of sight behind the counter, most likely dead.

I hadn't planned to grab for the gun. It all just happened, but the shooter didn't care. With the chamber empty, he struck out, yanking the barrel out of my reach to slam the stock into the side of my head. Hard. Sparks of light erupted in my eyes and the world tilted, awash in colors too vivid to be true. The cheap rubber floor reached up to slap the other side of my face as I toppled into it.

Useless.

He pumped the shotgun again, and I realized he was probably loading it or something, but I couldn't make my arms and legs work - or my brain. I couldn't even manage to scramble away. My head was spinning, the aisles were too far, and there was nothing between the criminal and me except the cold, hard, shiny steel of the gun. I raised my hand weakly, hoping to shield myself from the damage I knew would simply rip right through my flesh, and I wished for a miracle.

I got two.

First, dark swirls of putrid brown began to ooze from his skin like steam on a cold morning. The gunman paused, almost confused as the substance wafted out. A bewildered expression filled his eyes while the fog coalesced and moved toward me, drawn to my bared palm like a well-trained hound returning to its master.

Before I could react, a pale hand grabbed my wrist, owned by a third man who hadn't been in the store a moment ago. I had no idea where he'd come from or if my spinning head had concocted him, but he was here now, just when I needed him... like a miracle. The stranger moved so his body shielded mine from the gun.

"You made a mistake, Stephen," he said, his voice rich and lyrical like the songs of angels.

"I–" Stephen, if that was his name, paused as if entranced, the malice suddenly gone.

"You don't need the gun."

Struggling against the throbbing in my head, I forced my eyes to focus on my savior, the man with a voice so sweet even the robber couldn't resist obeying, but nothing about this made sense. The guy looked like a myth, in a dark hood that covered most of his face and a robe that concealed his entire body. His skin was so pale it was blue under the hard fluorescent lights, like the color of moonlight. He didn't carry a scythe, but I recognized him from countless poems and paintings. He was Death, and more enticing than I'd expected. Exactly the kind of hero I'd been hoping for: the vengeful kind.

"You're here for Jamal," I whimpered. That was the only reason I could come up with for Death to be here, but I wanted him to deny it.

He did. "I'm here for Stephen."

The gunman shook his head, stepping backward in his shock, but the dark fog still oozed from his skin. The difference was that now it wafted to Death instead of me. Lush, pastel lips smiled, and Death raised his free hand, slowly crooking a finger. Stephen immediately obeyed, stepping forward like a robot, as if his will had vanished with Death's subtle gesture.

"No one will hurt her," Death whispered, releasing my wrist to grab the man's face.

His hands weren't skeletal; they were strong and elegant with only a hint of calluses between his thumb and index finger. Completely normal hands, except for the color, but beautiful. Even his nails were perfectly manicured. Not quite the way I'd imagined Death, but better, terrifying and seductive all at once. No wonder classical artists had been obsessed with him.

When he touched the man's ski mask, more of the fog rushed out, streaming from Stephen's eyes, mouth, and skin like the faucet had been turned up. It took only a second, almost as if the robber had turned to liquid, but he hadn't. His body was still intact even as his essence rushed to do Death's bidding.

Then his eyes went blank, his fingers relaxed, and the gun fell to the ground, making me flinch in anticipation of it going off. It didn't, but his body followed shortly after. Dead. The man was dead! His eyes were open but empty, his mouth slack, his body so close I could almost touch it, but the man was totally lifeless. My addled mind realized what must come next.

"Oh fuck," I breathed, looking up. "Don't take Jamal? Take me instead, but don't take Jamal! He has a wife and three kids, and he's a good man."

Death shook his head, looking amused. Moving before me, he knelt on the filthy rubber floor and offered his hand, palm up. Even this close, I couldn't see his face. His hood tickled the top of his upper lip, hiding everything but that sensual mouth.

"I'm not taking you. I also won't let them hurt you."

"Taking Jamal would hurt me." I lifted my chin, daring him to deny it, and felt my head swim.

"Then I guess I'll have to make sure he lives, huh?"

"You can do that?"

A smile flashed across Death's lips, the perfectly white teeth proving the color of his skin wasn't my imagination. "Yeah, I can do that. What will you give me for it?"

"What do you want? I already offered you my life."

The strangest part was that I wasn't scared of him. I probably should've been – of the insanity of all of this, if nothing else – but I honestly believed this creature from classical literature had arrived

6

to be my hero. There was no other reason for him to be here. Stupid, probably, but I just couldn't shake the feeling.

Looking down at me, he inspected me from under that deep, thick hood. I couldn't see much, not with cloth that dense, but from this angle, I could just make out his eyes hidden in the shadows. They were filled with constellations, nebulas, and even galaxies. The entire universe was there, begging me to fall in, and I wanted to do nothing else. It was the most beautiful thing I'd ever experienced. Even more lovely than Death himself.

"I want you to have a very long life," he whispered, leaning closer. "A long, happy, luxurious life filled with grand ideas, but I'll give you Jamal in exchange for one thing."

"What?"

The corner of his lip quirked up. It was so human I had to look away from the depths of his eyes.

"One kiss."

I should have been scared. I should have been terrified! Poets had written about Death's final kiss, and artists had done their best to capture the pain and finality of it. That last touch was the comfort at the end of life. Oddly, I wasn't worried. Instead, feeling like I was in some kind of waking dream, my heart beat faster and my pulse dropped to the pit of my belly at the thought of those perfect lips on mine.

It made me feel a little brave. "Can I see your face?"

He shook his head, leaning even closer. "No, my precious little dove. I can see yours, and that is all I need."

His voice was breathy and rough, encouraging me to do this. His lips were so close to mine. I closed my eyes and pressed into him, my hand sliding under the hood to cup the side of his face as I brushed my mouth against his. His skin was like silk, those lips like warm velvet. A moan came from deep in his throat as he grabbed the back of my neck, pinning me to him. I sucked in a surprised breath. The scent of his skin was sharp and spicy, like nothing I'd experienced before, and so very addictive.

Then his tongue found mine, tangling with it in the most tantalizing way. I couldn't help myself. I wanted more, like he was some kind of drug I couldn't resist. I needed him to kiss me deeper, harder, and longer than any man before, but Death pulled away all too soon. I tried to follow, hoping to encourage one more kiss, yet it only made him sigh longingly.

"You are amazing," he whispered, easing me back. "Nothing like I expected, but you have to sleep now."

The perfection of sound and the throbbing in my temple commanded my mind to obey, calling for my body to relax. I fought it. There, with the pair of us on the floor beside the body of a dead man, I wanted to savor everything. If this was the end, I was determined to make it last as long as I could. While his hand still cradled the back of my neck, his thumb swept across the line of my cheek.

"Don't fight me now. I'm just trying to take care of you. I won't let anyone hurt you." The corner of his lip lifted again. "I swear it, Sienna. I will always be there when you need it, but it's time for you to sleep."

My body obeyed. The stars in his eyes were the last thing I saw before my lids closed to visions of endless worlds and soft blue lips on mine. His hands eased me to the floor, one finger tracing the gash of pain at my temple. The sensation was oddly comforting, like the mother I couldn't remember, promising his care even as I faded away.

Almost immediately, I woke to a blur of red and blue, sirens screeching in my ears and a legion of voices chattering. Some were metallic and distorted, others closer. Blinking, I tried to remember where I was and why I'd been sleeping at a party this intense. I blinked again when a bright light blurred my vision, first in one side, then the other.

"What's your name?" a woman asked.

"Sienna Parker," I replied automatically.

"Age?"

"Twenty."

She nodded to show she'd heard but kept going. "What day is it?"

"I don't know, what time is it? Thursday or Friday."

My sight cleared, my eyes finally adjusting to all the flashing lights, and I saw a paramedic leaning over me. It looked like she was moving. Tilting my head, I found chrome bars beside my elbow, holding me above the asphalt parking lot. Evidently, reality had returned, and I wasn't sure I liked it.

"It's not midnight yet," the paramedic assured me. "How do you feel?"

"My head hurts." I lifted my hand, trying to touch the throbbing spot on my temple, but she stopped me by easing it back to the side.

"You were hit, and that might need a stitch. Do you remember what happened?"

I blinked again, trying to get my mind in gear. Blue lips and stars. No, a shooter. "Jamal!"

"Who is Jamal?"

"Jamal Hussein. That's his store! Is he ok? Is he alive?"

She rested her hand on my shoulder, glancing up to look at someone before turning to me again. "The clerk? His name is Jamal?"

"Yeah. The robber shot him."

She nodded. "He's already headed to the hospital. His condition is critical, but he's still alive."

I closed my eyes and breathed a thank you. Not to God, but to Death. I'd never been religious, but I'd seen the shot and all the blood. I didn't know how else Jamal could still be alive except that Death had kept his promise. A kiss for a man's life. I tried hard not to smile, knowing the paramedic would never understand.

"What happened to the robber?" I asked, trying to lift my head enough to see the store.

She pressed me back again. "What do you remember?"

9

Everything. "He shot Jamal because he couldn't make the safe give him more money for ten minutes. I tried to grab the gun, but he hit me. I didn't mean to – I just didn't want Jamal to die. He's always been so nice."

"Nothing after that?"

I shook my head and the throbbing increased, making me groan. "No," I managed to get out.

"Ok. The police will want to talk to you." Someone on the other side made a gesture, and my stretcher slid toward the ground, then the paramedics lifted it, loading me into the back of an ambulance. The woman climbed in behind me, continuing as if we hadn't been interrupted. "We're taking you to County General. You might have a concussion or a fractured skull. There's a pretty good gash up there."

"It hurts like a bitch."

She nodded in understanding. "I bet, but you're pretty lucky if you just got a scar out of all that."

"What about my car?"

"The cops will take it to the impound."

I groaned. "I can't afford that!"

She patted my arm in sympathy. "They'll want to check for evidence, but by the time you're out of the hospital, they should be done. It's not like getting towed."

"I need to call work." I couldn't help it; the to-do list was starting to form in my head.

"One of the nurses will be happy to do that. Just let them know in the ER."

The doors at the back of the ambulance closed and the siren started up, barely audible inside the vehicle. I turned and looked around, seeing a man sitting on the other side. Something was tight on my upper arm. I checked and found the guy reaching for a stethoscope, evidently to check my blood pressure. The crackling of plastic on my left made me look back to the woman. She was opening something.

"I'm going to start an IV," she said, turning my arm so my palm faced up.

I closed my eyes, felt the pinch, then the adhesive to hold it all in place. It pinched again when she attached the line, and something cold flowed into my arm. I flexed my fingers and looked, impressed at how efficient the entire process was.

"Do you have any allergies?" This time from the man.

"None that I know of."

The woman made a noise in acknowledgment. "Then I'm going to give you something for pain. It might make you feel a little nauseous, but it will make your head feel better."

"Sure."

She wasn't kidding. The drug flowed through the clear line, into my vein, and my stomach flipped only seconds later. I swallowed, trying to silence it, and breathed deeply. The last thing I wanted to do was puke on the people trying so hard to be nice.

"This sucks," I groaned.

She chuckled in sympathy. "How's your head?"

That was when I realized how much it had hurt. The pounding had stopped and the line of fire now felt like a bruise: something I didn't want to touch but that didn't hurt if left alone.

"Better."

"Good. You probably have a concussion, and you may have some nausea, disorientation, light sensitivity, or memory issues. The pain medication may give you strange dreams. If you experience any of this, let your doctor or nurse know. We should be there in five minutes."

"Yeah." I swallowed, my mouth feeling a bit dry, and licked at my lips. My eyes were heavy and didn't want to focus. "Probably a good thing I didn't get to eat," I muttered.

I felt the tension on my arm release. "Just let me know if you're going to vomit," the man said.

"No promises, but I'll try."

I fell asleep after that. Flashes of the ER and a few faces, which most likely belonged to nurses and doctors, stuck in my memory, but the rest of the night was a blur. It had been the best day of my life and the worst, all rolled into one. It was like the world couldn't decide if it wanted to give me a break or double down on the crap it kept handing out, but at least Jamal was still alive.

Somehow, I knew he'd make it. Every time I asked, they always answered carefully, making sure not to get my hopes up, but I knew. I'd made a deal with Death: one kiss in exchange for the life of the man who'd been nice to me. Death wouldn't let me down.

2

Four years later...

*M*y pencil scratched on the paper, soft and sibilant, quickly producing tiny intricate lines that made up the whole. I rubbed my finger through the graphite, pushing it smooth, then dragged the eraser across it to accent the highlight. It had happened four years ago, but I could still remember the details so clearly.

I didn't know a thing about guns, but I could draw that shotgun over and over. Behind it, the man's eyes loomed cold and vacant in the ski mask. In the reflection of the barrel, I began adding the details of the hero: the thick cowl, the perfect lips. Working with just a pencil, I couldn't capture the color of his skin, but I knew it. Four years since I'd invented him, and I could still easily recall the exact shade of blue, so pale it had looked almost white under those fluorescent lights.

"Nice," a man said, dropping into the chair beside me. "Art major?"

"Yeah." I didn't bother looking up.

"Didn't realize art students took Calculus." He turned away from me for a moment to accept a stack of papers from the person on his other side, taking one and passing the rest to me.

I smiled a thanks and looked up, pausing with my hand on the papers. Whoa. The friendly student beside me was hot! Not kinda good looking, but the type of beautiful that made my mouth water. Blood rushed to my cheeks, and I quickly took a copy and passed the stack down the row, staring at the tiny words on the page to keep from gawking. *Calculus, Math 1810.005, Professor Traland, Monday, Wednesday, Friday.* Beneath that was a list of assigned chapters and subjects to be covered over the semester.

When my face felt a little cooler, I looked at the guy who'd claimed the chair to my left. His long legs were splayed before him, encased in loose jeans that somehow still managed to taunt me with every muscle underneath. He wore a black shirt with some logo. I couldn't make it out without leaning closer, and I wasn't ready to be *that* obvious. Just glancing at him was bad enough, but that shirt was so tight, the lines of his well-formed chest were easily visible and the sleeves strained across his biceps. I couldn't help but look. Then there was the long, dark hair that fell to the middle of his back, so black it was nearly blue, but without the harsh tone that came with dye. The ear closest to me was lined with rings.

He looked like he belonged in a death metal band, but it worked for him. Then again, pretty much anything would work for him. Yeah, and I had a fondness for the dangerous type. I couldn't stop my eyes from drinking in his unnatural beauty, and honestly, I didn't want to. When I reached his face, I found warm black eyes looking back, the corner of his lip lifted slightly in amusement. He knew I was checking him out. He had to; men that good-looking were always aware of it.

"So you just like math or something?" he tried again, amazingly long lashes brushing his cheek when he blinked.

I realized I'd never answered him the first time. "Oh, no. I'm a

14

biology minor."

"Art major, bio minor? That's a strange combination."

I brushed a stray lock of my ginger hair from my cheek, feeling overly self-conscious. "Medical illustration pays decently, and knowledge of anatomy helps with getting it right."

His eyes followed my hand, then he grinned. "Yeah, um, I think you..." He reached up and rubbed at something on my face. "You're wearing your work."

"Thanks." I didn't blush this time, but I did smile. I couldn't help it. He reminded me of someone, but I couldn't quite figure out who. I didn't exactly know anyone quite this gorgeous. Not even close.

He gestured to the sketch I was working on, my small art pad taking up most of the space on my desk. "That's a little dark for someone so vibrant."

"Huh?"

"A gun with... I think that's the grim reaper reflected in it?"

"Oh." I closed the pad and shoved it into my backpack. "It's Death. You know, like from the Dickinson poem?"

"Dickinson?"

I nodded. "*Because I could not stop for Death, he kindly stopped for me?*"

He nodded slowly. "*The carriage held but ourselves, and immortality.* Yeah, that's a pretty good one." He met my eyes. "Why Death?"

Quick, think of something! "Um, I wanted to play with reflections on a curved surface."

"So, you went for horror instead of a glass of water?" That almost-crooked smile taunted me like I'd seen it before.

"Death seems much more interesting." I shrugged, glancing up to the front of the class.

My new friend chuckled and leaned closer. "I'm not complaining. Just shocked to see a pretty girl drawing such a morbid subject. Nick Voland, by the way."

"Sienna Parker." I flashed him that nice to meet you smile, surprised to see an honest one returned.

"Maybe I can get you to help me with Art History." He opened a spiral notebook and flipped to a blank page as the teacher finally walked in. "I ended up in the class for majors, because the others all conflicted with one of my other courses."

"Tomorrow at nine?" I had to remember to close my mouth.

"That's the one."

Completely unbelievable. "Sure. I'm in that one."

He glanced at me and nodded, but he didn't really look surprised. "I thought all art students got that out of the way first."

"I'm a freshman."

His eyes slowly slid over my body like he was considering devouring me. "You look a bit over eighteen."

Wrenching my gaze away, I forced my face not to blush. Once a day was more than enough, thank you very much. "Yeah. Twenty-four. Um, I kinda took six years off to save up the money. I'm putting myself through school."

"That's the way to do it. I took a break for a few years, too. Got tired of the same ol' same ol'."

Before I could reply, the professor spoke up and the class fell silent. There were quite a few of us in the room, making the whiteboard seem a little too small from where I sat. Thankfully, being the first day of class, we didn't cover any material. He spent maybe twenty minutes discussing the textbook, the Professor's style of grading, and how he expected our homework to be completed, then released us thirty minutes earlier than I expected.

Glancing at my watch to confirm, I looked to Nick. "The first day always like this? My other class let out early, too."

He nodded. "This your first semester?"

"Yeah. I'm a college virgin."

His mouth quirked again. "Well, glad I could help with your first time."

I laughed at the devious glint in his eye. There was no way this guy was flirting with me. He was *way* too hot for a girl like me, but that was the only explanation for the fluttery feeling in my belly. Not that I could do much about it, but I'd let my ego revel in this for a bit. Wasn't every day that the male version of a supermodel smiled at me like that.

"Yep, awkward and fumbling," I assured him. "That's me. But at least I'm done early today. Gives me a bit before work."

"Yeah?" he asked. "Gonna let me buy you a coffee, then? You know, to celebrate your first time and all?"

He grabbed his bag and stood, waiting for me to do the same. The best part was that he looked like he was in no hurry to rush out of the class.

"Sure," I agreed. "Caffeine is my weakness. Know a good place?"

"The best."

Together, we left the room with Nick leading confidently. That was a good thing, because I didn't really know my way around yet. When we made it to the hall, it became impossible to miss the slavering looks tossed at him by passing girls. He pretended to be oblivious, but I swear every female in the building noticed this guy. I had.

Guiding me to a door at the side, he held it while I stepped into a stairwell I hadn't known existed. Together, we trotted down, all the way to a steel door that claimed to be the exit. The whole time, Nick somehow managed to match his long strides to mine, walking beside me as if it was the most natural thing in the world.

Outside, the heat was like an oppressive weight. Typical weather for the south in the fall, but it wasn't really helping me make a good impression. I could already feel my shirt starting to stick to my back. Luckily, Nick didn't seem to notice.

"The Kharma Kafe is the go-to place for good coffee on campus," he informed me, gesturing where I should go. "It's cheap, it's casual, and it's always open."

"Nice. Better than Starbucks?"

He shot me a dirty look. "Oh, yeah. You don't really consider that coffee, do you?"

"Hey, it's the best we had back home."

"Where's home?"

"Middle of nowhere, Oklahoma, most recently."

He raised an eyebrow. "And Starbucks is the best you could find? Yep, gonna have to teach you about coffee too."

"Oh, I see. You planning to make this a long-term relationship?" Inside, I was almost begging.

Nick looked across the street to the eccentric cafe he was leading me toward and licked his lips. "Pretty sure your boyfriend wouldn't appreciate that, but I do need a tutor for Art History."

I didn't say anything for a few steps. How had he known I was dating someone? I mean, I'd only been seeing Aaron about a week and it wasn't exactly serious. Maybe he was just fishing? A part of me wanted to claim to be single – especially with a man this good looking. I definitely enjoyed the attention, but I wasn't foolish enough to think someone like Nick Voland would be interested in anything resembling serious. He was probably unaware he was even flirting and had some porn-star girlfriend waiting at home.

"Tutoring I can help with," I assured him.

"But not the boyfriend, huh?"

I plastered a smile on my face and looked up at him. "Why, you need one?"

"Oh!" Nick grinned. "Put in my place already."

"Well, since you've been stalking me, figured I should start early."

His lighthearted mood didn't leave. He just took a quick step to reach the door first, holding it open. "Not stalking. Just figured a pretty thing like you wouldn't be single for long."

"Uh..." I stopped, my mouth hanging open. That wasn't accidental! "Did you just..."

He lifted his hand. "Just calling it like I see it. Lemme guess, he's also in some really impressive fraternity, huh?"

"He's not a frat boy." I rolled my eyes then turned to look at the menu.

"I'm betting Delta Phi." Was that annoyance I heard in his voice?

I didn't even bother to look at him. This conversation was trying hard to take a nosedive. "So what frat are *you* in?"

We reached the counter, giving Nick an excuse not to answer. I ordered a caramel mocha, extra-large, then Nick added on a plain latte. Before I could pull my wallet from my backpack, he passed across a credit card, paying for both.

"You didn't have to do that," I said, still digging.

His strong hand touched my arm lightly, halting my search. "I offered."

That was all it took for me to give in. "Thanks."

An impish light flickered in his eye. "Just don't let your man kick my ass for it."

Aaron? Kick Nick's ass? Not in a million years. Aaron was a decent looking guy, but he was at least four inches shorter and a whole lot softer. I shook my head and giggled, trying to envision it.

"I think you're safe." I was about to say more but got interrupted.

"Nick!" The voice belonged to a shock of magenta hair and stainless steel shoving its way through the crowd gathering behind us.

With morning classes over, the coffee shop was filling up quickly. Clearly, this was *the* place to be. Well, this, and the bar down the street that I called an evening job. Still, this guy stood out. It wasn't just his neon-colored hair or abundance of piercings. There was something about the set of his shoulders that begged people to look at him. Almost like a challenge.

"Hey, Sam," Nick called back, greeting the flamboyant punk. "What's up?"

Sam looked at his watch. "It's Wednesday. We have that thing in a bit." Then his attention shifted to me. "Hello, beautiful." And back to Nick. "You didn't forget?"

"No," Nick said, not sounding pleased. "Sienna, Sam, and vice versa." Sam smiled and stepped closer, but Nick put a hand on his chest. "And she's got a boyfriend."

"You could change that," Sam teased. At a growl from Nick, he held up his hands and backed off. "Or not."

"My roommate," Nick apologized, turning back to the counter just in time to accept our drinks. "And no frat. Not exactly my thing."

He passed me the caramel mocha, and the three of us moved to find a quieter space in the room. There weren't many, except for a couch in the corner, tucked out of the way. In my opinion, it looked like a wonderful place to hide from the world, but it seemed most students thought it was too secluded. Then again, college was supposed to be about hanging out, meeting people, and finding as many parties as possible. I didn't agree, but that seemed to be the general consensus, from what I'd heard so far.

"So," Sam said, claiming the chair to leave the couch for Nick and me. "What's a pretty thing like you doing hanging out with a guy like Nick?"

"Calculus." I shrugged. "Sounds like we also have Art History together tomorrow."

Sam nodded slowly, flashing a look at Nick that I couldn't quite read. "I see. What are the chances of that?"

"Slim to none," Nick said, casually taking a sip of his coffee. Something passed between them but damned if I could follow. "Anyway, we'd better get out of here if we're going to make that meeting." He smiled at me, the curve of his mouth tugging hard at something in the back of my mind. "Hate to caffeinate and run, but I'll see you tomorrow?"

"Yeah. Nine am."

The guys shared a look then stood. Sam didn't bother saying goodbye and, seconds later, I was sitting there alone, enjoying what was probably the best coffee I'd ever had, wondering if I'd just blown the chance of a lifetime. Nick really *had* been flirting with me. Sam too, but I got the impression he'd flirt with a rock if it wouldn't turn him down. Not that many would. He was cute, in his own way, and very aware of it.

Oddly, Sam seemed like the kind of person I could get along with, and it wasn't as if I had a plethora of friends. I'd only lived here for a little over a month. Just enough time to get a job, get a place, and get everything finalized for my first real semester of college. The boyfriend had been a fluke. Until a few minutes ago, I would've said a lucky one.

Speaking of my boyfriend, I pulled my phone from my bag. First, I checked for messages. Nothing. Aaron had promised to text me his plans for the day, and he knew I'd be out of class by one, but it must've slipped his mind. I sent him one instead, asking if he wanted to do anything before I had to work at four, then leaned back and tried to enjoy my coffee.

I was nearly done when my phone finally beeped, signaling a response. Swiping at the screen, I couldn't help but feel a pang of disappointment. *Ran into the guys, hanging with them. Will try to stop by the bar later.*

Men! Didn't he realize that when I was working, I couldn't exactly socialize? Probably not. Everything with Aaron was spur of the moment, without a thought to the consequences. I shoved my phone into my bag and sucked back the last of the coffee, throwing it into the trash to vent my frustration. I didn't even feel bad about not sending a response. My love life was such a joke.

Leaving the coffee shop, I turned for home. At some point, the campus had become crowded with students. Most of them were in groups of two, half of those being adorable couples that enjoyed spending time together. It never seemed to work that way for me. My boyfriend was a little too typical. It was like guys always thought dating a redhead would be fun and exciting, but none of them wanted to do anything more than get a piece of ass and blow me off until they were ready for more. I wasn't a prude or anything, but sometimes it felt like dating was nothing more than a series of one night stands with the same guy.

My shoes clicked on the sidewalk as I made my way home. Living two blocks from campus meant I didn't have to pay for parking. The downside was that I got a one-bedroom shack for the same price I could've gotten a much larger apartment. I didn't care. The only thing I did was go to school, go to work, and paint. Usually, I painted Death.

It was silly, but *he* was the reason I was never satisfied with the men I dated. I mean, swearing to protect me for the rest of my life was right up there in the swoon department. Maybe it was odd that I had a crush on a figment of my imagination, but it had felt so *real*. I could still remember the exact color of his skin, like a full moon on the ocean, pale blue but not the baby kind, as if my eyes couldn't quite see the full extent of the shade.

The doctors said false memories were common after the type of head trauma I'd received, but how bad could it have been if it didn't even leave a scar? Not that I'd told them exactly what I'd seen, just that I remembered some weird stuff. They said it was the brain's way of compensating for the error in memory storage and, likely, the drugs I'd been given for the pain had contributed. It wasn't abnormal to have hallucinations on opiates.

The only problem was that I wished it was real. I wished I'd been that brave, met a man that perfect, and could really take the credit for saving Jamal's life, but they assured me it was just the body's way of trying to cope with an extremely stressful event. It seemed *my* coping mechanism was making up a hero to save me and sweep me off my feet. Kinda embarrassing, in all honesty.

And thinking of Jamal, I needed to send him an e-mail. His daughter's thirteenth birthday was coming up. That was the strangest part of my little memory problem. I saw Jamal get shot at nearly point-blank range. I'd seen the wound in his chest, and I didn't know how it could be anything but fatal, yet he was fine. He'd been in surgery for a few hours and had the scars to prove it, but he had no lasting effects from the robbery. Not even the pellet lodged in his heart had caused any lasting issues.

Just like Death promised.

I groaned. Death. It always came back to Death. I was completely obsessed with him and it wasn't healthy. At least as an art student, it was expected. That and using a whole lot of drugs. I could handle the first, but I wasn't brave enough to try the second. Drugs weren't an option for me. I needed a degree, a plan for my life, and to get a job that would give me a path for my future, because there wasn't anyone else to do it for me. After all, opiates had already given me one obsession; I didn't exactly need another.

I turned the corner, almost home, but paused. Down the street, a shock of magenta hair caught my eye. It was on a guy walking to one of the massive historic homes that were almost my neighbors. Shifting my backpack on my shoulder, I tried to see if that was Sam. It wasn't like a whole lot of guys would dye their hair that color. It wasn't red, it wasn't pink, but more like the color of a very expensive neon wine. He climbed the steps to the porch, but the door opened before he got there. Another guy walked out. Even from here, I could tell he looked like some kind of underwear model, complete with the pretty blonde hair.

They exchanged a few words and, the longer I watched, the more I was sure it really was Sam. Huh, imagine that. Someone I thought I could get along with hanging out just around the corner. I smiled and started to look away when a third man joined them. This one had long, dark hair. He stopped and lifted his head, looking up the street – right at me. I sucked in a breath.

It was Nick.

Unsure if he'd notice from so far away, I lifted my hand in greeting. The fancy Victorian was halfway down the next block, so not exactly close. So when Nick waved back, my eyebrows nearly shot into my hair. Yep, I was smiling as I turned the corner and headed home to get ready for work. Maybe my guy problems were looking up. Now, if I could just convince Aaron that spending time with me at a bar only counted when I wasn't working.

3

---

*E*vidently, Jack and Coke was a college favorite. Either that, or it was the only thing most guys knew to order at this bar. I made another and slid it across the counter to a glassy-eyed man, taking a crumpled wad of bills in exchange. As sweetly as I could, I smiled at him. The smile was important. That was how I got tips.

Women liked to order fruity drinks; men went with either beer, shots, or Jack and Coke. I'd been working at Mac's for two weeks, and I had this figured out. Bartending in a college town wasn't quite like back home. There, my clients had been older and the atmosphere a bit more relaxed. Here, I was lucky if I could hear the order over the crowd. Having a good idea of what was coming helped me read their lips, and I didn't need to pretend like I cared what happened in their lives.

Granted, I could play the part of the shoulder to lean on, too. I'd done that ever since I'd started bartending. It made the tips flow, but a low cut top worked just as well here.

I turned to the next guy, shocked to see one of Aaron's friends. I'd know the guy's bland tawny color anywhere, even if I didn't know his name. He ordered a whiskey on the rocks, tossed a dollar in the jar, and retreated into the crowd as soon as he got it, never recognizing my face. I watched him go, a bit shocked to not even get a greeting – until I saw his destination.

Aaron and five of his buddies hovered around a table one row over. Four young college girls giggled between them. One leaned all over my boyfriend! The idiot hadn't even come by to tell me he was here. Nope, I was pretty sure he was either trying to ignore me or give me one hell of a hint. Maybe both.

I slapped the friendly smile back on my face and turned to the next guy in line, making his drink on autopilot while I tried to ignore the frustration. Too busy to see me after class and he'd try to stop by work? I should've known better! *He* should've known better! And if he thought I'd just ignore what he was doing? Oh, that boy was about to get a big wakeup call.

Aaron had picked me up on my third day of work. He'd flirted all night, convincing me he was serious, then he'd taken me out to an early breakfast when my shift ended. Two days later, we were officially a couple, things moving a lot faster than I expected. That was just over a week ago, ten days to be exact and, evidently, I was last week's news. I slammed the order onto the counter, sloshing half of it over the side.

"Shit, I'm sorry!"

"It's ok, dove." The voice was oddly familiar.

I finally *looked* at my customer and gasped. Nick smiled and offered me a twenty, grabbing a napkin for the sloshed alcohol with his other hand. I took the money and handed back his change.

"Let me make you another. I just wasted half of that on the counter."

He shook his head and dropped the change – over fifteen dollars – into the tip jar. "No biggie. Just means I'll come back faster."

His smile was honest as he stepped away, leaving me facing a tall blonde. "What do you recommend?" the new guy asked, leaning onto the bar.

The way this guy looked at me made me want to throw a drink in his face, but I resisted the urge. Even creepy customers could tip well. "What are you in the mood for?" I asked as nicely as I could.

"Something respectable."

I nodded, pasting on my best big-tip smile. "Traditional martini?"

"Perfect. With the olive."

"Coming right up."

I turned to make the drink but saw Aaron again. The girl was damned near in his lap. Her hands were definitely outside the friend zone. Yanking my attention away, I put my concentration on the order instead of the soon to be ex-boyfriend. When I went to spear an olive, I caught two and decided to just go with it, careful not to spill the drink this time.

The blonde paid me off and, like Nick, shoved a rather nice tip into the jar. What shocked me the most was that he headed off in the same direction. Taking advantage of a lull in the orders, I wiped down the counter, looking for my classmate in the crowd so I wouldn't have to see Aaron enjoying his near-hand-job right in front of my face. Of course, Mr. Martini led me right to what I wanted.

Sam and Nick sat at a table in the back, greeting the creepy blonde like a long-lost friend. Well, not everyone was perfect. It seemed even Nick hung out with at least one lowlife, but I wouldn't hold it against him. I wondered for a moment if it would be rude to mention my single status at the start of class tomorrow. Even if it was, the idea had me smiling honestly when I turned to the next customer.

They always knew when the smile was fake or real. "Two Jack and Cokes," the man said, "and whatever you want, beautiful."

"Drinking when working is a bad idea, but that's sweet of you."

He shrugged. "Was worth a try, right? Haven't seen you here before."

"Just started a couple of weeks ago. You were probably still enjoying the summer break." I slid the drinks across the counter.

He grinned. "Oh, fuck yeah, babe. You know it. Hey, if you get off work, me and some guys are hanging out over at the pool tables."

"Not gonna happen. I'm closing tonight. Maybe next time?"

He laid a five in the jar. "Oh, yeah. I'll be here all week." With a wink, he grabbed a drink in each hand, carefully making his way through the throng of people toward the back of the building.

No way would I take him up on it, but that was almost fifty bucks worth of tips in an hour. Pretty good wages for a struggling college girl, in my opinion. Things had certainly picked up with classes back in session. I was starting to feel a lot better about the night, right up until the fist slammed down on the counter behind me.

"Stop flirting with every dick that walks by, Sienna," Aaron growled. "And I need an apple sour."

"For your new girlfriend?" I tilted my head toward his table while I pulled down a glass. "Seriously, Aaron, if you're going to be a douche, at least find a table that isn't right in front of the bar?"

"What? She's with the frat guys, and we're thinking about rushing. It's like hazing or something. Don't get all paranoid. She's just a friend."

I shook the ingredients quickly, then poured it over ice. "Yeah. I buy that. No, really." Shoving the drink across to him, I didn't even try to smile. "Hope she likes her drink. Oh. Yeah. And friends don't shove their hands down your pants. That's kinda above and beyond, but you can let her know you're single."

I turned and walked away, heading to the other side of the bar where my partner in crime, Chris, was handling the orders. With a tap on the shoulder, I claimed a place at his side, helping him catch up on the overflow.

"Thanks for the assist," he said, glancing at my end of the bar.

"Ex-boyfriend problems," I explained. "Needed the excuse."

"Gotcha. Just lemme know if he gets to be a dick. We'll have Tom kick his ass out." He meant the bouncer. "Guess something happened?"

I nodded. "Handjob in booth five."

Chris sighed. "I'm sorry, Sienna. Hate to say it, but thought you could do better from the start."

While we talked, Aaron drifted away, taking the blatant hint. As soon as he was gone, I patted Chris again and reclaimed my space on the other end. It was starting to get late enough that orders were slowing down. That wasn't to say they were slow, but I had time to breathe between each drink instead of a constant line that went nearly out the door.

I let myself fall into the rhythm of work: smile, mix, smile, get tip. It was an easy job if you could remember how to make a drink, and I could. Oddly, while I disliked most people, I'd always enjoyed bartending. There was a certain disconnect over the counter that made the customers seem a little less real and a lot more like specimens in a zoo.

"Can I get an apple sour?"

I turned around, clenching my jaw. "Look, you can take your damned order a few steps down and..." I paused in the middle of my rant. "Oh shit, sorry, Nick."

"Right. Trouble in liquor land?" The smile on his lips was as devious as it was distracting.

I waved it away. "Apple sour, you said? Suddenly a very popular drink."

He chuckled, his dark eyes watching me a bit too knowingly. "Yeah. Haven't had it in a while and wondered if the pretty girl behind the bar could make a decent one."

"Still trying to get laid?" I teased.

He shook his head. "Nope. Still trying to ace something I'm probably going to fail."

"You never said what you're studying anyway." I mixed the drink, putting a little extra effort into it.

"Yeah, I'm a dork. Physics major." He shrugged. "Not exactly the best pickup line ever, I'm afraid."

"I dunno. I have a thing for smart guys."

He looked at me for a long moment, then glanced over his shoulder, right in the direction of Aaron's table. "Really?"

"Yes, really. I never said I could tell them apart from the dumb ones, though." I poured the drink, and this time managed to hand it to him without spilling half of it. "This one's on me since I wasted your last one."

"Nope, not unless you're sharing." He pushed the glass back with one finger. "You take a sip, and I'll let you buy. Otherwise, I'm paying."

I lifted the glass and took a swallow, just a bit larger than a polite sip, and handed it back. I did make a good apple sour. "Sorry, hun. Guess this means I'm buying."

When my tongue shot out to lick a drop from my mouth, his eyes followed it. "I think I can handle that. It was worth it for the show." He grinned, pulled a bill from his pocket, and dropped it in the jar, walking away before I could protest.

"Fuck," Chris groaned behind me. "*That* is the type of guy you should date. Anyone that tips you a fifty for a free drink is definitely better than that other loser."

"What?" I grabbed the glass jar and turned it, looking at the bill on top. A large five and a zero stared back at me from the corner, the same one Nick had so carelessly tossed in.

When I looked over at his table, he was waiting with a devious grin on his face. I pointed at the jar, and he shrugged, turning back to his friends to pointedly ignore me. The message was clear. It hadn't been an accident.

Unfortunately, Aaron didn't get the hint. For the next two hours, he kept trying to talk to me, alternating between groping the brunette right in my line of sight, laughing with his friends, and telling me it wasn't what I thought. I wanted to ignore him, but I couldn't help but try to listen in. Unfortunately, the only people I could hear at the bar were a pair of the fraternity boys he was trying so hard to impress.

"Pretty sure it's the same girl," one was saying.

The guy in front of him nodded. "Ok, and why aren't we doing anything about this?"

"Well, the plan is to let her see what kind of idiots they are, then get her to volunteer. No way she'd believe it unless she sees it for herself."

"Uh-huh. And how are we going to make that just happen?"

The first guy smiled wickedly. "There's a plan. You know how stupid he gets over his girls. Won't take much for him to show his true colors, and she'll run. The moment that bitch sees what horrors he can really do? She'll come begging us to help."

For a moment, I thought about warning the brunette that her fraternity buddies were sick puppies, then decided I didn't care. She was dry humping *my* boyfriend after all, and I wasn't completely convinced she was the same "bitch" they were talking about, but it was one more reason to stay as far away from Aaron as possible.

By the time last call was over and done with, I was happy to see the bar empty out. Nick, Sam, and their very eerie friend were among the last guys to leave. Sam waved, but Nick was deep in conversation, doing little more than lifting his chin in acknowledgment as they walked out, looking very sober considering the number of drinks they'd ordered – and tipped for.

Chris, Tom, and I cleaned up behind the counter. The two girls from the back handled the rest of the room. It didn't take long, no more than thirty minutes, before we were counting out the tips. Chris had managed a rather nice haul, nearly two hundred dollars. When he came over to brag, I was still counting.

"Five seventy-two," I said in awe.

"Holy shit." He grinned. "I won't tell if you don't."

I shrugged. "Sixty bucks for each of the cooks, and I'll split the rest with you down the middle."

"Nah." He patted my shoulder. "Make it seventy per cook to cover my share, and we'll call it good. You busted your ass tonight, even with Mr. Dumber-Than-Dirt playing the jackass."

"Deal, but you pay them." I passed him a wad of bills.

He nodded. "Fair's fair. Get out of here. It's almost three, and I bet you have class in the morning."

I groaned. "Yeah. Nine a.m." I shoved the money deep in my pocket. "See you next week."

"Have a good one."

I slipped out the back door and turned my feet toward home. I owned a car but never used it. It was pretty rare for me to go anywhere off-campus, except grocery shopping. That was good, since getting my car to start was always a crapshoot.

I was feeling pretty good about my night until I cut across the student lot. In the evening, it was open parking and filled up quickly with people hitting the campus hot spots. Passing the first row of cars, I saw Aaron leaning against the back of his truck, his arms crossed over his chest. It suddenly felt like an extra hundred pounds had been dropped on my shoulders. I really didn't want to stop. Having this conversation ranked right up there on my list of things I least wanted to do.

"What took you so long?" he demanded.

"Closing. Why are you here?"

He pushed himself away from the tailgate and stormed toward me. "I fucking *told you* I'd be here. I know you got my damned text."

I held up my hand to stop him before he could even start. "You'd better have one hell of a good story to explain why I should care after the shit y'all pulled in there tonight."

"What are you talking about?" This close, I could smell the beer on his breath.

I pointed back to Mac's, visible just behind me. "You already forgot that brunette with her hands down your pants? Don't play

31

me for an idiot, Aaron. You see, that whole thing about being my boyfriend and not just some guy I'm seeing on the side? That kinda means you keep your dick to yourself. I'm not sure what part of that is confusing."

"She was just joking," he said, trying to charm me with his smile.

I wasn't falling for it. "I sure didn't see you trying to stop it!"

"What did you want me to do?"

"Tell her you had a girlfriend! That would have been a pretty good start. Removing her hands from your crotch was another option. Or, hell, you could have tried both – *at the same time*." I shook my head. "I don't need this shit."

I started to leave, but he grabbed my arm, tugging me around to face him again. "Don't you fucking walk off in a huff. I don't know what the big fucking deal is."

Yanking hard, I pulled free of his grasp. "And that's the problem. You don't. I'm not looking for a piece of ass, Aaron." I waved my hands toward the campus. "There are about fifteen thousand men here, and most of them will put out, and half of them are better in bed than you. We're done."

Maybe I went too far. Maybe I was a bit out of line, but his reaction to my anger was even worse. Before I could turn away, Aaron shoved.

"Don't act like some high and mighty bitch," he snapped.

"Fuck you," I shot back as I staggered, caught myself, then braced up before him.

He hit my shoulders again. This time harder, knocking me to the ground. A sharp pain raced up my tailbone, and pieces of glass and dirt chewed at my hand, burning. I gaped up at him in complete and total shock. Yeah, I was pretty sure he was drunk, but that was most certainly *not* an excuse.

Before I could get back to my feet, a man somewhere to my right yelled, "Hey!"

I shook my head, trying to make reality settle back into place so

I could focus my attention enough to identify the new voice. Probably one of his friends. I should've been angry, and I knew I would be, but at that moment, I was simply shocked. That douche had seriously just pushed me? Damn, I could really pick them.

I also couldn't stop my mouth. "You fucking asshole! Go to hell, Aaron."

The look on Aaron's face was intimidating as he moved to grab me, but the new guy was faster, catching his arm to yank him back as I flinched away. When long, dark hair swung over his shoulder, I recognized Nick. Part of me was thankful, but mostly, I was embarrassed – and that fueled something deep inside that felt a lot like the anger I'd been missing. The fucker thought he could just push me around and I'd take it?

Nick pulled Aaron away as he shifted his body between us. "You really want a fight that bad? I'm more than happy to give you one." His voice was cruel and cold, like nothing I'd ever heard before. It was the voice of a killer. "Trust me, I'll win."

"I got this," I insisted.

Nick nodded but didn't move. I slapped my hand on the ground, aware it still burned, and propelled myself to my feet. I wanted to rant and rave, but that was pointless. Right now, I just needed Aaron to leave so Nick didn't end up arrested because of my stupid choices in boyfriends. If that meant keeping this short and sweet, then I could do that.

"Go home, Aaron. Don't talk to me again, don't call, don't text. The only thing I want you to do is *go to hell*."

"Fuck you," he shot back. "You think I'm scared of this pussy? I'll fuckin' show you scared."

Wallowing in his alcohol-induced anger, Aaron rushed toward me, trying to dodge past Nick. The look on his face was pure rage, pissed that he'd not only been rejected but also humiliated in front of some stranger. He never made it. Nick grabbed his shoulders and shoved, pushing him into the back of a car hard enough to crack the tail light. Aaron hit it and bounced off, but Nick grabbed him again. I saw the fist clenched at his side, the muscles of his arm bulging, and knew what was going to happen. If Nick swung, he'd end up the one in trouble, not Aaron.

"Don't," I screamed.

Nick froze – then pushed Aaron toward his truck. "Go home," he snapped. Every muscle was tensed, begging for an excuse to pound my ex into the dirt.

Like a miracle, Aaron went. He didn't say another word, but he looked back before climbing into the driver's seat. I knew he'd been drinking, but at that moment, the only thing I cared about was that he was nowhere near me. Slamming the door, Aaron pulled out of the parking lot, peeling out when he got to the street.

I closed my eyes and sighed, leaning against the car that had taken a beating in my little domestic dispute. "Thanks, Nick. Your timing seems to be impeccable."

He took a deep breath and moved beside me, his hip brushing mine. "Let me see your hand?"

"It's fine." I held it up. The heel of my palm was raw, but it was only minor road rash.

He took my wrist, his thumb tracing a line back and forth, careful not to touch the injury. "I didn't think he'd do that."

"Me, either." I chuckled. "Who knew he turned into a violent drunk? Damn, I suck at picking men." I patted the spoiler of the car with my good hand. "Wonder who gets to bill me for the damage?"

Of course, it wasn't a junker. Nope, the car that had taken the abuse from my asshole of an ex was small, red, and foreign, all signs that it was very expensive. I thought about sticking a note under the wiper, but Nick chuckled.

"Pretty sure I shoved the guy into it." He dug into his pocket and pulled out a set of keys. "Also pretty sure the owner thinks it was worth it."

"This is yours?"

He shrugged. "Can I offer you a ride home?"

"What is it?"

"Alfa Romeo."

"Can I drive?"

Nick laughed. "Can you drive a standard?" He dangled the keys in front of me.

I snatched them. "I'm a broke college student. Of course, I can. I can't afford an automatic."

"Black button unlocks," he said, walking around to the passenger side.

I pressed the button twice since only the driver's door unlocked the first time. Grinning maniacally, I slipped behind the wheel, shocked to find that I could barely reach it. As I fumbled around for the controls to move the seat forward, Nick talked me through it until I could not only touch the pedals but had also mastered the push-button start.

I backed out carefully, overly aware that I was driving something that cost more than I could imagine. The car still smelled new, too, but Nick didn't seem tense. Nope, he seemed amused.

"Guess this means I get to see where you live, huh?" he asked, leaning back in the seat and closing his eyes. "Since you've already scouted out my place, it seems fair."

"Or you can just stalk me a little more," I teased.

He sighed and turned to look at me. "I was just making sure I was sober enough to drive home. You solved the problem for me."

I nodded slowly, watching him from the corner of my eye. "It's ok, Nick. It's just that you seem to be in the right place at the right time today."

"Yeah." He leaned his head back again. "Funny how that worked out."

4

The next morning came way too soon. Art supplies in hand, I hauled my sore and tired body the couple of blocks to school, cradling my travel mug of coffee like a priceless treasure. Times like this, I was convinced that working the late shift would be the death of me. That, or getting knocked around by my ex in the parking lot. At least my class was on the first floor, so I didn't have to brave stairs in this condition, but when I walked in? There had to be over a hundred people in here. This wasn't a classroom – it was a full-sized auditorium! Wow, college was going to take a little getting used to.

Nick beat me to class, which wasn't surprising at all. That I found him kinda was. And he looked perfect. Freshly shaven and bright-eyed, he didn't give the impression of someone who'd been up until almost four in the morning. He looked like something that should be on the cover of a magazine: nothing but hard muscles and chiseled features.

What confused me most was the empty chair beside him. As hot as he was, a few women should have moved in on him already.

Then he lifted his head and waved. That was when I realized he'd saved the seat for me!

I headed toward him, and he greeted me with a charming smile before grabbing his backpack out of my seat. With a groan, I dropped into it, then took a big gulp from my mug. Sealing the lid, I tucked it under my chair, trying to be casual about sitting next to Mr. Beautiful.

"Morning," I said with a weak smile.

"It's definitely one of those. How's your hand?"

I lifted it, showing how quickly it'd healed. "Almost as good as new. Unfortunately, the rest of my body isn't as happy. Evidently, getting slung around like a rag doll uses muscles I didn't know I had."

He ducked his head quickly, but I caught the devilish twitch at the edge of his mouth. "Maybe you just need a good massage?"

"Is that an offer?" I pulled out my own notebook and folded down the piece of wood that made the chair into a desk.

That twitch turned into a full-blown smile. "Did you want it to be?"

"You are not allowed to answer a question with a question." I tried to sound stern, but the urge to giggle foolishly was too strong. The way he was looking at me? This was going better than I'd thought.

He sat up and leaned closer, tilting his head toward my ear. "Then yes, it's an offer. I'll even include lunch if you promise to be nice."

"Hey, I'm nice."

He raised an eyebrow. "So far, but I heard what you told that dick last night. Remind me not to get on your bad side."

I groaned and dropped my head to the desk. "Yeah. Breakups are always fun. Even better when the relationship can't get out of first gear."

"Mind if I ask how long you two were dating?"

"Ten days." I held up my hands, offering nothing. "Welcome to my love life."

"Sounds like you've been dating the wrong guys."

"Tell me about it."

He chuckled, the sound rich and pleasant as he reclined into the chair. "Well, you should probably look for a different kind of man. Someone a bit more laid-back, with a good sense of humor. I'd recommend the kind of person who specializes in the sciences – it does compliment your flair for the artistic."

My stomach flipped at least twice, but I struggled to play this cool. That had certainly sounded like an offer. Trying not to come across as desperate, I let my hand doodle in the corner of the blank page before me, but my teeth closed on my lower lip.

"You don't happen to know anyone like that, do you?"

"It's possible." His eyes flicked to the sketch I was making in my notebook.

Barely paying attention to what I was drawing, I focused on him from the corner of my eye, adding tiny feet to the small bird gliding across what would-be my notes so I wouldn't look like I was hanging on his every word. Something about Nick had me feeling like an awkward teenager all over again.

"Yeah? Like who?" I asked.

He didn't answer, not at first. Instead, he reached over and placed his palm on my hasty doodle. Staring at the page, his dark eyes were intense. Not good. I felt my heart freeze in its tracks. After a moment, he looked up.

"Someone that wouldn't try to make you fit into a mold." He lifted his hand. The bird beneath it looked nearly lifelike. "Someone who respects you and wants to get to know you better?"

"Yeah?" My reply was distracted.

We were both looking at the bird. I swore I could see every hair in its feathers, even though it had only been a rough sketch a few seconds ago. I couldn't remember drawing half the lines.

Nick calmly turned the page to a blank one, but he was watching me closely. "Someone who understands about your art."

The silly doodle was too good and finished too fast. People noticed those things. They might not admit it, but it always freaked them out. Always. Usually, it freaked them out enough they never wanted to talk to me again.

"I've been told it's a little too realistic," I explained.

"It's good." He didn't blink. "I'm almost surprised it didn't fly off the page."

My mouth had gone dry, wondering if he knew. It hadn't happened in over a year, and I'd almost convinced myself it was just one of those side effects from the knock I'd taken back in that robbery, but I was no longer sure of that.

"It's just a sketch," I insisted.

"I understand." He sounded too calm, just like people did when talking to an idiot. "Just make sure it doesn't fly off the page."

And there went the last of my hopes. He wasn't really flirting, just being a nice guy. Somehow, I managed to keep my expression looking pleasant as I assured him, "I think we're safe."

"So, lunch?"

His question caught me off guard. Just when I was convinced my weirdness had scared him off, Nick threw me a curveball. "What?"

"Can I buy you lunch? You know, like one of those almost dates that people usually do when getting to know each other. I figure I meet all the criteria. I've got a physics lab after this, but there's an amazing little Italian place just a couple of blocks over."

Holy crap, he wasn't trying to ditch me? I couldn't seem to stop the silly smile from taking over my face, which a big improvement on the pout I'd been trying not to give in to. "Yeah, I'd love that. I have Drawing next, but then I'm off for the rest of the day."

The Professor finally entered the class at that moment, carrying a stack of papers. We both turned to look, but Nick leaned close to my ear as the chattering fell quiet. "Well, if that goes well, maybe I can convince you to come to my place."

I nearly groaned. So he didn't really care if I was crazy, just easy. Unfortunately, I'd been hoping for a little more than just a hookup.

"Nick..."

He reached up and tucked a strand of hair behind my ear. "Not like that, dove. Hanging out and studying, that's it. I just enjoy your company."

Great, now I felt like a jerk for lumping him in with every other guy in my past. How did he manage to put me on such an emotional rollercoaster?

"Sounds like a date," I assured him.

"No, that's not a date. *That's* just getting to know you," he whispered as the professor started talking.

This was the first class where we weren't just handed a syllabus and turned loose. Dr. Adams informed us that we'd be covering a lot of material and couldn't afford to waste a single day, then dove right into his lecture. He went over the major periods of art history, breaking it into categories, promising we would discuss each in detail.

Nick took notes. A lot of notes. He wrote nearly every word that came from the man's mouth. Me? I turned back to the almost lifelike bird on the previous page of my notebook and added some shading to it. Most of the lecture was about stuff I knew by heart. Ancient art fascinated me, and the Classical period was my inspiration. It wasn't until the more modern eras that I actually heard anything I should write down. I took the reprieve to look at the gorgeous man beside me, trying to wrap my mind around what he saw in me.

He knew I was checking him out but politely ignored it. Only the upward twist of his lips hinted that he might even be enjoying the attention. Oddly, I didn't care if he knew. I wasn't exactly being subtle. Nope, I was acting like some high school girl with a crush – and not even ashamed of it. After all, I was single now.

Class ended with the professor passing out our testing schedule and syllabus. He'd saved that until the end to keep students from walking out early. Brilliant, but most of the class was muttering about him being a hard-ass. I'd already been warned that Art History for majors would be tough, so I wasn't surprised. Sadly, I expected Nick to admit he was dropping the course, especially since he only needed to take the easy version. But when we put our things away, he surprised me again.

"Ok, Art History might even be fun." He zipped his bag closed and stood, tossing it over his shoulder as his other hand pulled out his phone. "So, is there any way I can get your number? It'd make it a little easier to meet up with you in a couple of hours."

"Sure." I recited it for him.

He tapped a few keys, and my phone buzzed in the front pocket of my backpack. "That's me. Just making sure it worked."

I laughed and started shuffling out of the room, Nick following close behind. "Have a problem with getting the wrong number?"

"Nope. I don't usually bother asking, so figured I'm ahead of the game already." He paused at the stairs. "Your next class is here, right?"

"Yeah. Next floor up."

He took a step closer, moving out of the line of traffic. "Yeah, I'm across campus." When I leaned against the wall, he took yet another step, holding me there. "You sure you're ok? I mean, after last night."

"I'm fine, Nick. I bit the inside of my cheek and scraped my hand. Except for a few aching muscles, it wasn't a big deal."

"Was to me. I shouldn't have let him do that."

"You didn't *let* him do anything. Aaron was a jerk, and I kinda knew it from the start." I shrugged. "I just thought it was nice to meet someone so soon after moving here. Not exactly the best decision ever."

"Yeah." He reached up and ran a finger along the line of my jaw, leaving my skin tingling in the wake of his touch. "Lunch. I'll text you if I get out of class early."

I shifted my chin to keep the contact. "I'm betting they'll release us early, too."

"Good."

His voice was soft and deep as he quickly leaned in to brush his lips against my cheek. I sucked in a little breath, but before I could do anything about it, he turned away, leaving my mind spinning. Just before he passed out of sight, he looked back and smiled.

He was gone, but my heart was beating way too fast. I lifted my hand to where the memory of his lips still burned on my skin, smiling stupidly as I made my way upstairs to my next class. Holy crap, how did he do this to me? This guy already had me wrapped around his little finger, and I was pretty sure he knew it.

Up on the third floor, the rooms were studios. The floors were stained with years of splattered paint and the walls were covered in windows to let in the light. Easels were spread around the room with a stool behind each one. Most had already been claimed.

"Sienna?" A guy's voice pulled me out of the daydream I was having involving Nick with his shirt off and his hands on my body. A streak of magenta hair peered around a large pad of paper propped up on one of the easels, a metal-ringed eyebrow raised almost out of sight.

"Sam, right?"

"Yeah! Hey, come sit over here." He grabbed another easel and dragged it closer to his.

I picked up the stool and followed. Nick's roommate was as friendly as I'd expected, and I wasn't that shocked to see him in an art class. He looked the type with his mass of piercings and punkish hair.

"Think we're going to do anything today?" I asked.

"Nah." He gestured to the old-style chalkboard at the front of the room where the basic info for the class had been written. "We got a TA, and they don't want to be here any longer than we do. I'm betting it's grab syllabus, get the basics, and bail. Why, have a hot date or something?"

I chuckled. "Yeah, kinda. Nick invited me out for lunch."

"What happened to the boyfriend?"

I groaned. "He didn't tell you? We kinda had a knock-down, drag-out last night."

Sam sighed and shook his head. "Lemme guess, after the bar closed, right? Nick said he was waiting around a bit last night. Figured something was up, but didn't expect that." He looked over slyly. "He did point out the dick, though."

"You mean at Mac's?" Sam nodded, so I shrugged. "Yep. That's what I get for dating some guy that picked me up at work. Lesson learned."

"Yeah. Bitch wasn't even as cute as you. Don't know what the fuck he was thinking."

His comment caught me off guard. My head snapped back to gape at him with my mouth hanging open. "What?"

Sam grinned. "C'mon, Sienna. Pretty redhead or horse-faced bimbo with a body like a stick? Not even a competition." He blatantly looked me over, making it clear he enjoyed the view. "If Nick hadn't already made it clear he was interested, I'd be trying a bit harder to impress you."

I blushed brilliantly. I didn't need a mirror to know; I could feel it. "Thanks, I think."

"You're welcome, I think." Sam laughed. "You're really going to have to learn to take a compliment."

"Not exactly something I'm used to." To cover my embarrassment, I flipped open my sketchbook so my hands had something to do. Drawing was my go-to.

"Should be," Sam muttered under his breath. "Look, I'm not trying to move in on Nick's claim or anything, so don't take it wrong. I'm just... well, I say what I think."

I turned back to him. "Nick's claim? What, am I like a piece of meat now?"

He sighed and propped his elbows on the lip of the easel then pressed his head into his palms. "Don't blame him because I have a dumb-ass mouth, ok? I didn't mean it like that."

"Then how did you mean it?"

"Look, Nick's a good guy. He really is. He's also had this thing for some girl for a few years. He spent a lot of time trying to make it work out, but it just never did. If he's decided to ask you out, I'm not gonna get in his way. Owe him a few too many, you know?"

I shrugged and nodded, thinking that over. "Anything I should know about him? I mean, if he was obsessed with some girl for years, he probably has a few hang-ups, right?"

A devious glint sparked in Sam's eyes. "He has a pretty intense temper and doesn't know why chivalry ever died out? Um..." He scratched at his brilliantly-colored forelock. "He's a freak with the maths and sciences?" Getting no response, he shoved his hair back, exposing his eyes. "He isn't the kind of guy to be interested in a quick fling?"

"And what's the downside again?"

"He can get a little dark. Tends to freak people out." Sam quickly turned back to his sketchpad.

"Dark?"

He nodded, refusing to look back. "You know, deep conversations about what happens when we die, the meaning of life, and shit like that. Nick's a thinker, and it sometimes makes people uncomfortable."

"Well, not me. Besides, he's also hot as hell."

Sam chuckled. "I know, right?"

I paused and glanced at him again. "Um?"

He put on an expression that was much too innocent to be believed. "Hey, I'm not picky. That bother you?"

"You mean you're bisexual?"

Leaning closer, he whispered a bit too loudly, "More like try-sexual. I'll give anything a *try* once."

"You're a pig!" I huffed, but couldn't manage to sound honestly offended.

"Yep." He laughed. "Someone's gotta do it, right?"

I groaned and focused on my sketch. I'd learned my lesson last time. No more cute animals that would end up looking like they could fly off the page. I didn't need to take that risk in public. Instead, I lined out a simple number-two pencil. It was the symbol of standard education, right? An icon that was well past its prime in the digital age, but a necessity for most tests, even in college. It should be safe to draw.

While Sam looked on, I drew, trying to make it exactly life-sized, hoping I wouldn't embarrass myself again. So Sam was into both men and women? Well, there wasn't really anything wrong with that – except I found it to be kinda hot. I mean, he was cute. Not really my usual type, but he had the bad boy thing perfected.

His body was fit and toned, and he was probably no more than three inches shorter than Nick. Maybe five-eleven, if I had to guess. Plus, his face had this amazing bone structure that I was just dying to draw. Granted, he had more piercings than I'd seen on a single person before I started college. I hadn't found any tattoos on him yet, but it wouldn't shock me if he had quite a few tucked under his clothing.

He had the coolest-looking eyes, too. I glanced over at him, trying to be subtle. They were brown, but in a shade that reminded me more of eggplant than chocolate. Most likely, it was the pigment complimenting the color of his hair, but his eyes were almost plum – a raw, earthy, rich shade of brown that hinted at purple.

"Afternoon, class," a young woman said as she walked in.

She carried a stack of papers, marking her as the Teaching Assistant, or TA, for our Drawing class. I looked around the room while she started passing out the syllabus. There were only about twelve of us, so a bit more intimate than my other three classes.

Instead of passing out the paperwork the way I expected, she walked to each person, handing them four different pages. It took a while. While I waited, I worked on shading my drawing and started using an eraser to add reflections of light to the metal end, using the pencil in my hand as a reference. I'd just finished when she got to me.

I set my own pencil on the narrow lip and took page after page, barely glancing over each. When I got the fourth one, I tapped them together on my leg and turned back. My wrist brushed the easel just hard enough to bump it, and the pencil clattered to the floor, rolling toward Sam. After tossing an appreciative smile at the TA, I put the papers next to my sketch pad and paused.

The page was blank. My graphite pencil sat on the lip beneath it. I quickly shoved the syllabus over to hide the lack of drawing and turned to Sam, wondering what he'd picked up. He tilted his head to the side and offered me a pencil. A white, nearly-new, number-two pencil just like the one I'd been drawing.

"Gotta be more careful," he said, flicking the end of it at me. "Can't start flinging art shit at everyone."

"Yeah." I forced my lips to curl into something resembling a smile. "Thanks."

Before he could notice I was faking it, I turned back to my things. The goal was to close my sketch pad before he saw the drawing wasn't on the page. Thankfully, Sam reached into his back pocket and pulled out his phone, giving me the chance to hide the evidence. I mean, seriously. My art had just fallen off the paper! My heart was thudding in my chest so loud, I wondered why the whole room couldn't hear it, and my skin felt cold and clammy, but I tried to pretend that everything was fine. Nothing strange here, people; just move along.

It wasn't the first time it had happened. The bird on my Art History notes wasn't a fluke. Ever since the robbery, my beloved art had tried to claim a life of its own. Once, I'd made a kitten. It was just a silly doodle to distract me while I waited for a ride, but when I looked away, the page had turned blank. A few seconds later, I heard the tiny mews at my feet. A real kitten, just like the one I'd drawn, had appeared to rub against my legs.

Living things didn't last long, maybe an hour, but inanimate objects like the pencil seemed to turn real. Five times, it had happened. In four years, I'd made art come alive five times. I'd convinced myself it was happenstance. The kitten had jumped in through an open window. The coffee cup was one my roommate left out. The empty box could've been left from any delivery. The grasshopper wasn't anything unusual in an Oklahoma summer. Now, I had a pencil to add to the list. I wasn't insane because Sam had seen it too. He just hadn't realized it literally fell off the page, and I hoped to keep it that way. I sure didn't need to spend the rest of my life in a mental hospital!

Sam finished his text message while the TA gave us a very quick and concise description of what we should expect in the class. It didn't take more than ten minutes, but the white pencil lying next to my things made the time crawl. I wanted to hide it out of sight but knew that would only make more questions. At least I'd managed to put my sketch pad away before anything was noticed. After what felt like an eternity, the teacher dismissed us for the day.

"That went fast," I told Sam, aware my voice was a little tight.

"Yep." He flicked his eyes at me, hearing the tone. "Nervous about meeting up with Nick?"

"Yeah." That was as good of an excuse as any. "Just hoping things work out, you know?"

He nodded, watching me put both of my pencils in the front pouch of my backpack. "Yep. I have a feeling it's going to be ok. Relax." He looked up, those warm eyes sympathetic. "You're going to be ok, Sienna."

5

*M*y lunch date with Nick went really well. The restaurant was a converted home just around the corner from the bar, and it was as good as he'd promised. In two days, he'd already introduced me to two of the best-kept secrets in town: good food and good coffee.

Afterwards, he walked me home and ended up staying for several hours. He didn't seem to care about my crappy college furniture, or that I only had the couch to sit on. To me, it was just an excuse to be beside him. That night, we talked about everything from ancient art to quantum physics, and all of our classes. The conversation never ran dry.

Unfortunately for me, he was a perfect gentleman. I tried, but was pretty sure I failed at pretending to be a lady. Every time he moved, my eyes darted to watch the muscles flex. When he talked, I couldn't help but imagine what else his mouth could do to me. Then there were those sinfully dark eyes that would look so perfect in a bedroom. Sadly, my imagination was as lucky as I got.

When he left that evening, just after sundown, he again kissed me on the cheek. I'd been hoping for something more – like a tongue down my throat – but Nick was in no rush. He mentioned a few times that it had been a while since he'd met anyone he liked talking to as much, and only Sam's comments in class assured me that he wasn't trying to blow me off. I was used to men wanting to jump in bed after fifteen minutes, not a guy who savored every new experience as if it were a fine wine.

Truth be told, it made me a little nervous. Not that my last relationship had been great, but it just proved how bad I was at dating. Boyfriend after boyfriend, I either found a way to ruin it or picked the worst men. Sometimes both at once.

Needless to say, this time, I wanted to make sure it worked. Nick was great. He somehow managed to make me feel like I was important, but things weren't exactly progressing like I was used to. We talked, we flirted, and that was pretty much it. The guy hadn't even kissed me yet!

I mean, I liked getting to know him, but I wasn't looking for a guy to be "just a friend." I spent most of the weekend either at work, or hoping he wasn't the kind of man who had no interest in sex before marriage. Sometimes both. Hell, I was pretty sure I couldn't stay platonic for a whole *month*, let alone as long as it would take me to feel confident agreeing to spend the rest of my life with someone. I wanted a little intimacy to go with the amazing conversations I was quickly becoming addicted to.

When Monday rolled around, I was actually excited to get back into class, both to see Nick again and to enjoy the college experience. I'd spent six years saving up for this, so I trotted into my Creative Writing class awake and ready, claiming a computer near the back of the room. I wasn't usually a morning person, and it took quite a few cups of coffee to get me motivated, but I'd already finished off an entire pot before heading out. Granted, it would be a miracle if my bladder lasted through the entire class.

That was what I was thinking when the creepy blonde from the bar walked in. Maybe it was because I was early, or possibly because this time I'd gotten a chair in the back row instead of being stuck at the front like I'd been the first day, but I hadn't noticed him in here before. Something about this guy set off all my internal alarms, and I didn't want to be near him, not at all. Of course, that meant he claimed the chair right next to mine.

I couldn't take my eyes off him even though I was trying to be subtle about it. He grabbed a few things from his bag, set them at his side, then paused, looking slowly over his shoulder. Our eyes met, and I glanced away quickly. He was Nick's friend, I reminded myself, trying to ignore how his eerie green eyes made me feel uncomfortable.

Besides, he wasn't bad looking. More traditionally attractive than Sam, if I looked at him objectively, but not as beautiful as Nick. This guy was long, lean, and golden. His skin looked like it had been kissed by the sun, and his hair should've had a rating in karats. Where Nick was strong and athletic, this guy was muscled more like a dancer, fit and trim, but much more refined. Hell, he looked like he belonged in a suit.

I was just starting to convince myself there was nothing wrong with him when his near-twin walked in. Seriously, these guys looked like brothers – same size, same model-perfect faces, and even the same overly shiny hair. A few girls at the front turned, their eyes tracking the second one's every move, but I tried to shrink behind my monitor, hoping he wouldn't notice me.

Where the guy beside me was gold, this new one was brass. His hair looked burnished and his skin was just a slightly different shade. But their eyes? I swallowed, trying to calm my frantic mind. Their eyes were the same: a green so vivid it was surreal.

I felt a shiver run across my skin. There was something very unnatural about these two. Pulling my arms as close as possible so I wouldn't touch the one beside me, I wished the professor would start talking already. Nick's friend leaned toward me, but finally, something worked out in my favor.

The professor stood and began discussing the day's project. It was a simple short story. We could choose either a memory, a dream, or something that happened over the summer if we'd used too many drugs to remember anything beyond that. Like the rest of the class, I chuckled, amused that she knew college life so well.

She turned us loose, reminding us it would be due at the end of the hour, and we'd begin discussing technique on Wednesday. It was also the perfect excuse to keep the guy beside me from trying to talk to me again. Opening the writing program, I dived right in. It wasn't hard to think of something. I was an artist who had a crush on Death. There was so much material in that. All I had to do was pick something and make it sound like a bad dream.

Halfway through my essay, a flash of lightning reflected off my monitor. As if my day could get worse! I should've checked the weather before I left that morning, but I hadn't. So there I was, trying to make it through Creative Writing, watching the clock, and listening to the windows rattle at each boom of thunder. Naturally, I also hadn't done laundry and was wearing a thin white T-shirt with a comfortable but very purple bra under it – and my next class was on the other side of campus.

The goal was one thousand words. I hit almost two before finding a good place to stop. There were ten minutes left in class, but she'd said we could turn it in early if we finished, and I wanted to stay dry. Running through spell-check quickly, I hit print and listened to the machine spool up behind me. As it ejected the pages, I made my way over.

The brassy guy stared as I crossed the room, like a lion watching a gazelle with a limp.

I gathered the papers off the printer, stapled them together, and headed to the front. The professor looked up. "At least a thousand words?"

"Just over seventeen hundred," I assured her. "Dream sequence."

"Nice. Then I'll see you Wednesday." She nodded, giving me permission to gather my things and go.

Yep, that was good enough for me. I headed back to my desk, made sure I had everything, and tried to ignore Nick's creepy friend and his creepy almost-twin across the room. When I threw my backpack over my shoulder, Nick's buddy started to gather his things, and the printer whirred again. Damn it. That was my cue to go. I wanted to be as far from him as possible.

I was off like a shot. I didn't even bother putting my notebook away; I just scrambled for the door, down the steps, around the corner, and toward the exit. Outside, the clouds were dark and heavy, but the sidewalk was still dry. If I was lucky – and I was rarely lucky – I'd make it to the Edison building before the rain started, dry and hopefully with my pretty purple bra still a secret that only I knew about.

I shoved through the door, my eyes on the clouds, and hit something solid. The air rushed out of my lungs with a very unattractive grunt as my notebook slipped from my fingers, and all I saw was a pair of Greek letters in my face. My syllabus fluttered out and tried to take flight in the stormy breeze. The wall I'd collided with was solid, thick, about six feet tall, wearing a Delta Phi shirt, and had the most brilliantly platinum blonde hair. I hadn't even *seen* him.

"What the hell?" he snapped, taking a step back. "Seriously!"

"Sorry!" I gasped, bending over to grab my notes.

The next thing I knew, Mr. Abs-of-Steel was crouched beside me, snatching the loose papers easily. "Sorry," he said with a very plastic smile. "You just caught me off guard. Not every day I get tackled by an angel."

"More like a girl on a mission." I grabbed the papers and shoved them all into my backpack, once again feeling that irrational dislike of a complete stranger. I didn't even care that he was hot. I just wanted to be anywhere but near him. "Gonna be late for class."

"Seriously, what's your name?"

"Sienna." I tugged at my coppery hair, hoping this would be the end of it.

He held out his hand. "Mike."

I took it reluctantly, and his fingers closed on mine, lifting my hand to his lips. It was cheesy and completely transparent, but the Adonis before me was absolutely beautiful – in a toxic sort of way. The kind of way that made a girl not want his lips on her. Like a coral snake. Everything about him made my insides scream that I should be running as fast as I could.

This anti-social reaction I kept having to hot guys had to be some inner insecurity, but it was a hard feeling to ignore. Smiling weakly, I tried to pull my hand free, but Mike refused to let go, trapping me. Panic started to claw its way up my spine at the constraint just as the leaves rustled in a blast of cold air. The rain couldn't be far behind. I didn't want to piss this guy off, but right now, polite was ranking a pale second to my pretty purple bra.

"Leave her alone, Mike."

Nick appeared from out of nowhere. It was like a moment out of the Twilight Zone. Here I was, my copper hair whipping around my face, my fingers held by an evil golden god, looking at what had to be a fallen angel. They were both beautiful, but in completely different ways. Nick made the phrase tall, dark, and handsome seem blasé. Of course, that was when the rain started.

"Damn it!" I squealed, snatching my hand free to grab the last of my things from the ground.

As soon as I had the loose papers, I rushed back toward the building I'd just left, clutching my backpack to my chest. Desperately, I pressed my body beside the doors, hoping for some meager shelter.

"All yours, Nick," Mike said, winking as he darted inside. "See ya next time, Red!"

I groaned and rolled my eyes. First off, I hated being called Red. It was a thoughtless nickname that said nothing about the person under the hair color. Second, it was a *thoughtless* nickname. I mean, how hard was it to think of something new and different? I had blue eyes. Why couldn't someone choose a name that reflected that? Nope. It always came back to my mane of ginger hair – which wasn't even really red.

"Asshole," I hissed at his quickly retreating back.

Nick stepped beside me under the small overhang by the door and started pulling off his black leather jacket. The rain hadn't come lightly. Oh no. The skies had opened wide and were dropping an ocean on us.

"Yeah, um." He glanced at my shoulder, the corner of his mouth twitching, and held out his jacket. "Sorry, I don't have an umbrella."

Was he really offering me his jacket? "By the time I get there, you know this'll be soaked, right?"

"It'd be anyway since I'm going to the same place." He shrugged. "Pretty sure it's not going to lighten up before we get to Calculus. You really want to brave this, or blow it off?"

"I can't. Math is my bane. I need a C at least." But I wanted to. I really wanted to do anything to spend more time with this guy.

Nick smiled. "Ok, how about I make you a deal?" He tilted his chin across the street. "Let me buy you another coffee, we'll ditch class, and I'll make all those crazy numbers make a bit more sense."

"Really?"

He gestured to the open lip of my backpack. The spine of my Art History book was clearly visible. "Help me figure out the difference between Art Nouveau and Art Deco?"

"Deal." Art, I understood. Calculus, not so much.

Across the street ended up being a lot farther than it seemed. Granted, it wasn't as far as the Edison building, but by the time we scampered into the door of the coffee shop, I was soaked. Completely, totally, mascara-streamingly soaked.

So was Nick, but soaked looked good on him. His dark shirt clung to his amazing body, and I swear those jeans were using it as an excuse to tease me. Never mind the way his long hair hung down his back, one strand plastered to the side of his neck.

We paused inside the doorway to shake off the water, surprised to find the place nearly empty. I used it as an excuse to check and see how transparent my shirt had become. Very.

"Mind if I hang onto your jacket a bit longer?"

He looked at me with those dark eyes for a second, then a grin split his lips. "I was going to say yes, but..." He laughed. "No, it's ok. You want to grab one of the couches, and I'll get drinks?"

"Yeah, sure."

"Have a preference?"

Of course I did. "Caramel Mocha?"

"Can do."

Dropping onto the sofa, I checked my backpack. The plastic lining had kept my stuff dry, but my Calculus syllabus was a bit more wrinkled than it had been that morning. Not that it mattered, I thought, dropping my things on the coffee table. I just needed to be able to see the test dates.

I also checked my shirt again and wiped at the smudges under my eyes. I probably looked like a mess, but unlike most twenty-something girls, I didn't carry a mirror with me. My shirt, on the other hand, was a tragedy. The old, thin tee was wet nearly to my navel in a large V from my neck down. I should've zipped the jacket.

"Your dessert," Nick teased, placing the drink before me. He had a simple cup of black coffee. "So how do you know Mike?"

"I don't. I just ran smack into him while trying to beat the rain. Literally."

He nodded slowly, his eyes scanning me. "I grew up with him. Guy's an ass. Just thought I'd give you the head's up."

"Pretty much the impression I got. He was pulling out all the cheesedick moves."

"The hand kiss?"

I nodded. "Yeah, after helping to grab everything I dropped. Seemed like he expected me to just fall down and worship him or something."

Nick's jaw clenched. It lasted only a second, but I saw it. "If you're into that sort of thing, I guess. Look, he, um... He has a reputation."

"Ah. Can't say I'm really shocked."

"And a thing for redheads. Just figured you should know. Rape culture and all that." Nick grabbed his cup, took a long sip, then changed the subject. "So, what's got you stumped on calculus?"

"Well, I understand the part with numbers. The rest?"

Leaning back, he grinned. "Right. This is probably going to take more than an hour. How about we start with art, and I can meet up with you later this evening for calculus?"

"Uh." My witty responses abandoned me. "Yeah. Sure."

"Great. Your place, or mine?" He flashed me another of those panty-dropping smiles he did so well. "I'm pretty sure I'm not a stalker, but you might be."

I'd only accused him of that twice. "How about yours? I mean, since you've already been to my place, it only seems fair."

He looked at me again. It was like he could see right through me and was judging something. His face was a little too serious, and the set of his eyebrows made me think he was debating with himself. "You aren't intimidated to be alone with a bunch of guys?"

"To learn calculus? If you can really make this crap turn into something other than gibberish, I'll brave Sam's underwear on the chairs."

"Nothing like that. Promise. If you're not sure, I get it, but yeah." He nodded at my Art History book. "Fine Arts credits are kicking my ass."

"It's cool, Nick. Besides, I'm kinda curious to see y'all's place. What time do you want me there?"

"Six?" He leaned over and lifted a damp lock of hair behind my shoulder. "If you show up in purple, I might even be convinced to whip up dinner and make it a date." So, evidently, he had noticed the transparency of my shirt.

"Decide you've gotten to know me well enough?" Please, oh please!

Never mind that Nick wanted to cook me dinner? Not buy, not take me to, but cook for me? And the D word? A date with *him?* If I was lucky, that'd lead to a different D word. I certainly wouldn't turn down rolling in bed with *him.*

I had to be setting myself up for the biggest let down of the century - or maybe this was just how things worked in college. You know, a little studying, a casual hookup, and never hear from him again. But with the kind of guys I usually dated? Yeah. A casual hookup with a man who looked like sin incarnate was still a step up. Never mind that he'd been talking to me for half a week now. That was longer than some relationships I'd had, so would it still count as casual?

"Yep," Nick said. "Dinner and calculus. See, I'm a real catch."

His dark eyes met mine. The look was gentle but protective, and maybe a bit feral. He was all man, but nothing about how he'd acted so far set off my warning bells, unlike those other guys. Nick treated me with so much more respect than Aaron ever had. Besides, it was two blocks. If he went crazy, I'd be out the door and jogging like the devil was on my ass. That, or I'd end up in his bed. Let's be honest here, the second was more likely.

So what to wear? How the hell was I supposed to impress Mr. Beautiful? Kinky lingerie? I had none. Super-sexy short skirt? Dirty; I only had one of those. Jeans and a t-shirt. Yeah, that I could do.

He must have seen my mind whirling. "Just promise you won't change shirts, I'm getting fond of that one."

"Deal." I nearly sighed in relief. Jeans and t-shirt it was. "So. Art Deco?"

I grabbed the book and flipped it open, pointing out the nuances between the two styles. Nick asked question after question, picking apart the pieces as if he knew them. There was just something sexy about a man who liked to learn. Even better, he honestly seemed interested in my favorite subject.

He shifted closer, pointing at pictures while we talked.

Eventually, the book ended up in his lap with me leaning a little closer than I should. His arm rested on the back of the sofa casually, and his broad pecs were just inches from my face. Geometric patterns and bold colors slowly began to take a back seat to the unique spicy scent of him and the heat radiating from his damp shirt.

He knew it, too. I was probably acting like a desperate bimbo, but damn. When a man this good-looking – who didn't seem to be a complete douche – wanted to talk about my favorite subject, I may have turned into a little bit of a nerd. Not much. Ok, maybe a lot. It was like my tongue removed any connection to my brain and took on a life of its own. We went from Art Deco to Renaissance, slowly working to ancient history. Flipping back, page after page, I ran off at the mouth, discussing the nuances and inspiration for each, and Nick soaked it all in.

"The Ishtar Gate." My finger pressed into the picture. "Probably one of the most amazing things I've heard of. Glazed bricks and bas-relief. What I wouldn't give to see it in person."

"Which one?" His fingers toyed with the hair laying between my shoulders, nearly distracting me enough to miss the question.

I turned to look at him slowly. "The reconstruction in Berlin, not the replica in Iraq."

"Yeah." He smiled weakly. "I thought Art History was going to be about history, not stuff from a couple of decades ago. I love the old stuff, but the new eras? It all just blends together."

"The early twentieth century is not 'just a few decades ago.' It's a century ago!"

He grinned and shrugged. "So? It still looks the same."

I shook my head. "Nope. Art Deco is the industrial age. Nothing but modern designs, like the Chrysler Building. Art Nouveau is all organic and flowing. It came from the decades before."

"So the new is the old, and the decorative is the modern. I can do that." Nick pushed the book closed. "You're good at this, dove."

I laughed and pulled myself back to my side of the couch, deciding I liked the nickname. It wasn't the first time he'd used it. "You're so full of shit."

"Usually. So, dinner... Anything I should know about before I make big plans? You a vegetarian?"

"Nope. I'll eat just about anything that isn't mac 'n cheese. College diet, you know. I've been on it since I graduated high school."

"Pretty sure I can top that." He glanced at his watch. "You have another class?"

I shook my head. "Nah. Done for the day."

"Me too. You want another one of those super sweet things you pretend is coffee?"

"My turn to buy." I didn't want to seem like a greedy bitch, right? The least I could do was take my turn.

Nick had other plans. "Don't bruise my ego, Sia. I'm pulling the awesome gentleman thing here. Jacket for the rain and a coffee for a pretty girl."

Yep, that was it. I blushed. Not only had he called me pretty again, he'd also either messed up my name or just given me the first nice nickname I'd ever had. I managed to stammer something that sounded like an acceptance and excused myself quickly, heading to the ladies room.

When I pushed through the swinging door, my eyes went straight to the mirror. I'd just been caught in the rain with a drop-dead gorgeous man who'd just called me pretty. Why hadn't I checked to see how I looked before now? Because before now, he just wanted to know about Art History. It'd been little more than a way to blow off a class I hated and hang out with a man that had been sending too many just-friend vibes in between his flirting.

Now? I leaned into the mirror. Ok, it wasn't too bad. My mascara was smudged, but it looked more like a really sultry smoky eye and not like a drowned rat. The rain had tamed my hair a bit, and I looked rather ok. In fact, I looked like a typical college girl wearing a jacket that obviously was too big and a shirt that had dried enough to make my purple bra little more than a hint. I kinda looked good.

Walking back to our couch, I couldn't wipe the smile from my face. Maybe I needed to get stuck in the rain more often.

6

That evening, I jogged across the street, dodging the light traffic easily, and stepped through the pretty white picket fence. I was five minutes early. Enough to make it seem I was punctual, but not enough to come off as overly eager to see Nick again. I was, but there was no reason to let him know that.

The place was a lot nicer up close. That wasn't the only thing that was nicer. Heading to the front door, I couldn't miss the car parked outside the detached garage. I wasn't sure, but that looked like a little Porsche emblem. Nick's car had been really nice, too. Evidently, money wasn't a problem for these guys. I sighed, hoping to calm the nerves flipping in my gut. Calculus. I just needed to learn calculus. Anything else was just icing on the cake, right?

At the front door, I tapped gently, seeing something moving behind the beveled glass. It grew larger, and the handle clicked before the door swung open. On the other side, my worst nightmare greeted me. Unconsciously, I took two steps back. It was Nick's creepy friend.

"Can I help you?" he asked.

"Uh." Great. Perfect time to stammer, Sienna. "Yeah, Nick in?"

"Nick!" he yelled over his shoulder. "Company!"

Sam peeked around the corner. "Nice. Let her in, Luke."

Stepping back, he did, lifting an arm to welcome me into their place, but his eyes followed me like a hawk watching a mouse. "Thanks," I muttered, trying to stay just out of his reach.

"Yeah. How do you know Nick, anyway?"

I held up my textbook like a weak shield. "Calculus. Talked him into explaining it."

Sam dropped a hand on Luke's shoulder, almost like he was holding him back. "Nick's in the kitchen. Be nice, man."

I looked up the hall. "Where's the kitchen?"

"Show her," Luke grumbled, closing the door and heading into the room Sam had just vacated.

From the sounds, someone was gaming. The rattle of digital guns coming from the speakers was rather distinct. Growing up, I couldn't remember a time when I hadn't heard that. Granted, having foster brothers meant shooters were on the top of their list of entertainment. Peeking into the room, I saw a massive television, couches placed around it, and Luke sitting down to reclaim the controls.

Sam was looking in the same direction. When Luke groaned, he chuckled and gestured down the hall. "Yeah, that's what happens when you walk away mid-game, dude." Then he smiled at me. "Kitchen. Lemme show ya."

"Thanks."

The house was huge, which didn't help my nerves any. We walked past what had once been a parlor, at least one other living room, and down a long narrow hall before turning into a formal dining area – complete with the fancy furniture – and into the kitchen. Nick turned at the sound of our steps and smiled.

"Spaghetti ok?" he asked.

"Sounds perfect."

Sam slapped Nick on the shoulder. "Sounds like a date," he teased.

Nick shrugged. "Was hoping to make it like that, but there's knowledge on the line. Sia's calculus challenged." That was the second time he'd shortened my name like that.

"Then you're the one to teach her." Sam smiled at me. "Nick's got a thing for numbers."

"She's got a thing for art," Nick said.

That got Sam's attention. "You just draw?"

"Lately. I suck at poetry, but I enjoy writing, painting, and music. Not that I can sing, mind you, but did the band thing in school." Did I really just admit to that? Quick, save face. "I'm a certified art dork." Nope, that didn't do it.

"You ever go to the Thursday poetry thing at Cool Beans?" Sam leaned against the counter casually, but the corner of his lip was slowly moving higher. "Want to?"

"Back off," Nick teased. "Go find your own."

Sam gasped and shoved his hands over his heart dramatically. "You're killing me, man. Here I was, trying to flirt with the prettiest girl in the house, and you're totally cockblocking me."

"Yeah." Nick waved a tomato paste covered ladle at him. "Now I'm threatening you. Out, or you'll be cleaning. Tell Luke to stop being a dick."

"Luke's always a dick." Sam grinned. "Have fun, Sienna." Then he vanished around the corner.

"You tell them I was coming?" I asked when he was gone.

"Maybe." Nick turned his attention to the meal. "It's entirely possible that I told them if they acted like frat boys I would kill them in their sleep. Why do you ask?"

"Just curious." I shrugged, hoping I didn't look as nervous as I felt. "So, I guess it's dinner first, then my quest for knowledge?"

"Definitely."

He moved a pot off the burner and started turning dials on the stove. While he worked, I may have watched his tight shirt flex a bit. It was entirely possible that I was distracted by the curve of his ass. I felt like someone had taken my idea of the perfect man and put it all together in Nick. Granted, beauty was only skin deep, but it was a very nice skin to look at. The only thing I couldn't understand was why he was interested in me at all.

Here I was, having dinner with the kind of guy that wars were started over. Ok, maybe it was only women's beauty that got blamed for such things. I honestly couldn't remember, not with his incredible arms flexing as he drained the water from the pasta. And he cooked! The only thing better would be if he painted too. Holy crap, this guy was just amazing, and if I wasn't careful, I would definitely screw this up.

"So," Nick said, dragging my focus away from his muscles and back to the present. "Big choice of the evening. That massive table in the dining room or do you want to eat in the library?"

"Y'all have a library?" No fucking way.

"Yeah. It's a bit sparse, but technically it counts."

"You sold me with library," I admitted. "I'm such a nerd."

"I have a weakness for nerds. Besides, it's a bit less ostentatious. Follow me."

He grabbed two plates, both heaped full, and led me through an archway into a dimly lit room. It was the curved space at the front corner of the house. Made up almost entirely of windows, every open section of wall was lined in shelves. Only a few held books, a light coating of dust indicating that this room might be used less than the others. A small table was set in the corner, covered with a cloth. A bottle of soda and two glasses waited on top. Oddly, that was the touch that made my evening feel real: not wine, but soda.

"How'd you know I'd pick the library?"

Nick laughed and set the plates down. "I took a guess." He waited for me to claim a chair then slipped into the opposite seat. "Truth be told, I was hoping. This is the only room that isn't right off the main hall, and the guys don't need much of an excuse to give me hell."

"What, don't like your roomies?"

"Nah." He dismissed that by digging into his meal. "They're good. I just don't usually invite over beautiful women."

I couldn't help it. My brain and my mouth had short-circuited sometime earlier from nerves, and I still hadn't gotten around to fixing it. "Why not?"

He shoved a forkful of noodles into his face to delay his answer. Those dark eyes sparkled mischievously. "Earth girls aren't usually my type."

I nearly choked with laughter. "Oh, I see. So you *are* an alien. That's what's wrong with you. Guess you have a fetish for green-skinned girls, huh?"

Nick shrugged and reached for his glass. "That gonna bother you?" His tone was just a bit too serious. This guy had to think I was a complete nutcase. Granted, I hadn't exactly given the best impression so far.

"Nope. I figure anyone who's as hot as you had to be hiding something." Stupid mouth. Stupid, stupid mouth!

Thankfully, Nick didn't seem to mind, not from the smile on his face. "Everyone's hiding something, aren't they? Nah, the truth is that I'm just not good at the whole casual thing most people are into."

I nodded, trying to keep the panic from showing. I was in the process of crashing and burning so hard. "Yeah, I kinda get that impression from you."

He grabbed a piece of garlic bread and bit into it, looking completely unconcerned. He was either a saint, desperate, or a really good actor. "Well, now that you know mine, what's your big secret?" he asked.

Make or break time, right? Hopefully, he wouldn't run away screaming before we'd even finished eating. My big secret wasn't something I typically broke out on the first date, but he'd offered up something, so I wanted to do the same.

"I was a local media sensation as a kid."

"Yeah? Why?"

I took a long drink, the bubbles tickling my nose, but my mouth had gone dry. "Um, about nineteen years ago now, this kid was just abandoned at a fire station. No one knew her name, no records to track, nothing. Well, that was me. Seems I was just dumped off in the middle of No-where's-ville, Oklahoma when I was five."

"That sucks," Nick said. "So you do the foster system and all that crap?"

"Yeah. Even got the fake birthday to go with my lack of identity. They said I was addicted to something, but I don't remember any of that. Literally no memories of anything from before I showed up at that fire station." I shrugged, trying to keep it casual. "Kinda made me into a local pariah."

"How so?" Thankfully, he wasn't running away screaming. Not yet, at least. Or maybe I was more worried about my past than he was.

"It was all over the news, and you know how kids are. Their parents weren't really any better. Every big anniversary of it, they ran it again, making sure my life was hell. Nothing like having the whole town think of you as some kind of pity case to give a girl a confidence boost, you know?" Spaghetti into mouth. Impossible to talk with my mouth full. No need to come across as damaged goods right upfront.

"You ever find out what happened?" He seemed honestly interested.

"Nope. The trail was dead before they started looking, and I couldn't tell them a single thing, not even my name. CPS used my crazy blood tests to get legal custody, and I spent like a month in the hospital getting off whatever I'd been hooked on. They said it wasn't the usual stuff, so I dunno, maybe some junkies were feeding me designer drugs to test them or something. Never played with drugs because of it."

"Smart call." He smiled. "That shit will mess you up, dove. It's basically my area of expertise."

"Drugs?"

"No. Well, yes. I mean the whole chemistry thing and what can kill you." He leaned back, watching me. "I have a fascination with the death of the human body, which is why I got into the sciences. That's my big secret. I want to understand what it is that draws the line between life and death. Science has a big hole in the understanding of it all."

"So you're aiming to do research?"

"Maybe. You don't think that's weird?"

I shrugged. "Not really. I guess no more than you think me being a changeling is weird."

His eyebrows raised. "Not a word you hear often. You read fantasy too, huh?"

"A bit. Maybe a lot." Ok, so this was going better than I'd expected. All the rough stuff was out there, and we'd moved on to books. Nice. "It goes with the whole 'my parents didn't want me' thing. I was sure I was a fairy princess for a while."

Nick laughed. "No way. Fairies are evil, nasty things. Well, they used to be."

"Oh?"

He paused, his body tensing slightly. "You know, Brothers Grimm. Disney made them all happy and fluffy with butterfly wings. In folklore, they're nasty and conniving with bad attitudes, and that sounds nothing like you."

"Yeah, I grew up sitting behind a TV, watching the cartoons. Always liked Tinkerbell best, though. So, you read, too?"

"Voraciously."

We finished dinner over a discussion of books. Nick really was well-read. He'd devoured the classics, from Jane Eyre to Dracula, and was more than happy to brag about his virtual library. That was his excuse for the bare shelves – the ease of digital books – claiming he only bought hard copies of the ones he liked. Considering there were at least fifty books in the room, he seemed to like a lot.

After dinner, we moved into the parlor, textbooks in hand, and sat much too close. He started at the beginning, making sure I understood everything about calculus from the strange symbols to the reason behind the formulas. Slowly, very slowly, it all started to sink in. The way he phrased it turned the complicated ideas into bite-sized pieces, but sitting so close kept me a little distracted.

Later in the evening, Luke made another appearance, dropping a bottle of beer at Nick's elbow, but this time he said nothing. I wasn't going to complain either. He reminded me of one of those serial killers. The kind people said was so nice and normal before he got caught, but they knew there was something off about him. Well, I was sure Luke was off in a big way. Something about that man was just not quite safe.

When my mind finally wrapped around derivatives, I made the mistake of looking at my phone to check the time. "Oh my god, it's midnight!"

"Time flies when you're having fun," Nick pointed out.

"Yeah, but I have to get some sleep." I started shoving my things together before I could convince myself to stay any longer. "School night, you know. I'm horrible without at least six hours and a pot of coffee."

"More tomorrow?" He looked at me, almost pleading.

I wanted to. Oh, how I did. Any excuse to spend time with Nick sounded like a good idea to me – even if that meant more math. Just one problem. "I can't."

"Got a hot date?"

"No, not unless you count a six-hour shift at Mac's." I leaned back and stretched, hearing my back pop. "Gotta pay the rent, you know."

"Yeah. You want a ride home?"

"It's two blocks, Nick. More trouble to get there with all the one-way streets. I'm fine." I pulled myself to my feet.

He stood like the perfect gentleman. "At least let me walk you?"

"That's sweet, but it's *two blocks*. Two heavily policed blocks with more lights along it than on campus." I reached up to pat his shoulder. Wow, those were some solid biceps.

Nick shoved his hands through his hair and nodded. "Ok. So we'll do this again? Maybe I can get you through the next chapter?"

"You do anything besides math?" I asked as we headed toward the front door, hoping he'd give up on the perfect gentleman routine just a bit.

He chuckled under his breath. "Yeah. Um. I'm sure. How about a real date next time? Dinner and a movie? Mini-golf? Wild and kinky sex?" He glanced up through his long, thick lashes. "Usually in that order, but I'm not going to complain if you decide to skip ahead."

"Oh!" I laughed, opening the door. "Not even a first kiss, and you're already wanting to throw me into bed?" This was not an idea I wanted to discourage.

He followed me onto the porch, closing the door behind us. "That's a very loaded question." His voice grew soft, and he stepped closer. His hard body was a little intimidating but oh so amazing. My hand reached up to his chest before my mind knew what was happening. "I'm going to see you again, Sienna," he promised.

"I am perfectly ok with that." The words came out in a breathy whisper.

I looked into his eyes, the street lights reflecting in them, and swore I was falling into a sea of stars. His black hair cascaded around his shoulders, just tickling the tips of my fingers, and he leaned closer – slowly, giving me plenty of time to escape, but that wasn't what I wanted. Nick was beautiful, smart, and sexy enough that I couldn't resist. There was nothing to run from, yet he seemed to expect me to.

Then our lips met. Softly, his mouth caressed mine, one hand sliding into the hair at the back of my neck. Gently, delicately, with the power of his body looming over me, he kissed me like I'd never been kissed before. He kissed me like I was desirable. Like he worshiped me. Like this kiss had been brewing for years, and I couldn't stop myself from pressing my entire body into him.

His hand slipped behind my back, tugging my hips even closer, but he didn't make a noise. I did. Tiny whimpers came out, begging for just a little more as my hands slid over his broad chest. My fingers tangled in his hair as they moved higher, but he didn't seem to care. Just as I caught his neck, a car drove past, laying on the horn. The whoop of some drunk brought reality crashing back. I was supposed to be leaving, not getting seduced.

Reluctantly, Nick pulled away. "Right," he said softly, that deep voice rumbling right down my spine. "Early morning."

"Yeah." My heart was pounding in my chest. If he'd invited me to his bed, I would have gone like a needy puppy, trotting along behind him without another thought. Thankfully, he didn't. Thankfully, he really was the gentleman I expected. Damn him.

"I'm off Wednesday."

"Good to know. I had fun, Sienna." He smiled and stepped back, releasing me. "I have never enjoyed calculus so much in my life. Goodnight."

How the hell did he make that into a compliment? I almost stepped back into him before reminding myself that I really did need to sleep before class. "Night!"

I turned and trotted down the stairs, refusing to look back. If I turned around, I would find a reason to stay just a bit longer. I knew it. Hell, Nick probably knew it. Unfortunately, my classes wouldn't pass themselves, and good grades mattered a whole lot more when it was your own hard-earned money paying for the tuition.

The street lights sparkled on the puddles as I made my way home, feeling as if my feet didn't touch the ground. I didn't skip, but I may have spun and giggled a few times once I was out of sight. Flashes of lightning in the distance proved the storms weren't done, but it wouldn't matter if I got soaked now.

Like expected, I made it to my little shanty just fine. Unlocking the door, I stepped inside, flicking on the light. Tired old furniture in patterns that clashed met my eyes. All of it had been bought second hand, and none of it was elegant like the stuff at Nick's. I tossed my backpack into the closest chair and staggered toward my room to get ready for the morning.

Getting to sleep was going to be impossible. I felt like I'd just won the lottery. Nick Voland, the sexiest man I'd met since Death, wanted to see me again, and he seemed to be pretty damned real. And smart. And amazing. Which meant it was about time for things to start going really wrong, because nothing good happened to me without ten times more crap following right on its heels.

But for tonight, I was going to enjoy this while it lasted. Heading up the hall, I traced the edge of one of my paintings of Death. "I think you have competition, buddy."

*a*fter my face was washed and my teeth were brushed, I made my way into the kitchen to set up my fix for the morning. Without thinking about it, I used one hand to move the carafe to the sink. The other opened the cabinet and pulled down the plastic tub of grounds. It was too light.

Snarling a string of curses under my breath, I popped open the top to find nothing but coffee dust. Not even a whole scoop left to kick-start my morning. The problem was that I would never make it through the day without it. Considering it was already after midnight? I only had one real option. Thank goodness the corner store was open all night. Otherwise, tomorrow would be hell.

With a groan, I turned my ass around and headed for the door. My keys were on my desk. I had a pair of Crocs that would be good enough for a late-night run to the store, and I was certainly not going to fix my hair for this. I wouldn't be gone long enough to worry about it. And from the way the sky was flashing through the window, I'd definitely end up soaked before I made it back.

Thankfully, my antique little car started easily. That was a miracle in itself. The corner store wasn't far, no more than a ten-minute drive, but it was too far to walk. Especially in the rain.

As if my thought invited it, the first fat drop splattered in the middle of the windshield. The second came shortly after. Before I even reached the end of the block, it was coming down hard. Visibility was next to nothing, so I slowed down and leaned forward, peering through the window like some grandma out for a Sunday drive. The sound of the wipers flailing frantically was like a metronome that my heartbeat tried to match.

I hated driving in weather like this. Ok, I pretty much hated driving in general, but this flat out sucked. On both sides, student cars lined up like barriers. The water was coming down so fast it was flooding the street, sending out a spray from either side of my vehicle. Thankfully, the amber lights along the road kept me centered, and the stoplight at the end of the block made it impossible to miss the intersection. Granted, it wasn't like there was any traffic around to worry about. Any sane person was inside right about now.

By the time I reached it, the light was red. I honestly didn't mind stopping. Hell, I'd barely gotten over ten miles per hour, but when I wasn't moving, the rain didn't seem as bad. It gave me a chance to catch my breath. Out of habit, I looked at the cross street's light, waiting for it to turn yellow so I'd know when I had to put my car back into gear. It wasn't like I was going to sit here with my foot on the clutch the whole time.

When the light finally turned green, I eased forward slowly, overly aware of the mini-current of water my poor little car had to traverse to make a left turn. Halfway around the corner, movement caught my eye. I looked to my left just in time to realize that in the middle of the downpour, there was something else. Something moving fast – and right at me.

Something dark.

A terrible squeal made my eardrums hurt. I had just enough time to brace before the impact rocked the car. Glass shattered.

Metal cried out. I screamed, feeling my entire world wrenched sideways – and then it just stopped.

I tried to breathe, tried to move, tried to do something, but blackness took over.

I knew nothing else until cold hands touched my face. Slowly, I cracked my eyes open. Everything hurt. I'd been in a wreck. My car was probably totaled, but I needed to get out, or call someone, or do *something*, but I just couldn't. My body felt too tired. Weak. My mind couldn't focus on anything except how much I wanted to just sleep.

I opened my eyes again and saw *him*. Dark cloth covered everything, but there was no mistaking Death. He still didn't have a scythe, but the hood, the moonlit hand touching my cheek? It was him. Slowly, my eyes looked down, resting on crumpled metal and plastic. The door was crushed and folded around me. I was halfway into the passenger seat, but my body wasn't moving. I needed a nap.

"No," Death breathed. "Look at me."

I shook my head. At least I tried. Nothing really happened, but I knew I didn't want to look at him. This was not how we were supposed to meet again!

"I won't let you go. Just stay with me, Sia. You just have to help me a little."

Sia. Only one person had ever called me Sia. "Nick?" I asked, my lips not moving.

"Don't think about it. Don't fight me." His voice was gentle.

Someone poked his face over Death's shoulder. I couldn't quite see him, but his voice was strangely clear when he asked, "What the hell are you doing?"

"I'm not taking her soul!"

The second man scoffed. "Didn't expect you to. Stop fucking around and fix her already. The driver of the other car was mind-fucked, man. That means we'll have company if we don't move this along."

"Shit," Death growled. "Get their aether. I'm probably going to need it."

"All of them?" a third voice asked from a distance.

Death looked back, the set of his mouth proving he was pissed. "Right now, I don't fucking care. Just pull as much as you can."

His friends didn't respond for a moment. When the closest one did, his voice had lost the attitude. "There's two. The third might live."

"Unless I need it. They gave up any chance of compassion when they hurt her." Then he turned back to me. "I need you to stay with me, dove."

I nodded, feeling my neck actually obey. It wasn't much, but right about now, I was calling that success. "No kiss this time, ok? I want to graduate before I die."

"You're not going to die," he promised. Then he called over his shoulder, "Hurry up, you stupid angel!"

"Here," the second man said, holding out his hand. I could just barely make out his silhouette, but I was pretty sure the blob behind him was a set of wings.

Death reached back for whatever the angel held, but his eyes hung on me. I couldn't see most of his face, but I could feel it. Not even his thick hood could shield me from the intensity of his gaze. Unfortunately, a look wasn't enough to fix whatever had happened in the wreck. Deep inside, I felt something slip. Suddenly, I weighed less, and gravity had reversed. It was like the sky was pulling me, daring me to fall up instead of down.

"No! Not yet. Come on, dove." He palmed my face, forcing my head to look at him. "Stay with me, beautiful."

"I'm trying."

Slowly, deliberately, he pulled me to him. The shadows under the hood dared me to look, taunting me with secrets my mind wouldn't understand, but I wanted to. I tried to lean closer, hoping for another glimpse of constellations. Instead, I only saw his mouth move as he whispered the first word. After that, the pain was too intense to think about anything.

My weightless body slammed back home. The injuries hit me at once, each of them demanding my complete attention. It hurt so much that I didn't even realize the world had changed colors. No, all I could think about was that I would not scream before Death. I would not cry. I could take anything if it meant he'd just talk to me one more time, but it didn't hold back the agony. White light erupted in the back of my eyes, and all I could manage to do was breathe.

Then nothing.

I WOKE WITH A GASP. RHYTHMICAL BEEPS AND A MECHANICAL HISS chased the silence from the antiseptic room. Voices in the hall spoke softly. Around me, the lights were dim. A soft amber glow trickled beneath the edges of a curtain. Sitting up was more than I could manage, but I did get my head to turn.

"Sia?" Nick's voice sounded worried.

"What happened?" There was something I should remember, but couldn't. My mind felt so fuzzy. All I knew was that my head hurt.

"You were in a wreck. Your car's toast, but you're going to be ok."

There it was again, that tickle in the back of my mind. I could almost touch the memory, but it kept floating out of reach. Maybe it was the drugs? My head felt strange, so they probably had me on something really good.

"Why are you here?" I croaked.

"Because you don't have any emergency contacts in your phone, and I was the last number." He scooted his chair closer. "How do you feel?"

"Stoned."

Nick chuckled. "Well, could be worse, I guess. They said it's a miracle you made it out of that with nothing more than a minor concussion."

"It wasn't my fault. I had the green light, and they didn't even have their headlights on. I hope that bastard's insurance buys me a new car."

His hand ran across my hair gently, his fingers barely even touching. "No, dove, it wasn't your fault. The other driver had been drinking."

Dove. Nick always called me dove. Memories seeped back in slowly, oozing around my head before solidifying into coherent thoughts. Death called me dove. I'd seen Death, and his eyes were full of the universe, his lips so sensual. I'd asked him not to kiss me, and he'd agreed. He'd told me to hang on. He'd all but berated his assisting angel to fix me.

"Death saved me," I mumbled, unaware I was even speaking. "He killed those others to make me better, and I'll probably never get to thank him."

Nick huffed something that sounded like a chuckle. "Thank him? Sienna, I think you're enjoying those pain meds a little too much."

"Unh-uh. When someone saves your life, you should thank them." My eyelids felt so heavy, but my brain was on a tangent now. "He's always taken care of me. That's why I draw him, but he didn't kiss me."

"Yeah..." He chuckled. "Close your eyes, dove. The doctor said you need to rest."

"Mhm. How'd you get in here anyway?"

"Told them I was your boyfriend," he said softly. "And explained that you don't have any family. Makes me the closest thing to a responsible party that you have." His hand traced the line of my face, and he leaned closer. "Go back to sleep, Sia."

His voice sounded so good. The rich tone of it was soothing, convincing me to just breathe a little slower and stop trying to open my eyes. Giving in, I snuggled into the pillow, regretting the decision as soon as Nick pulled his hand away.

From a little farther away, I heard another man chuckle. "Not sure if she's trying to tell you something or is just so stoned she has no clue what she's talking about, but do you need to worry about her little death fetish? Never knew you went for the goth type."

"Shut up, Luke," Nick grumbled. "She's an artist."

"Duh," Luke teased. "And one who hates me, which is why I'm staying far enough away that she can't cut me down with those dirty looks. She's cute, though."

I couldn't take any more. I was also too stoned on pain meds to realize that silence might have gotten me a little more information. Nope, I just blurted out, "Not cute in the hospital, and I don't like your fucked-up-looking green eyes."

Both men froze. I couldn't even hear them shift in their chairs. Clearly, they'd assumed I'd just passed right back out.

"Well," Nick finally chuckled, but it sounded like he was forcing it out. "Guess I don't have a reason to get jealous this time, huh?"

Luke sighed. "Fine, I'll keep my hands off of your pretty little Muse, Nick. I get it. You're into her."

"A lot." Nick leaned over and caught my hand, his strong fingers sliding gently between mine as his thumb traced lazy circles on the back. "We should probably get out of here and let her get some sleep."

I felt his lips on my brow, and his fingers squeezed mine so softly. This time, however, I couldn't open my eyes. My entire body felt worn, like it had been through the wringer, but I didn't really hurt. Death had fixed that, and the pain medication handled the minor stuff. Mostly, I just needed to sleep. As I listened to Nick and Luke's steps leave my room, I stopped trying to fight it. Oblivion took me quickly.

"I'm here to draw your blood," a woman said, setting down something heavy.

I sucked in a breath, trying to remember where I was and why I was here. Morning light spilled through a gap in the curtains, proving I'd lost more time than I thought. Snippets crowded in my mind, but two things stood out. Death and Nick. They'd both done their best to take care of me. Now, it was my turn to take care of myself.

"I'm awake," I croaked, sitting up.

A woman approached, already wearing latex gloves. Her neon scrubs were glaring to my exhausted eyes, reminding me of the colors in Death's world. She clenched a pair of vials in her hand. "Ok, just put your arm up here. As soon as I'm done, there's a police officer wanting to talk to you."

"What?" Why would a cop want to talk to me?

"About the accident. The doctors refused to allow an interview until this morning. I'm not a nurse, so I really don't know anything else." She tied on the latex tourniquet as she talked.

I nodded, hoping that was enough of an answer and felt the prick of the needle. The tubes filled quickly, then it was done. The nurse – or whatever she was – pressed a cotton ball and clear medical tape across the puncture. When that was secure, she quickly put her things away and left without another word, her job with me done.

The door didn't even close before a man tapped at it, walking right in. "Ms. Parker?" he asked. The dark uniform declared him to be the cop.

"That's me." I tried to smooth down my mass of hair, knowing I looked like a mess.

"I wanted to talk to you about the accident last night. Is this a good time?"

I couldn't help it. I laughed just a bit, gesturing to the shapeless drape and the tubes extending from my arm. "Yep. I think I've been cornered. I'm sorry, I didn't have a chance to get presentable."

He smiled, lifting a hand to show he understood. "I'm not here to judge your fashion sense, Ms. Parker. I just wanted to get your side of the accident. Can you tell me what happened?"

I sighed and leaned back, digging up the memories. Everything up to the stoplight, that was clear enough, but afterward? It was just a blur until Death showed up, and I was most certainly not going to tell him about that.

"I was just running out to get some coffee." Ah, crap. I'd already missed class! "For my lecture this morning, which I'm going to need to make up." I groaned. "Crap. Crap, crap, crap. We were supposed to be doing perspective work in Drawing, and I'm going to need at least one example for the final portfolio!"

"I'm pretty sure you'll have a good excuse," he assured me, trying to bring my mind back on track. "So, you needed coffee?"

"Yeah. I live on Bernard. I'd just gotten in the car and made it, like, maybe a block, when it started raining hard again." I rubbed at my face, hoping to knock some of the crust out of my eyes. "So I was going about ten miles an hour, and I couldn't see more than a few feet in front of the hood of my car."

"Yeah, we got some pretty good rain last night. So, which way did you go?"

"Straight down to Avenue D. The light was red, and I stopped – so don't give me a ticket."

"None today. Go on?"

"Yeah. I was headed to the EZ Mart on Clemmens, and watched the other light, waiting for it to turn yellow. I was pretty sure no one else was out."

"Did you see any other traffic?" He was scribbling in a small notepad, glancing up at me with each question.

"No. It was raining so hard I couldn't have seen a person walking on the sidewalk, but I don't remember any other headlights."

"And then?"

I squinted my eyes and rubbed the bridge of my nose, trying to remember. "Yeah. The light turned green. I started easing forward to turn left. Something caught my eye, but it was dark. I wasn't sure it was a car until I heard brakes, or tires, or something, and then *bam.* That's all I remember."

"So they didn't have their lights on?" He didn't look up this time.

"I don't think so. It all just happened so fast, but I remember seeing something dark coming at me. Maybe he turned out of the apartments there and forgot to turn them on? I don't know. I mean, no one with half a brain would be doing more than twenty in that weather, but this guy was moving."

"I understand. Did you check both ways before you went?"

I picked at a tangle on the back of my head, trying to remember. "Maybe? I mean, I always do. I sat at the light for a few minutes. It had just turned red when I got there, so yeah. I had to have, but I can't exactly remember it."

"That's ok, Ms. Parker. Is there anything else I should know?"

I chuckled weakly. "I think my plates are expired. I was going to get them renewed, but I don't get paid until Friday."

"I think we can overlook that. Had you been out? Had anything to drink?"

"Soda. That's it, and that was a few hours before. I'm not a diabetic or anything."

He nodded. "Any recreational drugs?"

I shook my head. "No, sir. Don't touch them. Especially not when spending the evening learning calculus. I'm sorry, I'm kinda boring for a college student."

"Don't be," he assured me. "We're going to need to look at your medical records, though, to verify that. If you'd be willing to give us permission, that would make things a lot easier." He sighed and slowly closed the notepad. "Ms. Parker, the accident was a fatality. The driver of the other car and a passenger were killed on impact."

It was like a thousand ice-cold needles prickled through my skin at once, and my stomach clenched. I'd already known that.

How could I have actually *known* that unless Death was real? "Of course. Yeah. Look at anything you need to. Did anyone make it?"

"Yes, the passenger in the back seat. She's in critical condition. Your car didn't have airbags, correct?"

"No. It's an '84 Honda Civic CRX." I groaned. "Was. Damn, it's got to be totaled."

"I'm sure your insurance adjuster will let you know." He stuffed the pen back in his breast pocket. "I'm glad to see you're doing ok. That wasn't the kind of accident people just walk away from."

No, they didn't, and I shouldn't have either, but I had no intention of telling him how Death helped me. Instead, I just nodded my head. "I guess I've just used up all my luck for the year. Were they drinking?" Nick had said they were.

He opened his mouth, paused, then closed it. He licked his lips once before answering. "It's possible. We're waiting for the test results still."

"That means yes." I groaned. "Which means this is going to end up in court, most likely. Yeah. So what do y'all need from me?"

He lifted the small notebook and smiled sadly. "I think we have it. There are some mental health professionals located in the hospital. Did you need to speak to one about this?"

"Nah." I shrugged and tried not to look guilty. "Some random college kids died in a drunk driving accident. I probably didn't know them, never saw them, and kinda don't want to. I mean, it basically feels like a news story just trashed my car, and still feels a bit surreal."

I was probably being very insensitive, but it was the truth. I didn't know those people, and *they* hit *me!* It wasn't like I'd made them drink and drive, or made them crash into my car. Maybe I should've felt worse, but I just didn't. Then again, maybe it was the drugs they'd given me.

"I just wanted to make sure you knew the option is there." He laid a white business card on the table beside my bed. "If you think of anything else, call me, ok?"

"Yeah." He was almost to the door when I thought of something. "Officer? Where's my car?"

"The city impound. It's going to be reviewed for evidence."

Yep, I'd done this before. "I've got books and stuff in there. Am I going to be able to get it out?" Stuff included art supplies I'd purchased but never taken inside for fear of using them up.

He nodded. "Just stop by the downtown police station after 2:00 pm, and they'll be able to get your things. Thanks again, Ms. Parker."

8

———————

$\mathcal{T}$he rest of the morning ended up a flurry of tests and doctor visits, but all I could think about was how I was going to get home. I didn't want to walk, but my wallet was somewhere in my car, stashed carefully in my purse, and I didn't have a penny to my name. Thankfully, the problem was taken out of my hands when Sam strode into the room.

"So, heard you might need a ride," he greeted me. "How's your head?"

I could see a question lingering in his eyes. Nick had probably told him about my crazy talk the night before, but at that moment, I didn't care. He'd just become my hero, so he could think I was as loopy as he wanted.

"It's good," I assured him. "Doctors said a minor concussion, but that's all. I feel a little fuzzy and have a few bumps and bruises, but nothing worth complaining about."

He nodded. "Nick asked if I could give you a ride. Said you had a rough night. What happened?"

The look he gave me appeared honestly concerned - maybe even a little protective. It made me realize that without Nick overshadowing him, Sam really was a good looking guy. I just had to get past his crazy hair and piercings to see it.

"I forgot to pick up groceries so tried to make a dash to the corner store." Sighing, I gestured to the cheap, nearly paper scrubs the hospital had supplied to cover me until I got home. "Got hit by a drunk on the way. They ended up cutting my clothes off me, so I'm not only short a car, but my favorite jeans are toast."

It didn't make any sense but learning that my most comfortable pair of jeans – a pair I'd had since high school – had been a victim of the wild night hurt worse than anything else. Maybe I was just trying to hold onto a bit of reality to make the rest easier to set aside? Either way, I'd really liked those jeans.

"Yeah." Sam raised an eyebrow at the faded blue outfit I had on. "Definitely not the sexiest thing you've ever worn, but at least you're ok, right?"

"Something like that." I pulled myself off the bed and tilted my head toward the hall, not wanting to stay here a second longer than I had to. "Lead on, before the nurses try to put me in a wheelchair. I don't remember how I got here, and I'm definitely unsure how to get out."

We walked through the hospital side by side, Sam waiting for my ponderous, sore steps. After they'd taken me off the IV drip, my muscles realized what kind of abuse they'd taken. Needless to say, I was paying for it. The whole way, Sam didn't say much, but he kept glancing over to check on me. It was kinda weird. We didn't *really* know each other. I had no idea why he'd been willing to give me a ride, but I sure wasn't about to question it, at least not until I was home. Having no family and no friends was working against me one more time.

Just outside the lobby doors, he pointed to the right, leading me to the closest parking area. "Mine's the Porsche."

Figured. Sam looked like a wild child, acted like one, and evidently, he was the owner of that fancy car I'd seen in the driveway the night before. "Must be nice," I muttered under my breath.

Yeah, I might have been a little resentful. It wasn't really that I wanted some expensive car or a green Victorian mansion. Mostly, it was just that I knew missing a single day of class could cost me a few thousand dollars that I didn't have. My car was gone, I didn't have the funds to rent one, and could only guess how much trouble the insurance agent was going to give me before they paid out all ten bucks that my piece of crap had been worth. I wasn't jealous of the car; I was envious of the stability.

Like he hadn't heard me, Sam flicked his keys around his finger and chuckled. "I'd let you drive, but rumor has it you're stoned."

"Yeah. They loaded me up good. Heard one of the nurses say I should've been a goner."

He moved a little closer, looking like he wanted to put his arm around my shoulders, but he didn't. "Was that your car on the corner of Clemmens and Bernard?"

I nodded. "Yep, the white compact that got compacted."

He whistled. "Saw that. Cops everywhere and like three ambulances. Looked really bad. You sure you're ok?" He paused, pushing a button to unlock the car.

"I hurt all over, have the nicest stripe across my body from the seat belt, and they say I have a concussion, but that's it."

He pulled the passenger door open, offering me a hand to lower my abused body inside. Oddly, I was mostly aware of the fact that I wore stupid bootie socks, had no bra, and my tits were flopping under the paper-like shirt. Pretty, real pretty. At least it was the roommate and not the super sexy potential-boyfriend hunk, right?

"How'd y'all know I was here?" That was what honestly confused me. "I mean, I left around midnight."

He closed the door gently, nodding his head as he walked around to the driver's side. Sliding into the seat, he resumed the conversation, "Nick's phone rang at like 1:00 am, maybe a little after. We were finishing up the last round of Battlefield, so pretty late."

"Yeah, I ran out for coffee for my morning fix."

He nodded. "They said Sienna Parker – nice boring last name by the way – had been admitted, and this was the most recent contact. Wondered if we knew your next of kin." He looked at me, waiting expectantly as he started the car. "Nick said you don't have any."

"I don't. It's just me." I bit at my lip. "Hey, Sam? Thanks for the ride. I mean it."

"Yeah, no biggie."

"Kinda is to me." I shrugged and felt the delayed emotional outburst coming. Taking a deep breath, I turned to the window, watching the scenery pass by, hoping I wouldn't start blubbering. "Seriously. I know you don't owe me a thing, and yet here you are, giving me a ride home in your nice car."

"You like it, don't ya?" He reached over and caught my hand, squeezing it reassuringly. His words didn't match the action. "Ladies always love the car. Guys like it when I let them drive."

I knew he was giving me a chance to change the subject, and I appreciated it. Granted, having some chick that your roommate wanted to date bawling her eyes out on a trip home from the hospital did make a whole new level of awkward that I hadn't experienced before. I could handle awkward. Crying, not so much. A few deep breaths kept my eyes from doing more than welling up, but I was a wreck. The trick was to keep going, not look back, and never tense up. Awkwardness was easy to hide. I knew; I'd been doing it my whole life.

"Yeah. I love the car," I agreed. "Probably great for getting you laid."

He laughed. "You know it. So how'd Nick manage to score a real date with you, anyway?"

"He was a gentleman." I plucked at my lip, thinking about it. "It was after this weird encounter. I mean, I ran into some guy – he was an ass but thought a cheesy pickup line would be a good enough apology. Anyways, there I was, thinking about how to ditch him, and Nick just kinda showed up. I guess he knew the other guy."

"Ah, yeah. Told me he ran into Mike yesterday. We all grew up together."

"He said something about that. Anyway, we ditched class because of the rain, so I convinced him to help me with calculus." Ok, maybe I'd jumbled it all up, but it was close enough.

"And next thing you know, he's cooking you dinner?" Sam glanced over at me quickly before turning his eyes back to the road. "He played that off nicely. You gonna see him again?"

There I was, strapped into the front seat of a Porsche, sitting beside my crush's roommate, who I'd just realized was pretty cute, and trying to play it cool. Yeah, awkward and I were way too close of friends. "I'd like to. He's a nice guy."

"Nick?" Sam's eyebrows shot up. "Aloof, demented, and arrogant. Those things I can see, but nice?"

"He makes really good spaghetti?" I shrugged. "Seriously, he's nice."

"Isn't nice like one step away from dumped?"

"Maybe for the people you've dated. Granted, there'd have to be a bit more than helping me with calculus before there's dumping involved, Sam."

"Like making out on the front porch or having his friend pick you up from the hospital?" He laughed, pulling onto my street. "So which one is yours?"

"The rock shanty." I pointed ahead. "At least I got my keys."

He slowed and turned into the drive, turning the car off. "Need anything?"

"Nah." I opened the door, intending to pull myself out.

The car sat nearly on the ground, and it would be a long way up with every muscle screaming at me. I paused, taking a deep breath to prepare for the complaint my body was about to make.

Sam saw and jumped out, hurrying around the back to come grab my elbow.

"How about a big strong guy to help you up both of those stairs?" He looked me over. "Sweetie, you look like you got hit by a bus."

"Just don't tell Nick," I grumbled. "I was trying to keep up the hot redhead thing."

He pushed the car door shut with his foot and wrapped an arm around my shoulder, taking the keys from my hand. "I think you're ok there. Rescuing damsels in distress is my specialty. And Nick basically threatened me to make sure I'd give you a lift."

"He's in class?"

Sam shook his head, unlocking the door. "Nah. He'd ditch class for this. He had to talk to a guy about some business."

"Isn't that a euphemism?" I couldn't remember for what, and I was pretty sure I didn't want to think about it.

"Not this time," he assured me. "He honestly had an appointment he couldn't get out of. A time-sensitive thing."

He stepped inside with me, letting his arm slip from my shoulder as he looked around the room. "Damn, that's nice," he breathed.

I laughed. My mismatched furniture and second-hand things were not "nice." All I needed to make it into the stereotypical college pad was a table made out of plywood, but Sam was staring at the walls. My paintings covered them, leaving no space left untouched. Mostly, it was just to let them dry without getting smudged. Nothing was framed, and some of them weren't finished, but it was all my own work.

"The paintings?" I asked, pretty sure that was what had impressed him. The decor certainly hadn't.

He nodded, walking toward a piece I'd done called *Burning Brightly*. The canvas was filled with a close-up view of flames. "Yeah. Yours?"

"Most is stuff I couldn't sell or something I was trying to figure out. It's just crap, Sam."

"Not crap." His finger traced the edge of the canvas. "I like this one."

"You're welcome to it. It's a macro view of a match." I waved my hand back at it as I stumbled onto the couch. "Consider it a thank you for the ride."

Slowly, he turned to me. "Really? You're just giving me one of your paintings?"

I shifted onto my back, resting my head against the arm. "Really. I mean, it's kinda the least I can do. If you want it, you're welcome to it, but you have to find your own frame."

The look on his face would have been comical if it wasn't so sweet. He stared at me like I'd just given him a Monet. "Thanks, Sienna. That's probably the nicest thing anyone's done for me."

I paused, hearing nothing but raw truth in his voice. It seemed I wasn't the only person trying to make it through life on their own. Maybe that was why Sam felt like such a kindred spirit when we'd first met. Granted, a painting didn't seem enough to earn that kind of appreciation, but he probably thought the same about the ride.

"Then we're even, because," I grunted as I shifted again, trying to find a comfortable position. "I can't think of a lot of people who'd make sure I got home safe." I paused. "No, that's bullshit. Truth be told, Sam, I can't remember the last time someone did me a favor without holding it over my head."

"Well, that's one thing I won't do." He moved closer, sitting gently beside me. "When was the last time you ate, sweetie?"

"Last night." I shrugged. "Hospital food sucks unless you count the Jell-O."

"Lemme get pizza, or pick up some burgers or something? Nick said he wanted to stop by when he's done."

I shook my head. "No offense, but I just really want a hot shower and a nap."

"Nah, I get it. Can I do *anything* for you?"

He reached over and carefully palmed the side of my head, letting his hand slide down the back of my hair. For a moment, our eyes met. That hint of purple was still there. So was something else. It wasn't just concern. If I had to put a name to it, I'd call it protective, but the soft and sensual kind. The kind usually reserved for boyfriends, not *just* friends. I felt my heart beat faster in response. I was trying to date Nick. Sam was *just a friend*. Nothing but a friend, however at that moment, I realized he didn't agree. I also didn't mind.

I reached up to touch the ring in his brow, hoping to lighten the mood. "How many of these do you have, anyway?"

In answer, he stuck his tongue out. Two metal balls stood out on top. "A few," he said. "Like ten? Depends on if you count the ears. You thinking about getting some yet?" He smiled, but his eyes didn't waver from mine. "I'm voting for your tongue if you are."

"No," I groaned, wrenching my eyes away. "Sam, you're awful!"

His face softened, and he trailed his hand across the side of my head one more time. "I'm really not. I'm honestly just worried about you – and pretty sure Nick will grill me later. Are you sure you're ok here alone?"

"Positive. The only thing I'll miss is class."

He nodded. "I think Nick has notes from Art History, and I told our TA that you'd been in an accident. If you're out tomorrow too, we'll take care of it. It's the least we can do. Just text Nick so we don't worry, ok?"

That was sweet. Of course, everyone put on their best face at first, and it didn't take long before one thing led to another, and someone would be pissed about something – like that look in Sam's eyes. Friendships were temporary things, dependent only on what someone got out of it, and I just didn't have anything else to give. I'd been used up and tossed out as a child, and hadn't quite refilled yet. Keeping people at arm's length was easier. It kept me focused on the things that really mattered in life. Like my degree – which I needed to stay focused on.

Friends had never fit in my plans. They meant hanging out. Hanging out meant slacking off. Slacking off meant failing classes. Failing classes meant working more hours to pay for retaking them, which killed the hanging out, and would result in no friends. I figured it was easier to skip the mess in the middle and just move right to the end. That was what I tried to tell myself, at any rate, but it was lonely living like this.

And these guys were making it so easy to depend on them. Not once had they made me feel bad for their help, even when I knew it put them out. I already owed Sam big time, and Nick? He'd dropped everything to show up at the hospital last night. I could barely remember any of that, but I knew he'd been there. I also vaguely remembered talking about Death, but I didn't want to think about that right now.

"Thanks, Sam, but I'll be there." I smiled up at him. "I paid too much to skip classes when a few Advil will make it tolerable."

"And you're still allowed to change your mind. I'll get out of your hair and let you get some sleep." He patted my leg once, then stood, walking back to the painting. "You're serious about me taking this?"

"Yeah. It's actually kinda cool that you'd even want it, so definitely."

He grinned and pulled it from the wall, looking back once before leaving. The smile he offered made me want to blush. Lifting a hand, I waved awkwardly. He shut the door behind him, leaving me completely and totally alone. The silence around me was loud enough to ring in my ears. It also felt peaceful. Peaceful enough that I just wanted to close my eyes and nap, but I was still covered in particles of glass and grit. First, get clean, then I'd call work. There was no way I'd make it in. Hopefully, they'd let me work tomorrow. I wouldn't make it without the hours.

The shower came first. Heaving myself up, I began peeling out of the temporary scrubs on my way to the bathroom. I ran the water as hot as I could stand it and just soaked, letting every ache and pain seep from my body with the water coursing over my skin.

I stood there until the water ran cold, then wrapped myself in a thick, fluffy towel and staggered out. My stomach finally growled, making me glance at the clock. Not even dinner time, and I was totally wiped out. Staggering toward my bedroom for some clothes, I decided today was going to be a complete write-off.

That accident had been fatal. The way my luck went, they'd probably try to blame me for it somehow. The problem was that I was broke with a capital B. If this got expensive, I was completely screwed.

This would mess up all my classes, and I still had to work on top of that. Which meant that in a few days, I was going to be completely and totally fucked, and not in a good way, so I'd better take advantage of the solitude while I still could. Things were changing and, unfortunately, I was pretty sure I knew exactly where this was headed.

9

*W*ith the hot shower having loosened my muscles, I sat down and called work to give them the bad news. Oddly, someone had already taken care of that. I had a funny suspicion Nick was involved, but it was sweet. When the manager asked if I wanted to come in tomorrow instead, I jumped at the chance. Sure, I'd probably still be achy, but all I had to do was pour drinks.

Once that was handled, I gave up and crawled into bed. Dinner didn't even matter. I just wanted to sprawl myself out on something nice and soft. The mattress qualified. As the sun began to set, overly ambitious crickets chirped outside, but they couldn't keep me awake. The lazy rumble of cars on the street worked like a lullaby. It didn't take long before I was out.

Much, much later, a feather-light touch slid along my temple, following the line of my hair. It was dark, I could tell that, and my room was cool. Struggling to figure out what had jostled me from sleep, I pried my groggy eyes open. They flickered once before obeying, then I froze. The world was in shades of grey – and not just from the lack of light. Looking left, the clock was dim, just a dead black rock on a dead grey table. To my right was the only color in the room, but I didn't dare believe it. Moonlight blue shone under the deep black cloak of the man leaning over my bed. When my eyes landed on him, Death smiled sweetly.

"You were supposed to be sleeping," he whispered. I moved to sit up, but his hand touched my shoulder, holding me against the bed with the soft plea in his fingers.

"You came back," I gasped, not even ashamed of the relief in my voice.

With a rustle of cloth, he eased himself onto the bed by my hip. "I never left. You were supposed to forget me, not draw me. I just had to make sure you're ok."

"You saved me, didn't you." It wasn't a question. I knew he had, but I wanted him to admit it.

Again, that smile. "You're not even supposed to see me, dove."

"But I can." I reached up, sliding my hand under his hood. "Thank you for saving me last night, and Jamal!" There was so much I wanted to tell him. I'd waited so long, but seeing him again made the words vanish before reaching my mouth, leaving only the sight of his lips to torment me.

He pressed his cheek against my palm. Pale sparks from the stars in his eyes peeked from the depths of the hood. With one hand, he grabbed my wrist, holding it to him. "We have to stop meeting like this," he teased gently.

"Then how should we meet? I like *this* a whole lot better than last night or the robbery."

From the twist of his mouth, that wasn't the question I should've asked. "We're not supposed to meet at all. You're supposed to stay on your side of the veil, not mine. Little Muse, it's dangerous here. If you don't stop slipping over, someone might notice. I'm worried someone already has."

"Who? Wait, where?" I had no idea what he was talking about. Like in a dream, my sleep-fogged mind spun but got nowhere.

His soft, gentle finger slid to my forehead, tracing lazy spirals against the skin. "On my side of the veil. Our worlds may overlap, but we aren't supposed to meet. Sleep, little dove. I just wanted to make sure you were ok, not haunt you."

"Stalk me," I mumbled, feeling exhaustion pulling at my body.

"Definitely not that," he swore. "But you've been doing a good job of forcing me to come back. Dove, I have to protect you. I just need to make sure no one can get in. Sleep. Forget me. I wasn't here. This is all a dream."

It almost worked. My eyes closed, my breathing slowed, and my mind settled, but I wasn't willing to lose him again. I'd waited four years; I wouldn't give up so easily. With a breath, I wrenched open my eyes to see amber rays from the streetlight trickling through the blinds, the colors of the world as vibrant as ever. This was my world, not his. If I wanted to see Death, I had to figure out how to get back across. Sitting up quickly, I whipped my head around the room, looking for a hint. The time glared back at me on the clock in bold red numbers that didn't exist on the other side: 3:17 a.m.

"Damn it!" I snarled, pushing myself back against the wall, wishing that I could find the grey world of Death.

And I did.

That one little shove moved me through something, like breaking the surface of water, and I felt the world start to slide sideways. Instinctively, I grabbed at the mattress, locking myself to it, too shocked to do anything else. It felt like someone had turned on a fan – a very large one – and the wind was pushing me out of the room.

"Fuck," Death snapped, standing by my window.

With a flick of his hand, a wave of cyan and pink washed across the room, leaving tiny symbols as proof. They faded out quickly, but the wind died down, making this grey world into a colorless version of what I knew. There were still differences.

The more life something had, the more brilliantly it was colored. Death's skin might be pale, but it was almost iridescent.

His black robe was the same, rippling with midnight blue in its shadows. The cactus on my windowsill glowed in a neon shade of green. The plastic clock, however, was completely boring and grey. Under it, my wood night table held only a hint of color, proving that once it had been alive, but no longer.

Unfortunately, my inspection didn't impress Death. He scowled in frustration as he finished the strange letter he was drawing. I couldn't see it, not really. It was like a heat trail or the afterglow from a sparkler. The sigil hung for a moment, then faded, but the feeling of it remained. So did Death's anger.

"I said you couldn't be here," he growled, turning to glare.

He made another gesture and I felt a pull, tugging me into myself, but I fought it. I wasn't leaving. I didn't care who or what he was, he couldn't get rid of me that easy. I had questions, I wanted answers, and I wasn't giving up until I got at least one.

"You can't make me go," I warned him. "I will just keep coming back over and over if you try."

His jaw was clenched, the formless robe hiding the tension I knew would be coursing through his shoulders. "You felt that wind? Without my wards, it would blow you through the corridor until your soul was ripped apart. Are you that ready to die? Are you that desperate for my attention?"

"No. Yes." I tried to answer both questions in the order they were asked. "Death!" I crawled to the end of the bed, but he pointed back to the pillows.

"Sleep," he ordered. "Stay on Earth. Do not cross the damned veil again!"

Obviously, he didn't know me very well. His words didn't even slow me down. I knew I was barely dressed but didn't care. He'd seen me dying, so a t-shirt and panties wasn't a big deal at all. I kept going, crawling off the bed and storming to him with a purpose. I would not leave, not without seeing his face. I had to. I had to know what held those stars. It had become an obsession.

As I reached him, Death met me, ready to throw me back to

whatever hell I'd started in. Fine, let him try, but first... I grabbed the side of his hood and pulled, trying to yank it back.

His cheek shone in the dimness, but the cloth caught on something. I tried to tug again, but he caught my arm, pulling my hand away. "Please," I begged. When I tried with the other, he intercepted that one too, his strong fingers imprisoning my wrists. "Please," I said again. "I have to see you. I've spent four years wondering who you are. Just show me a glimpse, and I'll go back."

"You don't want to see my face," he insisted.

"Yes, I do!"

I pulled an arm free, but he pushed me back. Gently. Everything Death did with me was gentle, as if he was terrified I'd break. That was the only reason I managed to reach for his hood again, the back of my fingers grazing something hard – and he flinched away.

"Don't," he begged. "Don't look at my face. Please. I'm not human."

"I know." Once more, I lifted my hand, but this time it wasn't to pull at his hood. Feeling solid ridges hidden under the cloth, I breathed, "You have horns."

He froze. Stars peered at me from the darkness, but he didn't pull away from my touch. "Please," he whispered. "Leave me this one thing, Sienna. There's a reason I wear a hood, because what's under it isn't pretty."

"I didn't know angels had horns."

He took a breath, the air sliding through his barely parted lips as if he was bracing for the worst. "I'm not an angel."

"The Angel of Death."

"No. I'm *not* an angel." His fingers tightened on my shoulder. "I'm not divine. When humans see me, they call me a monster, so I wear the hood. Ask me for anything else, but not my face."

Standing there like that, with his cheek in my hand and my wrist in his, we were at a standoff. I could feel the vulnerability.

This strong, impossible creature had one single weakness. What he couldn't fathom was that I didn't care. I didn't want him to be pretty. I just wanted to know the man who'd made miracles happen to protect me, to put a face to all the dreams I'd had over the years. I needed something to fill the gap in my mind where his identity should have been.

"Do you at least have a name?"

The corner of his lip twitched in a hint of a smile. "A few. Death is one, and I like it when you call me that."

I huffed in frustration. "No face, no name, and you want me to be happy with that?"

"No," he said softly, stepping closer as he released my wrist. "I want you to rage at me like a woman, curse me to eternity, and then *stay on your side of the veil.*"

Oh, I heard what he was saying, but everything he did disagreed. So I called him on it. "Bullshit. I'm not sure what you want, but stop lying to me. I think you owe me that at least."

"Oh? Do I now? Dove, in case you forgot, it's you that owes me. I kept you from killing that stupid boy at the gas station because I knew the guilt would destroy you. I put your soul back together last night so you could graduate college, just like you asked. Tell me, what is it *you've* done *for me?*"

"Yeah, see, I'm not quite sure, but there's a reason you wanted my kiss. There's a reason you keep coming back. I may not know what it is, but don't treat me like I'm an idiot. You expect me to just obey your orders but give me no reason why. Well, in case you missed it, I'm not that kind of girl, so start talking, or I'll become the biggest pain in your ass you've ever seen."

He was supposed to be cowed, or at least chastised. Instead, Death was grinning at me like I'd just performed some adorable little trick. In frustration, I jerked away from him and turned back to my bed. I didn't make it a step before he caught my wrist.

"Sia..."

"Look, if you won't tell me anything else, at least tell me what you are."

He tugged me around so I faced him. "That's not any better."

"Ok, then where are we? Can you answer *that?*"

He dipped his head slightly. "This is the corridor. It exists in parallel to the reality you know, but it's not the same. It's where souls go to disperse when they die."

"Ghosts?" I asked.

He canted his head as if I was close but not quite right. "They can be interpreted that way. It's complicated, little dove, and I'm not sure I could make you understand. Your science hasn't gotten that far."

"Ok," I sighed, aware I wasn't getting much out of him. "Can you at least tell me what you were doing to my window?"

"Wards." For once, he made no attempt to avoid the question. "Twice now, you've almost made it through the veil without help." Then he tipped his head at me. "And once you've succeeded. The problem is that you have no idea how to deal with the winds. The walls wouldn't keep you from blowing away because they aren't really here. None of this is, but the corridor is thin enough to try to mimic the reality you know. So I used the structure as a foundation for a shield. So long as you're in your house, if you accidentally slip through without me around, you won't be torn apart."

"And killed?"

"And killed," he agreed. "It would be easiest if you forgot all about this place, but I'm not an idiot either. I know you will poke at the pieces until you think you've found an answer, and for you, that means trying to reach this place again. I'm trying to make sure you live long enough to realize that's a very bad idea."

I didn't like what he was saying. Not at all. "So what am I *supposed* to do, Death?"

"Make art. Inspire others. Create fantastical things and feed the fabric of life." Then he chuckled. "Well, that's what you *were* supposed to do, but I think your art has been winning."

The pencil. He had to know about the pencil that had fallen off the page. "Have you been watching me?"

His finger brushed the inside of my wrist soothingly where he held it. "Watching *over* you. It sounds a little less offensive like that. And no, I'm not always hovering around you. I'm trying very hard to leave you alone, but you have no idea what you've been doing, and it's like a beacon to those who want to make problems."

"Like that creepy guy in my Creative Writing class?"

His mouth split into a grin, and he ducked his hood in an attempt to hide it. "I like how you assume I know everyone around you. Just so it's clear, I don't."

"Ok." Evidently, I was on the wrong track. "So why can I even do this? Is this something that anyone can do if they knew this place existed?"

"You're special."

"Are we talking like short bus kinda special here?"

The laugh I got was the most amazing thing ever. If I tried to imagine what people said angels sounded like, it would be the same as his laugh, all deep, rich, and harmonious. "No," he assured me. "Most humans haven't evolved the mental awareness to traverse the planes of existence. You have. That kind of special."

"Are there others like me?"

His mouth opened, the smile faded, then it closed without a word. Slowly, he shook his head. "Not humans, no."

I tried to keep the accusation out of my voice for the next question. "Is that why you're watching over me?" I didn't want to be some kind of specimen.

He took a half step closer, ducking his head to look at me from under that heavy cowl. "It's why I noticed you. It's not why I watch. I just want to give you the chance to grow up and master your art. I want to see you shine so brightly."

"Why?" I had to know. I couldn't help myself.

Death reached up and cupped the side of my face. "Because I know what it's like to be trapped in a war you cannot win. Because there's this spark in your eye that challenges even me. Because in all of my very long life, I've never met anyone who can inspire me the way you do." Slowly, his hand slipped around to the back of my neck. "Because, my little dove, I love the sound of your laugh and can't get enough of that smile when you learn something new. I want to make sure you stay safe long enough to become the kind of person who won't resent what you've lost."

"What am I going to lose?"

"Everything," he said softly. "If you keep following me, you will lose anything and everything that matters to you. Maybe you'll gain more to replace it – I don't know – but playing with Death?" He offered a wry smile. "It's not a wise decision."

He had a point. Hearing it spoken aloud made it even more blatant. "So you're saying I should stop looking for you?"

Another half step put his chest almost against mine. "It would be the wise choice, but it's not the one I'm rooting for."

"Then what *are* you rooting for?" I'd intended to make that a demand. Instead, it sounded more like I was pleading.

He leaned closer. "A partner. A woman strong enough that she doesn't even fear Death."

I lifted my chin – not in defiance, but to bare my lips to his. "I'm not scared of you. I've never been scared of you."

"I know."

"But I am addicted to you, and I don't know why."

His thumb traced the line of my jaw. "Like calls to like, my little dove. You and I? We're not that dissimilar. Your tenacity is an addiction I can't get enough of."

I didn't know what that meant, but he didn't give me the chance to ask. There, in the darkness of my bedroom, Death kissed me, forcing all of the insanity away. Closing my eyes, I leaned in, pressing my entire body against his. While our mouths tangled like long lost friends, I felt the lines of his body. The very human lines, carefully hidden beneath the heavy fabric of his robe. His chest was broad and flat. His waist was lean. Using my hands, I found one hell of a sexy man locked away from my eyes, but I didn't care. He'd all but said he wouldn't leave me, and that was the only thing that really mattered.

10

$\mathcal{I}$ woke to the alarm screaming at me. I slapped at it, silencing the thing, and nearly went back to sleep but paused. The last thing I remembered was Death pressing me back into the bed. I'd been kissing him, letting my hands run all over his body, and then... Nothing.

"Damn you," I snarled, realizing what he'd done.

The bastard had magicked me back to sleep! He'd kissed me to distract me, then forced me back to my side of the veil and into a deep enough sleep that I couldn't come back. The problem was that I kinda had to give him credit for that. I mean, I'd basically told him I wouldn't give up, so he'd proven that I couldn't stop him. Was there something wrong with me to think that was a little bit sexy?

Probably.

There was something even more wrong with the fact that I wasn't freaked out at the idea of his abilities being magic. They probably weren't. Somewhere, there had to be a rational explanation for all of this, but it didn't really matter. There was this famous quote about how sufficiently advanced technology would be indistinguishable from magic, and I had a funny feeling it applied. Humans had been seeing ghosts for long enough that we'd stopped believing in them, but what if the reality was a lot more mundane? I'd have to get Death to break it down a little more the next time we met.

Wait. What if I was wrong? What if that hadn't been anything but a dream? The first time I'd seen Death was after getting smacked in the head with a gun and put on a pretty impressive dose of pain killers. Yesterday, I'd been diagnosed with a concussion and given some serious medication for the pain. Surely that was just a coincidence, right?

I couldn't shake the feeling. No one else ever saw him. I had absolutely no evidence that he was anything but one very amazing hallucination. The first time it happened, the doctors told me I may have seen things I thought were real, but it didn't mean they were. Magic? A sexy man in a hood that saved my life not just once, but twice? If that wasn't the kind of thing my demented mind would make up on its own, then I couldn't think of what would be.

I sat there in bed for a moment, trying to decide if I should call my old shrink. The problem was I couldn't afford her rates. Well, That was what I told myself. I also didn't want her to tell me I was losing my mind. Believing I was part of some bigger, super-special world? I liked that a whole lot more than thinking I was completely and totally nutso. So long as I kept it to myself, what difference did it make? I clearly hadn't gone all the way around the bend if I recognized this was insane. That meant I wasn't *totally* loopy, right?

Right.

Having mostly convinced myself, I tossed back the blankets and began my day. The strange thing was that I no longer ached all over. It seemed as if taking an extended nap was just what the doctor ordered, or should have. Unfortunately, that didn't get back my stuff from my car. On the upside, I had Creative Writing this morning and then Calculus. Everything I needed for those was in my backpack. Hopefully, Nick would be able to give me a ride over to the police station when we got out of class so I could pick up the rest.

I hated the idea of asking him. Even worse, I didn't know what I'd do if he had another of those meetings he kept running off for. Ask Sam? Probably not the best idea. After he'd been so sweet to me yesterday, I almost felt like I'd done something wrong, like I should tell Nick about it. We weren't officially dating or anything, but I sure didn't want to make him think he couldn't trust me.

Granted, what I'd done last night with Death? Yeah... I was going to write that off as a wild fantasy. I mean, it wasn't cheating if it wasn't real, right? Since no one else would believe me, and I *wasn't* actually dating Nick, it didn't count. Besides, admitting it would be so bad. The only way that would end would be with me in a white, self-hugging jacket.

Trying not to worry about it, I gathered my things and headed into the kitchen to fill my massive mug of go-juice. I was halfway there when I remembered that I'd never made it to the store. Not only was I missing my new art supplies, I still didn't have the one thing I couldn't live without. Just one problem; I could smell a nice fresh brew.

Peering around the corner into the kitchen, I saw the coffee pot pulled to the edge of the counter, the carafe half full of amazing brown fluid, and a bright red plastic tub sitting beside it. The light for the automatic brew was on, which meant it had been set up sometime yesterday. I hadn't done it, but it didn't take a rocket scientist to figure out someone had. But who?

Did Death make coffee? Sam? Had Nick stopped over while I was in the hospital? None of that made any sense! Death didn't live on my plane of existence. Sam hadn't left my sight the whole time he was here. No one else had keys to get in, and the door had been locked. Did I do it and just forgot?

Seriously, what the fuck?

I filled my mug anyway, adding a nice dose of creamer and sugar for that extra added boost, then turned the pot off and slid it back into the corner where it belonged. When I reached for the container of coffee, something blue caught my eye. Not royal blue, but moonlit – the exact color of Death's skin. Laying there beside the sink was a posy of wildflowers. The stem of one had been wound around the others, holding them together, but I couldn't take my eyes off those dainty little petals. The color was perfect. I had no idea what they were, but if I had to guess, I'd say forget-me-nots. They looked right, but it would take a Google search to be sure.

On a whim, I pulled down a glass, put a little water in it, and used it as a vase for my bouquet. They had to be from Death. I didn't see Nick as the flower kind of guy, and Sam? He would've gone for roses. Death was the type of man to handpick flowers and leave them where I'd stumble across them. The bigger question, though, was how?

I figured that out the moment I walked into the living room. Stacked by my door were both of my backpacks. Mixed among them was every single thing that had been in my car. My portfolio and art case were carefully leaned against the wall. A handful of books had been set beside it with two hoodies, both folded nicely and set on top of them. For a moment, I just gaped in astonishment. First, because I no longer needed to beg a ride to the police station. Second? Well, it seemed the line between my world and Death's was a very fluid one. No one else could have done this but him.

Third, I wasn't crazy.

Death was real. He wasn't a figment of my imagination, I wasn't going insane, and those things he'd said hadn't been just wish-fulfillment. I really *was* special, and for the first time in my life, I didn't have to doubt it. Shrugging my backpack over my shoulder, I left the house with a smile on my face. Everything was going to be ok. My dream guy was real. Things were finally looking up.

The smile stayed until I stepped inside the Language building. Coming in from another hall, Luke met me at the stairs, glancing over to make it clear he saw me. The groan that came out of my mouth was not intentional, but it was loud enough that he heard. Unfortunately, it wasn't loud enough to stop him from falling in at my side.

"Feeling better?" The way he asked that made it sound like I'd faked the accident or something.

I couldn't help the annoyed look on my face. I tried, but this guy just kept rubbing me the wrong way. "Remind me why you care again?"

"Hey," he gasped, lifting both hands in mock innocence. "Just making sure. You looked a little beat up when I gave Nick a ride to the hospital."

"I'm fine, thanks." And a bitch, but this guy just weirded me out. Besides, I'd rather be a bitch than a statistic. Sometimes, a girl just had to trust her gut.

He huffed in frustration but said nothing else until we reached the top of the stairs. I intended to keep walking past him, but his hand shot out, catching my elbow carefully. When I tried to pull free, he tugged, guiding me out of the flow of traffic. I went. I didn't like it, but I had no real reason to cause a scene. Not yet, at least.

"Is this because I didn't tip enough the other night?" The gloating look on his face proved he knew better.

I rolled my eyes, annoyed that he was making me sound like some cheap gold-digger. "No, ok?"

"Then what's it going to take to make you like me a little more?"

Right at that moment, his brass-colored impersonator walked past. I didn't know the guy's name, but his eyes crawled all over my body before he disappeared into our classroom. The look on his face was menacing, making me feel like I was under attack for no reason. When I looked back, Luke's eyes were locked on the asshole like the two of them shared some nefarious secret.

"Friend of yours?" I asked snidely. "Because the way y'all stare at me is getting old already."

Luke sighed deeply and lifted a hand to rub his brow. "Sienna, look –"

"I don't need to look. It's starting to get a little annoying that you and your buddy keep eye-fucking me in class. In case y'all missed it, that's not a real good way to make a good impression. I'm not exactly here for your amusement, got it? You've already screwed up being friends – let alone *anything* else – so you can quit already. The only thing I want from you is to be left alone. You can tell that to the goon squad." I waved my hand at the door the brass version had just disappeared through.

Luke's head whipped around, confusion on his face. "Gabe? I thought all chicks loved big, blonde, and beautiful."

"Yeah? Well, don't get your hopes up." The look I raked over his body made it clear he fit into that category, then I turned to head toward the room – but Luke grabbed my arm. His fingers were almost as gentle as Death's. That was the only reason I didn't scream.

"I wasn't," he assured me. "I don't typically have a thing for the same girls as my best friend." He barely lifted his eyebrow, daring me to beg him to explain.

I didn't need to. Sam had said something similar. "Figured Nick would have better taste in friends. Let me go."

His hand jerked back quickly, his jaw clenching in annoyance. "*Definitely* will tip better next time."

"It wasn't the fucking tip!" I snapped. "Has it ever crossed your mind that I might care about more than how much money you have, whether or not your buddy likes my hair, or how many times the weirdo over there eyes me up? I'm not into big, blonde, and *psychotic*, got it? You and your freaky twin over there act like I'm your next victim, and I've already played that game. I prefer men who have a little respect for the women they talk to, so all three of y'all can fuck off already."

From the expression on his face, he didn't have a clue what I was talking about. "I thought you and Nick were a thing?"

"We are! Your little carbon copy here, and this Mike guy y'all grew up with? Yeah, I don't know what family tree y'all fell from, but it needs to start branching a little, got it? Just stay the fuck away from me. I don't care if that's in class, when I come to see Nick, or any other time you think you could be around me. Don't. And stop *grabbing me* while you're at it."

Clutching my bag tightly, I stormed through the doorway. Yep, I was going to get to class early, but better that than having to be around this guy one second longer. When he followed me in a few seconds later and sat across the room, I decided he must have gotten the hint.

THANKFULLY, NICK DIDN'T ASK ABOUT MY PROBLEM WITH LUKE. When I got to Calculus, he was shocked enough to see me that it never came up. Then again, Luke may not have gotten the chance to tell him, but at least I'd be able to figure out why I disliked the guy so much. The truth was that I didn't know. Luke just made my skin crawl when he was around – just like Gabe and Mike. Getting to *know* them was something I had zero interest in, even if it meant I ended up acting like a shallow bitch.

But if being shallow kept me safe, then I could do it. I didn't owe those men a pretty little smile or sweet manners. I owed it to myself to get the hell out of Dodge when my freak-alarms went off, and they were screaming at me. The fact that Death was here to watch over me made me feel even more justified. He wouldn't bother if there wasn't a threat, right?

Unfortunately, I didn't really get the chance to talk to Nick.

After class, I had to rush home and get ready for work. A little makeup covered the bags under my eyes. A little more made me look ready to serve drinks on a Wednesday night. Not that the bar would be busy, but I needed every tip I could get. When I reached for a necklace, my fingers closed on a gothic piece made by a friend in high school. A tiny pewter figure looked into a mirror, and the reflection showed a skeleton. It seemed all too fitting.

Clasping the choker around my neck, I caught something from the corner of my eye. I spun – seeing nothing. I probably should've turned on some music to keep my mind from playing tricks on me, but it was too late now. I shimmied into the too-tight shirt that served as a uniform and grabbed my keys, heading for the door. I couldn't risk leaving late since I no longer had a car to get me anywhere. I sure as hell wasn't about to call for a ride.

Sam probably wouldn't mind. Nick would say he was glad to help, but I couldn't be sure if he was just polite or would actually mean it. I also didn't know their schedules. They had to have jobs. Renting a house like they had couldn't be cheap. As I put one foot in front of the other, heading back toward the campus, I thought about it. Just for a bit. Ok, for the entire two blocks. I made it with enough time to grab a burger and fries, shove it into my face, and still step behind the counter with two minutes to spare.

What I hadn't been able to do was convince myself that it was ok to put anyone else out over my stupid crap. For my entire life, I'd been the only person I could rely on. Just because a couple of good-looking guys had come to see me in the hospital didn't mean they'd be ok with acting like my babysitters. Besides, I had Death. He'd handle the big things, like making sure I didn't become some horrible statistic. With his help, I could handle this. I didn't need to drag anyone else into the middle of whatever weirdness my life was trying to become.

And today, the bar was hopping. Days like this, I wouldn't have to worry about my amazing interpersonal skills for at least a few more hours. Putting on my best impression of a flirtatious smile, I walked up to the next guy in line and got to work.

"What can I get you?"

The blonde turned – and I recognized his face immediately. I should've known. It seemed Murphy's Law was out to fuck with me a little. Mike, the guy Nick had gone out of his way to warn me about, the cheesy idiot with thoughtless nicknames, smiled at me over the counter. It was the kind of smile you'd expect a cat to have just before it broke the poor mouse's back. His eyes slipped to the necklace at my throat then to my cleavage, making no attempt to be subtle.

"Sex on the beach?" He looked up at me with vivid green eyes. I hadn't noticed the color before, but his eyes were the exact same eerie shade as the two creeps in my Writing class.

"Coming up." I couldn't even force myself to sound happy about it.

I turned, grabbed a bottle from the shelf, and whipped it together. Sliding the finished drink across the bar, I quoted him a price and moved on to the next customer as quickly as I could. Naturally, Mike didn't take the hint. Oh no, he found a chair at the edge of the bar, right next to where the glasses were kept, and planted himself there. That meant I had to pass right in front of him over and over.

I tried to ignore it. At first, that wasn't easy, but as I got into the flow, I became too busy to care. Mix, smile, give drink, smile, get tip. That was all I focused on, making sure I did my best to spend more time with the guys who weren't trying to flirt than those who were. Mike just sat there the whole time, slowly sipping his drink.

"Come here often?" he asked as I made about the fortieth trip down the bar.

"Yeah. It's called a job."

"Ouch. I'm striking out fast on this one, aren't I?"

Yes, yes he was, but I couldn't get away with that while on the clock. Being defensive was a bad habit I'd picked up in the foster system. If I wanted to keep this job, then I had to at least be civil, so I decided to make an effort. A *very* small one.

"Just trying to keep the clients happy, Mike."

"At least you remember my name." He pushed the empty glass toward me. "Maybe a Jack and Coke this time?"

"I can do that." What I couldn't do was convince my face to smile at him.

I mixed a few drinks for another customer then finished Mike's, taking it over to him. He slid across a few bucks. "Keep the change, sexy."

Wow, a buck and a few quarters for a tip. Such a big spender. It wouldn't have bothered me at all if he hadn't tried to make such a big deal about it, but this guy already had me on edge.

Why was it that when Nick called me sexy, my heart beat faster, but when Mike said it, my skin crawled? What had this guy done to make me hate him so much? For all I knew, he could be a decent enough guy, right? Maybe I had this whole thing all wrong. Clearly, I was the one with the attitude problem, but I was kinda ok with that. After all, the guy who'd put a gun to my head had been "decent" to some people, too.

Mike must have seen me pause. "So what would it take to get a date with you?"

"I'm not really looking," I said quickly, turning back to the next customer.

Being professional sure didn't mean I had to go *out* with the creep. As far as I cared, he should just be glad I didn't hose him down with the bar tap. Hell, the prick probably thought his tip had bought his way into my pants or something stupid, but that was *not* how I worked.

Unfortunately, he wasn't dissuaded easily. Biding his time, he didn't say a thing until I ended up back by his corner. "Tomorrow night? Let me take you out for dinner?"

I shook my head, already moving on to the next order. "Sorry.

Got a date tomorrow." I didn't, but lying was the best I could come up with to not be an ass about refusing.

I glanced back as the words were out of my mouth just in time to see the rage pass over his face. Mike stood, slamming his drink onto the counter, hard. Clearly, anything short of blind acceptance was not at all what he wanted.

"It's Nick, isn't it?" He leaned closer, pointing at my necklace, making me take a step back at the sudden change in him. "He's not what he seems, Sienna. That bastard is lying to you."

Thankfully, the jock I was trying to get a beer for decided to step in. Turning, he put the full width of his shoulders between me and the asshole who wasn't taking no for an answer. Then he crossed his arms.

"Back off, bud. If the bartender said no, then you need to respect that."

"Fuck off," Mike snapped at him. "This is between her and me."

"Not anymore." He looked over Mike's head and waved. "See, I know the bouncer at this place, and what you're doing? Not cool."

"Oh, I don't give up easily. I know what I want, Sienna," Mike sneered over the guy's shoulder.

The jock stayed there, planted like a protective shield until Tom came and escorted Mike out of the bar. The moment he turned back, I slid an ice-cold bottle of beer over to him. "Thanks, man. This one's on me for being my hero."

He lifted the bottle and tilted it toward me. "Anytime, hun. Try not to work too hard."

The truth was I didn't even care about that. My mind was stuck on something Mike had said. He claimed Nick was lying to me, but I had no idea what he meant. I didn't even know Nick that well. Oh, I wanted to, but we'd only gone out once. Twice if you counted ditching class for a coffee.

Clearly, there was no love lost between any of those guys. They'd probably dated the same girl at some time, or tried to, and were still fighting it out like a couple of high school boys. Nick, at least, had a little more class. Mike seemed to think treating me like a piece of meat was the quickest way into my pants, and he was oh so wrong. Nothing turned me off like a self-assured asshole, and that was exactly how Mike was looking right about now.

Maybe I'd been right to go with my gut after all.

11

The next morning, it started raining again. Walking to school in this weather was miserable. I half expected Nick to skip Art History, but he was there – and only slightly damp. The fashion of the day was shown off in party-colored raincoats and pocket-sized umbrellas. It was the wet socks that made it miserable. College air conditioning was set on "frostbite," and by the time class was over, I'd just started shivering.

With a promise from Nick for a ride home after Drawing, I hurried up the stairs. The storm outside made the light in the room drab and oppressive, lending an air of darkness to the still life set up. Sam and I were amused and spent the class trying to create something more macabre and ominous than the other. It wasn't easy to do with a roll of paper towels and some bad pottery. When the power flickered, it only helped maintain the ambiance.

The rain was still coming down hard when class let out. I figured Sam would get a ride home with Nick too, but he bailed, saying he had to meet with one of his professors. That left me alone and unwilling to brave the weather that had flash flood warnings dinging my phone. Ah, fall in the south, right? It was almost like monsoon season some days.

I had Calculus homework to finish, though, and a basic understanding of it after Nick's help. Heading to the common area of the Art Building, I decided that would be a good way to pass the time. Just inside the main doors, the foyer had a selection of tables set up for students to do their homework, and I had plenty to be done. I took a spot off to the side that was still visible from the entrance. Hopefully, Nick would see me if I got sucked into a calculation.

The area cleared out quickly. By the time I had my book open, the halls were quiet and classes had started, but Nick wasn't here yet. Granted, he was coming from the other side of campus, so I wasn't exactly surprised.

I'd almost finished two of the problems when the sound of the door made me look up. At first, I smiled, thinking it was Nick, but as the man headed toward me, I wasn't so sure. His long, rain-soaked duster was almost a robe. The hood was pulled low over his face. And those lips? The clothes weren't quite right, but I'd never forget those lips.

So many times, I'd seen him, but never like this. Never in my world. With each step he took closer, the more sure I became that this was really happening. I sucked in a breath, refusing to even blink for fear that he'd vanish.

"Hello, little dove," he said softly, his voice missing that strange resonance from the corridor.

And the thunder rumbled again. The lights flickered out, shrouding the building in darkness. Lightning flashed, the light coming through the large glass doors. The purplish-white glare illuminated his jaw like a snapshot. I couldn't even breathe. The color was all wrong, but the angles and lines were exactly right. It was him. It had to be *him.*

My mind whirled as I waited for the generators to kick on, but I couldn't think of a single thing to say. All I could do was stare with wide, shocked eyes. My breath hung in my chest as the man from my dreams stared quietly back. This was impossible, but he was real, and he was *finally* here.

For a moment, nothing at all happened. Only the sound of water dripping from his coat broke the silence. I couldn't even convince myself to speak, terrified I was wrong.

Slowly, he reached up and pushed back the hood, his lips parting in a smile so sweet I thought I'd have to die to see it again. The lightning flashed one more time as I sought his eyes. I found a beautifully dark abyss instead of the universe I'd expected. When it flashed a third time, my heart clenched painfully – just as the emergency lights clicked on, turning my fantasy world into a soft, yellow, and dim college foyer. Nick stared back at me. His face was carefully neutral.

I swallowed.

"You ok?" he asked.

I took a long, shuddering breath and nodded, my eyes locked on his lips. Why hadn't I seen it before? Maybe it was the difference in color, or maybe it was because I hadn't expected him to actually be real, but I couldn't deny it anymore. Words failed me, so I said nothing, simply reached into my bag for the sketchbook I always kept close. In the dim light, I had to dig. The sound of my rummaging was like a wild animal trying to escape. I was right. I knew it; I just had to prove it to myself.

Nick sighed and grabbed the homework I'd left open on the table, turning it around as he sat across from me. Reaching over, he grabbed my pencil, twisting it in his fingers as he smiled. Without saying a word, he just inspected the thing that had started out as a drawing before turning his attention to the problems I'd been trying to work through. He seemed oblivious to my inner conflict.

Finally, I found it. Frantically, I flipped to the first page, then the next, then the one after that, looking up at him between each. It was the same. In black and white - rather than color - the lines were the *exact* same. His lips, just like the ones in my sketchbook, curled, but his eyes never left my assignment. I was sitting across the table from Death. That, or I was completely and totally insane.

"You can't always make the world fit into the rules you want," he said softly, erasing something on the page.

"Nick?"

His eyes caught mine for a second, then returned to the page. "And you're probably going to need a little more help with Calculus." His voice was rich and soft. Like Death's, but without the resonance that came between worlds.

I swallowed. "Nick?"

That smile returned, his perfectly even teeth exactly like I remembered. "Not my best light?"

I dropped my sketchbook onto the table. Death's face looked back from under the cowl, staring up at his own reflection in Nick.

"I hadn't seen you in a hood before."

He looked at me again. "I think you have."

Ice flowed over my skin, pinpricks following in its wake, and my mouth fell slack, too shocked to even gasp. I swallowed and licked at my lips, begging my body not to fail me, hoping my voice wouldn't crack. "Why are you here?"

"I was trying to beat the rain. If you recall, I did offer you a ride home." The smile faded. "Are you scared of me now, little dove?"

"No. Should I be?"

"Never."

I nodded and pressed my fingers to my lips, looking around the room. We were completely alone. Everyone had either rushed home or was in the middle of class. "I'm losing my mind. That's what this is. I've finally gone insane."

"No," he assured me, looking back at the page to fill in a few numbers. "You just need to stop trying to fight what you don't understand. It's easy once you figure it out."

I giggled nervously. "Are we talking about the same thing?"

He laughed, no malice in the sound at all, but his eyes were still on the numbers. "No. I'm talking about your Calculus homework."

"What am I talking about?"

Those long lashes lifted slowly, his eyes so warm beneath. "Death."

"You know," I breathed.

"I was there." He paused, watching me like he expected me to run. "Which is why I'm here. How's Mr. Hussein, anyway?"

"Don't you know?"

He shook his head. "I haven't had time to look."

"Jamal's perfect. Just like you promised." I looked at my sketchpad, feeling like I was living in a dream. "You've spent so much time with me, but I don't understand why."

"Because every time I tell you to forget me, you just try harder. This was the only way I could think to keep you safe. You've been noticed, little dove." The homework was forgotten. His focus was riveted on my reaction.

Oddly, his answer made complete sense. It was exactly what I would have expected from Death. He was honest and caring, but powerful and terrifying, all at the same time. I didn't know why I hadn't seen it before.

"Why are you here?" I asked him again. "At college. Why is Death in my Calculus class?"

He shrugged. "I like math. I like art too, but I don't really know much about it. That's really more of Sam's thing." When I opened my mouth to protest the answer, he held up the white number two pencil he'd taken from my book. "We're here because you made a mistake."

"How?"

He spun the pencil in his hands. "Sam sees more than you think. He's not the only one. I'm willing to bet you don't know how to get this back on the page."

"I..." My throat pinched closed, the words stopping. I shook my head uselessly.

"The world doesn't fit into the simple rules you want it to, Sia. Most of it does, but not all. The problem is that when you do things like this, people notice, and not the ones you want."

"Like you?"

He shook his head. "No. I really am here to keep you safe."

"Why?"

He smiled and looked aside. "Your eyes are as iridescent as a peacock's feathers. Your hair burns with a flame that comes from inside." I watched him take a long deep breath. "You smell like spun sugar." He chuckled. "That. You make me – *me!* – wax poetic. Everything I've said since we met is completely true, little dove, but it's not all of it. I also hope you'll help me."

"With what?"

The world had just become crazy. I should've expected it, though. Nothing good ever happened to me without something twice as bad right on its heels. I met the most amazing man, and the next week, I went insane. Then again, I'd been on the edge of that for a few years, now.

Nick reached over to my sketchbook and flipped through the pages until he found a blank one. He took the pencil and lay it across the paper diagonally so it would fit, then slowly pressed it down with one long, strong finger. The shadows were deeper than those I'd drawn, but perfect for the dim light in the room. That was when I realized all hints of color had faded to shades of grey as the number two pencil returned to the paper it had come from.

"With that," he said. "With bending reality and creating something new."

I sighed. "I don't know how I do it, though."

"I do."

"Can you show me?" I heard the pleading in my voice but didn't care.

Nick smiled proudly. "That's pretty much what I was hoping you'd want."

Those words made reality crash back down. I'd been crushing

on Death for over four years. I'd been smitten with Nick since we met. I was going insane, right in front of the best man I'd ever known, but he wasn't here to meet the girl of his dreams. He'd been following me because he needed me to make something real. He needed a favor, not a girlfriend. Maybe we were both crazy, but our goals most certainly were not the same.

"God, I'm an idiot," I muttered, closing my sketchpad and book, then shoving them both in my bag. When I reached for my homework, his hand caught my wrist.

"Sia?"

"I'll help you, Nick," I assured him. "I owe you that for Jamal. I just..." I shook my head. "I should have known better. Guys like you? I knew it was too good to be true."

I tried to put my homework away, but he refused to let go, his grip light and delicate, more of a request than a demand.

"Can I take you to dinner?" he asked.

"Look. You don't have to –"

"I want to." His thumb traced the inside of my wrist. "Knowing you can help me has nothing to do with thinking you are the most amazing woman I've ever seen. You're not the only one who's had trouble staying away."

"What?"

He chuckled. "I was hoping to get another kiss. At least one. More would be better."

"Just a kiss?" I asked, feeling a nervous tingling in my gut that was so close to being a flutter.

Something devilish passed across his dark eyes. "To start. I figure this conversation just killed my chances of mini-golf, though."

I laughed, the joke convincing me this wasn't an elaborate prank as my heart picked up the pace. It wasn't fear. I'd never been scared of him, not really. I was terrified I was insane, but Nick had always felt like a safety net in either guise. It was hard to be frightened of the man who had not only saved my life, but had also been in almost every erotic fantasy I'd had over the last few years. Instead, this feeling was a lot closer to the giddiness I'd had when we first met.

Nick was Death. Death was real. This guy – who was both of them at once – was actually interested in me? There weren't words to describe this feeling, but I liked it a lot.

I bit my lip and nodded. "So Sam knows about all of this?"

"And Luke."

"The creepy guy?"

"My other roommate. Blonde guy? He's in your writing class."

That was the one. Wait. There was one of them in each of my classes, and he made it sound like that was intentional. So those guys were helping him?

"Why are y'all watching me?"

"Because you used the pencil." His response didn't exactly answer my question, but it said enough. "I can't be more clear than that, not here."

My teeth closed on the inside of my lips, pressing them together, and I nodded, mulling that over. "Then when and where?"

He pushed my homework back to me. "Since you're going to fail that anyway, how about now? I can help you with the math, too."

"So, the whole physics major thing? That's not bullshit?"

"I'm honestly enrolled as a physics major. I'm honestly fond of the sciences." He grinned deviously. "Still think I'm hot?"

"Yeah. I kinda like blue."

He looked away, a surprised smile playing on his lips. "That's even better than I hoped. Can I buy you a coffee while we wait for a dry ride?"

"You didn't drive?"

Nick shook his head. "Nah, I was going to get Luke to bring my car and play it all cool. If you're willing to come back to my place, um, we can finish this conversation. I'm going to bet my vague answers haven't satisfied your curiosity at all?"

"You're right." I put the last of my things away and stood, waiting for Nick to join me.

He looked up at me and smiled, lifting himself to his feet. His hand reached up for my face timidly. "I thought you'd be scared of me," he whispered.

"I thought you didn't want to see me again."

His dark eyes held me as his fingers traced my cheek. "No, I was trying to keep you safe from all of this." His voice had grown deeper, maybe even a little rough as he leaned just a hair closer. "But I think you've moved far past that."

My reply came out as a breath. "How far?"

"Far enough that I'm glad I no longer have to hide from you."

Then his mouth caressed mine, tender and careful, teasing me with the memories of the last time we'd done this. I pressed in for more, wanting to deepen the kiss, but Nick pulled away. His thumb swept over my cheek.

"As much as I'd love to continue this, we can't stay here. There's a reason I didn't want you to walk home alone." He grabbed his trench coat from the back of the chair. "And I think it's still raining."

I tried hard to play it cool while a million questions bottlenecked in my mind. The one I asked was, "Just tell me you don't melt?" Which proved just how shaken I really was.

He laughed as he settled the coat across my shoulders. "No. I don't melt. Would make it a lot harder to take care of you if I did."

Outside, the rain had let up a bit, coming down steadily instead of torrentially, but it was still enough to soak everything. Holding Nick's coat across my shoulders, we jogged across the street, ducking into the Kharma Kafe. Inside, the place was packed. Evidently, we weren't the only ones wanting to avoid the weather.

Nick pulled out his phone and sent a message. I could only assume it was to his roommates. In just a few seconds he had a response. "It's better to be around people, but the guys are coming. Um, can I get you a coffee while we wait?"

I shook my head. "As much as I'm an addict, I think that might be a bad idea. I kinda..." I sighed, not knowing how to explain that my guts might revolt.

"Yeah. I understand. This is a lot to take in. I'm sorry." He gestured to the corner. "Look, what do you remember about that night?"

"The gas station robbery?" He nodded and the memories flooded back. "Everything. They told me it was hallucinations caused by the head injury and medication."

"Do you know what happened to the gunman?"

I lifted my chin but dropped my voice. "You killed him. Just like you killed the people who wrecked my car."

His eyes held mine without remorse. "I did."

I looked around quickly, wondering if anyone had heard. "How?"

"What did you see that day, Sia? What did it look like to you?"

"Smoke. Brown, almost rust-colored smoke."

"When?"

It felt like the bodies around us were too close. Like every person in the coffee shop could hear what we were talking about. "When I reached up."

"That's not when he died." He sounded surprised. "You saw the aether?"

I nodded. "It came out of his eyes, and mouth, and skin. It was everywhere, like I would've expected blood, but almost like liquid-vapor."

He clenched his teeth and looked away. "Fuck."

"What?"

He pushed his hair back, pulling it into a ponytail at the base of his neck in frustration. "I can't believe you can see it."

"See what?"

"The fog," he said, dropping his hair. "You're creating already, and you can actually see it." He nodded to himself. "You're acting more like a demon than a human." He reached out and grabbed my chin, the kind gentleman suddenly gone in his intensity. "Have you ever inspired anyone?"

"What are you talking about?" I asked, stepping back.

"Had a painting made to honor your beauty, whistled a tune and someone made it better, made a comment that someone turned into a novel. Things like that?"

"No. Not that I know of. Why?"

He rubbed his hand across his mouth. "You shouldn't see that substance. Muses inspire, they don't create. You're acting like a demon."

"I'm not a demon," I told him.

My words snapped him back to reality. A smile flicked in the corner of his mouth, gone as quickly as it came. "Yeah, I know that, little dove."

"Then what the hell are you talking about?"

"I'm talking about that pencil we put back on the page." He gestured to my backpack. "I'm pretty sure you saw that."

"But there was no smoke."

"I know. The interesting thing is you didn't need it. Most of us do. Makes me wonder what you could do if you had it." His phone beeped, cutting him off before he could explain more than that. He read the message quickly. "The guys are here. Still willing to come over for a few answers?"

"Sure." His little tirade was making me feel a lot less sure of his mental stability, and my own was already in serious doubt. "I mean, it's not like I can get any more crazy, right?"

"Yeah," Nick agreed, gesturing to the door. "Pretty much. At least the rain slowed down for a bit."

That was all I needed to hear. I led the way, pushing through the people crowding the exit in my desire to get a whole answer I could understand. So far, everything he'd said only made me more confused and worried, not less. Trying to fight the anxiety, I just wanted to be someplace a bit less crowded where no one could hear him talking about murder – then have him assure me it was all going to be alright.

Shoving through the door, I ran face-first into a tall, beautiful, amazingly built blonde man. Something inside me snapped, sending every panic alarm into overdrive. The urge to run was instantaneous.

"Hello, Sienna," Luke said, grabbing my arm before I could bolt.

"*L*et go!"

I tried to pull free, but Nick's creepy friend chuckled, his grip almost bruising my arm. It didn't seem to bother him at all that I didn't want him touching me. He completely ignored my demands, turning me to face him as he looked directly into my eyes.

"Such a vibrant little lady. Definitely exotic, don't you think, Nick?"

I yanked again, but he held me. A step behind me, I heard the door thunk closed. "Let her go, Luke."

"No way. I know you can see that on her, which means any one of us could. I need to shut her down."

Nick walked closer and gently rested his hand on Luke's arm. "You think tormenting her is going to do any good?"

Standing so close to Luke, our eyes locked. I could see the yellow ring around his pupils fading to green closer to the edge. The color was at odds with the shade of his skin, like it wasn't natural. Like it was poisonous.

"I'll make you a deal," Luke said softly.

"No deals," Nick interrupted. He pushed us farther from the door, around the edge of the building. I stumbled along in Luke's grip. "Don't try that bullshit," Nick warned. "Not with her."

"And you actually call this dick a friend?" I asked Nick.

"Yeah." He never took his gaze from Luke. "She's already figured it out. Just let her calm down."

Luke smiled. "You scared, little girl?"

"I'm working on being pissed."

I wished I could pull the life out of this arrogant bastard like Nick had with the gunman. I wished I could force him to release me. I wished I could do something – anything – to get this asshole's hands off of me.

A tendril of metallic twists began to seep from his fingers where he gripped my arm. Luke gasped and stepped back, releasing me quickly. Without hesitation, Nick grabbed the substance, catching it in his hand like a butterfly before slapping it back to Luke's chest. When the jerk sighed in relief, Nick chuckled.

"Stop terrorizing her. I told you she's already figured it out. Next time I won't stop it."

"How can she pull aether?" Luke hissed.

Nick smiled. "And make the arts live? Sound familiar?"

Behind me, a third voice joined the conversation. "So she's really the Muse?" It was Sam. "She's not one of theirs?"

"Nope." Nick lifted an eyebrow. "She's what Michael's looking for, and I haven't exactly given her the whole intro to weirdness speech."

"What the fuck are you people talking about?" I demanded, turning to face them all.

Nick sighed. "Where'd you park, Luke? We shouldn't talk about this here."

"I'm not going anywhere with that asshole." I glared at Luke then turned and started walking back home.

I didn't give them a chance to talk me out of it. I wanted nothing to do with him. Sam and Nick had been ok, but Luke?

Something told every fiber in my body to get far away from that psychopath – even if that meant Nick, too. If he couldn't understand that letting his friend grab me wasn't cool, then I needed to seriously rethink my crush on Death. Stretching my legs with each step, I hurried without breaking into a run.

Behind me, I could hear the men talking amongst themselves, the debate hushed but intense. I couldn't help but be curious, yet I wasn't willing to risk being around that creep. Hopefully, Nick would understand. If not, was he any better than my ex?

All I'd ever wanted was to pass my classes, make good grades, and get a decent paying job when I graduated. I wasn't asking for much, just a normal life like everyone else took for granted. I'd even give up the idea of some great romantic love story if I had to. I didn't want to, but other guys *would* come along. My dream was to have a little stability in my life, and nothing about this entire situation was stable.

It also wasn't impossible. I'd seen enough to know there was more out there than what most people took for granted, but I'd also seen enough to know when to make a hasty exit. Looking down the barrel of a gun had that effect.

I made it almost a block, ignoring the random droplets still falling, and had just started to relax when Luke stepped in front of me. My feet nearly skidded on the sidewalk as I stopped and immediately began backing up. I'd just left him back by campus, but he'd walked out of nothing. Nothing! I tried to breathe, but my throat was closing and my heart was pounding way too fast. It was like someone had just changed all the rules of reality and I was suffering the consequences. I took another step back, searching frantically for a way out – and collided with something solid: Nick.

"I won't let them hurt you, little dove." The words were soft, his breath light against the side of my neck as his hands rested gently on my arms. Nick leaned closer, his lips brushing my hair. "And I'd prefer it if you didn't pull my life out."

"That's..." I turned to him, realizing he meant the smoke. "That's what that is?"

"Yeah." He pushed a wisp of hair away from my face, his dark eyes intent. "May I walk you home? You left the car behind, and it's only sprinkling now."

"Bring her to our place," Luke said.

Nick lifted an eyebrow. "Or that. Your choice, but I did promise to answer questions."

"What are you?" I lifted my chin, daring him to evade it.

"Nick Voland, college student, also known as the Grim Reaper or the Angel of Death, a misnomer –" Luke's laugh made Nick's lip quirk, but he went on, "Or Death, as you've dubbed me. I have many names, but Nick works for now."

"Did I do the same thing you did?" I looked over my shoulder at Luke.

Nick shook his head. "No. You did something much more impressive. I promise, Luci – er, Luke – will be a gentleman." He looked over my head. "If he doesn't, I will pull half the aether from his body and let you take the other half."

"Dick," Luke replied, his tone amused instead of offended.

Nick just ignored him. "Let us walk you home. It's not safe out here, not anymore. Too many people are watching us."

"I'll cook," Luke offered, moving a step closer. "I'm not always an asshole, just most of the time. Come over, we'll talk, and I'll cook to make up for earlier?"

"Is this some kind of trick?"

Luke rolled his eyes. "If it was, do you think I'd tell you? I make an amazing chicken parmesan, though."

"It's his turn to cook," Nick explained. "Your choice, dove. Just don't walk home alone."

"Why not?" I stepped away from Nick, well aware that his charm and good looks lured me in. I wasn't sure I wanted to be anywhere near Luke, not even with my eternal protector at my side, and I couldn't understand why I'd been fine walking to class but suddenly in danger heading home.

"I'd rather explain that inside."

Luke sighed. "We're not the only freaks in this town, and we think the others are looking for something. That something just happens to be you."

"And how do I know y'all are the good guys?"

Luke laughed. "We aren't. We're just the ones on your side." When he realized I wasn't amused, the smile vanished, and he shoved a hand through his close-cropped hair. "Our place is warded for it, which makes it safer than yours. You already know you can fuck me up, so you've got the advantage. The truth is, we need your help." He smiled, this time honestly. "May I please cook you dinner?"

"Where's Sam?" My mind was whirling, trying to keep up, but I wanted to know more. Curiosity may have killed the cat, but I couldn't stop the questions.

Luke shrugged. "He's taking the car home."

"More like he didn't want to piss her off," Nick muttered.

"Or that." Luke tilted his head. "You've already been over once and lived through it."

I chewed on my lip, debating. "How'd y'all beat me here?"

Nick offered his hand. "I'd be happy to show you."

"Show me, and I'll accept the invitation to dinner." I laid my hand on his, daring him to refuse.

His fingers closed on mine and he stepped back, pulling me just off my feet. It was like slipping underwater. The world changed just like it had the night before, but this time I could clearly feel the edge of the barrier on my skin. Unlike the inside of my room, out here, colors became more intense but buildings turned to shades of grey. Before I could adjust to it, cloth brushed my wrist, and I realized the hand I was holding now belonged to Death.

"This is what the corridor looks like when you're outside," he said, drawing my eyes to the hood. His skin was again the color of moonlight, and the black robe covered him completely, but he smiled with Nick's mouth. "Space works differently here, and I don't want to lose you. I need to be closer."

When I nodded, he stepped in behind me, wrapping his arm around my waist without releasing my hand. The other carefully clasped my shoulder. Then he stepped back, pulling me with him. For a moment, it felt as if the ground vanished. It was like dropping onto a chair that was lower than expected, and for that brief second, my body was convinced it would never stop.

Then we did.

Death tugged at my arm again, and the colors returned to normal as his robe vanished, leaving a dark-haired Nick in his place. I snatched my hand away and looked around. We stood on the lawn of a large, green, Victorian-style home. I recognized it. This was their place. We'd crossed almost two blocks in a single step.

"How?"

"Willing to come inside?" Nick asked.

I pressed my clenched hand to my chest, trying to make sense of it all. If I said no, they could out-maneuver me just by stepping through the corridor. If I said yes, they could grab me and take me wherever they wanted. With a sinking heart, I realized I was completely at their mercy. That, or completely bonkers.

"I don't really have a choice, do I?"

Nick took a step closer, and I retreated, keeping him out of my reach. He froze. "I thought you weren't scared of me."

"I'm a little bit freaked out, Nick. What did you expect?"

His face turned to stone. Smooth, beautiful stone, but devoid of all emotions. He nodded once. "I hoped you were ready. I'll take you home the normal way."

"And what way did you bring me here?"

Those dark eyes narrowed intently. "The fast way." He took a step toward the short white picket gate next to the road, pausing when I didn't follow. "Your home is only two blocks away."

"I know where it is!" I looked back at the house. "Why don't you just drag me in there if you want me so bad?"

Slowly, he turned back, frustration tensing his body. "Because you said you trusted me. You kept asking for this, and I actually hoped you could handle it."

"Is that why you saved me?"

Nick groaned and shoved one hand through his hair. The other was clenched into a fist as he closed the distance between us. I could almost see the power flickering in his dark eyes. "Yes and no. I can't explain it out here. That's like asking to be struck by lightning."

"Will you explain it in there?"

The anger vanished, dissipating as I watched. "I'd rather not."

"Why?"

"I shouldn't have interfered," he whispered. "I didn't tell them about it."

"Then why did you?"

"I didn't want to see you afraid." He pressed his lips together and met my eyes. "This, what you are doing right now? I intervened so this wouldn't happen. So you could have at least a bit of a normal life."

"Is that it?" I gestured to the yard around us. "All of this, and that's the best answer you have?"

"No." Something flickered across his face, but I couldn't read it before the smooth, calm mask returned, the one that reminded me of Death. "That's just the best answer I can give you now. I swear to you, Sia, we will not hurt you."

"But you could?"

He nodded. "We need your help, though."

A car drove by slowly, reminding me that we stood a few paces apart, braced as if fighting. I took a long, deep breath and made a foolish decision. I mean, since my life had already crossed the boundaries of weird, I might as well make it all or nothing. Besides, I really did like Nick, and I couldn't bring myself to actually believe he meant me any harm. Letting the air out, I felt my shoulders relax as I accepted the choice.

"Does he really make a decent chicken parmesan?"

Nick lifted his head and looked at me until the corner of his lip slid up. "Yeah. He really does. Would you care to come in?"

"Might as well, right? I mean, if y'all wanted to force me to do your bidding, I couldn't really stop you, so why fight it?" I turned for the steps, but Nick caught up easily.

"I have no intention of forcing you to do *anything.*"

He pushed open the door, waiting for me to enter first, then guided me into the room on the right. Three leather sofas were placed around a massive flat-screen TV. The gaming console lay on the floor before it, controllers dropped casually on the coffee table.

"Can I get you a drink?" he asked, gesturing to a chair.

"Something with sugar. Soda?"

He bowed his head and turned, leaving me alone. No sooner had my rump touched the leather than Sam appeared. He paused, looked me over, then took the seat across from me, leaning forward to rest his arms on his knees.

"Saw you tried to drain Luke." It was hard to take him seriously with the shock of magenta hair and the metal ring through his brow.

I shrugged. "He didn't let go when I asked."

"Told," Sam corrected. "You *told* him to let go." He looked me over again, his eyes seeming to trace my outline, as if he looked all around me but never quite at me. "Guess the rumors about redheads are true, huh? Spunky?"

"Something like that." I pointed at the lock hanging across his brow. "Tell me, is it working for you?"

He thrust out his lower lip as he nodded. "Yeah, sweetie, it is. Chicks love the hair, guys love the piercings."

I decided to ignore that and change the subject. "You know what's going on?"

"Yeah. Do you?" Sam toyed with the metal in his tongue, thinking. "You religious?"

I couldn't help but look at the door, worried I'd already crossed some line that would anger Nick – or worse, his well-dressed blonde friend. "No. Should I be?"

He countered that easily. "What religion recognizes Death?"

"All of them." Didn't they?

"As a god?"

He had me there. "I don't know."

"The concept of the Grim Reaper isn't exactly from religion. It's more of a folk story." Sam twined the longer hair by his forehead around a finger as he talked. "It's also not just one person. We all do it, but Nick's a little different. That's what I was trying to explain in Drawing that day."

"Ok? How so?"

"Most of us can catch souls, but he can ease them out. He's good at it, too - and you saw him. *No one* sees him unless he wants them to. You can only look up through the veils, not down - and from Earth, everything is down."

"What?!" He'd just completely confused me with that one sentence. I recognized all the words, but the order and manner he used them in didn't make sense.

That was when Nick timed his entrance, acting as if he'd been a part of the conversation the entire time. "You just jumped ahead," he told Sam, passing him a cold beer. He handed me a bottle of Coke then claimed the next closest corner, opening his own beer. "When you slip into the corridor, you pass a veil. I think you felt it?"

"Like sliding under water?"

Nick smiled and nodded. "Yeah. The corridor is a gap between two veils, like the buffer area between the doors at most stores." He held up his hands parallel. "Like Wal-Mart. There's one that goes from outside to the corridor, then a second from the corridor to inside the store. Two doors, two veils, and a gap in the middle. Same idea."

"Uh-huh."

He tried again. "Like the space between a set of nesting dolls? The smallest is inside, with the rest built up around it, but there's always a little gap of air. That gap is the corridor, and the veil is the outermost layer of each plane of existence, or world."

Now I was with him, but every answer made more questions. "What's on the other side of the corridor?"

"That's a somewhat complicated question." He gestured at my backpack. "Have paper in there?"

Once again, I pulled out my Calculus notes. A pen was clipped inside the metal spiral when I passed it over. Nick flipped to a blank page and began drawing a rough sketch. His hands were strong and calloused like someone who often used a pen or pencil, but not rough.

"There are five worlds that we know of, all in parallel dimensions," he began.

Sam snickered. "Dimensions sounds so science fiction, man."

Nick raised an eyebrow. "You want to explain string theory to someone with problems in calculus?"

"Nope." Sam sucked at his beer, waving his hand for Nick to continue.

He cradled the pen in his fingers lightly as he drew five circles in an upside-down V, then turned the page and drew them again but in a more circular shape. Flipping back, he laid it on the table between us, gesturing with the pen as he spoke.

"So, they exist in the same time and space, but different layers so that, in theory, they should not be aware of the existence of the others."

"Ok?" Sounding like a bad movie so far.

"So, the universe is constantly expanding. Big Bang Theory and all that, right? So is the multiverse, but it's moving away from the other dimensions, straining the bonds between them."

"Ok?" Still wasn't quite following.

"Here on Earth, you recognize only a few dimensions. Time, up and down, left and right, and forward and back. The thing you're missing is in and out. These universes aren't beside or around yours, they're inside or outside the reality you know."

"Uh-huh..."

Nick sighed. "Ok, it's complicated. It also doesn't really matter." He flipped to the second page. "All you need to know is that the planes used to be connected all the way around like this in an unbroken circle, so that no matter where we were, we all had a dimension open on each side. But, as the universe expanded, a part of the link broke. Now, instead of a circle, it's more like a mountain with Earth on top." He flipped back to the first page and tapped the point of the V. "So from here, you can only go down. Technically, out. All the way to the right is our world." He tapped the last circle in the diagram. "To the left is our enemy's." Then the last circle on the other side.

"What's between those and Earth?" I asked.

"Myths and legends." Nick tried to hide it, but the smile slipped through. "Between you and us is Vesdar, home of satyrs and dragons. The world next to Earth on the left side has fairies and unicorns."

I nodded slowly. "So you want me to believe that myths are real?"

"Yep," Sam said.

Nick just held up a hand. "I'm not really done yet. So, because the worlds are parallel, but different, things tend to have some semblance of continuity. As an example, all of the worlds have a sentient bipedal species."

"Humans, fairies, and satyrs?" I fought the urge to roll my eyes.

"And demons and angels," Sam said. "All the worlds, not just the inner three."

It felt like cold ice trickled down my spine when I realized what he was saying. Their world and their enemy's had demons and angels. I looked from Sam to Nick then back to the page.

"That's why they're your enemy? Demons and angels?"

Nick nodded. "Now is when you ask the next question, Sienna."

I licked my lips slowly, moistening the suddenly dry skin. "I don't think I need to."

Sam sat up. "Gonna see how Luke's doing with supper."

"Yeah." Nick shot him an appreciative smile, waiting for his friend to leave before looking at me again. "Can you even say it?"

"You're a demon?" The words came out no more than a whisper, but Nick looked pleased.

He closed his eyes for a moment, then nodded. "How'd you figure that out?"

"Luke said y'all weren't the good guys. Your world is next to that of dragons, while the other is beside fairies. I don't know how this works, but it makes sense to me that the cross-dimensional evolution – or whatever you call it – would be progressive, not random." I paused, then decided I might as well be completely honest. "I've also never heard of angels with skin the color of moonlight. They're always supposed to be brilliant and radiant, not soothing and ethereal. And you kinda admitted it the other night."

"Moonlight?" Of all the things I'd said, that was what he clung to. Nick glanced at me quickly, then waved it away. "Well, Luke's not a demon, but he's moved to our side."

"A fallen angel?"

Nick chuckled. "There's not really anything to fall from. They call him a traitor, we call him a friend."

"So why does he freak me out?"

"I don't know." He sighed. "Usually, humans feel comfortable around angels and try to avoid us."

"What's the fight over?" If any of this was true, I doubted the fight would be about human virtue or souls.

Nick pointed at the notebook again. "Let's not jump ahead. So the worlds of demons and angels used to be connected. During that time, someone – and none of us can agree on who – figured out how to cross through the veils. The wars started, and we've never really found a way to stop them. When the connection between Angelis and Daemin broke, the only way for us to continue fighting was to take the long way around." He traced the entire V, from end to end.

"So instead of giving up, y'all went through so many other worlds?"

He shrugged. "It seemed like a good idea at the time. We found ways to make permanent gates since not all of us can cross easily. This let us transfer entire armies across the worlds, stepping from one plane to another, but it also let the natives wander through." He raised his eyes. "Hence the legends and myths you know."

"So, knights really hunted dragons?"

Nick nodded. "Yeah. There was a portal in Europe that led to Vesdar. Knights would ride across, try to kill a dragon, and bring what parts of it they could home." He chuckled. "In Vesdar, there are some interesting tales of human myths."

"And fairies?"

Nick looked quickly at the TV then back to the page. "Yeah. Um, same thing, basically. The inner worlds are a bit different from the outer." He rubbed at his face, thinking. "On Earth, you live fast and intensely, and you breed easily. The farther out you go, the more males there are per capita. On Vesdar, they live longer, usually pushing ten thousand years, but have few children. Maybe one or two in that entire time. In the last three thousand years, the population has stayed pretty stable."

"Ok?"

"Fairies, well, they're on the opposite side but similar in many ways. They call their world Tyrnigg. Unlike Vesdar, the women tend to rule, but there still aren't a lot of them. Like Vesdar, they have similar lifespans and reproductive rates. Granted, where satyrs are humorous and pranksters, the fae are malicious and temperamental."

"And you?" I watched his face, but Nick refused to look at me. "How long do demons live?"

His answer was soft. "Those of us from the outer worlds are immortal."

13

"So the war is over land? Overpopulation?" I asked, trying to piece together the information so I could stay on track.

He shook his head. "No. We don't have children. We have no women."

"What about the angels?"

"The same." Nick shrugged. "They're lovely creatures, but like us, all male."

"So fairies must be pretty popular," I teased.

"Were." He sighed and leaned back. "There aren't many left. Remember that thing you pulled from Luke earlier?"

"The smoke?"

"Aether," he corrected. "It's what your science has yet to discover. Aether is what makes life. You can have all the right parts put together in the right way, but without aether, there is nothing living. A dead body needs something intangible to live. Pond scum needed something else to become bacteria. That something is aether."

"Which is why the robber died when you pulled it from him!" I sat up, looking into the other room, realizing I'd almost done the same to his roommate. "Can anyone do that?"

"No, but don't get too far ahead. Aether is a very powerful substance, and a few dozen million years ago, we made weapons from it. A few million later, we made defenses. Now, we have them in the veils."

"So, you made the veils?" My mind was spinning.

"No, we just improved them. In order to cross into Daemin, you must be allowed entry, like a key. This keeps angels out and slowed down the war. Unfortunately, the veils were altered with aether from outside our world, and we need more to maintain it." He tucked a lock of hair behind his ear. "The angels did something similar. The difference is they, um, harvest aether."

"What do you mean?"

"What happens when a Catholic is on his deathbed? He calls a priest to give last rites." Nick shrugged. "When you die, the aether in your body is released, and if someone is there ready to catch it, then it can be harvested. They created religion to harvest your souls."

"But we don't really have souls?" If that smoke was our souls, and it was what gave us life, did that mean there was nothing after death?

Nick guessed where my mind was going. "I've never died, Sia. I can't. I don't know what happens after and what consciousness you'd retain, if any. I don't even know if there is a god. I just know that if you're left alone, the aether will disperse from your body into the world. Just like carbon or oxygen, it's recycled."

"So what do y'all do with it?"

"Put it in the corridor, heal people, create things."

He stood and walked to a plant in the corner of the room. With a glance at me, Nick reached out and pulled at a leaf, his fingers drawing a greenish-blue fog from it as the leaf withered. Before my eyes, it turned brown and died, leaving the rest of the plant healthy. Nick closed his hand around the fog and returned, lowering himself gently.

"Plants tend to have less aether than animals. The more evolved the creature, the more intense the aether is." He opened his hand, showing me the mist that lay in his palm. "I have the ability to manipulate and use this, just like you can make paint become art."

"So anyone can do it with training?" Anyone could learn to paint and draw if they studied enough.

Nick tilted his head back and forth. "Somewhat. Any of us can learn to touch it, but few can master it." He lifted his hand, tossing the fog into the air between us. "Now watch."

He left it there, suspended, and grabbed his beer before leaning back. By the third gulp, the substance seemed thinner, more translucent. I watched while it simply faded from sight, just like the smoke it resembled.

"Where does it go?"

"Everywhere." He smiled. "You're missing the most obvious question, though."

Confused, I shook my head, hoping he'd explain.

"Why can you see it?"

My brow wrinkled as I thought back over the times I'd watched him do that. I'd always assumed that something he did allowed the substance to be seen, but that didn't seem to be the case.

"So not everyone can see that?"

"Not humans," Nick assured me. "Demons and angels see it as easily as you see water. If it's dense enough, it's obvious, but you don't see the vapor in the air, right?"

"Ok? But humans couldn't see that?"

"No."

I swallowed. "Am I human?"

"Yes." He leaned forward again, taking the last drink from his beer before setting the bottle on the table. "You're what we call a Muse. The rare exception to the rule, you can not only see aether – although most Muses can't – but also use it. Most often, this comes as inspiring others, or manipulating the aether inside of them. Some call it charisma – but not all charisma is from being a Muse. Some call it artistic talent, or beauty, or so many other things."

"Da Vinci?" I asked.

He nodded. "A very strong Muse. Humans have tried to explain it away for centuries now. The Greeks worshiped their Muses as near gods. Ancient man called them shamans or wizards. Each society tends to manifest a style, probably because of the culture. That's why the Classical Muses were all seen as goddesses of inspiration, but in other times they were wizards with destructive powers."

"And now?"

His black eyes bore into mine, seriousness written across his face. "I haven't seen a Muse in almost two hundred years."

My heart paused when the reality of his words hit me. "So what do I do?"

"Let me teach you?"

I looked around the room, hoping for something to give me the right answer. "Why you?"

My eyes found Luke leaning casually against the door frame behind us. I had no idea how long he'd been there, but it looked as if he'd been listening.

"He's the best there is. That's why he's the Angel of Death," a smile split Luke's lips, "even if he isn't an angel."

"How old are you?" I looked at Luke, but the question was for both of them.

Luke shrugged and turned back to the hall. "Dinner's ready."

When he was out of sight, I looked back to Nick. "You haven't seen a Muse in two hundred years. How old are you?"

"I don't know." He didn't move. Those dark eyes watched me cautiously. "We've always been, and we never thought to count. I used to come to Earth to look at the flowers, though, before the animals got so large."

"Large, like dinosaurs?"

"Yes, and other things. We thought they were like dragons, but in a few million years, things have changed a lot." He stood and tilted his head to the hall. "Dinner? Sam loves to describe the extinct species."

"So Sam's a demon, too?" I asked, just wanting to hear it.

Nick dipped his head in acknowledgment. "Yeah."

I pulled myself up, feeling slightly disconnected from reality, and followed him through the house, passing two other rooms before turning into the very large and very formal dining area. The table was laid out perfectly, but all four plates were set in the center to keep the conversation easy. When I entered, both Sam and Luke stood, waiting until I found a chair before returning to their seats. Their manners were impeccable if archaic.

"No one does that anymore," I said.

Sam grinned and reached for a dish. "We know, but it doesn't mean they shouldn't. Respect for women has pretty much vanished in the last hundred years."

"We did ask for equality," I pointed out.

Luke chuckled. "I don't really know how one affects the other." He passed a basket of bread and I tried not to flinch away, but he noticed. "I assume you don't discriminate for age, and yet you'd let an elderly woman go first in line, right?"

"Yeah?" I passed the bread to Nick, who'd claimed the chair beside me, then took the next thing Luke handed over. It was easier this time.

"It's called respect." He grabbed one more platter, offering it to me first. "Remember, women are still something of an intrigue to us."

I chose a piece of chicken and passed it along. "Why are you hanging out with demons? Aren't you supposed to be mortal enemies?"

Sam held up his hand and wagged his finger. "We save serious talk for after the meal. No sense ruining your appetite." He took a bite. "Delicious, Luke."

The angel grinned. "Yeah, I put in some effort. Trying to make a good impression."

While the food was handed out, the conversation lagged. I had so many questions and not nearly enough answers. Taking a bite of my meal, I paused. It really was good! Much better than anything I'd experienced before. Luke saw my expression and nodded to himself, but I had to take another bite. Could the stories about eating fairy food have any bearing on my current situation?

Nick glanced at me quickly, then looked over at Sam. "So, she seemed very interested to hear about dinosaurs."

Sam's eyes lit up. "My god, Sienna, they were huge. Some were bigger than dragons." He grinned. "Quite a few of them were brilliantly colored. Some had feathers, although they're just starting to figure that part out."

Luke nodded knowingly. "At first, they were insane colors, closer to fish. Of course, that's back when they were little things."

"Red and yellow lasted a while," Sam added, getting into the subject. "Eventually, they started changing to blend with the environment, but the world was evolving so fast. It was like every time I came back, a new species would just crop up. And the flowers!"

"Massive things," Nick said. "The first flowers weren't like what you have now, but more like clusters of leaves with pigment."

"Like a poinsettia?" They'd completely distracted me.

"Close." Nick glanced over to me. "White was common, and a lot were pale colors like yellow or pink."

"The sunsets were amazing," Sam said, leaning closer. "That crap about pollution making better sunsets is so much shit."

Nick chuckled. "Vesdar still has the best."

"Yeah. But Jurassic Earth was a close competitor."

They were either playing the best joke, or they had really been there. The way they spoke, in half sentences and incomplete descriptions, made it feel like nothing more than pleasant memories.

"What about early man?"

Nick took a drink before answering, his eyes distant. "At first, we thought they were like a pet. Similar to a dog, I suppose. They were smart but very bestial. Nothing like people now."

"Ok?" I wanted more than that.

Sam took another bite, speaking around his full mouth without being disgusting. "There were a lot of types, you know? Dark ones, light ones, big ones, and little ones. I mean, we could tell they were all some type of primate, but because all the realms were changing, we didn't know they'd eventually become our equal."

"Equal?" I looked at each of them, unsure I'd heard right.

"Close enough," Luke muttered.

Nick sighed. "Equals, Sia. Different, but one is not better than the other. We've just had the chance to learn more."

"And the fairies and satyrs learned faster than humans?"

They all nodded, but Sam's eyes were excited. "Satyrs aren't fauns. That got all messed up somewhere. They have horns – but we do too – and we all have normal feet, not hooves. They do tend to have more body hair, but fairies have those fragile little wings. Not quite like the insect knockoffs they show now, but more like feathers made of transparent panels. They live for centuries so tend to have a more advanced culture, even if the species isn't as perfected."

"Long life versus short generations," Luke explained. "Evolution happens quickly when you keep advancing. Think of watching bacteria evolve as compared to elephants."

That made sense, but Sam's comment made me wonder about one thing. "What do you mean about the horns?" I gestured at each of them. "Where do they go?"

Beside me, Nick ducked his head, but Sam didn't notice. "We stopped showing them here hundreds of years ago after the angels turned people against us."

"Angels did that?" I looked at Luke, hoping he'd explain.

Nick answered, his voice emotionless. "Angels started a

propaganda war, but humans feared us before then. We're monsters, Sia, so we use aether to build a skin. A way to change our appearance to look more like you. Something easier to accept. Centuries ago, we didn't bother, but now? It's easier to fit in, so we alter our bodies in each realm."

"If we're there enough," Sam added.

Nick nodded slowly. "Death was my first attempt, and it only works in the corridors beside Earth. I wanted to make something less terrifying to humans so I could ease their suffering at the end, but I had no idea how complicated it would be. I only got the job half right."

Sam grinned. "He lost a few bits but didn't change much else. That's why he uses a robe. The rest of us make an effort to put one on when we can, but we also don't reap quite as much. It also didn't take long before Angels figured out their own way of altering their appearance. Different technique, same end result."

That was a little more than I could process right now, so I focused on what I could handle. "Where does the robe go when you aren't there?" I asked, keeping my eyes on Nick.

"Same place aether goes." He shrugged. "It's just a framework that reorganizes the molecules. Some of it's from our own bodies, and the rest is taken from the environment around us."

"Beam me up, Scotty," Luke teased. "Same idea, different method."

"And I can do that?"

Luke shook his head. "Not yet. Building skins is one of the most complex tasks any outworlder can do. Making bodies is easier for an aethersmith, making alterations to one is easier for an aetherweaver."

"Aethersmith? Aetherweaver?"

"Mage," Nick supplied. "Demon or angel. It's a lot less hocus pocus and a lot more physics and chemistry, but close enough from your perspective."

"It's still an art form," Sam muttered. "I suck at it, Sienna. I have enough aethercraft to cross the veils, but I'm no magician."

I turned to Luke. "What about you?"

He winked. "Angel. Only demons do aethersmithing. We get different tricks."

"You want to explain that?" His attitude annoyed me.

Luke tapped at the side of his eye. "I can manipulate the aether inside a body, but not outside. It's called aetherweaving. In other words, I can give you mental suggestions, usually formed as a deal so your mind can accept it without losing its hold on sanity. That's how I got the reputation for corrupting souls."

"Too soon," Nick muttered, glaring at Luke.

They claimed to be eternal. They claimed that myths, legends, and religion were based on fact. They spoke as if they'd actually lived through history. That meant two things. Either they'd perfected this little ruse, or I was sitting across from a pair of demons and a fallen angel.

"Your name isn't Luke, is it?" I clenched my hands in my lap, terrified of the answer.

"It is now," he assured me.

"Has it always been?" Silence had fallen over the table. All three of them watched me intently.

Luke smiled. "That's not polite conversation for dinner, now is it?" The twist of his lips did nothing to hide the deviousness on his face. "Your toy doesn't like me, Nick."

"That's because you're being an ass," Nick shot back. "You want her to know, then you tell her."

"Like you wanted her to know what you did for her?" Luke asked.

"I had no idea she could slip across the veil." Nick slapped his hand on the table. "None of us did. We had no idea she was a damned Muse."

"But you hoped." Luke's eyes narrowed. "Why else were you so adamant we had to be there?"

Nick refused to blink. "To find out why the veils were bending. Then that kid got mind-fucked by an angel. Luke, she touches aether, and don't tell me you didn't think the same thing! Why else didn't you just stop at draining that malakim? You made sure he couldn't say a damned thing."

"What the hell are y'all talking about!" I jumped to my feet, making them all look at me. My teeth were clenched tightly. I was sick of being told I couldn't ask, then listening to them taunt me with things they all seemed to take for granted.

Sam propped his elbow on the back of his chair, his body completely relaxed. "Sit down, girl, and don't ask questions that you don't want answered."

"Or what?"

He lifted his chin. "Or we'll answer them."

"Nick?" I turned to him, refusing to sit back down like I was just some obedient bitch. My body begged me to run out of the room and not stop until I'd made it home, but my mind demanded to know more. "What are you talking about?"

Slowly, he raised his eyes, looking away from Luke and right at me. "I'm talking about why I helped you in that gas station."

"What do you mean, mind-fucked by an angel?" I'd heard that phrase the night of my car accident. My throat felt dry, but I would not back down now.

"Ask Luke."

"Sit down," Luke told me, looking more amused than concerned. "We make deals so your mind can accept it. Would you like a demonstration?"

Yes, but not from him. "Would I even remember it?"

He smiled, one eyebrow rising. "I can make sure of that." Leaning forward, he rested his elbows on the table. "Look at me, Muse. Look into my eyes."

"He won't hurt you," Nick promised.

It was all I needed to hear. For some reason, I knew Nick wouldn't let me be hurt, even if I had nothing to base that on.

Mostly, it was just that he'd been so insistent that they needed my help, and I couldn't do much if I was a vegetable. That was why I looked into Luke's eyes, noticing the catlike colors and nothing else. He stayed silent for a long moment, until I was completely transfixed.

"I'm going to make you a deal." His voice was deep and warm, almost sultry. "You will thank me three times for such a wonderful dinner, and mean it. If you can do that, I will never harm you intentionally. You will remember this offer, but you won't be able to stop yourself from saying the words. Do you understand me, Sienna?"

"Yeah."

He nodded and blinked, breaking the spell. "Then do you have anything to say?"

I wanted to prove him wrong, to show I was stronger than some cheap attempt at hypnotism, yet my mouth had a will of its own. "Thank you for dinner, Luke, it was amazing. I mean it. Thank you so much. If I hadn't come here tonight, I probably would've been stuck with mac and cheese again." I tried to bite my tongue, to make the words stop, but nothing could. "Seriously. It was really nice of you." I took a breath, but the last phrase tumbled over my lips. "Thank you."

"You're welcome." Luke lifted his glass. "I believe we have a deal."

"It's not a deal if I have no say in it!"

He shrugged. "Not exactly, but I'll still hold my end of the bargain. That, though, is what Nick means by a mind-fuck. It's how angels work. We call it weaving. I make the aether in your body resonate with the goal I want, and there's pretty much nothing a human can do to stop it."

I looked at Nick. "The guy that robbed the gas station?"

He nodded. "Yeah. He just happened to be the right person in the right place when the angel appeared to him. They can't help it.

152

That doesn't mean we can fix them, though. Once they're given a task, they do it – or they die."

For years, I'd struggled to get over the horror of that day and only the memory of Nick – Death – made it bearable. "He hurt Jamal to get to me?" I looked at each of them and stood, this time slowly. Suddenly, I didn't feel well. "Excuse me."

As I walked out of the room, I heard Sam. "This is why we don't discuss serious things over dinner, Luke."

"She asked."

I stumbled into the hall, turning left instead of right, hoping I could find a bathroom before I lost my dinner on the expensive floor. I pressed a hand to my mouth and inhaled slowly, sucking in long breaths while my feet moved on their own. I was the reason people had been hurt, and that was a lot to take in. My stomach slowly settled even as my mind revolted. The door at the end of the hall had to be a bathroom, right? I pushed it open cautiously, seeing nothing more than a very disorganized study. With a sigh, I stepped back until I hit the wall, then closed my eyes.

His footsteps were light, but I didn't have to look to know Nick had followed me. "I won't let *anyone* hurt you," he promised softly. "It's going to be ok. I promise."

"Why?" I pried my eyes open and turned to him. "Why me? What makes *me* so special?" I took a deep breath. "They destroy the lives of innocent people. Jamal. The college students in that other car. Why do they want to kill me?"

He reached up and dragged his finger down the side of my face, pushing stray hairs away from my eyes. "Because you aren't supposed to exist."

14

*N*ick's answer didn't do much to make me feel better. His presence, however, did. Just knowing that Death was Nick, and he'd come to make sure I was ok eased some of the guilt.

Some. Not all.

"What do you mean, not supposed to exist?" I tapped my chest. "I'm just a stupid college student hoping to pay her bills!"

Nick tilted his head to the door beside me. "Can I show you something?"

"Sure." I mean, why not, right?

He gestured to the office before walking in. When I passed through the doorway, it was like cobwebs tickled my skin, but before I could look, the feeling was gone. Nick hadn't paused. He headed to a long desk, the surface almost like a tinted mirror. As he reached it, he waved his hand across the top, and ghostly images rose like holograms. I didn't understand, and my mind was too full to ask. Stunned, I just moved to his side and watched.

He spread his hands and pulled, like a larger version of zooming and moving a photo on a tablet. When he stopped, I recognized the pattern. It was a map of the town. The neighborhood was mine. Unlike most maps, though, this one was encased in two overlapping, translucent bubbles. The inner one was pink, the outer one yellow.

"My place." Nick pointed to the outline of his house. "Yours." He gestured a few streets over then knelt, gesturing for me to do the same. Eye-level with the table, I could see layered peaks in the bubbles jutting down toward the city. The point of the yellow was centered directly down that of the pink. Nick glanced at me. "See it yet?"

"The funnel-looking things?"

He nodded. "Where are they?"

I looked closer. "Over your house?"

"Yeah. Look at the shape though, the whole shape."

That was when I realized the entire bubble wasn't a perfect circle. It leaned inward as if pulled by a vacuum toward the neighborhood we were in. Those peaks were just the most obvious part.

"The bubbles are the veils?"

He nodded slowly. "And something is bending them. That something seems to be in the exact same location you are. Always."

"I'm bending the veils?"

Nick shrugged one shoulder. "It's our working theory, but not even Merlin could bend the veils like this. We expected a weapon, not a human. That's why I was there when the robbery happened. I wanted to know what the angels were doing to alter reality. It was you."

I took a deep breath and looked back at the map. "Am I a weapon, Nick?"

"Do you want to be?"

That was not the answer I'd expected. "No!"

"Then you aren't." He pulled himself back to his feet. "Unfortunately, if the angels get their hands on you, you won't have a choice. They will make you a very bad deal, and you'll take it."

"Like Luke did?"

He chuckled. "Luke's deal was pretty good. He really can't harm you now, not without a few wounds from it."

"Wait." I rubbed my hands over my face. "Why not?"

Nick tapped his head. "Aether. Luke used his talent to create a cause and effect loop between the two of you. Think of it like holding a lion on a rope. You can pull, but it can always pull back. If you thanked him, then he must do something to complete the loop. In this case, refrain from intentionally harming you."

"And if he doesn't?"

Nick shrugged. "Then the deal is broken, and the backlash will happen in his mind, not yours, because of the way it was made."

"And if it was made differently? I mean, if he said that he'd protect me so long as I could fly, and I failed to fly, then I'd be breaking the loop, right?"

"Yeah." He took a deep breath. "And when you didn't fly, the loop would break, harder if there was a time limit on it. It could kill a normal human."

"But I'm not normal?" I wanted him to say I was wrong.

He didn't. He just pointed to the map. "In history, only a few beings have ever warped the veils. Humans called them gods, but we called them powerful. Many were the offspring of angels and humans or demons and humans. Some were fae or satyr."

"What am I?"

Nick shrugged. "All I know is that you pull at the veils as hard as Jesus."

"Like, the crucifix one?"

He laughed and shook his head. "Michael's first child. He was half-human, half-angel, and believed it when he was told his father was the one and only god. The poor kid never knew any better, but yes, that Jesus, and yes, that got to be a pretty big mess, but the angels loved it. They used the man to further their goals, letting him do his best to explain science far beyond anything people could grasp at the time. In the end, humans lined up to donate their aether, making our enemy so powerful they made it all the way into Vesdar and were battering the veil to Daemin."

"So y'all can have children with humans?" Of everything he'd said, I think that shocked me the most.

"Yes." He gestured and the map went dark, looking like nothing more than a reflective table again. "Don't worry. Birth control works with us as well as it does with humans."

I nodded and made my way to a couch set against the wall, then dropped into it. Nick watched while I took a handful of deep breaths, trying to make sense of everything he'd just told me. It didn't help. I felt my throat closing and pressure at the back of my eyes. This was all happening a bit too fast! I was supposed to be working toward a *normal* life.

"What do I do now?" I asked softly.

"What do you want to do?" He moved before me, squatting down to meet my eyes. The concern was clear on his face.

It was too much. I wiped at my nose, hoping it wasn't running because my eyes were threatening to leak. "I just wanted a degree." With each word, the tears pressed harder, like the dam was cracking. "I worked so hard for this. After everything I dealt with growing up, I just wanted to have a normal life. I wanted to prove I could succeed on my own! I didn't mean for anyone to get *hurt!*"

That was when the first tear broke free. The image of Jamal stained with blood hung in my mind as I struggled to hold the others back, but it wasn't going well. All of this was my fault. Me, the unimportant girl no one would even miss. People had died because someone else wanted to get me. More probably would, and my life would never be nice and easy.

Hearing all of this felt like being told I had cancer. It was terminal. It would never go away. There was nothing I could do except try to cope, but that was easier said than done. I was cursed, actually cursed, and everyone around me would end up paying the price.

Sitting there with an overfull brain, trying to decide if being special was worth all of this, the only thing I could do was give in to the moisture brewing in my eyes. The life I knew was over. Forget being cool and special – or even boring! If I wanted to keep people safe, that meant I had to spend the rest of my life all alone, and even that wasn't a guarantee.

Someone would always be chasing me. I'd never get the chance to have a family, to own my own home, or settle down into old age. If what these guys were saying was true, then it meant I would always be hiding, waiting for the next gunman or drunk college kids to try and kill me – or someone I loved.

"Hey," he whispered, pulling me against his chest. "Don't cry, dove. We won't let anything happen to you."

"Can you make it all stop? Can you make me normal?"

He crushed me against him, strong arms nearly suffocating with the pressure. "No, but I can teach you how to protect yourself."

I pulled back and wiped at my face. "Is that going to keep happening? Are people going to die everywhere I go?"

"People always die." He tried to make it sound reassuring, but the words were wrong.

"People don't always die because of *me!*" I took a long breath. It shook as it entered, and I looked down at my hands. "Can you make it stop? Just unmake me or something?"

He might not be able to change what I was, but he was Death. He could make my life end, saving those around me. Saving people like Jamal, or anyone else who got caught up in my bad luck. It wasn't like I had a future anyway.

Nick pressed his large palm against my cheek, his thumb smoothing away the line of tears. "I won't do that, Sia."

"But you can." I knew how to read between the lines.

"I *won't*."

"Why not? I'm a flash in the pan to you. I'm no more important than some fly buzzing around your head. Just pull the aether and stick it in your veil. If I'm something special, then maybe I have a lot of it or something."

"Could you just kill a butterfly because it landed on a flower?" He tilted his head, watching me, waiting for the answer.

"What?"

"I mean, it's easy to kill a wasp that's about to sting you, but a butterfly?" His thumb swept across my cheek again. "So perfect and gentle. So beautiful. It does nothing but exist, yet makes anyone who sees it a little happier. Could you kill it?"

"To save hundreds of butterflies? Yeah."

The corner of his lip twisted. "Then you're stronger than me. I will not, so don't ask me again."

"Then I'll ask Sam."

I tried to stand, but Nick's hand pressed down on my shoulder. "He wouldn't dare, even if he could. Stop acting like a child, Sienna."

"I *am* a child! I'm twenty-four years old, Mr. I-Walked-With-Dinosaurs. Not even a quarter of a century."

"And the strongest Muse in history." Nick's hand refused to let me up. "Do you know what you could do, even as a child?"

"No."

"You could banish demons and angels from Earth, preventing them from doing anything to any more humans. You could inspire acts of greatness that cure diseases and stop famines. You, Sienna, could make your world a much better place." He finally released me, his hand shifting down my arm. "And you could strengthen the gates of the veil to make Daemin safe from angels again."

With everything he'd said, I'd never thought his home might be suffering from the war. For some reason, I'd assumed it had been fought on the other worlds – like mine. Never in his own backyard.

I wiped at my eyes. "Is it bad?"

He nodded. "Daemin is eternal, just like we are. Nothing dies. Our food comes from plants that regrow and animals that regenerate. Aether from there is thick and strong, but always in use. There is no abundance and no way to make more."

"What happened?"

He rocked back on his heels and swallowed. "Angels came and tried to pull aether from our world. Beasts fell unconscious and plants wilted on the stalk. People were left in comas, unable to regenerate because there's no extra aether in the atmosphere." He looked up at me. "Many are still affected, their bodies protected by others, but they will never wake unless we can find enough aether to refill what they lost."

"Can I help?"

He nodded slowly. "I hope so. From the moment I realized what you could do, I've hoped that you'd be willing."

"Can I think about it?"

"Yeah." He reached up to my face again and wiped at the line of dry tears. "This isn't worth crying over, little dove. I saved Jamal. I'll take care of anything that matters to you. Those kids in the other car? They didn't deserve my mercy. They certainly don't need yours."

He was so impossibly beautiful. Everything about Nick Voland had been crafted to be pleasing, and even knowing it wasn't his real form, I still felt my heart beat a little faster when he called me his dove. Sitting so close, all I'd have to do is lean a bit and our lips would touch. My eyes flicked to his mouth, then back up, hoping he hadn't seen.

"Why did you save me that day in the gas station, Nick? If you'd done nothing –"

A chuckle came from the hall. "Yes, why did you save her, Nick?" Luke asked.

I jumped back, aware of how intimate our posture was, then glanced at the door. Nick leaned away as well, but slowly, as if he had nothing to hide.

"I didn't break any rules," Nick replied. "I didn't tell her anything they could use."

Luke made a disparaging sound and waved that away. "Like I give a shit, but I'm betting you didn't tell Sienna all that, did you?"

"She didn't need to relive it."

Luke raised an eyebrow. "She's stronger than you think. If you'd kept your hands to yourself, she might have drained him, saving you a lot of time talking."

"What?" I looked between them, but they both ignored me.

Nick lifted his chin in defiance. "I was simply stopping the angels' plan."

"Bull." Luke crossed his arms over his chest and leaned against the door. "I've broken every damned rule that exists at least once. No one gives a shit anymore. Why did you save the human, Nick?"

"Because it was the fastest way to stop Michael from harvesting her aether!"

Luke shook his head. "Try again."

"Damn it, Lucifer –"

"Whoa!" I stood up, turning so I could see both of them.

"Luke," Nick corrected, knowing it was already too late.

"Cat's out of the bag, now." Luke turned to me. "Scared now?"

"A little," I admitted. "You're really the devil?"

"No," Nick assured me.

This time, I was the one doing the ignoring. The creepy guy was Lucifer? No wonder I didn't like him! "I made a deal with the devil?"

"He's not the devil," Nick said again. "It's just propaganda to punish him for defecting."

"Are you the devil?" I asked, staring only at Luke.

He grinned. "Yeah. Too bad devils don't exist. It's just something angels made up to scare humanity. Here's what I don't get, though. We basically tell you that there's no heaven, no hell, and you're ok with that. You met Nick, named him Death, and were dying to stick your tongue down his throat, but you hear my real name and you act like *I'm* the bad guy?"

"If you're Lucifer, who's Nick?"

Nick shook his head. "We've used many names over the years. What I used to be called isn't important."

So he still wouldn't tell me. "Ok, then Sam?"

Luke answered, "Samyaza."

I racked my mind. "Nope, don't know that one."

"Demon of Seduction. He supposedly convinced the angels to lay with women," Nick said. "He didn't, and he was never an angel, but he did make a reputation in bed."

"And a few dozen kids," Luke added. "Unlike Nick, who keeps his hands off." He looked between the two of us. "You training her?"

Nick shrugged. "Hoping to, if you don't scare her off first."

"You'd better start." Luke looked up at me and winked. "If you ask real sweet, I can make you rich too, babe."

"What do you want for it?" I knew how this worked. Lucifer did nothing for free and couldn't be trusted.

He looked back at Nick quickly. "A favor in the future."

"No deal."

Luke pushed himself away from the door, walking in slowly. "Would you excuse us for a moment, Nick?"

"Leave her alone, Luke."

"I still can't hurt her, remember?" Luke looked back to me. "Ten minutes. Please?"

"Fine."

Nick sighed and left the room, pulling the door closed behind him – and my pulse quickened. Luke watched him go then walked right up to me, his chest nearly bumping mine, forcing me to fight the urge to step back. At my defiance, he laughed.

"I'll make you a very comfortable human. Plenty of money and everything your heart desires if you'll answer one question for me?"

"No."

He grinned. "I'll ask the question first, then you can decide." He leaned closer, and this time I did step back. "Why didn't you kiss him?"

"What?"

"You heard me. You were sitting so close, but you didn't do it. Why didn't you kiss him?"

I shook my head, not understanding why that would matter and trying to find a reason. "Because he's the Angel of Death?"

"Are you scared of him?"

I laughed at that. "No. I mean he's seen dinosaurs. I'm nothing more than a fly to him."

Luke looked at me, drawing out the silence, then whispered pointedly, "A butterfly."

I clenched my teeth, realizing what he was pushing at. "I didn't kiss him because not everything is about getting laid, *Lucifer*. Yes, he's the hottest man I've ever seen, but he already told me he made his body, tailored to fit his needs, right? The only thing I know about him is that he kills people and that nothing in this world makes sense anymore. I feel a bit like y'all are playing a very nasty joke on me, and that doesn't exactly make me wanna jump in bed with *anyone*."

Luke nodded. "Ok." He reached up and grabbed my chin, forcing me to look into his eyes. "Nick has been my friend for over two million years. He's the one who stood up for me when the Daemoni wanted to drain me dry. In all that time, he's done everything in his power to be invisible to humans." Luke tilted his head. "And he's accidentally broken a few who realized what he is. But you're different. He saved you because, for the first time, that demon wants to protect something, and that something is you."

"Why?"

Luke chuckled. "Why don't you want to kiss me, Muse?"

I laughed in his face. "Because you're a dick."

He nodded in agreement. "Exactly. Just imagine that you could never touch the beautiful things in life without breaking them. Imagine for a moment that your name was used to scare children into good behavior. Imagine that your face made people weep and beg for your enemy to save them, and then think about what it would feel like to have a delicate little butterfly seek you out. Imagine one frail little girl who fought against all odds just to find you again." He ran his thumb across my chin, refusing to break the gaze. "You aren't afraid of him, Sienna, and that's why he saved you. That's why he keeps coming back for you."

"Oh."

"Yeah, '*oh*.' So now here's the deal we're going to make. You look up the history of the phrase 'little dove.' Regardless of what you find, I will make sure that good things begin to happen in your life. Do we have a deal?"

I remembered Nick's warnings about making deals with Luke. "No."

"You already know you're going to do it." Luke turned my chin slightly. "Do we have a deal?"

"What will I get?"

He laughed, nearly breaking the gaze. "I'll make sure everything from that accident the other night goes away, just for starters. From there, I'll see what else I can do." He took a long breath. "Do we have a deal, yet?"

"No, Lucifer. I'm not making any deals with you. If you want to prove you're not a dick, you can do it without anything from me."

He smiled and released me. "Shame you feel that way, because Nick's coming back."

"Luke?" I wondered why he'd come in here, and why he cared what I thought.

"What now?"

"Is this how you're always going to look to me? I mean, like men?" I bit at my lips, trying to find the words to ask the question plaguing my mind. "Am I going to ever see your true forms?"

"True forms? You mean, what we look like in our own realms?" He shrugged. "Does it matter?"

I didn't want to explain, but I hoped Luke would answer. He was enough of an ass to be honest. "I don't want to be scared because I wasn't expecting it."

His impish nature dissolved, leaving a beautiful but serious man before me. Suddenly he was just a person, no longer terrifying, no longer something to fear. Luke looked at me as if measuring something in my personality, then nodded. "We'll talk about this more later, ok? Tomorrow?"

"Ok."

"Thanks, Sienna. Thank you for trying." He smiled weakly, the first honest one I'd seen from him so far, and I decided he might not be as bad as I thought.

"Yeah. Why'd you join the demons anyway?"

He looked back at the door quickly. "Because I believe in free will. Midworlders should be more than livestock, but the angels don't agree. They think you're nothing more than a crop for us to use. They think you're too stupid to understand us."

"Or fight back?"

"Or that." Luke pressed his lips together and took a step toward the door. "I should probably also tell you that the only person in five realms who can pull aether from me is Nick."

"But..."

He nodded. "And you. Not even the Archangel Michael could unless I offered it." He opened the door, nodding to someone on the other side, then left.

I wasn't surprised at all to see Nick standing there, waiting. "You ok?" he asked.

Oddly, I was. "I think Luke and I just came to an understanding."

He sighed. "Good. He really is a decent guy. I mean, he acts like an angel and all, but his heart is in the right place."

The irony of his words made me bite my lip to keep from laughing. "I thought demons were supposed to be the bad guys."

Nick shrugged. "Define good and bad?" He took a step closer. "Are you ready to head home yet, or did you have more questions?"

"I have so many questions I can't think of them all."

"I'm sure." He looked at his watch. "Just didn't know if you were aware of the time."

"Not a clue."

"Almost ten." He took another step closer. "We have a spare room if you'd rather keep going, or I can walk you home at any time. I'd just really prefer that you aren't on the street alone. The angels are moving into town, which means they know something. That's why Luke came when I asked for a ride. They have to have noticed the peak in the veils has stopped moving, and probably want to know why."

"And what about tomorrow when I walk to class? What about tonight when I'm asleep?"

He took the last step, standing just before me. "One of us will be around. The other night, you caught me warding your house. One of the many things I was blocking out was the angels. We will not invade your privacy, but we won't leave you unprotected, either. I swear it, Sia. I won't let them hurt you."

Unconsciously, I reached up and rested my palm against his hard chest. "And when are you going to explain calculus?"

He glanced away quickly, that surprised smile playing on his lips again. "You aren't running away from me yet?"

"I've spent four years trying to *find* you, Nick. I have no intention of running away anytime soon."

"Sia." He clasped my wrist, gently caressing the underside. "This is a lot to drop on you. You need to take some time to think about it."

"What?!"

Hearing the frustration in my voice, he smiled. "Dove, I'm not going to disappear again, but there's no need to rush things. You have an entire life to live. Go home, give yourself time to let this sink in. Think about what you really want. I don't want you to throw everything away because it seems exciting right now. I promise, it's not. What we're asking of you isn't a small thing, and I won't think any less of you if you'd rather live a normal life."

I couldn't believe him. "And that's it?"

"For *tonight*. One of us will keep an eye on you, but you probably won't even notice. Just give yourself time to process this, because if you get mixed up in our mess, there isn't any going back." He tilted his head toward the door. "And I'm going to be a gentleman this time and walk you all the way home."

I let him lead me out of the house, but I knew something he didn't. I wasn't exactly the kind of girl to change my mind. I was already committed. I'd found my Death, and I'd be damned if I just let him slip away. Besides, it wasn't like I had anything left to lose.

15

*M*y alarm went off much too early the next morning. I hadn't gotten any real sleep the night before. After everything I'd just learned, my mind refused to shut off – but that wasn't surprising. It wasn't every day a girl found out the world was a lot more complicated than she could ever imagine.

With a groan, I smacked the button and rolled over, hoping to steal just a few more minutes of rest. As I closed my eyes, the alarm on my phone chimed from across the room. It was clearly a conspiracy.

"Damn it," I grumbled, pulling myself out of bed.

A hot shower helped to get my mind in gear, but nothing would matter until I had at least twelve ounces of coffee in my system. I put a pot to brew and jumped into my morning routine with my brain still trying to make sense of what had happened yesterday. Nick was Death. I could handle that. He was a demon. Yep, that wasn't hard to accept either, considering demons were just a race from another dimension.

But there was the kicker – a race from another dimension. Something about that had my mind a little stuck. I could understand the science of it, in the most basic way, but that I was one of the few people who actually knew it was real? That was where the logic kept failing. Why me? What had I done to be chosen for this? How was this going to change my life?

The reality was that it wouldn't. Yeah, I may have freaked out when Nick dropped everything on me, but the more I thought about it, the less of an issue it seemed. I mean, so what if I had a big secret wallowing around in the back of my head? Was it really any different from the one I'd been hiding about Death? It wouldn't help me pass my classes. It wouldn't get me a degree. It most certainly wouldn't do much for keeping me gainfully employed and fed for the rest of my life.

In other words, it didn't matter. Regardless of what happened between demons and angels, I would still need a roof over my head and something in my belly to keep me going. That meant money, which was a hell of a lot easier when the crazy chick had a degree.

Besides, for all I knew, this could be one seriously intense practical joke. Maybe Nick was the crazy one? Yeah, that sounded nice, except I was the person who'd been dreaming of Death. I'd been chasing his memory since that first kiss. That Nick knew about all those little details from before we'd met? This whole thing might be preposterous, but the evidence suggested it really was happening. Who was I to doubt it? Weird was kinda my normal.

For now, all I could do was keep on keeping on. My first task? Get my butt in gear and get to class. By the time I was dressed and ready to head out the door, I'd already made at least five mental laps around everything I'd learned yesterday and still hadn't made any progress. Giving in, I grabbed my other backpack – this one filled with real books – and shoved my phone inside. Travel mug in hand, I stepped out, locking the door to my tiny little house behind me.

Something shimmered at the edge of my vision. Sucking in a breath, I turned, only to have it vanish when I tried to focus on it.

For a split second, I was convinced my little yard was haunted – but there was one problem with that. Ghosts couldn't be real, not from the way Nick described dying. To test my theory, I looked back to the door, trying to concentrate on my peripheral vision.

The shimmer was still there, right around the bottom of the stairs.

"I'm pretty sure I see you," I said, hoping there was no one close enough to hear me acting like a nut case. "God, I hope I'm not losing it."

A waft of air and a chuckle was my answer. When I spun around, Luke was standing right there, taking a drink from his stainless steel travel mug like he'd been waiting for me the whole time. Problem: I'd just looked. He hadn't been there.

Lifting an eyebrow, I let him know I expected an answer.

"The veil isn't opaque," he explained. "I was just going to follow you in the corridor."

"Uh-huh." Yep, today was going to take a whole lot more coffee to get through. "And you thought that was ok?"

"Uh, not exactly." He took a deep breath. "There was a threat of pulling out feathers if I didn't keep my eyes on you. Since you've made it clear we're not the best of friends, well, I figured it would be easier if you didn't know I was here. Think of it less like stalking and more like Secret Service."

"Funny, Luke. Real funny."

With a shrug, he gestured up the road toward the campus. "Lead on. I can either walk with you or follow in the corridor. I'll let you make that call, but bad things will happen to *me* if I let you out of my sight."

"Then stay where I can see you," I decided without hesitation. "Creeps me out to think you're watching me scratch my ass or something."

I didn't wait for him to answer, just started walking. Luke followed, casually sipping his coffee like he didn't even notice my attitude. The irony was that it made me feel a little guilty. Did everyone treat him like he was a dick? I mean, this was Lucifer, right? The worst of the worst. I had a funny feeling he hadn't exactly gotten a lot of praise over the years.

"Hey?" I asked. "Are we allowed to talk about this stuff out here? Or is that just an inside your place type of thing?"

Lengthening his steps, he fell in beside me. "Uh, yeah. That was mostly to contain the freakout." The bastard gave me an apologetic smile. "Which you really didn't have. So, it's not like certain words call attention to us or anything. The problem is more that screaming about demons and angels usually gets people locked away in a looney bin. We don't want to scare you off by heaping too much on you at once."

"Oh." Well, that was depressingly mundane.

"Why did you ask?"

"Because you said you'd tell me about your true forms."

"Ah..." He took another sip of coffee. "Theology. Yes. Demons tend to be massive things. Brutes, in their own way. Don't mistake that for stupid, though."

"Like Sam?"

Luke chuckled. "Sam's a lot deeper than he lets on. He's also a bit of a badass. If you ever get into a fight, you want that punk on your side. I'm pretty convinced he has a thing for pain."

"And you?"

Slyly, he looked over. "I've been working with Nick for a long time. Our skills are different but complementary. I was at the robbery, too, Sienna. And the accident."

"The angel over Death's shoulder!" Why hadn't I figured that out? "That was you?"

He lifted a finger, warning that I was getting too excited. "Yeah. I gathered the stuff Nick used to put you back together."

"And at the robbery? Why didn't I see you?"

He bit his lips together, looking like he was delaying the answer. "I wasn't inside. I was making sure the person pulling that kid's strings couldn't do it again for a while."

I nodded slowly, accepting that as nothing but the truth. Luke hadn't lied to me yet. None of them had, from what I could tell. It was just easier to believe Nick and Sam. For some reason, my instincts were convinced that Luke couldn't be trusted, but I wasn't exactly known to have the best ones, either.

"Thank you," I mumbled.

He huffed something that sounded like acknowledgment. "Nick was fascinated with you from the first glimpse. Then, on that day, we were watching you through the corridor, and you shined at us like a brilliant, iridescent beacon. He had to get closer, to see what could cause that." Luke shrugged. "I told him to deal with it while I chased off our angelic competition, never thinking he'd find a Muse."

"That's kinda a big deal, huh?"

Luke nodded. "It is now. Humans have evolved in a different direction, making the ability pretty rare. And one like you? Definitely rare. But when he told me what happened? He said you were pushing yourself through the veil so he had to stop it, and the moment you saw him, you smiled. Smiled, Sienna. Not a happy one, but the kind people give me. Dreamy, like you were completely entranced."

I nodded, able to believe it because that was exactly how I'd felt. "But what's the deal with his true form and name?"

Luke opened his mouth to answer, then shut it and shook his head. "Uh..." He tried again. "It's complicated."

"Give me a little something here?"

"You made a pretty big deal out of my name. His isn't any better. Most of ours aren't. Considering what humans are taught to think of demons? As often as you gape at him or make comments about how handsome he is? Do you really think he wants to give that up?"

"But he'd still be Nick, right? Regardless of what he looks like?"

Luke nodded. "But humans love beauty. You rate each other on it. Your entire society praises those who have it. It's only recently that angels haven't been able to just smile their way through everything. Trust me on that."

I did, actually. I'd seen how Mike and the creepy guy in Creative Writing almost expected people to drool over them. Hell, half my class was even blatant about it. "So the Nick I see here is merely based on the Nick he is there?"

"Loosely. He's about the same size, but that's another thing you need to know." Luke looked over at me and held up his coffee mug. Clenching his fist, the metal bent, crumpling easily under the pressure. He took one last swallow then snapped the lid closed. "We have to work very hard not to break you. Those of us from the outer worlds? We play by different rules."

"Oh."

He hadn't even struggled to bend the stainless steel mug. He'd crumpled it easier than I could a soda can! I walked with him silently, letting that sink in as we made the last half block to class. If Luke could do that, and Nick was quite a bit more buff, no wonder he was worried about me! There were at least two angels who'd taken an interest in me, and just one of them could snap me like a twig!

Then again, I'd basically asked Nick to kill me last night. Wouldn't that fix this whole mess? I wanted to think so, but that was just a stupid, gut reaction. If I was dead, who would do whatever it was the demons wanted from me? Nick already said they *needed* my help, which meant he couldn't do it on his own. Or not easily. Truth be told, it wasn't like the angels had really done anything to me. Not that I could prove, at any rate. Either way, giving up like some floozy with a broken heel in a horror movie wasn't exactly my style.

When we entered the Language building, Luke once again fell behind me. When I glanced back, he shook his head. Evidently, he didn't want anyone to know we were friends. Well, friendly. I wouldn't go so far as to say we'd crossed the buddy barrier yet, but he was definitely an acquaintance. He also didn't come off as quite so disturbing now that I knew his little secret. I was leaning more towards misunderstood. Since he wasn't human, I couldn't expect him to have the same empathy as a person who'd, you know, had to grow up.

I think that was what bothered me so much about the green-eyed creeps. They were amazingly perfect – and seemed to know it. Every one I'd met so far came off like he expected me to feel so graced by his presence. I understood why, *now*. They'd never had anyone laugh at them, been forced to suck up their pride, or those other awkward things normal people learned from. Nope, they'd convinced humans they were the arm of the divine, and had probably gotten very used to the swooning that came with it.

Luckily for me, Creative Writing passed quickly. Luke didn't sit beside me this time, but he did claim the spot right behind me. Just like Nick had promised, I was protected – and I had a funny feeling Luke's brass twin, who he'd called Gabe, knew it. Through the whole class, that freak glared at me from the second row. I wanted to punch him in the face just on principle.

When the professor finally released us, I took my time getting my things together. I didn't want to give angel-boy up there a chance to get his hands on me. I also didn't want to be late to Calculus, so I tapped the shoulder of the girl passing my desk.

"Hey? Did you catch what chapter she said had the extended list of plot types?"

"Oh yeah," the girl assured me, pulling out her notebook. "It's chapter twenty-four. She said we needed to learn the differences between the simple list and the extended one because we'd need to cite it for our midterm project."

"Thank you," I gushed, sticking by her side as we passed through the doorway. "You probably just saved my grade."

"No problem." With a smile, she turned the opposite direction from the way I needed to go.

Well, there went that human shield. Hugging my backpack to my side, I trotted down the stairs, keeping my eyes peeled for metallic looking psychopaths. I didn't see any, so I followed the flow of bodies outside and toward the Edison building for my next class. It didn't take long before Luke reappeared at my side.

"Good work with the student," he said softly.

"Thanks. Does this mean I get an escort to Calculus?"

His smile was perfectly devious. "Don't take it personally. I just like my feathers."

"Gotcha."

But he did walk me all the way to the door of my class. Waiting inside, however, was the one man I really wanted to see. Nick was bent over something on his desk, his face shielded by his long, dark hair as he scribbled intently. While I made my way over, I hoped he wouldn't be upset that I actually wanted to sit beside him. The last thing we'd talked about was me taking a little time to get used to the weirdness.

"This seat taken?" I asked.

He looked up and a smile immediately took over his face. "Saved it for you, dove." Lifting his bag out of it, he shifted to face me and offered a piece of paper. "Finished your homework. Hopefully, this means you still want to talk to me?"

"Uh, *yeah.*"

"Good." He almost purred the word. I loved how it sounded. "Luke still being a dick?"

"We're working it out." I dropped my bag between my feet and pulled out my notebook. "Hey, am I grounded all weekend?"

"Sia..."

"I'm honestly asking, Nick. I mean, I work tonight and have a lunch shift tomorrow, but I'm just not sure about this." I waved a finger between us. "Last week, you were taking me out for lunch. This week, you're telling me I need to stop and think, so I'm kinda hoping it's not the most epic brushoff ever."

"It's not a brushoff," he assured me, but his eyes flicked around the room. When he'd seen whatever he needed to, he leaned a little closer. "I have some things I need to do this weekend. They have nothing to do with you, and yet everything. Think of it more like bad timing."

"But Nick, I'm on board with this."

He lifted a brow. "Are you? Or are you just happy to figure out your little mystery? What if the man you've been obsessing over is nothing like the obsession? I've seen your paintings, Sia. I rescued you. Neither of those things has anything at all to do with the complications that come with hanging out with me, yet I'm sure it all seems pretty romantic on the surface."

He had a point. I hated to admit it, but it was a pretty good one. Unfortunately for him, I had a few, too. "And you think I'm just going to forget all of this? Maybe I should forgive the people who got one of my few friends in the world *shot.* Did you forget that I don't really like *them?* Even before I knew why, I didn't."

"I know." He reached over and clasped my wrist. "I do know, dove. I also know that your life speeds by so fast, and you all tend to make hasty decisions because of it. The problem is that this is something you can't take back."

"But I couldn't even if I didn't choose. Luke said I'm a beacon." I snapped my mouth shut.

Nick's eyes narrowed. "I see. So he's been telling stories, huh?"

"More like answering questions, and not very well. Look, my point is I currently feel like a fat rabbit in the middle of a pack of lions. Doesn't really matter if I like lions or not, they still want to eat me, right?"

His thumb made a circle against my skin. "I can always figure out something to help with that."

"You can?" Why hadn't he mentioned this before?

Nick sighed and pulled his arm back. "There've been Muses who were stripped of their talents. I don't want to because it's a one-way street, and I'm not completely sure it will work with someone of your strength."

"Oh." Well, there went that idea. "So I just stay the center of the Secret Service's protection until I graduate?"

"If you have to."

From the tone, I knew he was leaving something out. I also had a funny feeling he wouldn't make it easy to figure out what. That didn't mean I'd give up. Nope, as the teacher walked in and started writing on the whiteboard, I decided I just had to make sure I asked the right questions. Something in Nick's story wasn't adding up, which meant it was probably something I didn't really want to hear.

But I had a whole weekend to think about it.

When we finally got out of class, I wasn't surprised at all that Nick wanted to walk me home. What I didn't expect was for him to twine his fingers with mine. For some reason, I'd assumed that time to think about it meant time acting like Nick and I hadn't already made out a few times. Clearly, that was not the case.

When he dropped me off at my door, he didn't even try to come in. I got another of those tantalizing kisses, but that was it. He just told me to pretend like nothing at all had changed, promising he'd take care of the rest. All I needed to do was think about everything and give it time to sink in while he got his side of things organized.

He kept saying that. I just wished I knew what it would take to convince this demon that I'd already thought it all through. I'd made my decision. There wasn't a damned thing he – or anyone else – could do to scare me off. I'd already picked my side. I was totally Team Demon all the way.

16

My shift at Mac's on Friday night wasn't too bad. I blamed Sam for that. He showed up only minutes after I clocked in and tipped well the whole night. He also hung all over some busty blonde, but with the way she was groping him, I couldn't really blame him. Clearly, he had a way with women. Granted, I may have used his little public display as an excuse to check him out a little.

Sam was a demon with a body designed to be beautiful – and it was. Where Nick was tall, muscular, and chiseled, Sam was a different type of gorgeous, and it was growing on me. He was lean and lithe, with the body of an athlete. Under his tight black shirt, I could see the ripcords of muscles across his abs, and his arms were scrumptious. Not just his biceps, either. His forearms were also amazing. The whole neon hair and piercings thing he was rocking just gave him a dangerous air, and it worked for him.

Unfortunately, his show wasn't enough to distract me from another group on the opposite side. Five guys sat quietly at a table, all nursing their beers. That wasn't weird. That they all looked a little faded was what bothered me. Faded probably wasn't the right word, because they weren't all white guys with blonde hair or anything. Still, even the Hispanic-looking dude had this sun-bleached thing about him. It was like his hair perfectly matched his skin, as if the contrast had been turned down a little too much. I wasn't close enough to see their eyes, but I had this sinking suspicion that every last one of them would be green.

Then there was Aaron. That ex-boyfriend of mine who'd shoved me in the parking lot? Yeah, guess who he was friends with? The faded boys. He didn't sit with them, but he alternated between their table and another. The entire group all wore variations of the same fraternity shirt. The letters were Delta Phi. The same one Nick had asked about that first day.

They never once looked at me, though. Even when they got another drink, every last one of them went to the bartender working the other end of the counter. I honestly didn't mind. Sam, however, kept glancing at them. If anything was a tip-off, that was it. Even when his little blonde vampire was trying her best to suck on his neck, Sam's eyes couldn't stay away from the pack of weirdos.

That was why I asked Cody, one of the cooks, to give me a lift home. I told him I'd worn a blister on my heel. I hadn't, but since he was headed right past my place, he didn't care. I figured it just reduced the likelihood of giving some angels the chance to talk to me without revealing my bodyguards. From the way Luke had acted that morning, I was pretty sure they wouldn't do anything with normal humans around, so I was going to use it as much as I could.

The lunch shift on Saturday was more of the same, but instead of Sam seducing some college girl by the pool tables, it was Luke studying in a corner. He had his laptop and notes spread before him, and his fingers were typing furiously. When he came to the bar for a refill, I asked if that was his Creative Writing project. He wouldn't answer until I threatened to withhold his beer. Only then would he admit that he was working on a short story about a dragon hunter. Seeing the Devil blush completely made my day.

Well, most of it. I was home before the sun had even set and had nothing else to do until I headed back to class on Monday. All of my homework was done except Calculus. I didn't count that because I didn't understand it enough to finish on my own. The only thing I really had to do was make up that drawing I'd missed when I was in the hospital, but perspective work was easy. Typically, it was just a long hall with doors or windows to prove the artist could imitate distance.

Lucky for me, I had a hall in my little house. It wasn't a long one, but with the kitchen at the other end, it would do. Pulling out my sketchbook, I plopped down in the middle of the floor and got to work. When I started adding the details, my mind began to wander. One of the pictures in my hall was of Death. He was wearing the hood I'd first seen him in. As I replicated it on my project, I realized that I finally had an idea of what he looked like. It might be wrong, but it was better than always making him faceless.

That was how I ended up on a fresh page in my smaller sketchpad, doing my best to mix Nick and Death together. I'd never seen what was hiding under that hood, but I loved the idea of a challenge. I used Nick's face since they had the same lips, put the blackness of space in his eyes, lit only with a few stars, then started adding in the horns. I'd felt them, so I could make a pretty good guess what they looked like. Two large arcs, both curling against the side of his head like a ram's, they'd been thick and ridged, ending in a sharp point. I knew I had the mouth right, and the jaw, but everything else was just a guess.

The problem was I didn't need to focus on what I was doing. That let the questions start seeping in. Why did Death have the universe in his eyes but Nick didn't? Was that connected to their magic? Every angel I'd met had those freakish green eyes, but the demons were in varying shades of brown. Did *that* mean something? And if angels could only "mind-fuck" a person, then how could they craft weapons? How had they made skins? Those things sounded like they needed external aether to me.

As Death's face began to appear under my pencil, I finally did exactly what Nick wanted. I thought about it. About everything. This insanity was really happening, and I'd gotten caught in the middle. Would my life ever be the same? Did I want it to? What would I lose if anyone found out I actually believed in this? And the angels? I was getting the strong impression that unless I had my powers stripped, they'd never leave me alone.

But what did that even mean, stripping my powers? My art turned real. Sam had seen it happen and Nick had put the pencil back on the page. That made me think they could do something similar. If I gave up this special Muse thing they kept going on about, would I still be able to draw? I honestly couldn't imagine spending the rest of my life working in an office like a normal person. Something about the idea didn't sit right with me.

And if I didn't give up my powers? Would Nick, Sam, and Luke follow me around for the rest of my life? Sure, that was tempting, but how long would it take before they came to resent babysitting the human? I couldn't forget how easily Luke had crushed his coffee cup. He hadn't even tried! If they could do that, then how annoying was it to play human all day long just to keep me from going insane?

Yeah, I was getting nowhere. Now that I'd started thinking, each question just made two more. The only way to make this stop was to *finally* get some answers. I couldn't do that here. They were all kept locked inside a pretty little green Victorian mansion just two blocks away. And even if Nick wouldn't tell me anything, I knew Sam or Luke would. They might not tell me enough, but at least it would be progress.

Throwing my sketchpad into my backpack, I found a pair of shoes and my keys. If drawing was what made me finally think of the questions I needed to ask, then I'd draw at their place –

whether they liked it or not. Besides, it wasn't like I really had anything *else* to do. For most of my life, I'd been perfectly happy keeping to myself, but not now. All those hours had been spent with Death's memory, trying to recall some little detail that would help me find him. Now, I knew exactly where he was, so it was time to do something about it.

Before I could convince myself this was a bad idea – and it really was – I marched out of the house, pausing only long enough to lock it behind me. I had enough time to make it to the sidewalk before a sudden breeze made me glance back. Sam was mid-step and still pulling on his shirt. I caught a flash of some delicious abdominal muscles and jerked my eyes up. I was pretty sure he noticed, but the smile on his face convinced me he didn't mind.

"Where ya going?" he asked as he adjusted the hem over his waist.

"Uh..." I couldn't help myself. I had to check to make sure no one was around to see him step out of nothing. "Your place."

"Cool." Without asking, he reached out and snagged my backpack from my shoulder, shifting it to his. "Is this a walk it out thing, or a get there quick thing?"

"Walk it out, I think." So I had time to stop thinking about his abs.

He just nodded and gestured for me to lead on. "Nick probably felt the wards go off, too, so –"

"What?"

He paused, then gave me an impish smile. "You know how some stores have that little bell on the door so you can't miss when it opens? Same idea. If you pass through the wards, we get a little alert."

I stopped and turned to face him. "You know that's not cool, right?"

He just grabbed my shoulders and pointed me onward. "That's a conversation for inside."

"No, it's not. Luke already told me that's just to keep me from yelling at y'all, but you can't just invade my privacy like that, Sam! Regardless of why."

"Let's debate that *inside*."

"Fine!"

I trudged on a little faster, but the damned demon didn't seem phased at all. He even whistled like we were out for some evening stroll. It wasn't until I'd marched past the first block that reality began to sink in again. That, and I had to slow down because I was panting. The truth was Sam could've just followed me in the corridor. He could've hidden from me, still keeping an eye on me. He hadn't. He'd stepped out immediately, letting me know he was there.

He'd also clearly been in the middle of something else. He wasn't stalking me; he was trying to keep me safe. My *real* problem was that it was him and not Nick. For the last two days, Nick had put his roommates on my security team and fucked right the hell off. He said it was bad timing, but I was a little worried. I'd spent so long trying to find him, and now that I had, he was intentionally putting distance between us. I hated to admit it, but I was lashing out at Sam because I was afraid that this thing with Nick was nothing more than a figment of my imagination.

"I'm sorry," I mumbled just as he reached out for the little gate in front of their house. "I hope you weren't in the middle of something important when I decided to take a walk."

"I wasn't," he promised. "Just playing a little Battlefield. Wanna come in? Nick should be back shortly."

"He's gone?"

Sam pressed a hand to the middle of my back and guided me up the stairs to the porch. "In and out for most of the weekend." He opened the door and gestured for me to go first. "That's why Luke and I have been trading Muse duty." As soon as we were both in, he not only closed the door but also locked it.

"I, uh, had some questions."

He pointed toward the room they'd set me in the other day. "Make yourself comfortable. Coffee? Beer?"

"Coffee, please."

With a nod, he headed toward the kitchen. I did as I was told and made my way into what they called the living room. I was pretty sure it used to have some other name, but it didn't matter now. What did was the golden Adonis sprawled out on the couch in a pair of grey sweats and a baggy t-shirt. Luke looked exactly like every other guy I'd ever known in my life, if a bit more perfect. Not at all what I expected from the Devil.

"Your timing couldn't be better," he teased, refusing to glance away from the game on the screen. "Sam was kicking my ass."

Yeah, I wasn't going to let him distract me this time. "Where's Nick?"

"Out."

I groaned. "Where's out?"

His thumbs were tapping furiously. "Dunno. Could be Tyrnigg, could be Vesdar, could be India. He's somewhere in the five realms that does not include this house."

Not what I wanted to hear. "Ok, fine. Will you answer my questions then?"

"Sure." His lips flashed a smile, but it was directed to the screen.

"Why don't demons have green eyes?"

"Because it would be a waste of energy to change something that much. Demons tend to have dark eyes, so they go with brown shades. Angels have the fire of life in ours, so we chose the color that is closest on this world. Green, often with yellows or golds."

"But why?" I insisted. "Why does Death have the universe and you have, what, fire?"

"Dunno. Why do you have blue rings? We didn't really get to choose. I think it has something to do with our grasp of aether, but it's not something anyone's really studied. We've been too busy trying to kill each other for the last few billion years."

"Wait." He'd touched on my next question. "On your grasp of aether?"

"Yep." Luke was still focused on the game as if my questions weren't hard at all. "Simple explanation is that angels have control over what's inside while demons take over when it's outside."

"So you can't do anything with the free roaming stuff?" I asked, just as the front door opened.

"Not exactly," Luke said, but he didn't get the chance to finish.

Nick's voice cut him off. "What the fuck are you doing here? I thought I made it clear. If she leaves her house, you're to keep an eye on her. Do you have any idea what Michael will do to her if he's given half a chance?"

"Dude," Sam hissed, proving he was in the hall just outside.

But Nick was on a roll. "It was not a request, Sam. Stay the hell out of her way, but close enough that you can see if any of those feathered fucks are closing in. What part of that wasn't clear? Now where the hell is she?! I need to –"

I wasn't going to sit and listen while he ripped Sam a new one. Pushing myself to my feet, I peeked my head out the door and met Nick's eyes. "I'm right here."

He froze mid-rant. "Oh."

With a smile, Sam passed over my cup. "You two want to take this to, say, the library? Or should Luke and I ditch our game so you can scream in here?"

"Where's the library again?" I asked, giving Sam an apologetic look.

He jerked his head behind him. "Hall, left at the kitchen, far side, then right. Your bag's beside the couch."

"Thanks, but I don't need it yet." Then I glanced at Nick. "Coming?"

He threw up his hands, but he did follow. I almost found the right way, too. Almost. I forgot I had to go through the attached prep room, but Nick caught my elbow and steered me the rest of the way. What he didn't do was say a thing, not until we were behind closed doors and out of earshot.

"You scared the shit out of me, you know that?" he asked.

"Mm." I sipped my coffee as I crossed to one of the empty shelves. I used it to hold my cup, refusing to look at the way his muscles were bunched up with tension. I did not need to get distracted. "Well, this guy I know said I should take the weekend to think about it. So, I thought, then I ended up with questions, and I figured the answers were here. Made sense to come ask. Never mind that you *told* me to act like it was any normal day."

"And coming to talk to demons is normal for you?" he shot back.

"Yeah, pretty much." I dared him to deny it.

For a long time, he stared at me. Finally, with a heavy sigh, Nick nodded. "Ok, you're right. I'm sorry."

"Why were you pissed? What's going on that you're not telling me?"

He chuckled wryly. "A war." A shake of his head proved that was a lame joke. "They're converging, dove. Four years ago, an angel saw you and knows exactly what you are, and I have no idea if he's awake and talking again. At best they're making a wild guess. At worst?"

I could make a good guess. "They're looking for me."

He nodded.

"Ok, so what can we do about that?"

Shoving one hand into his long hair, he turned and paced a few steps. "Thursday night, you asked me to unmake you. You threatened to have Sam do it if I wouldn't. A few seconds later, you act like you're ready to dive right in and start fighting at my side. I don't know which one to believe."

"All of it! I say what I think, ok? Call it a lack of filter or whatever makes you happy. The thing is, I was talking without all the facts. In order to protect my poor little human sensitivities, you've kinda made me jump to a few conclusions. That's why I'm here!"

"And maybe I don't want you to get hurt. Has that ever crossed your mind? If they had any idea what you could do, hurt would be the least of your problems. Never mind what I could do to you."

"Break me? Yeah. I get it. You're this big strong demon, able to crush boulders with your ass or something. Luke gave me a demonstration with his coffee mug. The thing is, Nick, I'm still not scared of you."

"You should be."

"But I'm not." I stepped right into his face. "The *only* thing I'm scared of is that you're just using me. That you don't feel a damned thing for me, you just want this crazy ability I have. Is that it? Because if it is, speak up now. I'm pretty used to getting dumped. If that's what you're planning, tell me so I can have my little pity party and get my mind back in the game to learn this shit."

He grabbed my arms, staring right into my face. "What? What the hell are you talking about?"

"You all but chased me off this weekend. You go from asking me for a kiss to vanishing for years at a time. Just tell me, *right now*, is there really anything between us, or is it all just in my head?"

"Damn it, woman," he growled. "How could you even think that?"

"Think what? That you were into me? It's pretty much the human reaction to making out like we've been."

"That I'm not!"

I paused. "What?"

He moved closer. Our bodies were damned near touching. Then he bent to look right in my eyes. "You make me fucking crazy, Sia. I can't think about anything else when you're around. When you're not, I worry they've found you. Fuck. I'm supposed to be your teacher. To let you make your own decision about what to do with your abilities, but to do that, I have to keep my damned hands off you. Unfortunately, I tried to stay away from you, and *I couldn't*. What part of that is hard to understand?"

"Really?" I asked, my voice coming out as a whisper.

"For the first time in my life," he said, so close his breath caressed my cheek, "I've found there's one thing I can't stand waiting for. But I'm trying to be a damned gentleman, Sia. I'm trying to treat you like you deserve."

I tilted my head just enough to meet his dark eyes. "You don't have to. I don't want to lose my powers. I don't want to be normal. Most of all, Nick, I don't want whatever this is between us to be just in my mind. I just want to know you actually want *me*."

The response was his mouth crashing into mine as one of his hands tangled in the hair at the back of my neck. I kissed back, grabbing a fistful of his shirt to keep him from escaping, but this time he wasn't leaving. Nick pulled me closer until our bodies touched everywhere. His other hand was on my lower back, lifting me into him. He wasn't gentle. He didn't tease me. Oh no, he kissed me until I was breathless, savoring my mouth as if it already belonged to him. Those strong hands pressed into my flesh, proving that escape was not an option.

I didn't mind at all.

When I gasped for breath, he pulled back just enough to see my face. "You're my Muse. My girl. My miracle. I've worked so hard to keep my hands off you, and you just come storming in here, throwing it back in my face?"

"Nick..."

"No, this time you listen, little dove. I gave you the chance to take it slow, but you're begging to crawl into bed with a demon. Do you have any idea what that means?"

I couldn't help myself. A devious little smile took over my smart-ass mouth. "A really big dick?"

"Attached to a monster. The one thing you haven't yet thought about is what happens when you can walk between worlds. What happens when the beast that wants you isn't the pretty little human man you see now. I'm a *demon*, Sienna. A real demon, not a fluffy, cuddly thing that has a heart at the end of its tail!"

"Then I'd say it's a good thing I like blue, huh?"

He smiled, finally looking like the demon he claimed to be. "Yeah. It's a damned good thing. By the way, I hate mini-golf." Then his mouth was on mine again.

17

*H*e groaned and pressed me back, more powerful than I'd expected. Together, we crashed into the library wall, rattling the shelf that held my coffee. He didn't care. His lips crushed mine, his tongue making love to my mouth, and I never wanted him to stop. Pressing my body into his, I moaned softly as I writhed against him. He groaned to match. This crazy life of mine made absolutely no sense, but I'd wanted Nick since I first saw him. Resisting him was as impossible as expecting iron to avoid a magnet.

When his lips moved to my neck, I leaned my head back. The hand in my hair tightened, holding me there, and he paused. With his mouth hovering just above my skin, he held me trapped, and I made no move to resist. Lightly, the tip of his tongue tickled the tendon. Then he kissed. That became a nip. My pulse thrummed in the pit of my stomach, and I could feel the moisture between my legs, but he was taunting me, proving I couldn't do a damned thing to stop him.

I didn't want to. "Please," I begged.

"Not here," he said, pulling himself from my grasp. Before I could reply, he slid an arm beneath me, lifting me all too easily. "Just don't let me hurt you," he whispered.

"You won't."

He made it upstairs quickly, carrying me as if I weighed nothing. Walking to one of the many doors on the long hall, he pushed it open with his back. I caught a glimpse of soothing blues before he closed it again, leaving us awash in darkness. Gently, he laid me on the bed and followed me down. I opened my knees to make room for the width of his hips, welcoming his body against mine. One of his strong arms held his weight off me.

"God, I want you," he breathed, then kissed me.

That was exactly what I wanted to hear. Gripping the back of his head, I held him close, showing him what I wanted. My legs pressed against his thighs, locking him between my knees. His hand traveled down my body, tracing along my ribs to my hip, making me feel so small and delicate beneath him. Sexy. Desirable. Even wanton. So many times, I'd felt like I was just the easiest option, but that wasn't the case with Nick. He touched me like he wanted nothing else. His mouth moved down my throat, tasting my skin, kissing every inch of my neck with a desire I'd never felt from a man.

I surrendered to it, arching my body into him, grasping at his broad shoulders through the soft shirt to hold him closer. I needed more, wanted everything. Nick turned me on like no other man. I had to kiss his chest, to touch it. Yanking the hem of his shirt free of his pants, my hands slid beneath, feeling the skin at his waist. Slowly, I let them roam. Men like him were what women dreamed of. I'd never expected it to happen, though. Oh, I'd wanted this, fantasized about it even, but never honestly believed he would actually feel the same way about me.

My palms caressed the ridges of his abs and kept moving higher, making him suck in a breath. Then down, exploring the feel of him, trying to identify the imperfections I couldn't see. He was amazing. I'd waited so long to be here, with him, like this – and it was finally happening.

My mouth teased one nipple through the cloth of his shirt, then kissed the flat muscle above it as I sought his mouth. He met me halfway with a growl deep in the back of his throat. Damn, this man could kiss, but I wanted more. Sucking at his lips, tangling my tongue with his, I let my hands find their way down until my fingers tripped over the waistband of his jeans. That was what I wanted. I fumbled at the buckle of his belt, hoping to sneak inside.

He chuckled, breaking our kiss. "If you do that, I won't stop."

My answer was breathy. "I don't want you to stop."

"Thought you had questions."

I smiled in the darkness. "Only because I didn't think *this* would happen. Questions can wait."

The words removed his resistance, and he pressed his hips into me, rock hard through the fabric – and it felt so damned good. His mouth sucked at my neck as his hand slid under my back. Then he shifted, rolling over, pulling me above him. With me trapped on his lap, he sat up, but his hands were still moving. Taking his time about it, he guided my shirt higher, giving me every chance to stop him. What the stupid demon couldn't understand was that I was the one in charge here.

I grabbed the hem and wrenched the fabric over my head, tossing it out of reach. As the shirt fell away, he paused. I could see dim reflections in his dark eyes as he slid first one bra strap from my shoulder, then the other, drinking in everything as I reached back to release the clasp. The material dropped into my lap.

Nick sighed softly, the same sound people make when viewing a great work of art. It wasn't one I was used to hearing in the bedroom. Gently, tenderly, his strong hands moved to my ribs, meeting the swell of my breasts, his thumbs trailing higher. Slowly, the pads drifted across my nipples, making the flesh tighten almost painfully. Then he did it again, the feeling so exquisite.

"God," I whimpered.

"You don't need God," Nick promised, his hands worshiping my body. I bucked on his lap, unable to stop myself. "Just me, Sia. I'm the only god you'll ever need to know."

Again he rolled, tossing me onto my back, sliding the last of my clothing down over my hips before he reached for his own. His mouth kissed a line from my jaw to my navel as he eased back. The sound of fabric rustling on skin filled the room when he tugged his arms free of his shirt.

His touch was like fire, sparks igniting beneath his mouth, but it wasn't enough to distract me from the marks across his body. The trickle of light from the street was just enough to see them. Every curve of every muscle on his torso was branded with a symbol, like proof of his perfection, begging my eyes to see them all.

He moved away, breathing heavy. His eyes were filled with a need so intense I couldn't describe it. I lay there, panting, afraid he was going to stop again, and watched his hands slowly work the button of his pants. He raked his eyes across my naked body and bent his mouth to my ankle, dark hair pooling on the bed. His pants made a soft thud when they met the floor, but his mouth didn't stop. It moved along the outside of my leg, over my hip as he crept closer, up my ribs, until his tongue found one nipple, his hand the other.

I arched into it, moaning, hoping he wouldn't stop, feeling his lean, hard hips against my thighs. "Nick," I pleaded.

Releasing my breast, he moved to my mouth. His lips found mine for only a quick caress, then he paused. "That's not really my name." I could feel him right there, pressing into my cleft.

"It is now," I promised.

"And when you learn the other?"

I shifted, sliding my dampness against him. "I can guarantee the repercussions won't be as bad as the ones you'll get if you leave your woman this frustrated for much longer. Stop being a god damned gentleman, Nick. Shut up and fuck me."

He huffed a chuckle as he tilted his hips, prodding me, slowly pushing in. I sucked in a breath and tried to impale myself, but the demon caught my waist in his hand. Holding me there, he took his time, teasing me with every inch until I was mewling for more. Then he thrust.

For all I knew, I was surrendering my soul, but I didn't care. He felt so damned good, filling me as his rock-hard body pinned me to the mattress. I didn't believe in sin, didn't care about judgment. My life had been full of both. What I wanted was this, the man of my dreams entwined with me, slowly withdrawing just to slide a little deeper.

He kissed me, his tongue demanding my complete attention, and slid into me again, over and over, driving my body higher, teasing every nerve in my core. I clung to him, nails gouging his back, my voice tinting each gasp of air, thinking of nothing but the swell of pleasure building inside, wanting to have all of him.

"You feel so good," he whispered into my ear. "So damned good."

His voice was pure seduction, demanding that I surrender to it. I now knew the sound had nothing to do with angels. It was better. Made for temptation, and I had succumbed. I was finally with him, and our slick bodies ground together in perfect harmony. A cry of desire escaped my lips, smothered with his mouth, and his hips drove me to places I'd never experienced.

Slowly, deeply, tenderly, Nick caressed every sensation from me that my body could handle, filling me with pleasures I hadn't even known were possible. Worries about what the guys downstairs would think and caring about the sound of my passion vanished as my body worshiped him, every nerve completely under his control.

Over and over he thrust, and I took it all, delicate skin stretched taut with the size of him, sensitive nipples wonderfully tormented as they brushed against his chest. Each stroke sent flames along my nerves, burning away my restraint, quenched only by the sweat on our skin, until, with a throaty gasp, my body found release. I came, clenched hard against him. My eyes pressed closed to focus on the waves of pleasure running through me as he grunted in the back of his throat.

A few more strokes rode me to the end, then he shuddered as he came. When he tensed, our eyes met, holding each other for that one moment, just long enough to make this feel real, like it meant something before he relaxed. His head dropped to my shoulder, his elbows holding his mass off me while we both sucked back long gasps of air.

Languidly running my fingers down the mass of hair laying against his neck, I savored the moment, feeling so complete lying in the arms of my demon. The last flutters of my orgasm passed as I caught my breath, but I just wanted to hold him, to be close like this for one second longer.

It took a while before he shifted, kissing me as he withdrew. Then he moved to lie beside me on the bed. Nick took a long breath, chuckling in the middle. "That was not quite what I had planned for tonight."

"Oh?" I rolled onto my side to look at him. "And what was my big demon supposed to be doing?"

"Yours?" He scooted closer, reaching up to palm the back of my head.

I nodded under his hand. "I think screwing me means you're officially my boyfriend. Or do you disagree?"

"Mm. I do like the screwing part. The boyfriend part sounds interesting, too." His smile sparkled in the dim light. "And I can only guess that if I refuse, I won't be allowed to do that again, huh?"

"Exactly."

"Well, you drive a hard bargain, but it seems you have a deal, little dove. And I'm going to tell Luke to stop teaching you bad habits. The last thing I need to worry about is making deals with you."

I poked at his ribs, making him flinch back. "I will have you know that my bad habits are all natural, big boy."

He caught my wrist. "Sia? Did I hurt you?"

"Do I act like I'm hurt?"

"No, but..." He lifted my hand to his lips and kissed my knuckles. "I've never been with a human before. Sam said if we're not careful, it can hurt the first time."

With a laugh, I sat up. "You..." I couldn't finish without laughing again. "Nick, you're not the first guy I've slept with. Hate to break it to you."

"No, but..."

"And you were gentle. Trust me. I can take a whole lot more than that."

Another flicker of that smile appeared. "Yeah?"

"Oh yeah."

He released my hand and caught my hip, pulling me against him. Lying side by side on the soft mattress, he just looked at me, drinking in the moment. I didn't mind. It made me feel like I might matter for more than just right now, like this immortal creature beside me might even remember me when I was long gone.

"Help me get this right?" he asked.

"Get what right?"

"Us." His eyes flicked between mine. "You're not like any woman I've met before, on any world, and I'm a demon. I forget and do dumb-ass things. I can barely keep track of the rules you humans live by, and I'm going to make a mistake, but I don't want to lose you, little Muse. I want to keep you safe, make you powerful, and show you all of the wonders I've seen and, for the first time, I think it's possible. I think I've finally found someone who won't expect me to live a lie to make her happy."

"You mean you've never told anyone you're a demon?"

"Not if I could help it, no. Didn't matter if it was a fairy, satyr, or human. My kind are despised on every world." He inhaled deeply. "With good reason. Sia, we haven't always been kind to the midworlders."

"I'm sure they didn't necessarily deserve it, either. Never mind the angels and their lies." I grabbed his hand and laced my fingers through his. "And I don't give up easy, Nick. How about I tell you when you're out of line? I mean, it'll probably be at the top of my lungs as I'm throwing things, but I promise I'll let you know. Ok?"

He laughed. "*That* is a deal I will take." Then he sighed. "But I really do have things to do this weekend."

"Gonna tell me what?"

"Gather aether, prepare our next identities – including yours – and other rather boring tasks. The angels are coming. Right now, there's more of them than us. That means we need to be ready for anything. We need to build our defenses and make sure this place is locked from every possible plane. The war is coming, Sia. As soon as they realize what you are, we won't have the chance to do anything but keep them away. The moment you start working with aether, they will *all* know, and you'll be vulnerable until you can step between worlds."

In all of that, there was one thing I heard. "So you weren't ditching me, huh?"

"No, never that." He reached up and traced the line of my jaw. "I may have been a little worried that you'd change your mind, but I figured better now than later. I don't really want to fall in love with you just to end up disappointed when the rush of excitement wore off."

"What?"

He shrugged. "The idea of playing with the bad guys has its allure at the moment. We've seen it so many times, but it's not the kind of thing that lasts."

"No," I corrected. "What did you mean about falling in love with me?"

His hand paused on my cheek. "I'd like to have the chance to try. I've watched you for so long now. I feel like I know you, but I don't really, and I want to. You're the kind of woman I've waited eons to find."

"I wanna try, too."

"Yeah? You're willing to make this a long-term thing?" Smiling, he rolled closer. "I can think of a very good way to start. I do believe I've caught my breath."

I gasped, playfully swatting him away. "I'm not a toy, you big demon."

"Oh, yes you are," he said, dragging his hips across my thigh. He was getting harder very quickly. "A very addictive, beautiful, amazing toy that I plan to entertain me for a very long time. I just have to make sure I give you some very good reasons to keep coming back."

I threw my leg over his hip and pushed him onto his back so I was straddling his pelvis. "There's one that comes to mind. In fact, I think I could get used to this."

"I hope so," he whispered, running his hand down my spine. "I plan to make sure this is a night you will never forget."

18

Sam burst into the room only a few hours after we'd finally found sleep, waking both of us quickly.

"Nick, you've got that thing in an hour, get your ass out of bed." He turned to leave then looked back, his eyes settling on me. "Nice. So I guess this means we can keep her. Morning, Sienna."

I grumbled something incomprehensible and pulled the covers tighter around my chest, flopping an arm across my eyes. It was light outside, and it had that murky feel of early morning. That meant it was much too early to consider moving from this bed.

"Fuck," Nick groaned, sitting up slowly.

"Go away, Sam," I croaked, my voice rough from being abused all night.

He laughed. "Yeah. Going. Oh, and I'm brewing coffee." I closed my eyes until I heard the door click shut.

Nick sighed. "Good morning, beautiful. Planning to hang out here today?"

"Yep. I have some suppositions I need clarified."

He pressed me deeper into the bed. "Big words before lunch. I'm impressed."

"Just wait. I can do tricks too." I bit my lip and lifted my chin, daring him to kiss me.

Naturally, he complied. "You ok?" he asked softly.

"Yeah." I kissed him again. "Just a little sore. Not really used to a man who can go all night."

He chuckled and kissed me one more time before dropping back to his side of the bed. "I should probably feel bad, but I really don't."

"Good." I sat up. "Because I plan for that to happen again, but first I need a shower."

His fingers ran slowly up my spine. "It won't be today, little dove. I'm not that ignorant of the female body. Besides, I still have those things I'm supposed to be doing."

I yawned. "Ok, maybe you have a point. Wouldn't be nearly as much fun without you." I shifted to ease the dull ache between my legs. "I still need a shower, some clothes, and a damned coffee."

"Go shower. I'll grab you some clothes, Sam's brewing coffee." He pointed at the door in the back corner of the room. "Get up, or I'll keep you here, and I fully intend to watch you walk across the room."

"Beast," I teased, flopping out of bed.

I could feel his eyes on my ass but didn't mind. Nick clearly liked what he saw, so I had no reason to be embarrassed. I closed the door behind me, finding some massive, soft towels hanging from the rack. I petted one, enjoying the feel, then turned on the hot water while I located everything else I'd need. Soap, shampoo, and he even had conditioner – which wasn't surprising since his hair was almost as long as mine. Then I stepped into the most luxurious shower I'd ever experienced.

I'd only just rinsed my hair when the bathroom door opened. "That looks inviting," Nick said.

"It's hot," I warned him.

The glass door released and a hard, toned, muscular body stepped through. "I like it hot." He moved me from the water, his eyes devouring my body as he took my place. "I also really enjoy the massive amount of water and how frivolously you humans use it."

I grabbed the bar of soap, began lathering my hands, and slowly worked them across his chest. Suds trailed from my fingers as I caressed every symbol on every muscle, working ever lower. "So no hot showers on Daemin?"

"Only for the very elite." He gasped as my hands hit sensitive flesh. "Tease," he hissed.

"Already proved that wrong."

"If you start that, you won't be able to finish," he warned, grabbing my wrists.

I licked the mist from my lips and smiled. "Pretty sure I can finish, Nick. My hands work just fine."

He groaned and leaned back against the wall, his fingers moving over mine, guiding them. He was used to being in control, having things exactly how he wanted, and I didn't stop him from showing me. Pressure urged me to squeeze tighter. His hips thrust forward, and I slid on his wet, slick skin, faster, both hands working him savagely until Nick's eyes closed and he clawed at the tile walls.

But there was a power in giving, too. Being able to make this man, this impossibly gorgeous guy, writhe at my touch was my own dream come true, and I was enjoying this. My hands worked his body, but my eyes watched his face, trying to memorize every single detail.

It didn't take long before he was bracing himself, his dick thick and hard in my palms. The swollen head strained until a low, primal groan burst from his lips. His knees weakened and he spilled himself down my leg, the mess rinsed quickly to the drain.

"Damn," he moaned, lifting his wet lashes as the edges of his lips curled up. "I can get used to this."

With a giggle, I pressed against him, kissing his relaxed mouth. "That's exactly my plan. Now finish on your own."

"You already finished me," he pointed out. "Oh, you meant the shower."

I stuck my tongue out at him and turned for the door, gasping when he pulled me back. One tug transported me against him, and a rush of shock hit me at his true strength. Nick had always been so gentle. He'd never seemed like anything more than a well-built man until that moment, even though I'd known better. That didn't mean I'd actually wrapped my mind around it. Feeling him move me like that without even the slightest struggle? The reality of his power finally sank in, and I could tell he saw it written on my face.

"Sia, I won't hurt you." His hand pressed against my cheek. "Never, ok?"

"You're just stronger than I expected. I mean, I tried, but... Wow."

His black eyes pleaded with me. "Tell me that's not a bad thing?"

I shook my head, letting a little giggle slip out. "It's not a bad thing, Nick. It's kinda sexy." It was, but I also knew, for the first time, how easily he could break me.

The strange thing was that I honestly didn't care. Oh, he'd shocked me, but it was more because it had been miraculous than any kind of fear for my life. In fact, the more I thought about it, the safer it made me feel. This was *my* demon. My *boyfriend*. And Nick wasn't the kind of guy anyone in their right mind would fuck with.

Boyfriend wasn't the right word, but what else could I call him? I was pretty sure this thing between us wasn't love – or maybe it was? I didn't know yet, but at that moment he was mine, and "boyfriend" was something I could handle with everything else changing so fast. "Boyfriend" made me feel grounded, normal, and gave some weight of reality to all of this.

He might be Death incarnate, but I refused to skip ahead with our relationship. I wanted to date someone seriously enough to call him a boyfriend, have him turn into a lover, and maybe even a fiancée one day. No matter who he was, if he respected me, he'd let me take this at my own pace.

He stood there, letting the water course down his amazing body. "Dove, are you really ok with this?"

"Yeah," I breathed. "I'm probably just going to have moments, ok? Just things that make me realize this isn't some dream, and I'm not really losing my mind. That's not a bad thing. I'm sure you weren't any better when you first stepped into another world."

"That was a long time ago, dove."

"And I'm willing to bet you still remember the awe. Let me enjoy this, Nick."

"I'm trying, it's just..." He sounded almost nervous. "I haven't dated in a few years." He ran his fingers through the wet hair at the back of my neck. "Or so. I'm not good at this, and I have no idea what I'm supposed to do."

I stepped closer. "You're supposed to be yourself. That's it. I think courtship and that crap went out in the eighteen hundreds. There aren't any fancy rules to follow. It just takes time."

"Ok, maybe it's more like a few *thousand* years. I tried to avoid it."

"You trying to give me a hint or something? Well, bad news. You're stuck with me now." I turned to the door again, intending to make it to my towel this time. "I'm going to dry off, so you don't get any ideas, mister."

He chuckled as I closed the glass door between us. "I hope this is the same reaction I get on the next world. I've been told I look like a corpse."

"You mean the blue skin? Whoever said that had probably never seen a dead person. They tend to be more grey and lifeless. You're more like moonlight on a still lake."

"I honestly think it's the horns they hate the most. Or the wings. Maybe the tail." Something in his voice sounded like he was fishing.

"What color are the horns?" I asked.

"Bluish. Like a dark gunmetal blue."

I could hear him scrubbing shampoo into his hair and enjoyed the way his body was silhouetted against the glass. Damn, that boy had a figure to die for, regardless of the color. And his features had that biblical kind of beauty. His skin was this amazing sun-kissed color, but I couldn't be sure if he'd been trying to mimic some ethnicity or if he'd just gone for the perfect tall, dark, and handsome look. Rubbing the water from my skin, I did my best to imagine him with large bat wings, a tail, and a pair of horns jutting from the top of his head.

"Ok, that actually sounds kinda sexy," I admitted. "I'd love to see it."

He chuckled and turned off the water. When he pushed open the door, droplets clung to his skin. "And I don't really want you to. I'm enjoying having you think I'm beautiful, ok? Let me have that for a bit longer before you see the monster?"

"You're not a monster." I grabbed his bare bicep and let my thumb caress one of those strange symbols. "I bet your tail is cute. There's a little diamond on the end, isn't there?"

He grinned and turned into me, pressing me back with a smile. "I am not cute, little girl. I'm grotesque, monstrous, and terrifying."

"And really good in bed."

His smile turned sweet. "You think so?"

"Mhm." I slid my hands up his slick, bare chest. "Absolutely. Honestly, the best I've had."

"Good." His eyes dropped to my lips. "It's, um, been a while."

I pulled away to let him dry off, deciding to change the subject before I stopped caring about the ache I was still trying to recover from. "And you really fly?"

"Yeah!" He sounded appalled that I even questioned it.

"How does that work? You have some really massive wings or something?"

"Not made of matter. Well, not like you know it. Rather than just molecules of carbon, the further out you get, the more divergent our chemical structure becomes. Energy equals mass times the speed of light, but those variables change between the planes, and it doesn't account for the presence of aether. That means physics is a bit more complicated in the outer realms."

I was sure he'd just said something meaningful, but to me it was gibberish. "So how much can you carry when flying?"

"Uh." His forehead wrinkled. "Couple hundred pounds easily. I've caught Luke a few times. Why?"

"Will you take me flying one day?" I asked. "Just *once?*"

He focused on using the towel to dry himself. "I'll make you a deal. When you see my real body, if you still want to go flying, I'll show you what it's like to soar with dragons, ok? It's more work on Vesdar, but still possible. Wings are only good for gliding on Earth, though. It's why we didn't mind giving them up."

"It's a date," I promised. "And if I absolutely hate the way you look over there, I'll just screw you silly on this side of the veil. At least until I get used to it."

It took a moment before my words registered. When they did, he looked up at me, his lips slightly parted, and stepped closer to smother me in his arms. "I promise. I'll never force you to look at that."

"I said 'if,' Nick. Not when, *if.*"

Hearing how much he hated the way he looked hit me harder than it should. I knew that feeling. As a kid, I'd been the carrot-topped mess, always picked on for one thing or another. When Death had asked me for that first kiss? Never before had anyone acted like they wanted me that way. Maybe It was why I latched onto him so hard, but it also made me want to shelter him from ever needing to feel like that again.

"I'm trying," he said softly. "Damn it, Sia, I'm trying. I just never expected this to happen. You're *nothing* like anyone I've met before."

"I'm a Muse," I reminded him. "I'm not supposed to be, right?"

"Yeah." He leaned back, cradling my face in his hands. "And if you can stand Daemin, maybe we'll craft you a skin with wings of your own. I'll teach you to fly."

"You definitely know the way to a girl's heart." I kissed him quickly and stepped back, reaching up for the circle branded into his chest. "You gonna explain what this is?"

He looked down at my hand, his brow wrinkled, then he laughed. "Yeah. Um, that's my seal. Sam and Luke have one too, and you'll need one eventually. It's like a key for Daemin, and it will show on every skin you make."

I nodded slowly, accepting that. "And the rest of the markings?"

To prove what I meant, I touched one on his ribs, then just over his navel. They weren't as dense on his arms or legs, and he had none on his face or neck. That was probably why I'd never noticed them when he was wearing a shirt.

He grabbed his towel and rubbed the water from his skin, refusing to meet my eyes. "I forgot about that. Those are wards."

"On your body?"

He nodded, glancing up at me. "To prevent anyone from removing my aether without consent. I have no urge to lay asleep for thousands of years. There's only a handful of us that have never been drained, and most refuse to leave Daemin." He shrugged. "I didn't exactly plan for last night to happen or I would have told you."

"It's ok!" I assured him. "It's actually pretty cool. I mean, I just thought it was ancient body art or something. Didn't know you were covered in magic."

He nodded. "In more ways than you know. I'm trying not to hide anything from you, but it's going to take years before I can explain it all."

"It's ok, Nick. I've got plenty of time," I promised. "Clothes?"

"On the bed." When I turned for the door, he grabbed my arm, halting me. This time, his fingers were overly gentle. "Are you really ok with this?"

"Yeah." I turned back to him, not even ashamed of the flush on my cheeks. "In case you didn't know, there's nothing wrong with jumping in bed with some nefarious demon that wants to teach me the black arts."

"That's not what I meant."

"I know." I took a deep breath. "I hate that I no longer understand my own world, but that's my only complaint. I want to learn everything *right now.* Sam's fun, Luke's growing on me, and you?" I looked up at him slowly. "I'm pretty happy with this, even if I might be walking a little funny for the rest of the day."

He chuckled, avoiding my eyes as he wrapped the towel around his waist. "Tell me if I go too fast?"

"I can do that."

"Spend the night with me again tonight?"

"I'd planned on it."

He glanced up and grinned. "Marry me?"

I laughed. "Too fast."

He chuckled. "Ok. Least we settled that."

Then he walked past me to the bedroom, grabbing his clothes and pulling them on without a hint of shame. I looked at what he'd found for me, surprised to see my favorite t-shirt and a pair of jeans, clean socks, underwear, and even my running shoes all lying there, waiting for me.

"How did you figure out my favorite outfit?"

"Yeah, um..." He pulled a shirt over his head. "I've been keeping an eye on you, to make sure no angels tried to make a move, but those were on the dresser looking like you'd just washed them. I've seen you in that before, so assumed you liked it."

"So you just shifted into my house?"

He ran his fingers through his hair. "Wasn't the first time, either. After the robbery, I stopped by every so often. I needed to see if you'd been trained, but mostly I just wanted to make sure you were ok. Seeing Death messes some people up pretty bad."

"It did. I kept trying to figure out how to see you again." I shrugged. "But since I'm not really interested in dying, I only thought about doing something disastrous for a few seconds."

"Good, because I would've just put you back together." Then he met my eyes. "I didn't ward your house until after the accident last week. Before that, I tried not to snoop, but once angels were involved? The three of us have been keeping an eye on you since. I mean, not directly. Just making sure there aren't any of those assholes trying to move in."

"Thank you."

He lifted a brow. "You're ok with that?"

"Yes and no. You didn't hide it, Sam and Luke have been trying to be upfront, and I've already figured out that the other side hates me. I don't *like* that I have to be babysat, but I get it. So thank you for putting up with my bullshit and not making me feel like I'm the asshole."

He tilted his head to the door. "Speaking of assholes, you willing to spend the day with Sam?"

I rolled my eyes. "Sam's not an asshole, but sure. I'll pretty much do anything for a little coffee right now. Go do whatever nefarious stuff you have planned. I promise I'll keep a bodyguard close."

I kissed Nick again then opened the door, walking into the rest of the house. In the pit of my stomach, the first butterfly decided to start flapping around. It didn't take much to guess that Sam had already told Luke I was still here. It most certainly wasn't rocket science to figure out what we'd been doing last night, and a part of me worried what they would think. I shouldn't have. Shuffling into the kitchen, I found Sam pouring himself a cup of coffee.

"Morning, sunshine," he said, pulling another cup out of the cabinet. "Tell me you didn't abuse him too bad?"

"Not more than he deserved."

"Good." He filled the second cup, adding the perfect amount of cream and sugar to it. "Glad you two didn't try to avoid it."

"So you're ok with this?" I accepted the coffee gratefully, cradling it to keep my hands occupied. "No problems with Death screwing the Muse?"

"Well, I *guess* I can let you have him. Nah, Luke agrees. You're good for him, and we both like having you around to keep things interesting." Sam shrugged. "But this thing between us? Sweetheart, I know it'll be hard, but you've made your choice. Just look at what you've given up."

I laughed. Sam had never tried to be anything to me but a friend, which made his antics even funnier. "It's only because I didn't want to get shot down. Besides, Sam, if you want the girl, you need to do a little more than just be a nice guy. Flirting helps."

"Good to know. So, you do breakfast?"

I groaned and lifted my cup. "This is all I need. I'm also not used to staying up all night and waking at the crack of dawn. You monsters really need to learn how to sleep in."

19

*N*ick left without saying a word. I wasn't offended, not exactly, but it was still a little weird. The only reason I knew was because Sam muttered something about having the house to ourselves now. It seemed the wards on my place weren't the only ones he could feel.

Coffee in hand, Sam and I took over the parlor. That was not the room with the console in it, but the couches were just as good. It also had a lot more space to draw, and there was a certain demon who hadn't yet finished his second-week art project. While he arranged his supplies, I figured out where I'd left my stuff the night before and got to work on a few touch-ups to my own.

It was kinda nice having someone to draw with. It was also a great ending to one hell of an amazing night. Neither of us bothered talking until we'd made it through a few cups of coffee. Even then, we focused mostly on asking for an opinion, pointing out issues the other couldn't see and sharing our art supplies. It was after my third cup of the morning when I realized the house was still amazingly silent.

"Luke still sleeping?" I asked.

Sam pushed his hair back, leaving a smudge of charcoal behind. "Nah, he went with Nick."

"Oh." I added a few more details to my perspective piece from the day before, wondering how much he'd tell me. "You know where they went?"

Sam's hand stopped, and he looked up. "You probably don't want to know that, Sia."

"Why?"

He sighed and put down his charcoal. "Because you've spent your entire life believing in a certain set of rules. When they change, your body doesn't know how to react, so it tries to relate to what it's done before. In this case, worry."

That sounded like he was quoting something, and it wasn't making me feel any better. "Sam? Should I be worried?"

"Nope." He paused. "Well, not really. I mean, it's a dumb fucking idea, but –"

I groaned. "Just tell me already! You're not exactly helping."

"Luke set up a meeting with Mike yesterday." He glanced at his hands, thought about it, then wiped them down the legs of his pants before scooting back. "They're going to meet with the ranking angels in the area and see what's going on. Nick wants to know if they have any idea what they're chasing. They probably want to know what we know just as bad."

My guts clenched. "Fuck."

"See? Worry. I know it's hard to comprehend, but we're immortal. Not the vampire kind who end up dying to a whole list of things type of eternal life, either."

I heard him, I honestly did, but there was a very big grey area between perfectly fine and dead. A big portion of it involved a whole lot of pain, and I wasn't really fond of Nick suffering. Especially not when I was the cause.

"Why would he do that?" I asked. "Did he think they were just going to sit down and trade information to see which one's going to get me first or something?"

"Sia..."

But I was on a rant. "Don't 'Sia' me. He's probably walking into a trap right now. Those bastards can't be trusted!"

"Sia!" Sam snapped, grabbing my shoulder to make me shut up. "They may not know there's a Muse around. Nick thought it was a weapon bending the veils. Why would they think any different?"

"Because I've been face to face with a few of those creeps now. Why *wouldn't* they know? I mean, Nick figured it out! Luke said he could see it on me."

"Sweetheart," he said gently, his thumb wiping a smudge from my chin. "It doesn't work like that. Nick saw you pulling raw aether from a living man. *That's* how he figured it out. Most of the time, you don't look special at all. Just like any other beautiful girl. Your aura only flares when you're in a panic. Like when you couldn't get away from Luke – which was stupid on his part, but regardless. Otherwise, we can't see anything out of the ordinary. That's why Luke and I weren't convinced at first. Nick said you were a Muse, but we hadn't seen any proof of it, just a lot of hints. And we've spent a *lot* of time around you."

"Oh."

"Exactly." Sam bobbed his head slowly, watching me process that. "Which is why Nick wants to know if they're blaming us for the veils changing. They have to know about that. That's the only reason they'd be here, but it doesn't necessarily mean they know *why*. The peaks in the bubbles may point at you, but where have you been lately?"

"Here," I realized. "At your place."

"Exactly. With the enemy forces who might have a weapon. Us staying close just makes it that much harder for them to be sure and keeps you safe if we have to. Don't worry, sweetie, we'll take care of you and make sure you have nothing to worry about."

That only helped to a point. "They're still going to end up in a trap," I pointed out. "Y'all said you and angels have been fighting for millions of years, Sam. Why wouldn't they try to jump him?"

"They will," he admitted. "But this is Nick and Luke we're talking about. There isn't a whole lot they can do to them. Trust me. We've done this a few times since the worlds formed."

"Uh, and if they get shot, or stabbed, or whatever else y'all do to each other?" I could only imagine what kind of damage magic could do.

Sam cocked his head like he was weighing that. "Sure, that would be annoying, but Nick can heal almost anything they can do. Luke's not bad, either. Not exactly something to worry about."

"Oh. So if normal pain isn't a problem is there anything else I should worry about?" I got the feeling Sam was hiding something.

He looked away, proving I was right. "Aether drain. They'd have to break his wards to do it, which would be hard but not completely impossible. Anyway, if he's drained, he'd be in a coma – basically – until he can be refilled, and I'm not sure anyone can do that. Depending upon what world they're on, that could take a while."

"Why?"

"Natural aether will slowly seep in, but most places don't have as much as Earth. The outer worlds have nothing extra."

"So why can't someone just slap it back in like he did with Luke?"

Sam sighed heavily. "Those runes all over his body? I'm sure you saw them. They're wards. Nick protected his body to make it hard to pull aether. That means it's also hard to get back in. He's the best there is, Sienna, but if anyone figures out how to drain him, I'm not sure we could put it back."

"And then what?"

"Then he waits until someone is strong enough to break his wards or he gets it by osmosis. He can't die, but he can sleep for a really long time. Less if we bring him here, which is exactly what we'd do." He met my eyes and gave me a reassuring smile. "So stop worrying because it'll be fine. Nick's always fine, and he does a damned good job of keeping us fine. Let's just get our homework done and stop thinking about it for a bit."

I tried. I honestly tried, but I couldn't stop worrying. What bothered me the most was that it was all my fault. I hadn't exactly asked to be a Muse, but these guys were going through hell trying to take such good care of me. I didn't deserve that, but the least I could do was pay them back.

There was only one thing that could keep my mind off of waiting. That was Nick. In this case, his true form. I'd started drawing it yesterday but hadn't finished, and I was pretty sure Sam would know what he looked like as a demon.

"Hey?" I asked, pulling out my smaller sketchpad. "Will you look at something and tell me if I'm even close?" I flipped to the page that had Nick's head and upper body on it, then slid it over so he could look.

His eyes flicked from the page to me and back. "It's not bad, actually," he admitted after what felt like an eternity. "You didn't get the horns right, though."

"I was going off feel. He never let me see under Death's hood."

Sam chuckled and scooted closer, pushing the pad back in front of me. "See here? They attach a little farther back. Over his ears, not his temples. And there's another set on the top of his head." He gestured on himself to demonstrate the shape. "Same type of ridges, but a different arc."

"And the rest?"

He put his arm on the couch behind me and leaned in for a better view. I caught a whiff of something amazing and inhaled. He paused, slowly looking over. Our faces were a little too close.

"Did you just sniff me?"

My cheeks grew warmer. "You smell good. Shaving cream or deodorant?" Because that wasn't strong enough to be cologne.

His eyes dropped, and he chuckled once. "Demon."

"Oh."

"Yeah, uh..." He cleared his throat and tapped at the page. "His eyes are pretty close, but a bit bigger. You got the ears all wrong, though. Think sexy woodland elf or something."

"Sam?" I asked, overly aware that he still hadn't moved his arm.

He leaned a little closer to my neck. This time he inhaled. "I like it better when you use your own stuff, but Nick's works too."

This time, I refused to look. "Did you just smell me back?"

"Fair's fair."

Now I had to know. "What do *you* really look like?"

He didn't hesitate before answering, proving the problem with being a monster wasn't a universal thing. "I only have two horns. Like spirals that arc around the crown of my head. Thinner than his, little bigger than my thumb. Like antelope horns, I suppose."

"And your skin?"

He reached up and dragged one knuckle down my cheek. "Smoother, without the little hairs. Mine's like a dusky mauve color."

"Like a stormy sunrise?" I asked, finally tilting my face to see him.

He smiled. "Yeah. I like that."

Before I could ask the next question, something in the air changed, and footsteps sounded in the hall. Sam quickly grabbed the sketchpad from the coffee table and pulled it onto the floor, but that pushed him even closer to me. He didn't get the chance to sit back before Nick walked into the room. Luke followed a moment later.

"Studying?" Nick asked, looking between the two of us pointedly. We were much too close for this to be accidental.

Seeing him, my face wasn't getting warm. Nope, I felt all of the blood draining from it at warp speed. "Drawing, actually. Are you ok?"

Nick's jaw clenched, and he looked at Sam. "You told her?"

"Mhm. She asked." And That was when he finally moved back to his corner of the couch, acting for all the world like we hadn't just been sitting way too close to each other. "So how'd it go?"

"Mike brought friends," Nick said. "You aren't bothering her, are you?"

Sam shrugged. "Don't think so. She said I smell good."

Nick chuckled. "You do." Then he smiled at me. "And we're pretty sure they haven't figured out what you are. Means we have a little breathing room here, but it would be easier if you found a reason to postpone your studies for a bit."

I had to shake my head to make sure I'd heard him right. "You want me to drop my classes? For how long?"

"Until we get you trained."

"And how long is that going to take?"

He pulled his hand across his mouth, but it didn't hide the sigh. "Two years, maybe? If we push it."

What?! I'd already put it off for six just to save enough to actually do this. Now he wanted me to be a twenty-six-year-old freshman? To graduate at thirty if I was *lucky?* Yeah, not going to happen! I'd been ok with this whole demon war thing so far, but that was pushing it just a little too much.

Never mind that all of this hinged on me blindly trusting a group of guys I'd just met. Oh, sure, all signs pointed to them being right, but the proof? I had none except for getting annoyed at pretty blondes with green eyes. I might be a little impulsive, but I needed more than hearsay before altering my entire life plan.

"No."

"Sia," he tried, but I didn't let him finish.

"Two years of being stuck at some craptastic job, letting my life pass me by, struggling to make ends meet? Not going to happen, Nick. Maybe where y'all are from, you can just camp out under a tree and live happily ever after, but in case you missed it, on this world, we need jobs. To get a good one, that means I need a degree, and I'm *already* behind the curve. So, no. This is not negotiable."

"We'll take care of you," he insisted.

I used both hands to point at my chest. "Do I look like a damsel in distress? No. Already got my fill of living on the system, thank

216

you very much. So here are your options. I help you while I get my degree, or I get my degree. Am I understood?"

Again, he sighed, but this time he nodded. "We'll figure out a way to make it work."

Luke shifted around Nick to look into the room. "Hey, Sam? I need help with something, I'm sure, in some other room, far away from where those two are."

"All over that," Sam agreed, quickly shoving his things into a bag.

I couldn't help but notice that he also grabbed my sketch pad, flipped it closed, and put it well out of sight. When he hopped up to leave, he caught my eye and winked. I wasn't sure if I should feel guilty for something I hadn't really done, or appreciate that he was keeping my drawing a secret. I could only guess that Nick wouldn't be too thrilled to know I'd been fretting over his demonic body after all but hanging on his friend.

I waited until they were both in the other room before asking, "Are you really ok?"

He nodded. "I'm fine. We have a few days to get some protections set up now." He looked at me for a moment. "You were really worried?"

"Is that bad?" Oh man, it sounded like I'd already offended him.

The look on his face removed all my worry, though. "No, it's not bad. I've just never really had anyone worry about me before."

"And there wasn't anything with Sam. It's not what it looked like."

He tossed me a smile and moved to claim the cushion beside me. "I'm not worried about Sam, little dove. You shouldn't be either. It's ok."

"You're not mad?"

He wobbled his head as if thinking about that. "I'm a little annoyed that my big date idea just got screwed up, but I think we can work around it." Then he leaned closer and kissed me. "I do wish you'd drop your classes."

"Nick, I've only really known you a couple of weeks. There are so many what-ifs that I don't feel comfortable doing that. No, ok? Getting my degree is something I've spent my entire life working toward."

"Even if I told you a few choirs are moving in?" he asked. "We've spotted three archangels, at least a handful of malakim, and there were four cherubim there today -"

"I don't even know what that means," I broke in.

He nodded. "Exactly. Sia, these are angels, and they won't use the same tactics you're used to. Time is one thing that is always on our side. So long as you're not using aether, they're winning. Getting you to use it for their purposes is just icing on the cake."

"Ok..."

"Which means their first attack will be trying to drive you away from us – and our protection. I mean, if I told you I'm the Prince of the Watchers, does that mean anything to you at all?"

"That I have a crush on royalty?"

Nick chuckled but shook his head. "Often, biblical references actually match our threat levels. That's why I asked. I'm trying to be serious, Sia."

"I'm trying to make you stop that, Nick."

He cupped my cheek, making me look at him. "Listen, dove. I have no idea how you missed all the religious basics growing up, but there's something you need to know. Once Michael figures out what you are, he'll do everything possible to make you afraid of me. For all I know, he already is." He paused and clenched his jaw. "And I'm worried it might work. All he needs to do is get you to run off once. One time, and he'll be able to take you so far out of reach that I *won't* be able to bring you back."

"Then I won't run off without one of my big strong protectors," I promised.

Using both hands, he rubbed at his eyes. Clearly, I'd missed the mark. "Sia, do you know why I use the name Nick?" I shook my head, and he went on. "Old Nick is what they called me, back in the Middle Ages."

"Ok?"

He shifted uncomfortably. "And the angels all know my real name. Most of them don't call me Nick."

I shrugged. "So? What's the problem?"

His answer was a little too controlled. "You didn't like hearing Luke's name."

"I didn't *expect* to hear it," I corrected. "It's not every day you're told you're talking to the Devil."

"Luke's not the Devil."

I lifted my hands and let them drop again. "I know that now, but c'mon. You guys did drop a lot of stuff on me the other day."

"Sia." Nick took a deep breath and wrapped his fingers around mine. "Michael will do anything to turn you against us, so I'd rather you hear this from me. The first name I knew? Satanael. The second is a little more common. Satan." His dark eyes met mine. "Luke isn't the Devil. I am."

"And I'm an atheist."

His head twitched slightly, taken aback by my answer. "What?" he asked, shocked.

"Well, I've seen an angel, I've met some demons, and you all insist that I'm pretty much the same thing as some ancient Greek godling. Right?"

"Yeah?"

I smiled and shrugged. "So, evidently history is a little murky and myths aren't based completely on fact. Who knew?'

"But –"

A wave of my hand cut him off. "But you just spent the morning with a very famous archangel, broke the bad news that you're some kind of royalty, and screwed my brains out last night. I get it. Things aren't what I had planned. Most of my life hasn't been. I'm still not going to drastically change everything for a guy I started dating last night." I bit my lip, then added, "And teach me how to refill your aether?"

His eyes closed and he cursed under his breath. "Sam told you?"

"Yeah. I figure if I can pull aether from Lucifer, then I can probably refill the Devil, right?"

"I think I prefer it when you call me Death."

Reaching up, I turned his face toward mine. "I happen to think that Satanael is a perfectly good name, but I'm a little partial to Nick."

"I'm getting to be," he admitted. "But my name really doesn't bother you?"

I lifted one shoulder in a halfhearted shrug. "I was kinda expecting it, in all honesty. I think the only thing I'm not thrilled about is how you keep expecting the worst from me. You assume I'm going to believe something someone else says instead of what I've experienced myself. I get it, but that doesn't mean I like it. You're still a good guy, Nick. I've already figured that out."

"I'm trying," he promised. "And I'm doing everything I can to keep you safe."

I scooted closer and rested my head on his big, strong shoulder. "You know, you can protect me the most by showing me how to take care of myself."

"I know. I'm working on that. I really am." Slowly, he let his eyes close as he rubbed the bridge of his nose. "I'm sorry all of this happened."

"Well, I'm not."

"But you could die!" His eyes flicked open, complete surprise on his face.

I patted his arm in understanding. "That's not an if thing, Nick, it's a when." I shrugged. "And when I do, I want to have made at least a little difference."

20

That evening, Nick had to go out again. I stayed up late waiting for him to come back. Luke told me it wasn't anything dangerous, but that only helped so much. Sam had already proven that their idea of dangerous and mine wasn't quite the same. Unfortunately, I passed out before he returned. Sometime in the middle of the night, I woke to find him curled up against me. It was a feeling I couldn't describe, but one that had me smiling as I went back to sleep.

Monday morning, he and Luke walked me to school. And then nothing happened. Gabe glared at me a couple of times in Creative Writing, but for the first time, I realized he spent as much time giving Luke eye-daggers. Maybe Sam had been right and they really had no clue what I was?

After that was Calculus. Nick was a little more tense than normal, but I figured he was just on high alert. Granted, remembering that we had a quiz just before I sat down sucked, but I managed well enough. At least I got some sort of answer for every problem, and I recognized most of the funny symbols. I was willing to call that a win.

Then, Monday night, I had to go back to work. That was when I realized the extent of the angel problem in town. On the upside, it seemed that a plethora of good-looking creepy guys drew an equal measure of desperate college girls into the bar. Mondays were usually slow as hell, but not this time. The tips were flowing, and my shift was over before I knew it. Flirting with Nick the whole time made it that much better.

But when he gave me a ride home, I made him take me back to my place. For once, I honestly needed to get a good night's rest. I'd been stressed out for too many days in a row, and it was finally catching up with me. When my alarm went off the next morning, it hadn't been nearly enough. Rolling over to see the tiny little blue flower on my night table, though? That made up for everything.

Or so I thought until I stepped out my front door. When I turned to the sidewalk, I saw a shock of magenta and recognized Sam. The last time we'd talked had been when he'd helped me with my drawing of Nick. I still didn't quite know what had happened between us, but I was pretty convinced one of us had crossed a line. What bothered me the most was that it might've been me.

"Morning," he said, lifting a paper cup. "Peace offering?"

I closed my eyes and groaned in appreciation. Coffee was exactly what I needed, and from the label on the cup, it came from my favorite place. "What is it?"

Sam grinned. "Caramel mocha with a little extra espresso, and probably better than whatever you have in that mug."

"Sold." Sealing the lid, I shoved my travel mug into my backpack and gestured for him to join me, more than willing to be bought with caffeine. "I'm a cheap friend."

He chuckled. "Wrong kind of cheap, sweetheart."

"Wrong kind of friend," I tossed back, hoping he got the hint.

He shrugged and passed over the coffee, falling in beside me. "This big sexy guy gave me a lecture last night about invading your personal space. Said something about freaking you out by being too touchy-feely." Sam pointed at the cup. "I figured I'd try the whole bribery thing to make up for it. You cool with that, or is Nick gonna drop me from a cliff?"

"From a cliff?" My eyes widened as I waited for an explanation, then realized I hadn't answered. "No, bribery is ok, especially caffeine. What do you mean 'drop you from a cliff?'"

He shoved his crazy hair out of his eyes. "Yeah, um, I guess like smacking your fingers with a ruler, but Daemin style."

"What's it like? Daemin?" Not only did I really not want to talk about my slip up, but I also got the impression that our worlds were completely different, even if parallel in many ways. Unfortunately, I wasn't sure Nick would talk about it.

"My home?" Sam asked. When I nodded, he went on. "A bit like primordial Earth, I suppose. Lots of volcanic stuff and rocks. Plants aren't anything like what you're used to. I think the closest would be like vines. We don't really have trees." He sucked at his own coffee, but I was hanging on every word. "It's pretty sparse too."

"What do you mean?"

He pointed to a tree. "Two squirrels and at least five birds, right? Not where I'm from. Seeing a bird a day is impressive. Granted, they aren't really birds, but still. I mean, we have a few plants, but not enough to make anything resembling a lawn. More like cactus in a desert. That's why I like it here. Daemin is nothing but valleys and cliffs. We live in modified caves because the rock helps keep temperatures constant."

"What about seasons?"

He shrugged. "Two. We have hot and cold."

"So Hell does freeze over?"

Sam grinned and nodded. "Yep, at least once a year. There's actually a city with that name, and it's in the northern hemisphere. So winter is pretty much the same as here."

"I'd love to see it."

Sam paused, missing a step before he caught back up. "Why would you want to see Daemin? It's basically a wasteland, Sia."

I shrugged. "Dunno, because it's different? I mean, look at Hawaii. It's all volcanic leftovers, but people spend a lot of money to go there for vacation."

"It also has oceans," Sam pointed out. "And a lot fewer demons."

"Feathers or leather?" I asked, shifting the topic a bit. I was pretty sure I knew the answer.

"Luke has the feathers. Shit falls out everywhere. Leather all the way, baby."

I nodded. "So are your bones hollow? Nick said physics is different, but that's a little over my head."

"Not hollow," he assured me. "See, the easy way to think about it is that outworlders are made of more aether than matter, so we have a density that isn't made of mass. Prevents us from breaking yet allows flight. The farther inward – toward Earth – we go, the stronger we seem by comparison."

I grabbed Sam's shoulder, making him face me as I stopped. "What's it like to fly?"

His brow wrinkled as he thought about it. "The closest is like swimming, but easier to breathe. It's also really hard to explain having another set of limbs. I mean, imagine trying to describe what your arm feels like to someone born without them or what it's like to paint?"

"Ok, I can see that." I refused to let him go. "But really, is flying cool?"

He plucked at his lip, watching me, then grinned. "Yeah. Maybe Nick can make you a skin for Daemin and teach you?"

"Is it hard?"

Sam shrugged. "Is walking hard?"

"It was when I was a baby."

He chuckled and together we started moving again in silence. It wasn't uncomfortable but this pressure still hung between us. I had the feeling there was something important Sam wanted to say. Most likely about getting caught flirting when Nick had left us together. Considering that I hadn't really talked to him since, it could've just been my guilty conscience, but when he spoke up, he proved I wasn't the only one who hadn't forgotten that little moment.

"Hey, um, about Sunday?"

I felt my shoulders drop. There was no way this could go well, so I tried to deflect. "Yeah? I appreciated your help with that drawing. Nick is convinced I'll think he's a monster, but I can't stop wondering about it."

"I didn't tell Nick about the picture but, um, we did talk." He hefted his bag higher on his shoulder. "Look, you're a one guy type of girl. I get it, and I wasn't trying to make some smooth move or anything. Nick chewed me out for making you feel pressured, but I just -" He pulled in a long breath. "I guess I just forget that you're not one of us sometimes. I mean, you're different. It's like we've stumbled upon the only female demon in existence, and I sometimes forget that the way we act might seem weird."

That was not what I'd expected. "The way y'all act?"

"Yeah." He laughed at his feet. "After a few million years together, we don't really have a lot of hard lines, you know? I didn't mean to treat you like some kind of object. I honestly didn't even think of it that way. I was just getting closer to look at your drawing until you sniffed me."

"I smelled something nice so was going to ask what brand of cologne you used, then realized it wasn't strong enough," I explained. "I'm not upset. I promise. I just don't want Nick to think I'm going to cheat on him the second he's out of sight. Let alone with one of his friends!"

He reached up and clasped my shoulder. "He's not worried about that. Nick knows me. We've spent too many years together to worry about things like that."

"Yeah, but -"

He shook me gently. "Stop thinking you know the answers and just listen for a second. He knows you're a Muse. He's well aware that people will be drawn to you in one way or another. Some innocently, others not so much. When Nick walked in and you looked scared to death? He assumed it was because you felt like I'd trapped you. *Not* because he thought there was any other problem. He was worried you wouldn't trust me enough to run *to* me if something happens." Ducking his head, he caught my eye. "Not once when we talked did he have a single concern about you cheating."

"I just... I don't want to screw this up, and my track record with men isn't the best."

Sam shook his head. "You won't. I told him about you asking what smelled good and he thought it was funny. When I mentioned that you compared my skin to a stormy dawn sky, he liked it. Liked it, sweetheart. He said you were dead on and was impressed because you'd never even seen what I really look like. I told him about how I was sniffing you back, and he agreed that we like your shampoo better. He knows I get all touchy-feely with people I get along with, but if I do and it makes you feel weird, just smack me around a bit?"

"No, it's not that," I insisted. "I've never had a problem with you, Sam. I'm pretty sure you flirt with everything." I chewed on my lip and ducked my head. My next words were almost mumbled under my breath. "The problem was that I *wasn't* offended."

"Oh," he said, sounding a little shocked. After a minute he added, "Then we're ok?"

All I could do was nod. My face was already starting to feel a little warm and saying anything else would turn it into an inferno.

"So, like, I can still hang out with you and shit?" Since we were almost to the Art building, he shifted closer and dropped his voice. "You know, without any weirdness? I mean, if Nick's ok with it, and you're ok with it, then I don't have to pretend to be Mr. Goody-Two-Shoes, right?"

I giggled, mostly to ignore the awkwardness of this. "Sam, you wouldn't be the same if you tried to be good. And I promise if any of the bad guys show up, I'll be running right to whichever of my friends is closest." I stepped over and bumped his shoulder with mine. "That includes you."

"Good." With a gallant gesture, he pulled the door open for me, saying nothing until he was beside me again. "Because our friends have been closing ranks, so keep your eyes open today."

"Which friends?"

"All of them." He shrugged. "You know, typically blonde, always beautiful, none as friendly as Luke."

"Luke's an ass," I reminded him.

Sam nodded. "Yeah, and he's a nice one."

"So what do I do if they try to mess with me?"

"Play dumb," he said. "Seriously. You don't know shit and it's just a normal day. If they think you're ignorant, they'll assume you're just our latest pastime."

"Pastime?" I stopped, my Art History class only a few doors down. "Is that really how you think of women, Sam?"

"It's how *they* think of humans." He patted my shoulder. "And if one of them tries to put his hands on you, scream as loud as you can and drain them dry, sweetheart. It hurts like a bitch, and they *will* let go." He paused. "Yeah, but don't do that in the corridor. If someone gets you in the corridor, just hang on for dear life."

"Why?"

He took a long breath, looking guilty. "Um, if you don't know how to get out, you could be swept away. It's almost impossible to find a lost human between realms."

"Right. Drain before slipping through. Gotcha."

"That's my girl." He playfully punched my arm. "And if you tell Nick I was sweet to you, I'll get you another coffee when Drawing is over."

I punched him back lightly. "Does that count as sweet?"

"Nope, but you're lucky I have a thing for redheads."

I grinned and pulled open the door for the lecture hall. Sam winked and headed the other way, vanishing before some big, sexy guy could drop him from a cliff. What he didn't know was that the big sexy guy in question couldn't see the door from where we sat. Not in a class this big. With a smile lingering on my lips, I made my way down the aisle until I saw Nick, then shuffled over to claim my chair. When I dropped into it, his eyes landed on my coffee.

"Sam?" he asked.

I took a long sip. "If I tell you he was nice to me, I get another after class."

His mouth split into a smile and a chuckle followed after. Evidently, Sam wasn't going to be getting dropped anytime soon.

"He doesn't bother you, does he?"

I shook my head. "He's sweet. I just figured you'd get the wrong impression about him all but crawling into my lap this weekend."

Nick shook his head. "I'm not worried about it. Of all the people in the world, I think I trust Sam the most. He does his own thing, but he's honestly a good guy."

"Yeah, he is. Plus, having someone to walk with from my house to class lately is kinda nice. You know, I'm actually enjoying having a few friends in my life for once."

"Good, because we're not going to stop anytime soon." His expression turned serious. "Notice anything different today?"

"What do you mean?"

Leaning closer, he used the width of his chest to hide his hand pointing behind and to his left. "See that guy over there? The pasty kid with the black glasses?"

"Yeah?"

"Malakim. Lesser angel. There's another in the front row and a third hanging around the back of the room. Think of them like grunts of the feathered type, and they're usually sent out to watch and report back." Nick leaned back in his chair, his body relaxed, but his voice wasn't. "I think they're starting to figure it out."

"Figure what out?" I asked, careful to keep my voice as quiet as I could.

"That you're a Muse and the veils are tied to *you*, not us."

"Ok. For a second here, pretend like I just found out about all of this stuff a few days ago, and break it down *real* small for me? Sam said I don't look any different most of the time. How would they know?"

That got me another of those amazing smiles. Damn, I loved this guy's mouth. Then again, I had been obsessing over it for a few years now.

"Because they've probably been tracking the peak. While there's always a demon around its location, it isn't always the same demon. However, one thing is constant with it. You. Granted, I'm only guessing here, and I sure don't want to prove it to them. I just want you to be extra careful."

"Ok. But what good am I? You said Muses inspire people. How would that help them any?"

"Most Muses are inspiration," he clarified. "It's a minor form of influencing the aether inside a person's mind. Similar to what they do but with fewer repercussions. Harnessing that ability, they can get more out of the resources they already have. You, however, aren't most Muses. Your art comes off the page. That means you can take inert matter and jump-start the vibrations."

"Vibrations?" I was doing ok up until that point.

Nick waved that away. "Sorry. In layman's terms, you're a very beautiful little battery. Almost all of our technology runs on aether, and your talent basically multiplies whatever is already there. You can't make something from nothing, but you can make a single seed into a forest." Then he leaned into my ear. "With the right training, of course."

"Of course," I mumbled, but my mind was struggling to accept what he'd just said. "So what do they want with me?"

"To make the angelic version of a nuclear weapon, most likely." His eyes flicked over my shoulder, checking the people around us. "Sia, they need aether. The things you can do with it? If they can get their hands on you, they'll force you to create until you use everything you have. Then they'll make you drain the aether from every other world we know of. A nuclear holocaust is nothing in comparison to a world without the basic building blocks of life, and they want them all."

"And y'all?" I asked. "What do your people want from me?"

His eyes flicked between mine, searching my face. "Most of my kind are so worried about surviving they don't have time to worry about anything else. Those of us on the front lines? We'd love for you to make a shield. A defense against intrusion. Me?" He carefully trailed a finger over my ear, pushing back a lock of my orangey-red hair. "I'm hoping you can come up with a way to stop all of this. Whether that's by inspiring us all to make peace, creating something that will fix our problems, or whatever other thing your brain can devise, I don't care. I just think that you might very well be the one person who can change everything."

My breath fell out in a rush. That wasn't at all what I'd expected. Nope, I'd braced for him to say something about keeping me safe or some other fancy words that basically meant nothing. That? He wanted me to make miracles? No pressure or anything!

"Nick, I'm just a college student."

"For now," he agreed. "But you won't always be, and I'm not planning to go anywhere. Right now, we're all just watching you – because doing anything else isn't as easy as just snapping our fingers. There's a little bit of magic that has to be worked first. Just don't let them touch you. Not now, and not ever."

21

---

*W*hen Art History let out, Nick followed me up the stairs to the room for Drawing. I was worried it would make him late to his own class, but he told me not to worry about it. When that wasn't enough, he reminded me he could travel the fast way, meaning through the corridor. Then, he pointed out that he already had a few dozen degrees so wasn't all that worried about this one. Yep, it was the more mundane aspects of this strange new reality that I was having the biggest problem acclimating to.

But Sam was waiting for us in the hall. The guys clasped hands and shared a look, then Nick bent to give me a quick kiss. Not a word was said. With a smile, he turned and trotted right back down the stairs we'd just walked up. I felt like the baton in a relay race. They'd completed the handoff, and now we were on the next stretch.

"You must've said nice things," Sam teased as he escorted me into the classroom.

"Oh? How can you be so sure?" I tried to make that sound as menacing as possible – which wasn't much.

He flashed one of those impish grins. "He didn't threaten me once. Means I'm out of shit."

I was giggling as we claimed our usual easels and started setting up for class. Pulling out my large sketch pad, I found a blank page and clipped it in place. When I bent over to get the tin of pencils from my backpack, I noticed bare feet and legs at the back of the class. The cluster of students and easels blocked most of my view, but there was only one reason for an art class to have a partially dressed guy waiting in it. It seemed we had a model for the day.

I barely finished setting up when the instructor moved to the center of the class, drawing all of our eyes. "Due to a scheduling conflict, we're going to start on nudes today." She turned slowly, looking at all of us. "Remember, our models are people too, and not paid enough to be teased or harassed. Any rude remarks, directed to the model or not, will have you dismissed."

I tuned her out. Of course, there'd always be one person who turned into a juvenile at the sight of a naked body. I hoped it would be different in college, but I wouldn't bet on it. Looking at the faces behind the easels, I could already see a pair of girls with immature grins. What would they think when they saw the type of person who typically posed for the freshman level courses? I'd been hearing the horror stories since I was in high school.

"Now, I'd like to introduce you to Mr. Raphael Daniels." The teacher gestured to a collection of blocks in the middle of the room, her eyes locked on the man at the back of the class.

Sam tensed and sat up straight, drawing my eye. His jaw was clenched, and he stared toward the model. I wondered if he was revolted or turned on by the idea of some guy stripping for our artistic needs. He did claim he'd try anything, and now I finally knew why. It was his demonic nature.

I'd seen nothing but feet and the lower portion of the model's robe, so when he moved into the center of our circle of easels, the stupid smiles finally made sense. I sucked in a breath, just like every other woman in the room, but not for the same reason. Mr.

Daniels was lovely. Eerily so. With a haunting smile, he dropped the robe and draped it over two of the blocks, then reclined across it as if waiting to be handed grapes. He'd situated himself so that he was facing me and the door behind me, baring himself for anyone who happened to pass in the hall outside.

From the instant my eyes landed on him, I knew he was an angel. This guy was damned near as good looking as Nick, but his eerie green eyes made me want to avoid him at all costs. His beauty looked poisonous, like some rainforest frog, toxic to the touch. The problem was I couldn't let on that I knew what he was. Sam said to play stupid, so that was what I would do.

Biting at my lip, I let my eyes roam over his body then turned to the teacher. "Any specific media?"

"Your choice." She was too busy looking at the naked man to focus on my question.

I could feel my cheeks burning as I grabbed a graphite pencil and sharpened the tip, hoping Sam didn't notice. Mr. Daniels' body was sculpted to perfection. I could count every muscle in his abs, and the trail of hair from his navel to genitals was the same rose-gold color as his hair. He didn't say a word, but his eyes watched me. Not the class, just me.

Even knowing what he was, I couldn't put my finger on why he – and the other angels – made me so uneasy. Maybe it was the intensity of his gaze? The unearthly beauty of him? But why didn't Nick or Sam bother me? They were both very easy on the eyes, and I'd liked them immediately. It seemed angels always made me feel paranoid. Even more so now that I knew what they were. I couldn't even blame religion since I hadn't been raised with any. It was nothing more than an instinctual reaction to their metallic appearance so far as I could tell.

Now, I just had to act like any normal girl who had no idea that angels and demons existed. Unfortunately, I'd never really been a normal girl. I gently traced a few shapes on my paper, trying to size out the finished portrait while my mind wandered. In school,

I'd been the dork, always too absorbed in art and reading to care about making friends or impressing boys. After I graduated, I'd done nothing but work. The handful of relationships I'd had were always short and dramatic, most commonly ending in a misunderstanding. Aaron had been a perfect example of the kind of guys I ended up with.

Then again, I probably wouldn't get another chance to draw an angel, so I should make the most of this. Glancing at Mr. Daniels again, I shifted my supplies so I could see him easier, daring to meet his eyes quickly before looking back to the page. I knew I was blushing but hoped he'd think of it as nothing unusual. Out of the corner of my eye, I saw him smile slightly as I looked at his body, letting my gaze linger between his legs longer than was polite. He'd clearly put a little effort into building that skin to impress!

What the poor guy didn't know was that I'd always preferred brunettes to blondes, and Mr. Daniels didn't look nearly as good undressed as Nick. That didn't mean I had a problem with looking. My pencil scratched at the page, building the man from rough shapes into a Babylonian god. Every arc of his body drew the eye up to the scowl I couldn't help but inscribe on his mouth. I tried to capture the desire to touch him and the dangerous game of seduction in the shape of his face. Line by line, smudge by smudge, and glance by glance, the minutes ticked by.

Sam sat silently beside me. I could hear the scratches on his paper, but I didn't dare look over. All I needed to do was make art, and that was the one thing I'd always been good at. Before I knew it, the teacher was talking again, explaining that if we hadn't finished, we'd have another chance next week. In other words, the angel would be back. She tried not to look at Mr. Daniels, but her eyes strayed as much as the rest of ours. I got the feeling the angel enjoyed every second of it.

I started packing my things, putting the tin of art supplies back in my bag before grabbing a can of cheap hairspray from the shelf and spraying the page to prevent smudging. When I reached up to close the sketch pad, a pair of arms closed around my waist. I tensed, expecting the worst.

Just as I was about to pull at his aether, Sam whispered in my ear, "Do you have any idea how hard it was to keep my hands off you that long?" Then he made a production of nibbling at the side of my neck.

Holy crap, he was good at that - but we'd just talked about this. The problem was that he was *really* good at that. I sucked in a breath and turned, making no attempt to push him away. I should, but a thought trickled into the back of my mind. I was supposed to run *to him* when angels were around, and right now I had no problems with that at all.

Our eyes met. The look in his wasn't the playful demon I'd gotten used to. It was intense and pointed. Slowly, he reached up and cupped the side of my face. For a split second, I wondered what he was doing, then I remembered he was the demon of seduction.

That was when he leaned in and claimed my mouth. Not sweetly like Nick. This was Sam. He sucked at my lower lip, pulling it between his teeth, then released it to truly kiss me. I knew what he was doing. I did – but *damn!* When his tongue sought the secrets of my mouth, I grabbed at his neck, trying to remind my knees that this was just theater.

Until I moaned.

Sam noticed. Oh, that sound hadn't been subtle at all. Hell, the angel in the room must have heard – which was probably the point.

Sam chuckled and pulled back. "I promised you a coffee. Get your things, sweetie, and let me seduce you." His eyes flicked toward the door before coming right back.

I decided to just go with it. "Coffee's a good start. The rest you can finish later." I grabbed my things and turned from the room, but a man's voice stopped me.

"How'd it turn out?" The angel had moved closer, standing beside the teacher only a few paces from the door. He looked right at me, his green eyes trying to capture mine.

I bit my lip and glanced down, feigning the shyness that I should have had. Now I knew why Nick had let Luke make a deal with me. It was so I'd know what it felt like and how to avoid it.

"Good," I mumbled to my feet. "I had a little problem with the proportions, but I think I'll get it next time. Thanks again, Mr. Daniels."

"No problem." He smiled at me, but when he reached out, Sam shifted between us. The angel snatched his hand back, unable to hide his look of distaste. "So you're an artist, too?" he asked Sam.

"Oh yeah. Always wanted to try it." Sam tossed his arm over my shoulders and turned me to the door, walking easily out of the class.

And that was it. The monster didn't try to stop us. He didn't call out. We just walked through the building like we had so many times before. Well, mostly. After kissing Sam like that, being tucked under his arm was an entirely new experience. One that made my mind dwell on muscles for some reason. Lean, ripped biceps specifically.

Neither of us said anything important until we were outside the building. Only then did he tilt his head closer and whisper, "There's a line of windows overlooking the street from that room. Just go with this, ok?"

"Yep, going."

And secretly taking complete advantage of the situation. Dear god, even his hands were nice. Why did Sam have to have sexy hands?

He steered me back to the coffee shop, which wasn't the same direction I'd use to go home, but I wasn't foolish enough to complain. Once we passed through the door, Sam sighed and removed his arm. "Grab a couch, I'll get drinks."

"I have work in an hour."

He shook his head. "Not if Raphael's taken an interest in you. I sent Luke a text when we were in class, and he's supposed to tell Nick and meet us here. You might be late, but you will not be *alone*, ok?"

With a sigh, I grabbed the strap of his backpack, pulling it from his arm to swing it over my other shoulder. When that was balanced, I flapped my hand for his portfolio. "Thanks, Sam. Next time it's my turn to buy."

"Yeah, not gonna happen." He laughed and moved toward the line, shaking his head at me.

All I could do was turn toward my favorite couch in the corner. It was getting to be my go-to place with these guys. The best part was it was always empty and no one ever hung around close enough to listen in on the weirdness that we seemed to spend so much time talking about.

It didn't take long for Sam to return, carrying a large paper cup in each hand. He offered me one then dropped into the chair beside my couch. "Talk about bad timing. We just work out our unquenchable attraction, then end up making out all over again." His purple-brown eyes met mine. "Sorry. He was coming over, and I didn't know what else to do."

I was starting to hate how easily I blushed. If it was going to happen this often, I really needed to learn how to do it attractively. "It's ok. I figured it was something like that."

"Good." Sam looked relieved. "I mean, it was pretty hot and all, but Raphael will assume you're still clueless –"

"And you know him?"

"Uh, yeah. He's one of the bigwigs on their side. One step down from Michael, equal to Gabriel. Basically, the guy who took Luke's place when he bailed."

"Oh shit. *That* Raphael."

Slowly, he bobbed his head in agreement. "Exactly. Looks like all the big names are showing up." At that moment, Sam's phone dinged in his pocket. He immediately looked up and let out a relieved sigh. "The cavalry has arrived."

I turned to the door and saw both Nick and Luke stroll in. Seeing them made me feel a bit less like I was about to get jumped. One big strong protector was good. Three were a whole lot better. Hell, I was even happy to see Luke! They headed right over. Nick claimed the spot beside me; Luke took the cushion on the other end.

"What's up?" Nick asked.

Sam grabbed my sketch pad, flipping it to the nude. "How's that for up close and personal?"

Nick's jaw clenched, but Luke pulled the drawing from his hands. "That's about as blatant as it gets." He grinned. "Sam, you should try doing this the next time we go to college. Could get a few dates."

"Oh, I'm gonna," he agreed. Then he nonchalantly added, "So, the thing is, I basically made it look like Sienna was my latest conquest."

"Raphael's not going to like that," Luke said, but both of them were watching Nick.

Nick blinked his gaze over to Sam. "What happened?"

"Raphael was heading over, so I decided to make out with your girl. She didn't seem to mind. Played right into it."

Nick huffed out a chuckle. "You're good at what you do." Then he looked at me. "You still ok with this?"

My mouth was hanging open in shock. "I just kissed the shit out of your roommate, and you're asking *me* if I'm ok?"

He nodded once. "I am."

"Trust me," I shot back, "it didn't hurt. I figured Sam had a plan, and I just kinda went with it."

Sam chuckled. "She moaned. I mean, totally, right there where everyone could hear it."

Nick waved him off. "She does that. I'm a little more concerned with why Raphael was in your class."

I spoke up before they could start embarrassing me again. "Our class schedule changed. We weren't supposed to do nudes for a couple of weeks, but a 'conflict' came up, and things got moved around." I shrugged. "He probably did the same thing Luke did to get y'all in my classes?"

Nick tried to hide it, but I saw his eyes widen slightly. "How'd you know about that?" He looked at Sam.

"She's not stupid," Sam muttered.

I rolled my eyes. "Trust me, I would notice a bunch of amazingly hot men in my classes on the first day."

Nick looked back at me. "You didn't seem to think it was strange that I was there."

"Yeah, I kinda did. I kept wondering why someone like you would bother talking to a girl like me. But one hot math student in a big class? It could happen. That you had Art History with me? That was really pushing it. Math and Art don't go together, but your excuse was halfway decent." I shook my head. "Halfway. Right up until I realized that Sam's also an artist. Then, having one of your blatantly good-looking roommates in every one of my classes and going out of their way to be nice to me? That's suspicious. Casually ending up at my work and tipping too much? Trust me, I'd been wondering how I'd gotten so lucky since you slammed my ex into the back of your car."

Sam slapped my shoulder. "You're so good for my ego, sweetheart."

I never looked away from Nick. "It's pretty blatant. You made these skins to be the ideal, right? Good looks can get you places and all that?"

Luke pressed his fist to his mouth, his eyes sparkling over Nick's shoulder. "No."

"What do you mean?" I looked back to Sam.

He was grinning. "Nick just removed our inhuman traits and pigmented the skin. We lost the wings and accessories, but this is what we look like. Normalized our features a bit, but pretty much the same."

"No shit?" I turned back to Nick feeling warmth rushing to my face. "Ok... I really thought you'd like..."

"I gathered" he grumbled. "You assumed we'd been designed to entice women."

"Is that bad?"

Luke stood up. "Hey, Sam?"

He nodded. "Yeah. Coffee. I'll help you carry. Sienna's gonna need another anyway. She's a fucking addict."

I watched Nick's face while the guys disappeared around the corner. He looked annoyed, and I had a feeling I knew why. "You *told* me y'all were monsters."

"It's ok, Sia."

"Clearly, it's not. Especially if those two vanished like that. They always do when things get sensitive." I lifted a brow, daring him to deny it.

When he dragged his hand down his face, he looked exhausted. "I don't care what the myths say. They're myths. We are not out to subvert souls or take advantage of anyone. I did not design these skins to do anything but blend in."

"Well, then you made a few mistakes, Nick, because from what I've seen, you and those blonde creeps kinda stand out."

He immediately leaned closer and dropped his voice. "And your immediate assumption was that I'd done it intentionally, right? That I'd made our appearance into some type of weapon?"

I couldn't believe what I was hearing. "No," I shot back. "I thought that maybe you were just like everyone else and wanted to have the chance to enjoy a little vanity. Trust me, if I had the power to choose how I looked, I'd be a fucking knockout."

He reached over and palmed the back of my head. "Human ideas of beauty change too fast to worry about that. I just wanted to make us look believable." Then he shifted so I was tucked in at his side. "I'm not mad, and I'm very glad you trusted Sam."

"I was worried you'd be pissed about it," I admitted. "I just want you to know I'm not trying to cheat or anything."

He chuckled, the sound rumbling against my side. "Let's worry about keeping you out of angel hands first. I promise I'd much rather you were alive to dump me than chained in Angelis being drained dry." Then he kissed the top of my head. "Besides, he's almost as good at getting inside your head as an angel. I think Luke's been teaching him bad habits."

Those words gave me an idea. The moment the other two got back, I caught Luke's eye. "Hey, can you make me a deal?"

His face wrinkled in confusion. "Yeah, but why?"

Looking up at Nick to make sure I was on the right track, I explained my thought. "Can you convince my mind to not be persuaded by any other angel?"

Behind me, Sam laughed. "Oh, she's *good.*"

"Do it," Nick agreed. "That's one more layer of protection."

Luke grinned devilishly. "Can I have your soul?"

"No, I'd rather Nick used it for the demons."

He chuckled at that. "Ok, fine. What do you want in exchange for being my pet?"

"How's this? You and only you can control my mind, on the condition that your intentions will be good?"

Glancing at Nick, Luke mulled that over. "Yeah. Look at me, Sienna." I did without hesitation. When everything around me faded to nothing, Luke began to speak. "I want to make you a deal, little Muse. You will only listen to suggestions from me, no other angels. Your mind will not succumb to anyone else's attempts at control, only mine. In exchange, I will do everything I can to only persuade you for your own benefit. By letting me, and me alone, have access to the aetherial mechanics of your decisions, I will repay you with protection and friendship. Do you agree?"

"Gladly."

Between us, Nick chuckled softly. "You're getting soft, Lucifer."

Luke blinked, releasing me, and glanced at his friend. "I've never actually met a Muse before, Nick. I think I've been inspired."

"I think you're both smitten," Sam muttered. "Women! Our eternal bane."

"Just yours," Nick teased, but Sam waggled his finger between the three of us on the couch.

"So." I tried to pull their attention back to me. "I'm no longer angel bait, right?"

"You're still bait," Sam said apologetically. "You're just not quite as easy of a catch."

"Which means we'd better barricade the house," Luke said. "Get what you need fast, Nick. I have a feeling playing dumb won't work for long."

Nick turned his focus to me. "Dove, so long as you're in public, you're pretty safe. In this day and age, it's just too easy to prove their existence, and they won't want to risk their religion. That means they have to touch you to pull you into the corridor, and they won't want to lose you unless they think there's no other option."

I nodded. "So make sure they can't touch me. I can do that."

2 2

*A*fter my little fright, it wasn't hard for Nick to convince me to hang out at his place. My one holdout was losing my job, but he promised Luke would take care of it. That didn't mean I got to spend a lot of time with my guy. Nick was in and out for a good portion of the afternoon, often locking himself in his study for a while before he came to socialize, but someone was always there. Unfortunately, that was part of the problem. Being alone with Sam? Even the idea made me nervous.

I couldn't forget how easily I'd given in. The moment his mouth had touched my neck, I'd forgotten all about Nick – the man I'd been chasing for *four years.* Nope, at the first hint of affection from a guy, my brain completely clicked off, sending my hormones into overdrive. Mostly, I was ashamed of myself. That Nick didn't seem to mind only made it worse. It made me feel guilty.

Not guilty enough to be stupid. I understood why Sam had done it. The angels wanted me, the demons would protect me, and I had to trust them to make this all work. I did. I honestly did. I just didn't trust myself. That was why I avoided being alone with the guy I'd started to realize was a little too tempting. It was fine when Luke was around, but the two of us unsupervised? We'd already proven that was a bad idea. Twice.

And that kiss? My mind kept jumping back to it. He'd held me there and taken what he wanted, knowing exactly which buttons to push to get it. Something about that was so hot, and I couldn't stop replaying the memory over and over. Each time, I recalled some new little detail, like the feel of his tongue piercings or the way his fingers had pressed just behind my jaw. Nick could take my breath away with his mere presence. Sam? He'd go straight for my panties.

Should I tell Nick I'd liked it too much? No. That would only strain their friendship, and Sam had only kissed me because of the angel in the room. It wouldn't do anyone any good and might screw everything up. If Nick had to choose between his close friend and me, I wasn't sure I'd be the winner. My life was just too short for something like that.

So I had to make sure I got over my stupid infatuation before anyone noticed. It was a completely normal reaction. I mean, it wasn't like I was used to having a bunch of hot guys pay so much attention to me. Who wouldn't feel a little overwhelmed?

Sam made it easy. The only time we were alone was when we passed in the hall. He gently touched my arm and smiled, but never stopped walking. A part of me hoped the look on his face was longing, but I wasn't quite that full of myself. Then, when Nick said he needed an assistant, Sam immediately volunteered. Luke wasn't as much fun to hang out with, but at least he was nice and safe. For now, that was the best thing I could ask for.

Granted, cooking with Luke was much more entertaining than I'd expected. He danced between three different pans, stirring, sampling, and adjusting as if it was a highly choreographed ballet. Across his chest, a very frilly, flower-patterned apron – too small for his well-muscled frame – completely ruined any chance of him looking evil. It made me laugh, which I was pretty sure was the point, and together, we managed to make one hell of a meal. It was ready just as the guys got back.

The four of us ate together, and there wasn't a hint of awkwardness. What they didn't do was talk about where they'd been. I kinda got the impression that was top secret demon information, so I didn't pry. Whatever it was, it had to do with me, and I was more than thankful for everything they were doing.

After dinner, Nick and I retreated to his room. His excuse was homework. I had some too, but the truth was I spent a lot more time with my mouth locked to his than with my nose in a book. Somehow, I still managed to get caught up. Since I didn't remember doing half the Calculus problems, I was pretty sure I had a little help, but I pretended not to notice.

To be honest, spending time with Nick was a lot more interesting than math of any kind, and it wasn't like I'd use calculus a lot as a medical illustrator. Unfortunately, spending time with him didn't include the naked kind. I was reading the required chapter for Art History when I heard his breathing even out. Rolling over, I found the most beautiful sight I could imagine.

One arm was curled under his head, acting as a pillow. His eyes had closed, letting those long, dark lashes rest on his cheeks, and his mouth was relaxed. Blue-black hair spilled across his shoulder haphazardly, and his shirt had ridden up at his waist, revealing one of those strange rune-shaped wards. For a long moment, I just watched him sleep, unable to believe that the guy I was dating wasn't just the sexiest man I'd ever met, but also the sweetest – and notorious for his power in more than one world. I, the crazy little orphan girl, had somehow ended up as something special, and it honestly felt really damned good.

I didn't bother to wake him. Whatever Nick was doing had taken a toll, so the least I could do was let him rest. After I finished my chapter, I got his boots off and eased him under the covers. Halfway through, he mumbled something I swore was in another language and smiled. I finished tucking him in, changed, then slid in beside him. When I wrapped my arms around his waist, he caught my wrist and pulled it closer, hugging my arm in his dreams.

The next morning, Nick was fully dressed when he woke me. Struggling to steal a little more sleep, I rolled over and found his side had already gotten cold. That meant he'd been up for a while. With a groan, I gave in and sat up.

"Stick close to Luke today," he said as he sat beside me on the bed. "Staying here would be even better."

"Can't get my degree here," I mumbled. "Nick, I know you don't understand, but without an education, what will I do when you disappear again?"

He bit his lips together and nodded. "I understand. I don't agree, but I understand what you're saying. That's why I'm not trying to keep you here. Just be careful, Sia? You have no idea what angels are capable of, and I don't want to lose you."

"Mm." I scrubbed at my face, trying to wake the rest of the way up. "I'll have the Devil with me. Pretty sure there's not much that can fuck with him, and there will be people everywhere."

He leaned closer and kissed my cheek. "*I'm* still the Devil. He's just the fallen angel who gets all the credit. Tonight, I want to try something with you. I've been gathering aether and should have enough today. Now get up, little dove. You only have half an hour before your class starts."

"Why can't school start at noon?" I grumbled as I flung back the blankets and padded over to my clothes. "I mean, we invented artificial lighting for a reason. It deserves a lot more use."

He laughed, watching as I got dressed. Then, once I was completely covered, he stepped in to steal a kiss. I didn't even try to resist, just melted into him, letting his powerful body hold me up. Nick made a pleased noise but still pulled back, slowly, pausing to look in my eyes.

"Coffee should be done. I hate to do this, but I have to go if I want to make it back before Calculus." He pulled me a little closer.

"Sia, if anything seems off, come back here. We can convince your professors that you never left, so don't worry about that. Just be safe, ok?"

"Promise." I pressed a sweet peck onto his lips and stepped back to cross my heart.

For Nick, that was his cue. He gave me one last smile and stepped back, slipping under the surface of absolutely nothing to vanish right before my eyes. I'd never gotten the chance to see someone step *into* the corridor before. It was a little disturbing, in all honesty.

It also left me alone, smelling the scent of a nice dark roast wafting up the stairs. Grumbling about needing to be awake at this ungodly hour, I gave in and headed for the kitchen. I wasn't alone. The first thing I saw when I walked through the open archway was Sam wearing a pair of plaid pajama bottoms and a very thin, very tight, white shirt.

He heard me and turned with a smile. "Morning."

"Hey." I smiled, mostly to hide the stupid rush of guilt welling up.

Sam's lips curled to match, then he reached into the closest cabinet, pulling down one of those fancy travel mugs the guys used. Without asking, he filled it with coffee and began mixing in my preferred blend of cream and sugar. He passed it to me before leaning back against the counter.

"You still ok with this?" he asked.

I knew what he meant. He wasn't talking about angels. He was talking about me being weird every time he was around. Slowly, I nodded.

"I will be. I just feel like I've done something wrong."

"Promise, you didn't." Ducking his head, he chuckled dryly. "Pretty sure the stupid was all on me. Raphael wouldn't've believed anything else, so I just went with it, hoping you'd understand."

"No, I get that," I assured him. "I really do."

"But?" he asked.

A heavy sigh slipped out. "That moan?" I paused, convinced that admitting this was the dumbest thing I'd done in my life. "It wasn't fake."

His head snapped up, and his eyes met mine. "Oh," he whispered. Damn, I loved that almost-purple color.

Before I could say anything even more stupid, Luke walked in. "Good, you're up," he said, moving to the counter for a cup of his own, completely oblivious to the tension between Sam and I. "That means we won't be late to class."

I laughed, pushing my guilt to the back of my mind. "Like *you're* worried."

"I am when Nick tells me to keep an eye on you or he'll make me regret it." Luke shrugged. "That, and he's got enough to worry about."

"Why do you make that sound bad?" I sucked back another gulp of my coffee, nearly choking when Sam offered me my backpack. The last time I'd seen this one, it had been at my place. Demons were going to take a bit of getting used to.

Luke tilted his head to the door, suggesting we head out. "Um, he's pretty sure you won't approve of what he's about to do."

I turned that way, looking back to ask, "And what is that?"

Luke fell in beside me. "I'm not sure I should be the one to tell you. Seems you already have enough to feel guilty about."

Which meant he'd noticed the tension in the kitchen after all. I groaned and rolled my eyes. Thankfully, this was a topic I was a whole lot more comfortable with.

"Ok, Lucifer. Enough with the mysterious. Is he headed off to perform some kind of evil mystical ritual or something?"

"No, probably more like a hospital. Possibly a nursing home."

"Oh." Death was off to collect his souls. That was how Nick got the resources to protect me. "So, he's going to find some people on their deathbed and ease the aether from them so the angels can't get me?"

"Pretty much."

I walked for a bit in silence, mulling that over. It didn't really bother me that much, oddly enough. I'd seen Nick work. He'd killed the gas station robber and made him feel at peace. Was it wrong if he was easing someone with a terminal illness? Did it make it bad simply because we needed what they could no longer use?

"How does he pick?"

Luke pursed his lips, trying to choose his words carefully. "Pain and suffering color the aether. Outworlders can see that as an aura on humans, so he tries to find those where the pain is stronger than the urge to live and releases them from the misery."

"Sounds kinda noble."

Luke looked at me, his eyebrows nearly to his hairline. "Noble? He's killing people, Sienna."

"So?" I shrugged that off. "When I was a kid, one of my foster families had a dog that got hit by a car. They had the vet put her down because her back was broken. I've always wondered why we call it a kindness when we do it for our pets but cruel when someone thinks about the same thing for a person." I lifted my hands slightly. "I mean, we say we don't want a dog to suffer, but we want Grandma to? Maybe it's because I never had a real family, but it doesn't make much sense."

He latched on to the tidbit of my history. "You know anything about your parents at all?"

"Nope. I know I was left at a fire station on Parker Street. That's how I got my last name. I was five and supposedly a handful, even at that age."

"Foster homes, huh?"

I nodded. "A few of them. I kept hoping one would want to adopt me, but it never happened." I paused. "Um. Luke?"

"Yeah?"

"My first foster parents were devout Christians. I don't really remember them, but I stayed there for just over a year. They sent me back because I refused to go to church."

"Good call," he teased.

"No, you don't understand." I tugged at his arm. "Luke, when I went into the church, I lost it. I was terrified of the angels. I don't remember it, but my CPS advocate showed me the note in my file. All my life, I assumed it was like how some kids are scared of clowns. I mean, I never had to go to church because of that little note. I was also never one of those people who collected angels or anything like that. They just seem..." I paused, realizing what I was about to say. "They seem creepy. A shrink tried to convince me it was a phobia, but I'm not really scared of them. I just don't *like* them." I licked my suddenly dry lips, my mind whirling. "Luke, I didn't really like *you* that much when we first met, and I had no idea what you were."

"I wasn't exactly being nice."

"Even before that. Like that night at Mac's." I took a deep breath. "I don't like angels, and it seems I never have. When did I start warping the veils?"

He turned to watch me. "The veil has been slowly bending for just over twenty-four years. The peak started four years ago. It's still changing."

"Pulling toward me?"

He nodded. "The veil is a bubble, like a membrane around the dimension. It should be a perfect circle but, all your life, it's been distorted to something more like an oval, and not just on Earth. Whatever you're doing crosses the planes of existence."

"Oh shit."

He nodded. "Exactly. I assume Nick showed you the map?" When I nodded, he continued. "So the spike that points at you? Yeah. It started the night of the robbery. It was little back then, but we can't stop the inertia. It's growing, Sia."

We'd reached the Language building, and Luke grabbed the door. As I stepped through, I asked, "So why have the angels only taken an interest in it now?"

He steered me to the stairs. "We don't really look at the shape of the veils that often. Four years ago, one did, but we chased him off and made sure it would be a while before he could tell anyone else. Back then, they assumed the change was because of something we were doing, and it worked for a while because you liked to move around."

"And now I'm not." We were almost to our classroom.

He looked at the open door and shook his head, holding me back. "Sienna, I'm pretty sure they're worried about a lot more than just the peaks. They're up to something, and not all of it has to do with you. Mike's got angels watching Nick."

"But Nick's not here," I whispered.

Luke nodded. "I know, so don't worry about our problems today. You're just a student, like everyone else. You have no idea that the three guys trying to seduce you are anything but normal."

I nodded, and he turned me to the door. Even though we walked into class together, four different girls still looked up at Luke with smiles. He pretended to ignore it, but I could tell he'd noticed. Finding a pair of computers at the back of the room, we made ourselves comfortable, saying nothing. Just as the professor was moving to the front of the class, Gabe walked in, smiling sheepishly for being late.

I tried not to stare, but couldn't help it. His hair was swept back to reveal those freakish green eyes, and his shirt was just a bit too tight. From the late entrance to the outfit he was wearing, everything was designed to make people look. Like every other woman in the class, I did – but unlike them, I wanted nothing to do with him. When he flashed a sneer at me, my heart stalled out in my chest. I should've taken the chair beside the wall – not the one by the aisle.

Gabe made his way toward us, but the only empty computer was on the other side of the room. Trying not to stare, I watched the other students instead, hoping to mimic their reactions. A girl in the row ahead of me wasn't even trying to hide her interest. A pair of women in the front had their heads together, their giggles hard to miss. A very nicely dressed guy next to the windows was smiling a little too much, his eyes shifting toward Luke instead of Gabe. No wonder they thought we were livestock, I thought, trying to force my attention back to the professor. We didn't try to hide that we worried more about sex than anything else.

While Gabe found his seat, the professor paced back and forth across the front of the class. Her heels clicked softly on the rubber tile floor while she explained how our midterm projects would be graded. That got everyone's attention. For the next two weeks, it was all we'd be working on, and it counted for a quarter of our grade. The irony was that she wanted us to produce a work of fiction. I'd tell her mine was, but I planned to write a very vivid story based on nothing but fact. It wasn't my fault no one else would believe it.

23

Five minutes before class ended, we were instructed to print two copies of our rough drafts and give one to the professor. The second was to be self-edited before the start of our next class. When we were done, we could leave. My fingers furiously finished the last paragraph, worrying more about completing the assignment than forming coherent thoughts, then hit print twice.

To my left, the machine hummed and whirred, announcing its intention to vomit up my work. I made my way over just as the angel pushed his chair back, turning to the same printer. Of course, since he was closer, he reached it before me, lifting the page from the tray to scan the first few lines.

I smiled politely and waited a pace away from him, knowing the story in his hands said a little too much. Thankfully it was only *based* on reality, not a play by play of what I knew. It was still enough to incriminate me.

"Nice." He smiled and shoved his hand toward me. "Gabe, by the way."

"Sienna." I couldn't figure out a polite way to refuse, so clasped his hand quickly.

His fingers closed on mine. "Any way I could convince you to join me for lunch?" He smiled charmingly, but it didn't reach those cold green eyes.

I tried to pull my hand free as I shook my head. "Sorry, I already made plans."

The smile faded, but he still didn't let go of my hand. Just as I started to panic, I heard the printer whir again and steps approached from behind me. Gabe looked over my shoulder and stared.

"Excuse me," Luke said, reaching over our clasped hands, forcing Gabe to release me.

"What made you decide to transfer to school here, Luke?" Gabe asked, his voice dripping with malice.

Luke smiled at him sweetly. "Friend of mine is testing a theory. How've ya been?"

I looked between them, hoping I was acting normally but afraid it was too late. "You two know each other?"

"Gabe's my cousin," Luke said. "Distant relative."

"Oh."

He went on before Gabe could speak. "Yeah, haven't seen him for ages. We need to catch up."

"Gotcha." I smiled up at Gabe innocently. "I need to turn this in."

Walking to the front of the class, I could feel the tension between them. I hoped Gabe hadn't gotten far enough on that page to realize what I knew, and for the first time, I wondered why I was chancing it. Maybe I should just quit my classes. Maybe I could convince Nick to teach me all the aethersmithing stuff so I could protect myself. Yes, I wanted a degree, but was it really worth the cost of my life? I'd promised I wouldn't touch them, but that freak had figured out how to put me between a rock and a hard place a little too easily. If I didn't take his hand, he'd make a scene. If I did, I was risking my life.

It seemed there were no longer any good answers, and I was smart enough to know when I'd been outplayed.

I'd just turned in my paper on her desk when the professor stood and announced, "Ok, time's up. Turn in what you have."

Around the room, the printers spooled up, and students began moving around. Some grabbed their things and left, others milled, hoping to make their work print faster. Gabe and Luke still spoke softly at the back of the class, braced as if ready to throw down. I retrieved my backpack and was heading over to Luke when someone bumped me in their rush to get their printout. I stumbled one single step.

Luke and Gabe raised their heads in unison. Vigilance covered Luke's face, but Gabe's was angry – and I was too close! The angel's eyes lit up, and he struck, reaching out for my arm like a snake. As soon as our skin touched, he pulled, and I felt the wave. Desperate, I threw my free hand out to Luke like a lifeline. He grabbed it just as the veil washed over me and the colors changed. The room shifted to shades of blacks and greys. The students became neon-colored ghosts, ignorant of our presence.

"Let go," Gabe demanded, yanking me toward him.

"Don't let him drop you!" Luke screamed at me.

I tried to hang onto Luke, but the pull was too hard, the angel too strong. I felt my hand slipping free, so snapped my head around to look at my new enemy. Instinctively, I clung to him, my fingers wrapped in a white robe that had appeared with our entrance into the corridor.

Crushing my arm in his, Gabe wrenched me back, and I felt the world drop away from my feet. A pain at the back of my head hung like a weight attached to my hair. I didn't scream, but this trip seemed to last forever. Winds buffeted us as the world sped around in a blur, but my eyes stayed locked on the angel holding me.

His skin had turned perfectly smooth and metallic. The green of his eyes had changed to an eerily sick flame, and brassy hair billowed around his head in the winds. He reminded me of some kind of comic supervillain, and the massive wings at his back did nothing to ruin the image. Neither did him swiping at the weight on my hair until I couldn't feel it anymore.

And then we stopped.

Saffron skies and fuchsia grasses told me we weren't on Earth anymore. The air was crisp and warm, but I could breathe it. With my feet firmly on the ground, I pulled, slipping my arm from the angel's grasp. This time, he let me go with a laugh.

"You don't seem overly shocked, girl."

"Don't fucking touch me again," I warned him.

He took a step closer. "Or what?" His face was cruel and terrifying. Quickly, I staggered backward, not wanting his hands anywhere near me, but he seemed amused. "Oh, don't be scared. I just brought you to Heaven."

"Oh, shit," I breathed, daring to look around. "Oh, no. No. This can't be real."

Angelis, as Nick called it, was the home of the angels, hence their name. I also remembered Nick saying the veils here were locked to demons. I took another step back, my mind spinning. That meant I was alone here, unable to cross the veils on my own, with no way for anyone to rescue me.

"What do you want?" I asked Gabe.

"I want to know what your little friends are doing. Oh, we've seen you with all three of them, and after reading your story, it's clear we've been going about this the wrong way."

"And if I don't know?"

He jerked his hand to the right, one finger extended. "Then you're useless."

I looked. A clump of blue trees sheltered something that looked like a pile of firewood, except it wasn't. The breath caught in my lungs and my heart faltered when my brain finally understood what it was I was seeing. Bodies. Stacks upon stacks of bodies, discarded like refuse. Not all of them were human.

"Those are people!"

"No, that's fuel, you stupid girl. First, they give us power, then they feed the plants. Start talking – or I'll let the trees eat you."

I stopped retreating and lifted my chin. "Try it, you narcissistic fuck."

He snarled and reached for me, but I was reaching back. This Muse wouldn't go down easily. Before his hands could touch me, I slapped my fingers around his wrist and pulled. I pulled with every fiber in my body, hoping I could drain every last tendril of smoke from between his cells. Swirls of brassy fog writhed around my hand, and the angel shoved, desperate to break free, but I wasn't done. I pulled with everything I had.

Aether flowed into me and twined around my hands, spiraling up my arms. Like warm and weightless powder, the essence of the angel was tangible but had no mass. The feeling wasn't like anything else I'd experienced before. I had no idea what I was doing, but I refused to stop pulling.

"You shouldn't be able to do that," he gasped.

Gabe staggered, weakening before my eyes. I wanted to run, but I didn't dare let go. Not when I was winning. They couldn't die, but Nick said there were still demons devoid of aether, stuck in a coma. I only hoped angels would react the same way, so I kept pulling as hard as I could.

"Sienna!" The voice came from above, sounding both panicked and overjoyed. I looked up and saw the most brilliantly gold man with unrealistically white wings, plummeting quickly. "Run!" he yelled. It sounded like Luke.

I shoved at the angel, and he collapsed to the ground, unable to get up. His aether clung to my hands, but I ran. A part of my mind knew how precious the smoke was so I tried to gather it while fear pumped my feet faster. Somehow, I managed to do both, the aether moving with me, seeping into my skin. I caught nearly all of it when a mass hit me from behind, hard, knocking the breath from my lungs. My feet went flying. Literally. The ground was moving away, but I was too shocked to do more than watch.

"I got you," Luke breathed in my ear, his gold arms tight around my torso. "Please don't puke."

He turned in mid-air, pointing me toward the sky, and we fell, the world around me blurring as we crossed the veils. I closed my eyes and relaxed, knowing he was taking me back home. Nothing else mattered. He must have been the weight on my hair. That was how he'd found me. Luke had wings, and he'd promised to protect me. He'd saved me, and we were flying. Everything would be ok now.

"Thank you, Luke. Oh, thank you."

He chuckled and held me a bit tighter. "I guess this means you like at least one angel, huh?"

"Forever and ever," I promised him.

The snap of his wings signaled our arrival. We were still more than twenty feet in the air, far enough that I didn't want him to drop me, but not high enough for the fall to be fatal. The flapping of his wings felt like a raft on rough water, the two of us bobbing in the corridor while he oriented himself. With a strong push, we tilted. My back was pressed against his chest, the ground sprawling ever closer before it blurred quickly, clearing after only a breath to show the lawn of their home.

"Go straight inside," Luke said. The wind from his wings swirled my hair around his face as we descended. "Don't knock, don't stop, just get inside."

"Got it."

As soon as our feet touched the ground, he tugged me into reality, and I obeyed. The first step back on Earth was a staggering one while my mind tried to compensate, then I jogged up the stairs and pushed open the door. When I turned to close it, I realized I was alone. Luke was gone.

"Nick?" I called out, pushing the door until it clicked, aware I felt funny.

Footsteps from the second floor made me hopeful, but it was Sam, not Nick who peered over the banister. "What are you doing here?" he asked.

"I just got yanked to Angelis. Luke followed and brought me back."

"Oh, shit." Sam ran down the stairs, taking them two at a time as he hurried to my side. "You ok, Sienna?"

"I..." I held up my hands, a trace of brassy mist still clinging to my fingers. "I told Gabe to let go."

"Keep those to yourself," he said before scooping me into his arms. "We need to get you lying down. How much did you take?"

"I don't know. How do you measure it?"

He carried me upstairs, and for some reason, I didn't really care. My eyes were locked on the last trace of aether, trying to draw it inside myself. I didn't know why, but it seemed like the right thing to do.

"Was he standing when you let go?" Sam asked.

"He kinda fell down. I think still crawling, but barely."

Sam nodded. "That's a lot, kid. You took more than half of him."

"So what do I do now?" I waggled my fingers, and Sam leaned his head away.

He turned his back to a door, pushing it open, and carried me to a large bed covered in a luxurious red comforter. "Nothing. A nap would be great. You're not supposed to try that for your first time."

"Try what?" I asked as he laid me in the middle of the bed. "Oh, that's soft."

Smiling, he shifted a pillow to be more comfortable under my head then sat beside me. "You're not supposed to absorb that much aether, sweetheart. It's pure life, and a little intoxicating."

"So I'm drunk on life?" I couldn't quite get the last bit inside.

"You're about to be." He looked up at the sound of the front door slamming. "Just close your eyes, ok?"

Feet tromped up the stairs, sounding rushed.

"Can I give this to a demon?" I asked.

Sam nodded, gently brushing a strand of hair behind my ear. "Sure. If that's what you want to do with it."

"Ok." My head felt a lot lighter than it should. "I don't want to lose the last little bit then. Maybe we can wake one up."

The feet paused. "Oh, dove," Nick said softly. "Luke found me. Are you ok?"

"She tried to drain Gabe," Sam warned him. "And she's feeling it."

I grinned. "Sam said we can give this to a demon."

Large, warm hands closed on mine, and I watched the last traces of brass mist sink into the pores of his skin. "You couldn't even absorb it all, but it clung to you?" Nick asked in awe.

"From Angelis," Sam added. "Luke flew her back."

"And she still had aether clinging to her?"

Sam nodded slowly. "And was standing, Nick."

"Fuck."

Sam rested a hand on Nick's shoulder. "She's filled to the brim. You're going to need to pull some of that off her."

Nick's fingers tensed on mine. "Uh," he stammered.

"Or I can," Sam taunted. "She's human. You know what will happen if you don't. Promise, it won't be any kind of inconvenience for me."

"What?" I asked, barely able to keep my eyes focused.

Sam chuckled and patted my shoulder, then stood. With one last look, he left, pulling the door closed behind him. Nick's fingers traced the back of my hand, but he said nothing for a moment. When he finally spoke, it was almost clinical.

"The body is like a balloon when it comes to aether. If you take in too much, too fast, you can rupture. If that happens, it's a bitch to find the leak and fix it, and while we look, your life seeps away." He swallowed and nodded. "Since you're human, it could kill you."

"Can I just give you some?"

I saw the smile before he turned away. "Yeah." He cleared his throat. "You should know that donating aether can get intense, little dove."

I giggled. "Which is why Sam didn't want to."

"Oh, he wants to," Nick mumbled under his breath.

"But he doesn't want to mess with his buddy's girl, huh?"

"Something like that," Nick agreed, tugging at his shirt.

He pulled it over his head, and I smiled. "I will never get used to that," I breathed.

"They're just warding symbols," Nick said.

"I meant the muscles."

He paused, glancing down. "Um, flying takes good core strength."

Unable to tear my eyes away, I bit my lip. "Can I touch?"

He laughed and leaned closer, bracing one arm above my far shoulder, the other grabbing my wrist. "It's required." Gently, he rested my palm on the intricate circle branded across his left pectoral.

Pressing my skin against his, Nick's fingers locked my hand in place. He closed his eyes and whispered words in a strange language, the letters crisp and discordant on his tongue. The sound was hypnotic, the feel of his chest so hot and sensual. He stopped chanting, and something flared against my palm, hot enough to burn but without the pain. When I tried to pull back, he held my hand tight.

"Relax," Nick whispered, leaning a bit closer.

My eyes went to my hand. "What did you do?"

"I just gave you the key to my soul. You're the only one who can reach the aether inside me now." His index finger tapped the back of my hand. "So try to push some of that excess out?"

I took a deep breath and tried, imagining the process of pulling it but in reverse. Nothing happened. Closing my eyes, I tried again, but still absolutely nothing. I felt Nick shift and lean closer, so scrunched my eyes tightly and pushed with everything I had.

"I said relax," he whispered again, then his lips met mine.

I relaxed. His mouth was as soft as velvet, warm and inviting, but tender. I reached up to his neck with my free hand, locking my fingers in his long hair to pull him closer as my tongue caressed his full lower lip. Nick moaned, his mouth parting, and his tongue met mine. His hand pressed even tighter on the wrist caught between us. Except for that, he only touched me with his mouth, but I refused to let him go, feeling connected to him in a way I didn't think possible.

Where we touched, my skin flared to life, feeling like something deep inside was thawing. I wanted to melt into him, to never leave him, to bind him to me forever. Nothing had ever felt like Nick's touch, and somehow, I knew that nothing ever would. What started as a gentle kiss quickly turned insistent, his mouth devouring mine while my head slowly cleared. I sucked in a breath and leaned closer, but he retreated, keeping the distance between us, teasing me with his perfect body.

"Sia," he whispered, releasing my hand. "Look at me."

My lids felt heavy with desire, but I forced them open. Black eyes, like pools of eternity, were waiting. He smiled gently and slid his fingers across my cheek, the moment over but not forgotten.

"How do you feel?" His voice sounded deliciously rough.

I chuckled once and glanced at the closed door. "You sure you want me to answer that?"

He nodded slowly. "I am."

"Horny?"

"Mm," he murmured. "So better."

"And whose room are we in?"

"A spare." He leaned closer and kissed me again, this time less passionately. "But I have to go, little dove. I can't hold this much aether for long, and you did want it to refill a demon."

I groaned and pressed the heels of my hands to my eyes. "I was thinking..." I sighed. "Never mind."

Chuckling, he pulled one hand from my face, dragging it to his lips to kiss the inside of my wrist. "You need to rest, Sia, and *that* would not be resting." He let me go and leaned back, smiling like a pleased cat before standing. "You shouldn't be able to hold that much aether yet, let alone pull it. What you just did is impossible."

"I'm getting used to impossible."

"Good. Stay here. I'll be back in an hour."

"Where are you going?"

He opened the door. "To wake up Beelzebub." Then he was gone, vanishing as he stepped through the doorway.

"Damned demons," I complained.

Pushing myself up in bed, I was well aware that the door was still open. With an annoyed grunt, I thumped both hands into the soft mattress then swung my legs over the edge. For a moment, I sat there trying to regain my composure.

A tap sounded on the doorframe. "Still alive?" Sam asked.

"Seems like it," I muttered, not even trying to hide my frustration.

He chuckled and tilted his head downstairs. "I brewed coffee, and I'm sure we have something to eat. Just you and me for a bit."

A wash of nervousness hit me, but I decided to ignore it, gesturing for him to lead the way. "You know y'all have fucked up my entire life plan, right?"

Halfway down the stairs, he paused. "Yeah. We do. The thing is, Muses are *not* common. Muses like you? Unheard of." He shoved his forelock back and nodded to himself. "Sia, you just took enough aether from an angel to make Nick struggle to hold it, and you're still not down to normal. You shouldn't be able to walk, let alone anything else."

"So why am I?"

He shrugged and continued down the stairs, leading me into the kitchen. "Too much caffeine?" He pulled down a pair of cups, filling them both. "Did Nick really say he's going to wake Beelzebub?"

"Yeah, why?"

He glanced at me quickly then focused his attention on pouring the cream into the cups, not around them. "Because a few thousand years ago, Gabriel drained him dry. Completely devoid of aether. Instead of having demons harvest what we could and trickle it into him, we focused on healing up more of us that were just a bit under the level for consciousness."

"Us?"

Sam nodded. "Michael got me a few decades before the whole Jesus thing."

"Shit, I'm sorry."

He waved that away. "It's not a biggie, just disorienting to wake up and things are so different. Luke and Nick got the aether, though, filling up on some war and rushing over before it dissipated."

"But Beelzebub has been out for a while?"

"Yeah. It'll take a bit for him to get his bearings, but if we have him on our side again? Yeah, those feathered fuckers will be running scared." He stirred the coffee and handed me one.

I sipped at it gratefully. "So, what's the deal about transferring aether?"

He turned and leaned back against the counter, smiling before he sucked at his cup. "Like that, did ya?"

I blushed. Clearly, he could tell I was a little sexually flustered. "Stop dicking around and explain it?"

He raised an eyebrow and took another drink, taunting me. "Ok," he said finally. "Incubus, you know that one?"

"Yeah. Fake, right?"

He made a noise and tilted his hand. "Yes and no. When a human willingly releases aether, it's a little um," he grinned, "seductive. We'd sneak in at night, drain half of them, and leave them thinking it was a really good dream."

"But..."

Sam tilted his head and shrugged. "Humans can regenerate, so it's not a big deal. But tell me you didn't feel a little turned on?"

"Fuck off."

He winked. "Exactly. So, you play Battlefield?"

*I*t was nearly dark when Luke finally returned, and none of us had heard from Nick yet. Sam destroyed me over and over in his favorite game, but he never once gloated, nor did he take it easy on me, so I accepted Luke's return as the perfect excuse to stop dying.

"Hey, you're back!" I said, dropping the controller.

"Yeah, sorry." Luke flopped onto the couch beside me. "Had to pull a few strings."

"Want to explain that?" Looking between Sam and Luke, it was obvious I was the only one out of the loop.

"He found a few of his angel friends," Sam said, turning off the console. "How'd that go?"

Luke sighed. "Not as well as I hoped."

The way he was looking at me, I knew he was avoiding something. "Spill it," I demanded.

"Might as well," Sam agreed. "And if you show me yours, I'll show you mine."

"So, Uriel is still pretty neutral." Luke glanced at me. "Um, he said Mike's pissed she got away. Gabe's fucked up, and they had to drain a few of their slaves just to find out what happened."

Which meant kill. Oddly, the death of strangers didn't really bother me as much as I expected. I was more upset at the idea of humans as slaves.

"What's the deal with the plants?" I asked, remembering the stack of bodies.

"Fairy plants," Luke explained, but my blank look made him go on. "They're almost sentient. Compost from human bodies allows them to grow, and the plants can be harvested for aether, their dead leaves feeding more slaves."

"Oh."

"Yeah." Luke sighed. "Sounds like they're trying to make another portal from Angelis to Earth. The idea is that the atmospheric aether can be siphoned off, and if the portal is high enough, only flying creatures will stumble through it."

"Planes?" I asked.

He nodded. "Free delivery of new slaves if it happens."

"So how do we stop them?"

"That's a question for Nick." He lifted his chin at Sam. "Your turn."

"Sia pulled so much aether from Gabriel that she couldn't hold it all, but it clung to her on your flight home. Nick siphoned a bit off and went to wake up Beelzebub."

"Oh fuck," Luke groaned.

"That's a *good* thing," Sam reminded him.

Luke just shook his head. "You're not the one who'll get his wings broken."

I lifted a hand, drawing their attention. "You and Beelzebub, not so friendly?"

"No," they both said.

Luke sighed. "In the great war, um, two thousand years ago, or so? Well, I ended up face to face with him. It was a wound I inflicted that let Gabriel drain him." Luke lifted his hand slightly, then let it drop. "So, for him, that was a couple of days ago. For me, not so much."

"Well, I won't let him break your wings."

"Uh," Sam shook his head. "He's not really the kind to listen."

But I'd already figured one thing out. "He will be, or I'll drop his ass back to the ground."

Luke chuckled and rubbed the top of my head, mussing my hair badly. "I like it. And you can learn to heal when you put me back together."

"Deal."

"Wait." Luke held up a finger as he looked back to me. "You pulled aether from Gabriel. Nick is waking up Beelzebub. How?"

Sam leaned back and kicked his feet onto the coffee table, grinning. "There was a little sucking face upstairs."

"Yeah," Luke said, ignoring that. "But Nick's locked."

"Not to her."

I realized Sam wasn't about to explain so gave it my best shot. "He did something and spoke a language I didn't know, and um, I guess it worked?"

Luke yanked at the collar of his shirt, pulling it low enough to expose his chest. "Have anything to do with this thing?" A circle of symbols was branded on his chest, just like Nick's.

"Maybe? I was touching it." I bit my lip and looked at Sam.

"It's our seal," Sam said, lifting his own shirt to expose not only his but also a pierced nipple. "Every immortal has one. It's our key to the gates."

"Mine's keyed to both Daemin and Angelis," Luke explained. "Because I helped craft the system, they can't really undo it without my cooperation." He looked at me, waiting, but when I didn't say anything he groaned. "Sia, the same applies for Nick. He can't stop you from pulling aether from him now. Not unless you agree to be locked back out."

"Or pushing it in," Sam added.

"Ok? But I don't have a seal thing."

Luke dismissed that. "You do, just not marked. We all do. It's the pattern of our aether and the basis of all magic. Nick was locked to everyone but his own seal. That's what those runes are on his body. We all have some sort of protection, but Nick went overboard. Where ours are like chain-link fences, his protections are more like Fort Knox."

Sam chuckled. "Luke's freaking out because Nick's been locked from everyone for pretty much ever. Only he controls his aether, and he never took a snooze because no one could get through his wards. He also had to be conscious to repair or he was pretty fucked."

"And he can't change his mind?" That sounded like a big deal from the way these guys talked.

"Not without your help," Luke said. "Don't tell anyone else, not even Beelzebub, about this, ok?"

"Yeah." I ran my hand across my mouth, trying to remember what had happened. "Why did he do that? Why didn't he just take it from me?"

"Beer?" Sam asked Luke.

"Sure. Get the Muse a coffee?" Luke suggested. I started to complain, but Luke shook his head, waiting until Sam was gone. "He's just giving you privacy. Pulling aether is a tricky business. It's also not a pleasant experience. With that said, giving aether is the opposite. They are not at all the same. The only analogy I can think of is like the difference between sex and rape, but it's not quite that violating."

"And when he does his Death stuff?"

Luke cocked his head in what was meant to be a shrug. "He encourages, but it's always a gift. That's why Death's portrayed as a lover in so many poems. The few a reaper can't finish off? They remembered the seduction of it. Nick's so powerful because he's learned a way to all but force them to give. He slips halfway over and lulls their minds." He paused. "But his trick doesn't have a stop button. It's all or nothing, usually."

"But if he's locked, how do they give?"

Luke shook his head. "It's not the same. They release and he catches before it disperses. They don't push it into him." He grinned mischievously. "Think of it like a hundred dollar bill. If I stole it from you, that would hurt. If I found it laying in the grass, that would be awesome. If you pressed it into my hand, I'd be really touched."

"Ok, I get it," I admitted. "And donating always feels good?"

He smiled slyly. "Tell me, how hot and bothered were you by the time he was done?"

"What does that have to do with anything?"

"Everything," he assured me. "Giving your aether is one of the most intimate things you can do, even if your human body doesn't understand. It's life. No different from nurturing a child or lying with a lover. The exchange is just as basic, which means it feels just as good."

"Oh."

He nodded slowly, green eyes amused. "So, how do you feel about him stalking hospitals now?"

"I don't know, Luke. I can't even understand half of what y'all try to explain. Thinking that Nick gets off on killing little old men kinda freaks me out, but I saw him do it, and he didn't act like that. I dunno. I feel like a five-year-old listening to grown-ups talking about how babies are made."

"Good analogy." He leaned back and tossed his arm over my shoulder. "Long ago, before other worlds had developed a sentient species, the only form of care we knew was sharing life – aether. That doesn't mean it was seen as sexual. Just like caring for a parent isn't. It's still nurturing. No one is disgusted when a mother loves her child. We innately understand that it has to do with care and protection. Aether transfer is the same, but care and protection can be arousing in the right circumstances, with the right person."

I nodded, finally understanding. "So, do demons even feel love?"

"Yes, of all types. The problem is that outworlders are all men. We may only have a single gender, but we are still *men*, and have the same desires. We probably wouldn't have known what we were missing except that someone figured out how to cross the veils." He sighed. "So when we saw women, we liked your kind just as much as any human man would. Well, most of us. There are gay outworlders who are only attracted to men, just like there are gay humans."

"But Nick said –" I tried to bite off the sentence before Luke noticed. It didn't work.

"Finish that," he encouraged. "I know almost all of his secrets, but I'm not sure which you're referring to."

With a sigh, I gave in. I could always apologize later. "He said he'd never been with a human before."

"Nope. He preferred fairies. First, because they don't die so fast and break our hearts. Second, well, I swear that beast has a thing for sharp-tongued ladies. Even when he fell for a satyr, he always picked the strongest will he could find. Like you."

"Really?"

Luke lifted one shoulder in a partial shrug. "He's not some kind of sweet virgin, Sienna. He just isn't attracted to screaming or crying women, and that's the response he tends to get from humans. For centuries, you've all been taught to fear the Devil. Fairies weren't as concerned with what others said about him, and they didn't really take to religion. And those women are well known for their sass. He just happens to find that amazingly sexy."

"Yeah, I can see that." It actually explained quite a bit.

"But you really aren't like the other women. Well, other humans. You're doing pretty good with all of this, and your questions make sense. You haven't worried about going to Hell, if we've seen your grandmother, or anything like that. You're acting more like a demon – just the facts."

"Good, because I feel like I'm losing my mind."

"Sucks having your world turned upside down, huh?" He looked down at me fondly.

"It kinda does. I'm pretty sure I can't even go home, not with all those angels out there, and Gabriel is going to be pissed when they fill him back up." I groaned. "And I can't finish my degree, not if the veils are pointing me out to anyone that can read them!"

"We have a spare room," Luke offered. "Rent's pretty cheap too."

"I don't really have an option, do I?"

"Not a good one," he agreed. "Let us move your stuff over, have Nick teach you the basics of working with aether, and we can go from there."

I hated the idea. I really did, but I also knew it was the only way to stay safe. That these guys had become friends made it a lot easier, but inside I wanted to scream that they couldn't make me do this. The problem was that they weren't. The angels were, and if I wanted to stay alive and in control of my own life, then I had to put on my big girl undies and suck it up.

"Can you take care of my job, classes, and lease?"

His hand closed on mine. "Promise. If you didn't ask, Nick would've."

I nodded, looking up shyly at Luke. "I really do like him. You know that, right?"

"Yeah, I do." He pulled me against him in a friendly hug. "Just remember he's not human, ok?"

"Ok?"

He smiled at me weakly. "The demon thing. Seeing it scares women off."

"But you look the same, just gold and shiny, but that's about it."

"You missed the wings?" He gasped, making a production out of it. "Big white things? C'mon, you had to see them!"

"You know what I mean."

He laughed and nodded. "Yeah. You're right. Angels got the

shiny, but demons come in more colors. They get horns and tails to go with the wings, but the main stuff is all the same."

"Then I don't understand what the big deal is about."

Luke shrugged. "Being told your whole life that Hell is a very bad place, mostly. That, and the horns are a little intimidating."

"Great defense." Nick stood in the doorway, exhaustion written across his face.

I couldn't help but surge to my feet when I saw him. "You're back!"

He nodded slowly. "Beelzebub sent you a message, Lucifer."

"I know. He's going to kick my ass."

Nick shook his head and staggered to the couch. "Nah. He said he understands, and if I trust you, he'll give you a chance." He tried to smile, but his lips didn't quite make it. "He also said if you fuck up, he's chopping you into tiny pieces and feeding you to hatchlings."

"Baby dragons," Luke told me. "I think I'm ok with that."

"Good, because he's stopping by tomorrow." Nick leaned his head back. "I'd kill for a coffee."

I was the closest to the door. "I can do that." So I hurried into the kitchen, nearly colliding with Sam. "Nick needs coffee," I said.

"Yeah, I felt him come back." He handed me the coffee and a beer. "Give that to them, I'll bring you another."

"Thanks, Sam."

I'd finally started to find my way around. I still hadn't found a bathroom on the first floor, but I could make it from the coffee pot to the living room without getting lost. Returning, I passed Luke the beer and moved to sit beside Nick, careful not to spill the overfull cup.

"Thanks, dove." He sipped at it gratefully. "I didn't expect you to be up and around."

"Really?"

He shook his head. "Not with that much aether or after that much excitement." He leaned his head back again, closing his eyes.

Luke tapped his chest, then gestured to Nick. It took me a second, but I realized he was suggesting I give him a little more aether, the only problem was that I didn't know exactly how. I chewed at my lip, trying to remember what had happened before while Sam made his way back in.

Luke took that as a sign to start talking. "Uriel said Gabe's fucked up."

Nick nodded and moved his hand to my knee, draping one of my legs over his. "Good. One less thing to worry about tonight."

It seemed so casual, just hanging out on the sofa, talking about destroying angels and reviving demons. Like this was no big deal at all. Just a normal day's work. Somehow, that also made it feel a little more real.

Shifted sideways with my leg draped across Nick's muscular thigh, I tuned out their plans to stop the portal. Instead, I found myself trailing my fingers down the back of Nick's neck. His long, silky hair slid through my hands like ink. He leaned into the touch, but his attention was focused on the larger threat.

It didn't take long before I realized he'd already become more vibrant. Unfortunately, he did, too. His hand reached up to catch mine, and he pulled it away slowly. "Stop that," he whispered.

"Feel better?"

His attention had shifted completely to me, shutting out both Luke and Sam. "Much." A roguish smile teased his lips, drawing my eye. "The problem is you don't know when to stop."

"And when should I stop?"

Nick's eyes held mine. "Before I tell Sam and Luke to leave."

Sam laughed, breaking the mood and pulling me back to the present. "You want to screw the Muse, you take her to your room or we get to enjoy the show."

"One of theirs, at least," Luke mumbled.

Nick's head whipped around in surprise. "*One* of ours?"

"She's moving in," Luke said. "The red room, I think."

"I like red," I agreed.

Sam chuckled. "Good, because it's next to his."

Nick looked back at me. "When did this happen? You ok with this?"

"While you were playing back home, and ok is a good word to use." I shrugged, trailing my fingers down his neck one last time. "I can admit that I was wrong. And I'm pretty sure Gabe is going to be *pissed.*"

"To put it mildly," Luke added.

"I don't have any family who'll miss me, and I'm not the type to just make friends –"

"Thanks," Sam teased.

I waved him down. "Human friends. Luke can fix shit at school, and I really need to learn how to use this stuff." I wiggled my fingers. "Which means I don't have time for college anyway. Not if I want to stay alive, and I kinda do."

Nick nodded, but it wasn't enthusiastically. "I'm sorry, little dove."

"It's ok. Who knows, maybe I can gather enough aether to wake up some more of your friends?"

Nick grabbed my hand. "No," he said. "You're not reaping the dead."

"Why not?"

Sam whistled softly. "Uh oh," he muttered.

"You have no idea what that would do to you." For the first time, Nick looked intent enough to convince me he was a demon.

I wasn't scared, though. "Then explain it."

"You really want to see hundreds of people die, at your touch, just so you can wake up a legion?" He shook his head, long hair waving against his chest. "Over and over, they beg you to fix them, and you can't."

"There are things worse than death, Nick." I gestured to Luke. "Angels are a pretty good example, I think."

"Hey!" We both ignored Luke's protest.

I went on. "I'm a Muse, right? Well, what am I supposed to do if not help?"

"Inspire people. Change the world. Protect humans. Create poets. That's what you're supposed to do, Sia. Not worry about *our* war!"

Grinding my teeth, I lifted my chin. "Then why were you looking for me?"

"Busted." Sam raised his beer in tribute to my argument.

"Stay out of this," Nick snapped.

Luke tapped his own bottle to Sam's. "A lover's quarrel, how cute."

I grabbed Nick's face and turned it back to me. "Let me make this real clear, Satanael. You can't stop me. Every Muse is different, right? Every Muse is influenced by her culture? Well, this is mine. Humans suck, demons are my only friends, and I fucking hate angels. Not you, Luke."

"Thanks."

I smiled quickly but went on before I lost the point. "I have a talent that is impressive enough to alter physics, and if I understand correctly, it's kinda a big deal. Well, that means that no matter what I do, I'm fucked." Sam choked, trying to swallow his beer before he spit it across the floor, but I ignored him. "If the best aethersmith in Daemin is willing to teach me how to use this little gift, then the least I can do is help y'all wake up your friends, protect your home, or whatever it is that my *friends* need."

Silence hung in the air as Nick just looked at me. His eyes flicked between both of mine, and the corner of his lip lifted a couple of times as thoughts shuffled through his mind. I refused to look away, but I hoped he wouldn't leave me hanging too long – and that I hadn't upset him.

Finally, he nodded. "On one condition."

"What?"

"You learn how to control it first, then reap one, and only one, soul. If two days later, you still want to do this, I'll teach you everything I know."

"A deep red," Luke said to Sam.

"Silk," Sam agreed.

"What?" I looked at them, completely confused.

Luke smiled back. "Your robe, Lady Death. They always expect you to have a robe. I think every demon wears one in the corridor."

"You're a little ahead of yourselves," Nick told them.

Sam took another long drink. "You wish." He gasped as he swallowed. "This one's not like the others."

"The others?" I asked.

"Muses," Luke said.

"Y'all hang out with a few?"

"Oh no," Sam assured me. "Most Muses are annoying, spoiled, temperamental brats. People adore them and shower them with everything they ever desired."

"Wait." I sat up, pulling my legs from Nick's lap. "I was ridiculed as a kid. The stereotypical redheaded stepchild type thing. Well, foster child in my case."

Sam shrugged. "Redheads are hot; kids, not so much."

"I wasn't showered with gifts or even liked by anyone."

Nick looked at me slowly. "Go on?"

"I was abandoned at a fire station on Parker Street. That's how I got my last name. They never figured out who did it, but it wasn't like they had surveillance either."

Nick nodded, his attention hanging on every word. "And then?"

"Um, I supposedly got bounced from my first foster home for hating angels. I refused to go to church because of the pictures of angels, but I don't remember any of that. It's just what they put in my file."

By this time, Luke and Sam were sitting up, listening as closely as Nick. I swore I'd told them most of this, but realized it had been pieces to each of them.

"What else?" Luke asked.

I lifted my hands in surrender. "There was some deal about me being addicted to something when they found me, but they couldn't figure out what from my blood work. I mean, I was *five*, so not like still latched onto the tit, right? Whatever it was, I had to be taking it, or given it."

"Shit," Sam breathed, but Nick held up his hand, urging me to keep going.

"So, I got picked on for being a freak as a kid. I didn't do so well in school, but I kept my grades high enough to graduate, and when I turned eighteen, I moved out. Well, it was a pretty clear agreement between my foster parents and myself. Soon as I turned eighteen, I moved out or they'd kick me out."

"But you always liked the arts?" Nick asked.

"Yeah. Took ballet as a kid and had the little solo bit. Did gymnastics when I was twelve. Played clarinet in band. That sorta thing. Um, I'm a failure at sports, but learned to play the piano in junior high."

"Poetry?" Sam asked.

"A little here and there in high school. Mostly dark, brooding, angsty crap. You know, pretty typical for a teenage human girl."

Nick grabbed my arm gently. "How long did it take you to break the addiction, and what were your symptoms?"

"I dunno, a couple of months, maybe?" I realized they were all looking at me a little too intently. "Why?"

"What symptoms, Sia?"

"Um, they said I acted drunk half the time, and that I'd throw things, break things, and just have crazy tantrums. I guess I was pretty evil." I tilted my head, lifting my eyebrows. "Why?"

He still didn't answer, looking over to Luke instead. "As a five-year-old?"

"She's warping the veils," Luke said, sounding unsure.

"How many people did you hurt?" Sam asked.

I looked up, sure the guilt was on my face. "A few. It seems I was a spoiled brat who couldn't be controlled until I was like seven or eight. Again, I don't remember hardly any of that. I was *little*."

Sam grinned, glancing to the others before he nodded. "How?" he asked me. "What did you do that hurt people?"

"I would have these tantrums, and I guess I threw things? I know I broke one foster mom's arm when she tried to stop me, but that's about it. Why?"

Nick reached over and grabbed Luke's beer, taking a long sip before answering. "You weren't addicted to a drug." He chuckled and took another drink, then passed the bottle back. "Sia, you've been pulling aether since you were a child. You were high on life, little dove. No wonder you can drain a damned angel."

25

Something about my revelation inspired Nick to start teaching me that night. Luke promised he'd tie up all my loose ends, and Sam swore he'd help move my things over in the morning, then both retired. Listening to their evening routine was oddly comfortable. For my entire life, I'd lived with people I barely knew, and I'd always felt out of place, but not here.

Luke had become someone I thought of as a friend, and Sam was the partner in crime type. They didn't look down on me for loving the arts. Nope, they said it was a sign of my abilities. They didn't care that I was poor, wore clothes that weren't exactly fashionable, and tended to say what was on my mind. They looked beyond those things and made me feel like I actually was a welcome part of their group. It made the idea of suddenly moving in with them easier to accept.

And then there was Nick. As I followed him across the house to his study, I remembered how perfect he'd seemed that first day. He was beautiful – insanely beautiful in a way that no human could ever match – but he was a bit overprotective. It was cute, in a frustrating sort of way. A part of me liked having someone care enough to stand up to me, but he always tried to pick the wrong fights. That, or I did. I wasn't exactly sure which, yet.

Most of it came back to my new reality. Nick expected me to freak out. Hell, in some ways I wanted to, but what was the point? I'd always been more of a doer than a freaker. I figured a lot of that was because I'd always had to take care of myself. Spending time bawling my eyes out only made things worse, so while all of this stuff might be crazy, it was also happening. I mean, I'd just seen "Heaven." It didn't get much more real than that, and if I wanted to make sure I didn't go back, then this had to become my new normal, and fast.

Grabbing coffee when we passed the kitchen, Nick pointed out the guest bathroom, his lip twitching to fight a smile when I thanked him. He listed off a few other rooms, making me aware of exactly how large the place was before stepping into his office. Again, my skin tingled when I crossed the doorway.

"Warded?" I asked.

He smiled. "Yeah. So if I blow something up, Luke's whole house isn't lost."

"Yeah, that would be a waste. This place is huge and has to be like a hundred years old. So it's Luke's?"

"Yep." He sank into a plush leather chair, carefully setting his cup on the desk, and gestured for me to take the couch. "Sam owns a castle in Europe. Romania or someplace."

"And you?"

He glanced away, but smiled. "I have a couple of places. Cute little cabin up in northern Ontario that we built in the 1800s, an apartment in Dubai, and the island."

"An island?"

He sipped at his coffee, those dark eyes smiling at me. "Just a little rock in the water. Nothing special. We've inherited or acquired a few safe spots over the years."

"Like a whole island?"

"Yeah. Claimed it in the fifteenth century when ocean travel was so dangerous, and I just keep transferring it to new identities. It's my sanctuary."

"Damn." I couldn't imagine owning a house, let alone an entire island.

"It's easy to accumulate things when you have a few thousand years to build it up." He shrugged. "It's a lot harder to keep track of it. We have specialists to handle most of our financial issues, though, making sure bank accounts stay topped up and passing things down when one alias is old enough to die. That's what I was doing the first week of classes. Making sure I had a verifiable identity."

"So other demons handle that? Do you know all of them?"

He nodded. "There aren't that many of us. I mean, we aren't all friends, but after a few million years, it's hard not to at least talk to everyone once."

"How many?"

He grinned. "Guess."

"I dunno, six hundred and sixty-six?"

Nick lifted his cup and took another sip. "Exactly. Same number of Angels."

"How many are sleeping?"

The enthusiasm drained from his face. "Three hundred and forty-two, I mean forty-one."

I sucked in a breath. "So more than half."

He nodded slowly. "Only about seventeen angels are unaccounted for, and those bodies are lost."

"Lost?"

"Yeah, we don't die, but in order to be refilled, we need to know where the body is. Sometimes they turn up on one plane or another. Or if they were in pieces, it takes a while for the molecules to reform. Longer on worlds with less aether."

"Wait." I made a circle with my hand, begging him to go back. "You mean, if y'all were chopped into bits and spread across the Earth, that still wouldn't kill you?"

"Nope." He shrugged. "Immortal, Sia. I mean, we're unconscious, but still alive. Eventually, the extra pieces degrade and the main one grows until there's an entire body."

"How do you know what part will be the main one?" I couldn't help it; I was completely fascinated.

He tapped his chest. "The seal. It lies over our heart, which is the center of our body."

"Not the mind?"

"Not the mind," he agreed.

Cradling my cup in my hands, I leaned back, mulling that over. "And humans have a seal too?"

"Yes."

"How do you know it?"

He tilted his chair back and kicked his feet up on the desk. "Your seal is your pattern."

I nodded, accepting that as nothing more than the truth. "So how do you key your wards to me?"

The smile returned. "Good. You're already thinking the right way." He turned his chair quickly and stood, pulling off his shirt as he walked across the room, tossing it back to his chair. "Every seal is different," Nick said, kneeling before my knees.

I couldn't take my eyes off him, but he didn't seem to mind. "Ok?"

"Well, in order for the veils to recognize us, we need them marked on our skin." He traced the outer ring on his broad, flat chest. "It's our resonant structure. Like DNA, but made of aether. It's our personal signature, and the seal makes it into a key."

"How's it decided? I mean, I've never seen marks like that before."

He raised an eyebrow. "You've also never seen Daemonic before."

"True. So how do you know mine?" I set my cup on the small table in the corner and leaned closer, looking at the strange brand on his skin.

Nick moved my hand to his chest, resting it across his seal. "Close your eyes, little dove."

I obeyed without thinking, feeling his heart beat against my palm. His skin was so warm and smooth, the raised edges of the seal tantalizing against my fingers. He laid his hand above mine, holding it to him, but said nothing. His thumb gently swept back and forth across my skin, a smooth, comfortable rhythm that my mind embraced.

"Could you draw it?" he finally asked, his voice barely more than a whisper.

I opened my eyes. "Yeah. I could."

"But you can't see it. You never looked long enough to know every line." His thumb moved again, soft and soothing. "How could you draw it?"

"Because I know what you feel like." Astonishment tinted my voice, but it was true. I knew Nick. Completely. It was like I could feel him in my bones when I tried to imagine who he was. That was why I wasn't scared of him.

He nodded, those dark eyes holding more than just the knowledge of aether. Something smoldered deep inside him, contained and harnessed, but begging to break free. "That's how I know your sign, Sia. That's how I keyed this room to you."

"And to your body."

His hand slid up my arm, releasing me without breaking the contact. "Exactly."

"So when do I get a seal?"

Reluctantly, he leaned back. "Before you try to cross the veils." Then he stood and grabbed his shirt, wadding it tightly before tossing it onto his desk. Then he dropped back into his chair. "It hurts."

"If I'm marked, can I still enter Angelis?"

"Yeah. They chose who to lock it to, and you weren't on the list back then."

"Damn." I grabbed my coffee again and took a long swallow, my brilliant idea a bust. "So the angels and demons set up your veil protections backwards? I mean, they're open to anyone but their enemy, and your world is closed to anyone but your friends."

"Right. Angels have to bring their slaves over, and our way would prevent that."

"So I can't go to Daemin?"

He flashed me a wicked smile. "You will. I'm one of the demons responsible for keying the veil to our friends."

"Like Luke?"

"Exactly." He shrugged. "You'd have to be marked so the veil protections can read it. The only problem is you have to be able to stand in the corridor – where angels can try to stop us."

"And I'm too weak right now."

"Unstable," he corrected. "Weakness isn't your problem, considering you just pulled enough aether to fill a demon from empty to almost half full."

"Is that a lot?"

He nodded, his eyes watching me intently. "That's like five humans. But in the corridor, the laws of physics are shifted. The aethereal winds between worlds push at us, and unless you know how to balance, you can be swept away."

"Oh. How much aether does it take to regain consciousness?"

"Between a quarter and a half. Everyone is different, but we all have a buffer level." He sipped at his cup again.

"Three hundred and forty-one," I said to myself. "That's three thousand, four hundred and ten people that need to die."

"Approximately. About a hundred thousand humans die every day." He sipped again, letting me work it out.

"So, if we could revive a demon each, every day, that's just over six months to wake them all."

"But we can't." He raised a hand, stopping me before I could disagree. "It's exhausting, and I cannot do that every day. I can only guess you can't, either."

"But you're the strongest aethersmith in Daemin, right?"

He shrugged, nodding slightly. "And dumping that much aether nearly knocked me off my feet but didn't even slow you down. I'm not a Muse."

"So I need to hold more." And needed a plan to make me feel in control again. Waking demons seemed like a win-win to me. "Like a balloon, I can stretch and learn to hold more."

"But there's more to aether than simply waking demons." He set his cup on the desk and stood, gesturing for me to move over. "It's the force of life. It's the building blocks of the world." He claimed the corner, kicking his shoes off before sprawling languidly against the well-padded armrest. "Come here."

He tugged me back against him, one arm wrapped lightly around my waist as we lay back. Nick's bare chest became my pillow. He held his hand before me, palm up, and reached around me to touch the tips of his other hand to it. Slowly, he pulled. Pale blue, frosty tendrils swirled between his hands.

"Aether makes us like gods." With a flick of his wrist, he broke the substance free, letting it float before my face. "It's life and beauty, and anything you desire." His hands played around it, guiding the fog without quite touching it. When it condensed into a tight ball, he closed both hands, shielding it from view, and took a deep breath. "It's complete power, and can corrupt you completely if you let it."

Opening his hands like a book, I saw a tiny butterfly grasping his finger. Black and blue wings flapped slowly, displaying an intricate design before it took flight, slowly flitting across the room.

"Complete power," Nick said again, snatching his hand in the direction of the butterfly. It vanished, and when he twisted his wrist and opened his fingers, the aether had returned, swirling just above his skin as if the butterfly had never existed.

"Wow."

His lips brushed against my ear. "How much do you want to learn?"

"Nick, I want to know everything." I turned to look at him. "I can do this."

"I know." He glanced away. "But how far are you willing to bend? How much are you willing to give up for people you didn't even know existed a month ago?"

I looked back at his hand, the aether still dancing on his open palm. Reaching up cautiously, I touched it, taking the time to finally feel the hot and powdery surface of concentrated life. Twining my finger through his essence, I felt his heart against my back, each beat heavier than the one before.

"If I'm going to make sure those bastards can't hurt any more of my friends, then I'm willing to bend exactly as far as I need to," I whispered, trying to mimic what he'd done.

Where my finger touched it, the aether solidified, tinting green and turning woody until a delicate red flower bloomed at the end, growing from the air just above his hand. Manipulating it was no different than the pencil that had started this whole thing.

"I am *not* going to just sit here and let everyone else worry about keeping me safe. You say I have a powerful talent? What I hear is that one day I'll be able to take care of myself, and that's all I ever really wanted."

I trailed my finger down the petals, touching the leaves and tracing the stem to the end, leaving nothing but wisps of blue behind my touch. Then I pressed my palm to his, driving the aether back into his skin, returning it to the home where it belonged.

Nick gasped, his fingers spreading beneath mine. "You don't play fair."

I giggled and shifted enough to see his face. "No, I don't."

With a devious grin, he grabbed my arm with one hand, flicking a glob of aether into his other. "Let's see what it's like for a Muse."

He pressed his hand to mine, a trickle of his essence caught between our skin. His eyes watched my face. The warmth met my skin first, like sun-baked powder, smooth and soft in my palm before it began to seep in. The sensation radiated from inside, down my wrists, to the core of my being, feeling like a feather against my skin: sensual and seductive but reassuring and comforting.

It was like an embrace after being apart. The kind that was so tight I never wanted to let go, so perfect I couldn't stop smiling. Like a teddy bear to protect me during the night, a friend to promise it would be ok, or that warm feeling that comes when someone loves their gift. It felt like love, and the sensation lingered after the substance was absorbed. From the smile on Nick's face, he knew I'd felt it.

"I think you like that." His eyes dropped to my lips.

"I think you're a tease."

He shifted, forcing me to face him. "I think you've learned more in one night than most demons learn in a week, and yes, I'll tease you a little if this is the result."

"Only a little?"

He leaned closer. "Define a little."

"An impossibly beautiful man with his arms around me, cuddling with me on a couch." I glanced down. "The lack of shirt is well outside that definition. I think it may constitute torture."

"Being held by a horribly scarred and single-minded monster?" His tone was light, but his eyes betrayed him.

I traced a symbol along his waist. "They aren't scars, and your wards are beautiful. Like works of art."

"And proof I'm not human," he reminded me. "You've only seen the good parts, Sia, not the demon."

"Then show me the demon, Nick. Give me a chance? Let me reap the dead, let me see your wings, let me visit the rest of these crazy worlds I keep hearing about."

"After you're sealed."

I pressed my hand to his chest. "Then get me a seal."

He nodded slowly. "When you're ready, and not before. It never comes off, little dove, not in any of your skins."

"Isn't it just a key?"

"Not always." His hands were sliding down my back, trying to distract me. "It's like a focus, but it works both ways. While being sealed will concentrate your abilities, it's also a beacon to those who know how to find it." His fingers slipped under the edge of my shirt, resting against the skin of my back. "It's how ancient witches used to summon us. If they get it right, we feel an annoying pull."

I heard what he didn't say. "But one you can ignore?"

"To a point." He grinned. "Usually, we'd show up just to destroy the binding because it's irritating, like a fly that keeps landing on the end of your nose. Not harmful, but it sure gets old fast."

"Nick?"

His dark eyes flicked to mine, hearing something in my voice. "Too weird?" he asked.

"No," I assured him. "I just... I mean, are you really like all those myths? Is anything in the Bible true?"

"Yes." He flicked his gaze between my eyes. "Yes, dove, most of it is in one way or another. The problem is how it's portrayed. Like witches. They were just flirtatious girls who didn't shun our attention." He sighed. "And yes, we seduce you. Women are like a drug to most of us. You appeal to something we shouldn't have, and," he smiled, "we have a hard time resisting."

"And the sins?"

He groaned and tilted his head back. "That's complicated."

"I've got plenty of time," I reminded him.

He sighed. "Ok. So Luke makes deals. He loves to trade good fortune for someone's soul. That's the conglomeration of aether in your body. Your life, I guess. Anyway, the catch is that even if someone gives him the right to their soul, he has to be there to catch it, and all he does is what nature would do anyway. He releases it into the world so angels can't use the power against us.

Granted, sometimes that's releasing it exactly where he wants, but still."

"And that whole thing about encouraging evil acts?"

"Like thinking outside the box?" He shrugged. "Yeah, um, did you know that when I taught the first man about complex math, it was assumed to be evil? Stop and look at those sins, Sia. Eating pork? Jealousy? Cosmetics? Angels wanted to keep humans primitive and ignorant. We want to encourage your evolution, to find an ally. I'm not ashamed that I introduced physics to Earth. I'm sure Sam isn't upset that he created the condom and invented the idea of family planning."

I paused to think that over and couldn't find anything nefarious about it. "What about the whole thing about enticing people to commit murder? Or starting wars, or all of that?"

"Angels." He caressed the side of my face, making me look at him. "War brings aether, and a whole lot of it. Look at how many were fought for religion – a concept angels found to be successful for domesticating your kind." His thumb brushed my cheek. "We're not perfect, Sia, but we're not a force of some all-powerful evil. We're just people who happen to disagree with what the angels are doing. Good and evil aren't tangible. They aren't inherent because of where we were born. They're just a matter of perspective which changes depending on whose story you listen to. From our point of view, we didn't do anything at all wrong."

"So why do you reap the dead?" I tilted my head and kissed his palm, assuring him I was merely curious.

He smiled, his eyes following my lips. "Most demons do it. It started as a way to release the aether before they could get it. If we pull it into the corridor, it flows so quickly that it's free. Eventually, it will leach through the veil, back to Earth."

"And now?"

"For me? Because, I can make it better. When I ease the release, it comforts them, and I like humans, Sia. I always have. I'm also part of the group responsible for maintaining the veils of Daemin.

We need aether like you need oil. Our society depends on it to function."

"So, you're harvesting us, just like the angels are?"

"Yes and no. I'm harvesting only those of you who no longer need your souls. They're harvesting you as soon as the life has grown to full. Bombings, wars, and so many man-made tragedies cut lives short, and all too often it's just for the aether that will be released. They collect it in mass. We collect it inside ourselves, soul by soul, when the humans no longer need it."

"Ok, I think I like your way better," I conceded. "But Nick?"

He laughed. "You're insatiable, little dove."

"Maybe, but I need to do this. I need to learn everything so no one else I care about will get hurt. That means I need you to teach me. No matter how I feel about you – and I really do like you, Nick – I still need you to let me do this. Please don't try to protect me so much that you make me weak?"

His expression sobered, and his dark eyes met mine. "I don't think I could, dove. Not even if I wanted to."

26

*T*he next day, we slept in late and then headed over to my little shack around noon. Luke had already taken care of all the details, like breaking my lease and quitting my job. Considering he had a knack for that, I was more than happy to let him. Granted, no job, no home, and I'd only known these guys a little while? For me, this was a *really big deal*. I was giving up every single thing I'd spent my life trying to prove I deserved.

Angels had a way of changing priorities.

But Luke couldn't make everyone forget my existence. That was why Nick and I walked over, so the neighbors would see us enter while Luke and Sam just slipped through the corridor. I was a little sad about the idea of losing my own place. I'd worked so hard to finally afford my privacy, but the trip to Angelis was all the convincing I needed. Privacy was nothing when a group of psycho angels were after me.

We walked in the front door, and I stopped, looking at how much stuff I'd acquired. Second-hand furniture, a used laptop, countless art supplies, and more canvases than I could count. I pressed my hands to my head, trying to decide where to start.

Luke walked out of the kitchen and saw my anxiety, so decided to make it easier. "All the paintings go to our place. You want to keep the furniture, put it in storage, or give it away?"

"How long do you think I'll have to stay with y'all?"

Luke looked over at Nick. "Well, that's hard to say. A couple of years easily, if you really want to master your craft." He looked back at me with a knowing smile. "I can make sure you have a large enough bank account to buy something better, just in case you ever need it."

"She won't," Nick grumbled, moving to look at some of the paintings hanging on the wall.

Luke tilted his head toward him, grinning at me. "But his places are all furnished pretty nice."

"It's not that," I said, hoping Nick would understand. "It's just that I hate the idea of needing to rely on everyone else. I mean y'all have already done so much, and I kinda feel like a mooch."

"Money's not a big deal," Luke assured me. He tilted his chin over his shoulder, calling to Nick, "Hey, how much is in your bank this year?"

"I'm not talking money," Nick said.

"Just fucking tell her."

Nick turned from the painting to look at me. "About seventy million."

"Uh." I swallowed, trying to digest that. "You're rich?"

He shrugged. "I made a few investments that paid off well."

"Like a few hundred years ago," Luke teased. "Nick convinced us we should buy into that whole electricity thing. Then there was that drink Sam was obsessed with, called Coca-Cola. Not to mention that we have some very good financial advisors."

"The demons who handle your accounts?"

They both nodded.

"Look," Luke said, gesturing around the room. "Anything you want to keep, we'll keep. If you just want to feel like you aren't giving up your independence, we can do that too. If it's just feeling bad because you think we're broke college guys?" He lifted his hands in defeat. "None of us are hurting, and this is a big favor for us."

I took a long, deep breath and nodded. "Trash the furniture. Art I want to keep. The laptop has stuff on it." I started walking through the house, aware of how tiny it was compared to theirs. "Everything in the dining room is for my work."

"I got that," Sam said, stepping out with a box of paintbrushes in his hands. "Sorry, was snooping. Figure we can turn the red room into a studio?"

"Really?"

I wanted to hug him, but his arms were full. That one little sentence made so many of my misgivings vanish. They hadn't made me ask for a place to work, but were offering one up front? Even though this wasn't really an optional thing, and Nick and I weren't even close to ready for the whole live-in commitment, the guys were already making me feel like family. There weren't words to describe how reassuring that was.

Sam grinned, nodding like a proud child. "Of course. I mean, it's not like you'll be sleeping there, not with the sounds I've been hearing at night."

I stuck my tongue out at him. "You're just jealous."

"Damn right, I am." He winked and started to step back, disappearing before his foot touched the ground.

I pointed to the empty spot. "That's freakish. Y'all know that, right?"

"You get used to it," Luke assured me. "Bedroom, Sia."

I looked at him quickly, realizing all of the guys had adopted the nickname Nick had given me. "Guess that's gonna be a universal thing, huh?"

"Oh yeah," Luke agreed. "You want to just stack all the drawers in the red room then bring them back empty?" He raised his eyebrows, trying to give me control even though I knew his idea was pretty good.

"Yeah," I sighed. "Y'all really don't mind all the heavy lifting?"

Nick laughed behind me. "We're fine, little dove." He glanced toward the bathroom. "So, should I put that stuff in the blue room or the red one?"

"Hm," I turned toward him and leaned my back against the wall. "Depends. Where do you think I'll be sleeping?"

"The blue room," he said, taking a step closer. "There's no need for you to have to walk naked through the hall just to get the shampoo that smells right."

"Oh? Don't I get a say in this?" I couldn't wipe the smile off my face.

He placed his hand against the wall, beside my head. "No."

Luke cleared his throat. "Still here. You two remember that, right?"

"Then slip something over," Nick suggested, his eyes never leaving mine.

Luke said nothing, just grabbed a drawer and dropped it on the bed, pulling out a second to stack on top of it. Shaking his head, he lifted them both. "Just don't be naked on the bed when I slip back for the next load?"

"Won't happen," I assured him. "Mine's not nearly as comfortable as the ones at your place."

Nick dropped his head and laughed as Luke disappeared. "They like you."

"Is that abnormal?"

He nodded. "A bit. Now that we don't have to marry a girl to get her naked, it's a lot safer to vanish before the inconsistencies show up."

"Then why hasn't either of them brought home a girl yet?" So far, the only woman I'd seen around them was the one Sam had at the bar, and I was pretty sure he hadn't taken her home.

Nick leaned over and kissed my neck. "Because they've been focused on you."

I groaned, knowing it was true. "Remind me again why they don't hate me?"

He kissed a little higher. "Because you're charming, beautiful, and willing to help save our world."

I pushed him away gently, enjoying the attention but wanting to get the moving done. "Ok. That's a fair point, but I still feel bad for cock-blocking them."

He chuckled. "Pretty sure you're not the only one to blame. A bit of that is on my shoulders too."

"Well, then I'll just have to make sure my boyfriend doesn't regret it."

He caught the back of my neck and leaned closer. "It's been four hundred and eighteen years since I was one of those, and that was just to stop a war. I 'accidentally' died before we had to get married. I promise, Sia, I don't regret any of this."

My guts flipped in excitement, but I tried not to show it. "Over four hundred years, huh?"

"Yeah."

"No wonder you're so good in bed. Lots of pent-up frustration." Time to change the subject before I got all mushy. "And what are you moving, since I can't exactly slip through the corridor yet?"

He released me and backed toward the bathroom. "Girly things. I'm pretty sure there's something embarrassing in these cabinets."

"Tampons," I called after him. "Razors, maxi-pads, and face cream. All sorts of embarrassing things."

He pulled open the medicine cabinet. "Birth control?"

"Nope."

He paused. "Sia?"

"They make that in shots now. Don't really keep it in the house."

I watched his shoulders relax, and he sighed. "You just scared the shit out of me, dove."

Laughing, I turned to the kitchen. "Consider it payback. You already mentioned you have no interest in kids, and I'm not ready to even think about it yet. You're safe, Nick."

WHILE THE GUYS WORKED ON CARRYING STUFF THROUGH THE corridor, I was rummaging in the cabinets, filling a box with things I wanted to keep. A few coffee mugs from art museums, a very large insulated travel mug, and a hand-painted plate that one of my foster sisters had made for my twelfth birthday all went in. The cheap dishes and tarnished silverware stayed. I'd climbed onto the counter, sitting perched precariously on my knees, when I heard someone rap at the front door. A split second later, it creaked loudly as it opened.

"Sienna?" I recognized the voice but couldn't quite place it. "Are you here?" the guy called out.

"Who is it?" Annoyed at the intrusion, I hopped down and marched into the hall, pausing when I saw Aaron – my ex-boyfriend – standing in my living room. "What are you doing here?"

"You moving out?"

Damn it, why didn't I think to lock the door? "Remind me why you care again? Never mind that. Why did you think it was ok to just walk in?"

He ran his tongue across his teeth, debating his answer. "You didn't return any of my calls. I came by last night, too, but it was locked. Look, can we talk?"

"No. I blocked your number. In case you forgot, we broke up!" I stared at him in complete disbelief. "You were messing around with that chick in the bar, then you *pushed* me, and you think I'd want to talk to you?"

He sighed, his eyes on the ground. "Look, the guys started drinking early, and well, I had too many –"

"Not fucking good enough. Get out of my house and don't ever walk in it again."

"Can we just talk about this?"

Heavy steps approached behind me. "No," Nick said.

"Who the fuck are you?" Aaron demanded.

Nick's voice was cold when he answered. "Your replacement."

Aaron looked from Nick, to me, then back. "You're the bastard from the parking lot." His hands curled into fists at his side as he turned back to me. "Don't you dare act like I did anything wrong, you little slut. The same guy from the bar is here, and you're fucking him now?"

"Yeah," I snapped, stepping into his face. "The guy that stood up for me asked for a date. Guess it's a lot better way to get laid than trying to smack your bitch around. Maybe you should try it."

"Sia," Nick warned, "don't touch him."

"Not gonna. Bastard doesn't deserve it."

Outside, a man laughed, his voice ringing like chimes. "That isn't what he meant, little girl." He leaned against the open door frame, a beam of sunlight making his hair glisten like white gold, and he smiled. "Here I was hoping you'd be alone."

"Michael," Nick growled, pulling me back beside him.

"Is it Nick?" Mike taunted, completely ignoring Aaron. "Is that the one you're using now?"

"This year," Nick said, lifting his chin.

"Hmm, gave up on Satan?"

I could hear Nick's teeth grinding. "You made sure that lost its appeal."

Mike chuckled, his voice too charming. I wanted to claw his eyes out. "Aaron said his girlfriend fell in with the wrong crowd." He looked at me and smiled, but it wasn't kind. "Do you even know what you're playing with? These demons will steal your soul and damn you to Hell."

I laughed, seeing through his false charm so easily. "There is no Hell, asshole."

"Hm." He gestured for Aaron to come closer. My ex obeyed like a drugged puppy. "I see what you mean. She's completely brainwashed. What do you think we should do?"

"Get her away from him," Aaron mumbled, sounding like he was quoting it.

"Brilliant idea." Mike shifted his gaze back to me. "Such a wonderful plan. I'm afraid it's going to take a few more buddies, though. I doubt they'll go down easily."

Nick pushed himself before me, the fingers of one hand splayed before his thigh. "There are not enough angels in the world to take her from me, Michael, but I dare you to try. We'll drain all of you back to dust."

"We?" Mike laughed. "You have a lot of faith in that pet of yours. Is this like the thing with the fairy? I assure you, now that we know there's a Muse, the poor thing doesn't stand a chance. We'll either keep you running, or we'll get her, so you might as well just give up."

Through the open door, I could see more men walking into my yard, approaching from all sides. I counted six but had a feeling there were more. Even if Luke and Sam returned, we'd still be outnumbered. Aaron just stood there, his blank eyes watching the wall like an empty shell.

"She's nothing like the fairy," Nick said softly. "I'm not going to let you kill this one."

"This one?" Mike looked at me, trying to distract us while his friends closed in. "*This* one? You honestly believe she'll be *loyal* to you?"

"Fuck off," I said. "Nick, angels on all sides. We need to go."

"You can't," Mike purred. "You hit the corridor and you're ours. It took us a bit to break the wards, but you've been a good girl and kept him distracted. I had the Seraphim keep all of them except the protections against us, and Satan's ego meant he never suspected a thing. Go ahead, Satan. Look. He knows it's true. He also knows why Samyaza and Lucifer aren't back yet."

"There's more," Nick told me. "Probably ten on this plane, and at least that many in the corridor. He's just biding time until more mind-fucked humans show up who can cross the threshold."

"So you *do* remember this game." Mike braced an arm on each side of the open door. "Give me the Muse, Satanael, and I'll forget you were ever here."

"Do it, Nick." I moved to his side, sliding my hand in his.

Mike shook his head. "Slip, and we'll yank her from your grasp. She'll be lost in the winds between worlds forever, and you don't want to risk that." He held his hand out to me. "Or you can come willingly. I won't hurt your lover if you give yourself up."

Nick looked down at me, his eyes sad. "You can't drain them all, Sia, and he knows it. That means they've stored aether, knowing you'll drop a few of them."

"So you're just going to let me go with him?" I felt his fingers tighten on mine. Any more and he'd bruise the skin. "Everything you said about showing me the mysteries of the universe? Was that just a lie?"

"I can't fight them all," he whispered.

I nodded, looking deep into his eyes. "I see how it is. You told me all those things, over and over, and none of it matters."

I didn't mean any sweet promises like I wanted Mike to think. I meant the stories about other worlds. How he looked as a demon wouldn't bother me, not even if he was hideous. Nothing mattered except getting away from these angels, and I hoped he understood.

His eyes flicked to my mouth then back to my eyes. "Yeah."

"Don't try it, Satanael," Mike said, pushing as far into the door as he could stand. "We will find you. It's *impossible* to hide her."

Nick tugged, pulling me against his chest as we slipped across the veil. His hands clamped around me before the corridor even came into focus. Dozens of shimmering, winged men immediately moved to surround us. One grabbed for me, but Nick was too fast. He took another step back.

I nearly cried out at the feeling of falling, but Nick's arms around me assured me I was safe. My eyes squeezed closed. The winds buffeted my body, almost as if it was trying to pull me from his grasp, feeling like hands on my arms. I wondered if it was the angels and hoped Nick knew what he was doing. It didn't take long, but those eight heartbeats felt like an eternity.

Suddenly, the feeling of the air changed, and Nick staggered, leather snapping as he released me. My lids were pressed tight against the glare of the brilliant sun, but I planned to keep them like that. Unfortunately, without Nick's arms around me, I had no balance; we'd shifted here too quickly. Without looking, I couldn't compensate for the lack of movement, but this wasn't how I was supposed to see the real Nick. This hadn't been planned, and keeping my eyes closed seemed like the best way to prove my trust.

I still knew I wasn't on Earth. Hot summer sun pounded on my back as I dropped to my knees, hearing the breath of wind in the distance and sounds I couldn't recognize as either animal or insect. Even the smells were different! Something pungent and almost like citrus tainted everything. It smelled more like broken pine needles than fruit, but was pleasant in its purity.

Hearing Nick move behind me, I slowly opened my eyes, keeping my gaze on the ground. Deep green sand, like crystals of jade, pooled around my legs, soft and cool. A lilac sky framed the edge of my view. It was like a fantasy. Everything was so close to what I knew, but whimsical and amazing. I laughed, shoving my hands deep in the verdant crystals, looking up for a cloud, wondering what color it would be.

"Sia?" Nick asked, taking a step toward my back. The sand slushed softly. "You ok?"

"Yeah. Which world is this?"

"Vesdar." Leather shifted.

"*This* is Vesdar?" My voice dripped with awe.

"Yeah. We've got a bit, but it won't take them long to figure out what world we shifted to." He took another slow step, keeping behind me. "To get you home, I need to touch you again."

I let the grains slip through my fingers, filling the other hand full. "Nick?"

"Yeah?"

"Do you want me to close my eyes again?" I released another handful, entranced with the variations of green and the soft feel of it. "I don't think I'll care, but I know you're worried."

He stepped closer and crouched down behind me. One strong hand touched my shoulder. I didn't look at it, keeping my eyes on the unnaturally colored sand. His fingers brushed my neck, and I heard that strange rustle again. It was impossible to hide my smile.

"I just found you," he said softly. "I don't want to lose you already."

"It's going to take a lot more than green beaches and purple skies to scare me off, Nick. Unlike your last girlfriend, I've watched movies."

A long, muscled tail flicked around me, laying directly in my field of view. The tip was flattened, nearly diamond-shaped, and the skin was the color of clear moonlight, so pale it looked like ice. I held out my hand, hoping to touch it, and he moved the end toward me, lifting it into my open palm. The skin was soft, and the flared end was supple, nothing like the spike it resembled. As my hand caressed it, his tail curled around my wrist, clasping it as easily as his own fingers would.

"That's amazing," I breathed. "You're so soft."

He moved just a bit closer. Slipping his arms around my waist, he pressed his lips next to my ear. "I will never hurt you, Sia. Do you trust me?"

"I do. Completely." I smiled and lifted his tail to my lips, kissing the gentle bend across the back of my palm.

He took a quick breath. "Please don't be afraid."

Leather rustled again, and pale wings moved around us. One was held open, the other brushed against my knee. "Are they sensitive?" I asked.

He chuckled. "Yeah, but not very delicate."

Reaching up slowly, I felt the bones just under the skin then slid my hand down the flight membrane. It was like buttery leather, nearly as smooth as silk. At the next joint, a claw twitched, drawing my eye, and I tugged the wing back as if it were an arm, wanting to see more. Shifting it exposed a thumb and forefinger. The remaining digits made up the expanse of his wing.

"It's beautiful," I breathed, turning to the open wing. "Like stained glass but as soft as silk!" I laughed, brushing my palm against the membrane. "I want to paint this!"

His tail tensed, pulling me to the right. "You're not scared?"

"No. You're beautiful. What am I supposed to be scared of?"

"The Devil." His hand slid down my shoulder, resting on my bicep. "Did you want to see the horns?"

I nodded. "More than anything."

"Turn around, Sia."

Slowly, I did, my eyes trailing across his body. He wore dark pants and tall boots – I still didn't get how that worked – but his arms and chest were bare. His skin was a uniform color, the wards present even in this form. Except for that, Nick looked just as he had before. The same size, the same build, with what almost seemed to be a second set of biceps extending from behind and below his shoulder blades.

They made the base of wings, giving them the same functionality as his arms. He didn't quite have bat wings, but more like *really* large, webbed hands. The soft leather started at what I could only describe as his second elbows, leaving room for his wings to tuck tightly to his back. Peeling my gaze from them, I looked up, my eyes trailing up his throat to his full lips, lingering in his dark, star-filled eyes until I saw the horns. Then I smiled, reaching up to caress one.

Four of them grew from his head. Two were paired above his forehead, curving back just above his skull. The other two began just above his ears and curled like a ram's, the points hanging at the edge of his jaw. Beneath and between them, his long hair was closer to midnight blue, but exactly as thick and lush as I remembered.

"You're beautiful," I gasped, letting my fingers slide along one of the lower horns. "Holy shit, I expected something atrocious."

He ducked his head to hide the boyish smile, exposing a long, nearly elf-like ear. Two rings pierced the top, making me wonder what other adornments he wore. I tugged at his horn, turning his head back to me. Even without an iris, I could somehow tell when the stars focused on my face. Nick's gaze looked shocked.

"You're ok with this?" he asked.

I could only think of one way to explain how I felt. Leaning closer, I kissed him, pressing him back into the jewel-toned sand. "I like this better than the other version."

27

He pulled me across his chest, clinging to me tightly. One taloned hand trailed across my shoulder blade, the other palmed the back of my neck. Then he kissed me. Desperately. I felt long fingers on my lower back, a thumb hooked into the loop of my jeans and, slowly, his tail caressed the back of my calf. I sucked in a breath, realizing those long fingers were his wings, and pulled back just far enough to look over my shoulder.

"I'm sorry," he gasped, releasing me.

I grabbed a horn and pulled his face closer. "Stop that. You're sexy, and I'm not afraid of you, ok?" I grinned. "It's hard to be scared of a guy that flinches every time I dare to *look* at him."

He reached for my face, claw-like nails slipping through the hair at my temple. "I'm trying, but we've been terrifying to humans for thousands of years, dove. You're supposed to scream and run from me, not want to kiss me."

"Or wonder if lying on your wings hurts?" I tilted my head to the side. "Or be surprised they work like hands?"

His forehead wrinkled, and the bright points in his eyes swirled. "How are they supposed to work?"

I kissed him again, my lips tight with a smile. "I don't know. I've never had any and I'm curious! It's a little strange, but you look like you, just with some amazing special effects, so stop *worrying*."

Finally, he laughed. Pushing me onto my back, his body loomed over mine. This time, he was all demon. A massive, splendid, magnificent demon, more perfectly designed than anything I could've imagined.

Slowly, he spread his wings like a vulture shielding its feast, letting the shade cover us both. "No, it doesn't hurt to lay on them any more than it hurts to lie on your shoulders." He flexed the tips, closing the winged fingers, then opened them again. "Thumb," he wiggled the short, thickly clawed digit. "First finger." That was the longer grasping claw beside it. "And the rest of the fingers." The soft leather folded and expanded again before he shrugged – lifting his winged shoulders, not those of his arms. "They're just like hands but with longer fingers."

Lying on my back, pinned by a monster from biblical nightmares, I lifted my hand without fear. "And you can grip with them?"

"Yeah, a bit." His right wing took my hand, moving beneath his natural arm.

The thumb slid across my palm. That long grasping claw rested on the back of my knuckles. The rest of the fingers in the wing were longer than my entire body, but he managed to wrap them gently around my forearm like an adult holding an infant's hand. The tips of his wing bent against the sand, extending far past my arm, but he didn't seem to care. His touch was delicate, like gossamer, but the tips of those claws teased at my skin, sharp, deadly, and oddly seductive.

"That's amazing," I breathed, clearly unable to think of a better word.

He leaned closer and kissed me again. "You're amazing. My wings are no more special than my arms."

"Those are pretty amazing too," I pointed out, grabbing a well-muscled bicep in my other hand. "All four of them. Tell me about your horns?"

"What do you want to know?" He shrugged. "They grow slowly, but they do grow."

"Do they have feeling?" I released his wing and reached up for the one by his ear. "Can you feel it when I touch them?"

He sighed. "They're like fingernails. When the tip hits something, you feel the pressure on your finger, right? I feel it on my head, but it's the same thing."

"Does it hurt to catch them on something?"

He shook his head slowly. "No. The ones across the top are used to gore anything that attacks my back."

I nodded. "Vulnerable wings, right. That's amazing."

"You keep saying that."

I laughed, my finger tracing the ridges of his upper horn. "Because it's true. What about your tail?"

He blinked slowly, setting the stars whirling, and I felt a touch sliding up my leg. "Think of it like a rudder. Aerodynamics and all that." Thick muscle wrapped around my thigh, sliding between flesh and sand easily before wrapping back around to brush across my hip. "Strong, sleek, flexible," he paused, the tip of his tail sliding under the hem of my shirt toward skin. "Smooth."

"Prehensile."

He laughed, the tip of his tail flaring against my ribs. "Among other things, yes. The flight vane works very similar to other parts I know you're more familiar with. Increased blood flow swells and flattens the end, but the lack of sharp edges is extremely useful."

My teeth closed on my lip as my mind fell into the gutter. "Sensitive?"

His lids dropped but didn't quite close. "Very."

"How soon do we have to be back on Earth?" My pulse was a little too high.

He groaned and released me, pulling his wings in before flopping onto his back. "Too soon. I'm guessing we're already missed, and Michael probably has everyone looking for the peak." His tail unraveled from my leg and flicked across his own. "I thought we'd only be here a few seconds." It twitched again, like an irritated cat.

"Damn it." I sat up, brushing the green sand from my arms. "Because I'm really curious about that tail of yours now."

He closed his eyes and smiled. "You can certainly kiss it again. I wouldn't stop you."

The next time it flicked closer, I snatched it, my fingers curling around the thick muscle. "Really?" My hand slid toward the end, my tongue dragging after.

Nick clawed at the sand, sucking in a gasp of air as his body arched. "Sia! Dear god."

"There is no God," I reminded him jokingly, kissing the flared edge.

He moaned, gently pulling his tail away. "Oh there is, and right now, I'm convinced it's your mouth." He turned his head, looking at me with a lazy smile that showed perfectly human teeth. "If we aren't back, Luke will check here. It would be very awkward to get caught like that."

"And yet you flaunt your tail openly?"

"Think of it more like a man's nipples. Not obscene but still sensitive. One of many erogenous zones. Being seen without a shirt is fine – is pretty typical for people with wings. Being seen with your lover pinching or fondling them is a little more personal." He sighed and pulled himself to his feet, those massive wings shifting with his body for balance. "Come here, dove. Let me take you back to Earth."

"Already?"

He folded his wings tight to his back, the tips brushing his calves like a cloak. "We just had a group of archangels corner us. There's probably a freaked-out demon wondering if we're ok, and maybe even a demented angel. It would be rude to keep Sam and Luke guessing."

I took the hand he offered with a sigh. "Will you bring me back?"

"I promise, dove. I will bring you back to Vesdar, show you what it's like to soar with dragons, and seduce you in my real body." Starry eyes glowed as he smiled down at me. His wings relaxed, moving to my clasp my hips. "Completely, like a woman should be," he breathed and brushed his lips against mine.

I kissed him deeper, needing more. With our tongues entwined, he stepped back, his hand tightening on my arm, his other grabbing my wrist, and I felt the veil pass over. Cloth suddenly brushed against the side of my face.

"Demon, Death, and a very good-looking man," I said, glancing up into his starry eyes. "Remind me what you were so worried about?"

"Losing you," he replied, pulling me back to Earth and simultaneously shifting into a man. "Get inside. We'll key the house to you tonight."

I jogged up the steps, half expecting angels to appear before I could make it through the door. Nick was right behind me. As soon as I stepped inside, I called out, "Luke, Sam?"

"Thank God," Luke said. "They're safe!"

"Damn you, Satanael," Sam yelled, storming up the hall. "Stop fucking around. Seal her, key the wards, and get over the whole wings thing already. I'd rather you didn't get laid than..." He trailed off when he saw the grin on my face. "What did I miss?"

I shrugged a little too innocently. "I went to Vesdar. Oh, and had a few angels at my place."

"I know!" Sam exclaimed. "Michael brought all the big names. They didn't expect us to be coming in through the corridor, but when we saw twelve... Wait."

Luke laughed. "He's been a little worried."

Sam ignored that. "You went to Vesdar?"

I nodded. "Green sand, purple sky?"

He looked up at Nick. "And how'd that go?"

Nick shrugged, trying to act nonchalant. "I think she wanted to dissect me."

"Is that what we're calling it now?" Luke asked. "She didn't even flinch when she saw me, and we already know her opinion on angels."

The corner of Nick's lip twitched. "She liked the tail."

Both Sam and Luke laughed a little harder than I would have expected. Sam leaned closer, "Very sensitive to catch the air currents. *Very* sensitive."

I felt my face heating up. "Yeah. So, angels?"

"Gone," Luke assured me. "Slipped out in a hurry."

Nick nodded. "Probably trying to figure out where we went. They'll be back, so I need you two to get the rest of her stuff later tonight."

I lifted my hand. "What about my ex-boyfriend?"

Luke sighed. "I'm going to bet he's just gone missing."

"Stupid fuck," I muttered, heading into the kitchen. I refused to acknowledge the pang of guilt. Wasn't my fault he'd gotten messed up with angels. Besides, he was an asshole anyway. "Someone want to tell me what we're going to do next? Luke, can you still control the Angelis veil?"

He watched me leave, calling to my back, "Um, technically, but it's nearly impossible with just one person, why?"

"To lock me out. If they can't take me there, then half of their threats are null and void." Yep, I was yelling through the house like a teenager.

When I heard footsteps, I looked up, shocked to see only Sam. "Can't do it," he said. "You and Luke are the only ones on our side that aren't locked out. It'd be better to have Nick give you a crash course in aethersmithing, and um, figure out how to lock them inside."

"Is that possible?"

Sam toyed with his magenta forelock and shrugged. "In theory. It's a dream the demons have always had, to lock them away from the other realms. You're strong enough. It might finally be possible."

I dropped grounds into the basket and closed the lid, pressing the button to start the coffee brewing. "Sam? Just tell me something? Nick's thing for me?" I turned, pressing my back against the counter. "It's not just because I can warp veils and all the other crap, right?"

He looked at my hands, my fingers a little too tight against the granite. "He saw you the first time when he was looking for a weapon." His voice was calm and sympathetic. "Maybe a year before the robbery? Something like that. You were young but at the age where girls start to become women. They used to marry you off by then, and um, he was intrigued."

"Because I had this power?"

Sam reached up and rested his hand on my arm. "He didn't even know you were the reason why. This was *before* the robbery, Sia, and we can only see your power when you use it. Nick just liked your hair – I know because he told me all about it for a year or so – but you kept talking to angels."

"I did?"

He nodded with a wry twist to his lips. "A counselor at the school, an employee in town, a guy on the street. We'd all figured out there was something about that little town, but Nick was the first to realize it was a who, not a what."

"What? Those were angels? No wonder I hated them – well, at least that counselor. But that's beside the point. Sam, is he just with me because I'm a Muse?"

"I really don't think so, sweetheart." He looked over his shoulder, back toward where he'd left the others. "I think he's been lonely, but no matter what you call him, Death or Satan, he's not something people tend to welcome."

"But he looks human. Wasn't that just from back before y'all had skins?"

He chuckled once and leaned beside me. His shoulder just

bumped mine. "We all use the corridor to collect aether. We've all been called the Grim Reaper at one point or another. Nick? He's the most powerful of us all, and that means he uses more aether because of it. He's reaped so many lives that it clings to him, slowly changing his pattern. Only his seal holds it in place. Most people can feel it, like intuition that he's dangerous."

"They aren't like that with you?" I hadn't seen people look at Sam with concern.

He tilted his head and smiled. "A bit. That's why I prefer the punk look. It gives people an excuse for what they feel, and most of them write off that gut reaction. The thing is, Nick's had a few bad experiences in his life. Then you come along? He's loving every moment of this."

I breathed a sigh of relief. "Good."

He bumped against me playfully. "So, about the whole demon thing?"

"Yeah?"

He laughed. "Don't play innocent, human. Didn't freak you out? Not even a little?"

"Nope." The coffee pot beeped, signaling it was done. "He's gorgeous, Sam. I mean, skin like the moon on water, iridescent horns, and his wings are so soft! I thought they'd be awkward or something, but they're like hands." I couldn't keep from smiling at the memory.

"I know. In case you forgot, I have a set of my own. Granted, he did get an impressive rack of horns."

"Is that a good thing?" I pulled down a cup, touching a second as I raised my eyebrow.

"I'd love one," he said. "And yeah, horns are basically a symbol of power, not to mention sexy. The more aether we wield, the bigger they grow. The more potential we have, the more horns. There are demons with one, demons with just nubs, and a couple with three. Only a handful have two full, matched sets, and Nick's are the most impressive rack I've ever seen. I mean, the outer set nearly curls all the way around!"

"And his wings are huge!"

"Mine too, baby." Sam winked.

"Ugh, I'm so jealous." I stirred the cups and passed him one while sipping gently at my own. "I can't wait to see what you look like as a demon."

He smiled down at his cup. "Hopefully, you'll approve. Not a lot of people are enthusiastic about it."

So I'd gathered. "Bet you terrified people back before you wore a human skin," I teased.

Sam waggled his eyebrows, the line of metal rings bending awkwardly in his left. "Yeah. I could swoop into a little village, spread my wings, and demand anything. It's how I started my fortune."

"By terrorizing humans?"

"Yep. Stupid, bigoted humans. I miss the days of the Inquisition. There was nothing like waking a priest in his sleep, convincing him I was only a dream, and having my way with him."

"Raping some guy?"

He flapped his hand at me, dismissing that. "No, trust me, it wasn't rape. Those men were seeking witches because they wanted men. They didn't hold back in their 'dreams,' so I got to have a whole lot of fun." He took a long drink, his amused eyes peeking over the rim. "Tails do make for a great reach-around, you know."

I nearly choked on my coffee. "What?"

"You know, bend them over, flick your tail around, wrap it nice and tight with the flat vane lying against the underside..." He paused. "What?"

"Y'all jack off with your tails?"

He wrinkled his brow. "Uh, yeah! Feels better than a hand. I told you our tails are sensitive."

I dragged my hand down my face, trying not to laugh. "You're such a pig, Sam. You know that, right?"

"Yep." He laughed and pulled himself from the counter. "Nick's in there making plans with Luke. That means it's going to be nothing but training for the next couple of weeks. You know that, right? I mean, no way is Nick going to chance you getting dropped in the corridor by an angel or leaving you defenseless."

"Yeah." I'd realized things were about to get a little more intense but hadn't really wanted to admit it. "So I'm stuck in the house for a while, huh?"

"Looks like." He tilted his cup to his lips, draining the last of the coffee, then placed it in the sink. "But the faster you learn, the sooner you get to reap the dead and take a trip to Daemin to wake up more friends."

"Ok, now that I can handle." I grabbed the coffee pot again, and Sam turned to leave. "Thanks, Sam," I said, meaning it. "I always wanted a friend like you. The kind of person I can trust."

He paused, one hand on the door frame. For a moment, he said nothing, then just sighed. "Yeah. You're cool, Sia. We'll see how long it takes before you're sick of me."

"Not gonna happen," I promised.

He left, but not before I saw the warm look in his eyes. I wasn't quite sure what was going on between Sam and me, but it was still there, lurking every time we were alone. Not that I'd do anything about it. It was just hard to miss how sweetly he treated me – or how good these outworlders looked.

Yeah, he was sexy, but so was Mike. The difference was that I didn't like to see Mike smile. These guys? It made my day. All three of them. So long as I didn't do anything stupid and kept my hands on Nick, maybe I could finally have that happy ending I'd always wanted. Since Sam wasn't trying to change my mind, I didn't have anything to worry about. This was completely ok. I hadn't done a single thing wrong.

I mulled things over while filling my cup again. Most likely, Nick would keep me up all night, teaching me to use aether, so a little extra caffeine wouldn't hurt. Dumping out the last dregs from the pot, I turned on the faucet, placing the carafe beneath it, and heard heavy steps on the hardwood floor of the hall. It seemed Nick was done plotting with Luke.

"Hey," I said without turning around.

A deep chuckle made me spin in place. The man standing behind me was massive, even taller than Nick, and twice as broad. The problem was that I didn't know him. His skin was a deep umber, his jaw was beautifully square and strong, and the muscles across his upper body convinced me he wasn't human. Unfortunately, I was too busy sliding along the side of the counter to bother looking at the color of his eyes. It really didn't matter. This guy was scary as shit!

"Hello, pretty," he said with a strange accent as his hands slammed onto the counter on either side of me. I was trapped between the trunks of his arms. "Nice of them to leave me a welcome home gift. Been a long time since I've seen a woman."

Black. His eyes were as black as his skin, which meant he wasn't an angel.

I lifted my chin defiantly. "You touch me, demon, and I'll make you regret it."

He leaned closer. "Will you scream? Demand I marry you when we're done?" He chuckled as he pressed closer. "If one of my brothers hasn't already, I can do that. It's ok. We don't mind sharing the good ones. I'll make sure you like this just as much as I do."

"Don't you dare come any closer," I growled in his face.

"Sia?" Nick called, hurrying into the kitchen. "Someone just..." He saw the man leaning across me, and his words fell away – but his feet never slowed. The dark man looked up with a smile just as Nick grabbed him. Wrenching the asshole away from me, Nick shoved him hard into the side of the fridge. "Don't touch her."

"Samyaza won't mind. He never does." He laughed, the sound empty. "And he'd rather I do the marrying."

Nick slammed him into the appliance again, the monster's body bouncing off the stainless steel. "She's not Sam's, Beelzebub."

"Then Lucifer's! Ah, well, he owes me a few."

Nick glared. "Mine."

There was something about seeing my man turn into a protective beast that was just a little too gratifying. Plus, knowing I wasn't completely helpless? Yep, that made this whole thing amusing instead of terrifying. I giggled, having figured out that this was the man Nick had just woken from a *very* long nap.

"Good morning, Beelzebub. If you're a dick, I'll pull out all the aether I just gave you."

28

*B*eelzebub froze, the malicious amusement draining out of him at my threat, but his eyes were on Nick. "She got the aether? So she's... You have the Muse in your home?"

"And sometimes in his bed," I added. "Nick, is he ok?"

"Nick?" Beelzebub asked. "Like, Old Nick?"

"Yeah." Nick looked at me. "He's a little behind the times. Women's rights are probably something he hasn't even heard of yet."

"Satan, you're going by Nick? I thought you hated that name."

Nick sighed. "Yeah, well it works, and I've gotten used to it in the last thousand years or so. Leave the Muse alone?"

"Didn't know she was your pet," Beelzebub muttered. "Just thought I'd gotten a welcome back present."

"She's not a pet!" Nick clenched his jaw and gave him one last shove before stepping back.

"Sorry!" Beelzebub held up his hands. "You marry her or something?"

I groaned, not sure if I was amused or disgusted. "Bel..." I decided to go with a shortened version, since I couldn't say his name the same way they did. "Bel, it doesn't work like that anymore. Women get married if and when they want. We sleep with who we want, and we basically don't need men to dictate our lives. Trust me, offering to marry someone out of the blue is a good way to get kicked in the balls."

"No sift?" he asked.

"Shit," Nick corrected without thinking.

Beelzebub nodded, his lips lifting into a smile. "No shit, then. I didn't get that part in my research." He scratched at his head. "Wasn't really looking for it either, though. Never thought women would really do it."

"Research?" I asked, letting the rest of that just slide on by.

"Yeah," Nick said. "We try to make sure we can blend with the cultures a bit. Draws less attention. There are demons who do nothing but keep track of cultural shift across the five worlds."

"Nice." It sounded like a really well-run system, but my introduction to the new guy hadn't gone unnoticed. Sam and Luke stood there watching, but neither wanted to interrupt. Probably because they'd seen Nick's reaction. "Well, now that we all know each other..." I tried.

"You good?" Sam asked.

Beelzebub heard the voice and smiled. Unfortunately, turning exposed the angel in the room. "You let the bird into your house?"

"He's cool, Beelzebub," Sam assured him. "And if you try to make a scene in the house, Nick will be pissed."

Nick chuckled. "I'm not the only one." He tilted his head to me.

"So, I should probably warn you," I told the big guy, "if you try to hurt Luke, I'll drop you back into oblivion. He and I made a very unofficial deal."

Luke chuckled at that, earning a scathing look from the black demon. "Babe, you may be a Muse, but no human can knock my ass out," Beelzebub grumbled.

"She can," Nick said.

The big man scoffed. "Whatever. This is between Lucifer and myself. Not you or your girl, Satan, and I'll keep it outside."

Nick crossed his arms over his chest and leaned beside me, his body placed perfectly to work as a shield. "She pulled your aether from Gabriel. *All of it.* I couldn't even hold everything she withdrew, and she was full when she started."

"No human can do that." Beelzebub sounded uncertain.

"None before now," Nick agreed. "I should also mention that she doesn't like angels."

"Except Lucifer," I added. "Well, now."

The dark demon looked at the ground for a long moment, his head bobbing as he thought. When his eyes flicked up to mine, his expression was serious. "And you intend to help us?"

"I'd planned on it."

I couldn't quite get a read on this guy. He'd scared the hell out me when he'd arrived, acted like he was an old friend of Sam's, clearly respected Nick, but couldn't seem to pick a side of the fence. Then again, he had been napping for a few thousand years. I couldn't even imagine what it had been like the last time he was here, but one thing was clear. I didn't trust him any farther than I could throw him. Did I mention he was huge?

"You ever seen a demon, girl?" he finally asked, lifting his head to look at me. "You know you'd be playing for the minions of Hell?"

I shrugged pointedly. "There is no Heaven and Hell. Y'all are just an evolutionary effect of multiple dimensions and altered time streams." Then I smiled. "And yes, I've seen a demon. I happen to like the whole tail and horns thing. Looks pretty kick-ass."

That earned me a smile. "How old are you?" he asked, sounding impressed.

"Twenty-four."

"How long have you been playing with aether, child?"

"Intentionally? A couple of weeks. Unintentionally? Nick thinks I always have."

Nick smiled at me and reached up to tuck a strand of hair behind my ear. "She bends the veils."

"Damn," Beelzebub said. "Both, or just Earthside?"

"All of them." Nick's mouth curled into that lopsided smile. "Daemin, Angelis... *all* of them. Gabe's aether clung to her hands from Angelis to Earth – in flight!"

"Shit," Beelzebub breathed, pulling himself away from the wall. When he looked at me this time, it was with awe. "And she's helping *us?*"

I nodded slowly. "That's the plan. First, I need a seal, and to learn to walk in the corridors."

"Satan, you need to take her to Daemin. If she's here..."

"I know," Nick said. "The house is warded."

"That won't stop them!"

"I *know*," Nick said again. "We need to seal her, key the gates to her, and train her. I can't take her to Daemin until she's keyed in, because as soon as she's outside wards, the angels are all over us. That means we have to figure out a way to get her stable in the corridor first."

Beelzebub nodded slowly, looking like he finally understood. "Which is why you wanted me here."

"Wait," I interrupted. "Why?"

Beelzebub grinned smugly. "No one can down angels as well as I can, girl. *No one.* He wanted you to have a bodyguard."

"Another," Sam added.

Luke huffed but was smart enough not to say anything.

I let out an awkward laugh, looking at the four of them. Sam and Luke were quiet, Beelzebub looked full of himself, and Nick seemed embarrassed. Yeah, I'd have to ask about that later, but if I had a bodyguard, that implied something very important.

"Does this mean I won't be stuck in the house forever?"

"Eventually," Nick promised. "It'll take a bit, then we can move you to a safer place. First, we seal and lock you. I'm not about to take any risks, little dove." He turned to face me. "You mean too much to me."

"Us," Beelzebub corrected with a knowing chuckle. "If she's as strong as you say, that girl's good for more than just keeping your bed warm. Means you're going to have to share her." He paused to scratch at his closely shaven hair. "Just can't believe you went and fell for the Muse. Damn, Satan, you never do anything by halves."

"No," Nick admitted. "I don't. Seems she doesn't either. Yeah, and she's serious when she said to leave Luke alone. He got her out of Angelis. Sia's pretty fond of him."

Beelzebub nodded in understanding, finally giving Luke something other than a terrifying glare. "Satan told me that fight was a long time ago for you, and that you only did it because you had no other option." His eyes flicked over to me, but it was almost too fast to notice. "And the Muse says I can't take my pound of flesh. You owe me, though. Alter my skin to blend in with the people here, and I'll call it even."

Luke chuckled. "Don't need to."

"Three days ago, I was terrorizing people as a Nubian. Maybe you've forgotten, but I certainly haven't, and while it may amuse you to see people shrink in fear of me -"

"Black is normal," Luke cut in, refusing to let him finish. "That's what the race is called now. About twenty percent of this country looks like you. Yeah, there's still some prejudice, but it's not socially acceptable. You're fine, Beelzebub."

The new guy looked over at me. "Is this true? You were scared when we met."

"Oh, no no no," I told him. "Some guy twice my size walks in and threatens to fuck me? *That* was the problem. Not the color of your skin. It's that you were acting like some misogynistic prick."

"Mis-og-o... What?"

"Sexist," Nick supplied. "Person who thinks men are better than women. Doesn't work like that anymore. Gender and racial equality are a thing now."

Beelzebub's eyebrows shot up. "They have advanced a lot."

"Yes, they have," Nick agreed. "Sam? Why don't you let our friend watch some TV? Might help him more than just talking."

"CNN," Luke suggested, heading back down the hall with the other two.

Once they were gone, Nick sighed and finally relaxed. Neither of us said anything. I was pretty sure we were both waiting for the fight to break out now that their boss – Nick – was out of sight. It didn't happen. Instead, I heard the new guy laugh outrageously when the television was turned on. Considering it sounded like the news, he was probably more impressed at the concept than anything else.

"So," I said, leaning my shoulder against Nick's, "were you really going to beat the shit out of him?" The thought was oddly pleasing.

He looked at me sheepishly. "I didn't really think about it. Just saw some guy grabbing my girlfriend."

I bit my lip to keep from grinning like an idiot. "Gotcha. So I guess this Bel guy didn't get the complete debriefing, huh?"

"No." He lifted his arm to drop it over my shoulder. "The only people who know that you're the cause of the warped veils are in this house. When we figured out it was you, the three of us agreed that the fewer people who knew, the less chance there was of the angels hearing it accidentally."

"Spies?"

He paused, sucking at one of his incisors. "It's always possible. We're people, little dove. We make as many mistakes as anyone else."

"Just have more time to do it," I said, understanding what he meant. "Nah, I get that. Just trying to wrap my mind around the bigger picture because it seems like I'm kinda a big deal all of a sudden."

"All your life," he corrected. "And I do want Bel, as you call him, to keep an eye on you. With the way the house is warded, we'll know if anyone is inside, so he doesn't need to hover over you or anything."

I nodded, but my mind was replaying all of those little bits that had been thrown out. At the time, I hadn't gotten the chance to even think about half the things the big demon had said, but now? Oh yeah, Beelzebub had dropped quite a few interesting hints.

"So he and Sam had a thing going a while back?" I asked, watching Nick's reaction from the corner of my eye.

He reached up to push his long hair back and sighed. "That was a very long time ago, Sia."

"Not for Bel. He made a comment about how he and Sam used to share. I'm just wondering if that was both fucking the same girl, group sex, or if there's a relationship there I kinda need to know about. Sam already told me he's into guys."

Nick's head whipped over, his eyes just a bit too wide. "Sam told you that?"

"Yeah. When we first met, he agreed that you were hot then told me he was a try-sexual." I paused, aware of the apprehension on his face. "Why?"

"Some of the things we've done were out of ignorance. Humans weren't very civilized when we first met them, and it can often take us a little longer to adapt. Lack of generations and all that."

He was clearly avoiding something, and I was dying to know. "Like orgies?"

"Among other things," he reluctantly admitted. "We only started using skins here regularly around the Bronze Age. Before that, the fear of our appearance was one of our best tools. We looked like monsters. Rape was considered an acceptable way to claim a girl at one point. Just take her, and she was yours." He sighed. "Even the women didn't know any better, and they weren't given the option to consent. Once they were, it got harder for us. Then we realized some were drawn to the idea of danger."

I could see where this was going. "But not enough to go around, huh?"

"No," he agreed. "Many demons found a solution that kept everyone happy."

I noticed how vague he'd made that. "Were you one of them?"

"Sia," he groaned. "It was a long time ago."

I giggled. "Which means yes. So, I guess a few guys got together and made agreements or something?"

"Look, it wasn't anything as devious as that. It was just that if a woman was interested in more than one of us, we never questioned if that was normal. We came from a place where women didn't exist. It only made sense that we wanted her happy, and sometimes that meant she wanted more than one lover, so friends learned to share the same woman. Sometimes at once, sometimes she had separate relationships with each one. For *us*, there were no social connotations to it. Regardless, they spoiled and pampered her." He glanced up. "On the midworlds, the women were used to it, but humans? Those girls loved the attention. From their point of view, it was a good deal. The additional lovers made sure no one abused her, and they all kept her in luxury."

"But surely you saw that other humans didn't have the same types of relationships, right?"

His tongue flicked across his lips. "We did. We also saw how angels treated men. Back then, angels enslaved men, and those men enslaved their wives. We had no interest in making love into some kind of torture."

I thought about women's place throughout history, and I could see why their offer would be so appealing even if society didn't approve. "You know, that all makes sense. So why didn't you get in on the good deal? I mean, you already told me you haven't slept with a human before. Overly jealous?"

"Um..." He glanced to the far side of the room. "I only said I've never had *sex* with a human."

"But you've made out a time or two, huh?"

I saw a smile flash across his lips. "Or so. My work kept me closer to Angelis. I spent a lot of time on Tyrnigg with the fairies.

That, and my name? The demon of seduction was tempting. Satan?" He shook his head. "The church simply had too much power, and I've earned a place as their enemy. For good reason."

Nope, I was not letting him derail this. "So y'all had like, fairy gangbangs?"

His head dropped to his chest. "Dove, it was a very long time ago, ok? We weren't trying to take advantage of her."

"Nick..." I giggled. "I'm not pissed. I mean, the idea of you and a couple of demons getting kinky?" I flashed him a devious smile. "C'mon. That's hot."

"You're not...."

I shook my head. "This is the twenty-first century. We humans have figured out there are more options than heterosexual monogamy. In fact, we ladies? Believe it or not, sometimes we think the idea of multiple hot guys being into us might even be a good thing!"

"Bel's into you," he said softly, glancing over to check my reaction.

I nodded. "Haven't made up my mind about him yet. I'm not convinced that he isn't a dick, but he's pretty."

A little smile was curling one side of Nick's mouth ever higher. "Sam's into you."

That actually got a laugh. "Sam's into anything with a pulse, and I'm not sure he requires even that."

"Seriously," Nick said. "Does that upset you?"

"Um..." Yeah, my opinion on Sam was dangerous territory. All of a sudden, I wasn't so sure this had been a good topic. "It's flattering?"

"Sia?" He turned to face me. "I told him to be more respectful. He's a good guy, but he doesn't always like to stay on his side of boundaries."

I scrubbed at my face. "He's a friend, ok? I'm not upset if he flirts, and I'm most definitely not going to cheat on you. I promise! Nick, you deserve to finally have a woman who is devoted to you, and I want that to be me. I mean, I spent four years trying to find you. Now that I have? Nope. Nuh-uh. Not going to screw this up."

Moving closer, he pressed a hand to the back of my neck. "There's nothing to screw up, little dove. I'm ok with us. I'm *more* than ok with us. I just know that you make my friends happy, and I don't want to lose that either. We've all been through so much together, and I like how we're finally able to all be happy together."

"I know. And I'm just a flash in the pan, right?"

"A year is still a year," he told me as he pressed his forehead to mine. "A day passes the same to me as it does to you. Once you learn to control aether, there's no reason you won't be able to maintain your life."

Sucking in a breath, I looked up, still shocked to see darkness instead of stars. "What? If I learn how to do this aethercrafting stuff, I can live longer?"

"It's the internal aspect. Luke will have to show you that, but yes. Many Muses used their talents to live a few lifetimes."

"And be young? Not like some two-hundred-year-old wrinkled old lady?"

"You can age if you want, or not." The smile on his face was almost confused. "You'd really want to live longer? Most don't. They give up after a few generations."

"Why the hell not? Of course, I like the idea of living as long as I can."

He tilted his head slightly. "And when everyone you love has gone?"

Thrusting my arm out, I gestured around the house. "Luke, Sam... *You!* Nick, I have no family. My friends? They're a joke. The only people I give a damn about kinda can't die. Duh!"

He was nodding, but not looking quite as thrilled as I felt. "And when the world has changed so much that you can't recognize it?"

"Nick!" I gasped, shaking his shoulders to make my point. "I don't recognize Vesdar or the other places either."

"Maybe not, but they've all still given up eventually." With a relieved sigh, he pulled me against his chest and wrapped those amazing arms around me. "But I'll take all the time with you I can get."

With my cheek smooshed against his pecs, I managed to mumble, "Then stop suffocating me and start teaching me, demon!"

29

*A*fter that first day, Beelzebub was completely respectful, and he never made a move to get even with Luke. Once he began to realize how much the world had changed while he slept, he even apologized for his rudeness to all of us. Me, more than the rest. The last time he'd been on Earth, women had been treated as property, raised and trained to submit to their men. The concept of birth control amazed him, resulting in many embarrassing questions. The idea of equality thrilled him in a way I never would've expected. In less than a week, we'd even become tentative friends.

While Beelzebub threw himself into learning modern culture, I focused on mastering aether. Then, one evening, after surpassing every challenge he set, Nick finally agreed that it was time to take the next step. With a sigh, he pulled me into his lap, wrapping his arms around my body protectively.

"Before you try to cross the veil, you need to be sealed," he said gently.

I nodded. "Ok. How do we do that?"

"It hurts." One finger pulled the hair away from my neck. "It's a brand, little dove, just with aether instead of iron."

"Pretty sure I'll live. How do we do it?"

He kissed the side of my neck, trying to distract me. "You willing to let Luke help?"

I pulled away and turned to him. "Stop avoiding the question, demon."

Nick laughed, the sound warm and melodious. "Angel, demon, human. The three of us can weave aether together, calling to the pattern of your own life to raise the symbol on your skin." He shrugged. "It means lying naked with the two of us standing over you, doing a little chanting to keep our weaving synchronized."

"You just want to get me undressed," I teased.

He chuckled, avoiding the implications completely. "Sealing your pattern will be stronger with his help."

"Like, completely naked?" He was serious? Yeah, that suddenly didn't sound like as much fun as I'd hoped.

"We can do something for modesty, but um," he chuckled. "It's better to not have your clothes burn off your body. The sealing generates a lot of heat. That's why it looks like a brand. It basically is."

"When?"

He caressed the side of my face, smiling guiltily. "Now?"

"Thanks for the warning!"

With a devious look, he lifted me back to my feet and stood. "One more thing." He shifted around so he could see my face. "Your seal will mark you in the worlds like a tether. It's tied to you, and you alone, but..." He paused, glancing away for a split second. "If you're willing, I'd like to bind a set of stones to us afterward."

"I don't know what that means, but it sounds important."

He chuckled softly, then reached up to rub a hand over his betraying mouth. "Um. Think of it like a homing beacon. One for you, one for me. I'd wear yours and you mine. With a little concentration, you'll be able to track me down anywhere in the five realms, and vice versa."

"Ok?"

He moved his hand to clasp one of mine. "Once you're sealed, we'll be able to inscribe your pattern on a gemstone, locking it to you. If you're willing to let me wear it, then anytime I touch the stone, I'll know where you are. The same would be true in reverse."

"And that's a big deal?"

He shrugged. "You won't be able to hide from me. When I piss you off, you can't just run to Vesdar and spend a week on the beach without wondering when I'll show up."

I nodded. "And if the winds in the corridor sweep me away?"

"Then I can push to where you are and pull you from the current. That's why I want to do this, so you'll never end up lost so bad that I can't come save you. So if you ever need me, you can summon me. So that no matter where we are in all of the five planes, we'll never truly be alone."

"And when you get tired of the boring old human and decide to spend a weekend with a hot new replacement, I can show up to chase her off?"

He grinned and shook his head. "Not going to happen."

"This coming from the man who says he's never dated a human?"

He tapped the end of my nose. "Human, Sia. Spent a few centuries with a fairy, though."

"I heard you liked them better."

"Nothing of the sort. I happen to be pretty fond of *you*. Want me to prove it again?" He tugged me against his chest and kissed my neck with a laugh. "It's just that human relationships always had those annoying complications. Fairies not only were more willing but also stuck around longer."

"What's the longest?" I knew I shouldn't ask, but I was dying to know.

"Seven thousand, eight hundred and twenty-one years, five

months, and two days." He shrugged with an impish smile. "Not that I was counting. She died about a few million years ago."

"Damn."

He nodded. "And she grew old with me, and I still loved her." He let out a heavy breath as his arms relaxed on my sides. "And when Michael destroyed her body, I took her aether."

"I'm sorry, Nick. I shouldn't have asked."

He smiled sadly. "It's ok, dove. Was a long time ago, and I honestly don't mind telling you. Makes me feel a little more permanent when you want to know about my past."

I bit my lip and smiled up at him. "I dated a guy for two months once."

"Did you love him?"

"I dunno. Kinda thought so, but I'm not sure. I mean, he made me feel special, and I thought that's what love was supposed to be." I shrugged. "Now, I think it was just hormones."

"Then not love." He wrapped his arms around me again. "Love is something you can't miss. It burns so deep inside that it almost hurts and drives you to do things you'd never expect. It's something miraculous, not just hormones."

"Mostly, I just had pretty shallow relationships. I dunno, I guess I was waiting for something better. I mean, does love at first sight really exist?" I figured he'd seen everything. If anyone could be sure, it would be Nick.

He smiled knowingly and pushed me to my feet. "Yes, but it's not a good thing. Love at first sight is based on nothing but lust. Not that initial lust is bad, mind you; it's just not enough. Love that starts slow and grows into a wildfire? That's the kind that lasts an eternity." He gently pushed a lock of hair from my neck. "Real love starts as chemistry, builds into friendship, and blossoms into something so magical that it makes everything else feel worthwhile, even the bad parts. Sia, should I order the stones? Even if it's little more than a glamorous leash, will you let me do this?"

I nodded. "They already think I'm your pet. I figure this way will basically make you mine back, right?"

"Definitely." A little smile teased his lips. "And, if you ever change your mind, for any reason, I swear I will return it."

"Ok. Then the same goes for yours."

He eased away. "I can't think of a single reason I wouldn't want you to have a piece of my soul. I should go tell Luke to get ready."

Stepping into the hall, he left me standing there with my mouth open. I'd known this was important to him but hadn't truly understood why he was acting so serious about it. That man had just offered me a piece of his soul and asked to carry one of mine. He'd already keyed the wards on his body to my touch, and now this?

A part of me wondered if he was rushing into things too fast, but the other half knew better. He was the strongest aethersmith in five realms. I was a Muse, supposedly unlike anything that had existed before. From the stories they told, I was different, special, and something to fear, but so was Nick. Together, we were supposed to be able to do miraculous things. It only made sense that we worked together. It was even nicer that we happened to get along so well.

And we did get along. The sex was amazing. Granted, a few billion years of practice might have that effect, but it wasn't just about sex with him. Nick made everything exciting and comfortable. He was honestly my friend as well as my lover. We could talk for hours about inconsequential things then dive so deep into my lessons that the sun would take us by surprise the next morning. Just being with him made me happy, even if it was across the room, completely dressed, unable to speak. He was like an addiction I couldn't quite satisfy.

Luke's laugh in the kitchen pulled me back to reality. I knew Nick would be talking to him about performing the sealing and wondered what was so funny. Considering I'd just been told I was going to lie naked between them, I was feeling a bit overly sensitive about jokes right about now. Making my way there, I stopped just around the corner, listening.

"You're giving her a binding stone?" Luke asked, sounding shocked.

"Yeah. Already found a place with a set in the right colors. Just need to buy them and have them shipped." Nick tried to make it sound uneventful.

Luke laughed again. "When was the last time you let someone have that much control over you, let alone a Muse as strong as Sienna?"

"There's never been a Muse like her."

"Mhm." Silence hung for a moment. "There's no reason you need to give her your own stone, Nick. She won't be offended. Keep hers, just in case she fumbles in the corridor, but why? Why hand over the key to your existence?"

Nick sighed. "How can I expect her to trust me if I'm not willing to trust her?" A cabinet opened, the thunk of a heavy coffee mug following. "I'm not worried about it, Luke. I want her to have it."

"You love her?" Luke's voice was quiet; I almost wasn't sure I'd heard.

That was my cue to enter the room. I didn't want to hear the answer, not when it was someone else asking. "Fresh coffee?" I asked, striding around the corner.

Luke glanced up, his face never leaving Nick's, but his eyes were on me. "Yep." He smiled, well aware that I'd heard.

"You going to help with the thing?" I tapped at my chest.

"Sealing, and yes." Luke flicked his eyes back to Nick. "When was the last time angelic and demonic weaving happened?"

"I don't know, when was the last time we did it?"

Luke shrugged. "Never for a seal."

Nick grinned. "Exactly. Hopefully, it'll make her that much harder for anyone to crack."

"What am I getting myself into?" I looked from one to the other, more amused than concerned.

"Dark magic," Luke teased. "Although, there's not really any light magic, so I guess that's a moot point, huh?"

"Yeah. So what's the deal with the seal, and why is Nick so damned worried about getting it perfect?"

Nick lifted the cup to his mouth, sucking at it as he turned to face me, looking completely normal and mundane. He swallowed and cradled his coffee between his fists. "It's so you won't need the wards, dove. If we get the seal right, you won't need to scar yourself like I did."

"Oh."

"Would be a waste," Luke teased, gesturing for Nick to hurry up. "I mean, have you seen the marks on him? Every bare spot has some kind of rune now."

"I like it."

Luke groaned. "You would." He rolled his eyes playfully.

"You mean you don't have wards?"

"You've never seen him without a shirt?" The twisted corner of Nick's mouth told me he was teasing.

"Well, once, but he was kinda swooping down to save my life. Not really a good time to look, ya know?"

"Right." Nick chugged at the coffee again, then paused. "Oh. Probably should mention that caffeine seems to help with aethersmithing."

"Really?"

He nodded. "That's why I offered you a coffee that first day of class. Figured you'd already have a taste for it."

"How? I mean, how does it help?"

Nick sighed, but Luke had the answer. "Caffeine expands the vessels in your brain. That means more aether can flow through, and well, it's like unclogging a drain. It's not going to make a weak smith into a great one, but it makes complex tasks a little easier. No different than filling up before you take a test to help you concentrate."

"Gotcha." I shoved my lips together, mulling that over. "That's actually kinda cool. So is Earth the only place that has it?"

Nick shook his head. "Nah. Caffeine is out there, but Earth makes the best kind. Coffee, chocolate, things like that. On Vesdar, it's in a very bitter weed, and you have to chew it. Not worth it."

"Fairies had a flower whose seeds had it. Tasted like ass and wasn't enough of anything to make it better." Luke shrugged. "So, we're all addicted to coffee. I mean, tools of the trade, right?"

"But Sam isn't an aethersmith?"

They both hemmed a little before shaking their heads.

"But he drinks it?"

Luke held up a finger, signaling he could explain. "Sam and Beelzebub are warriors. Sam is neither overly large nor overly skilled with working aether, but he found a way to make the two work well together. Beelzebub's like a Mack Truck, but he has enough smithing to cross the veils and use aether weapons. Unfortunately, not enough ability to be classified as an aethersmith. It makes them like badasses at angel ass-kicking."

I giggled. "That's a lot of ass."

"Sam likes it," Nick said, setting down the cup. "Ok. Give us ten minutes, Luke, then meet me in the gold room?"

"Yep."

Nick grabbed my hand and led me out, dragging me upstairs. He opened the door of the first bedroom to expose gold decor. Instead of a bed, a large marble table was centered in the room. He looked back at me as he closed the door.

"So, this is our dark little secret."

I laughed nervously. "Um, you perform sacrifices in here or something?"

"Something. Clothes off, dove, then you're up on the table." He moved to a closet on the far side, pausing with his hand on the handle. "How modest are you?"

I sighed and pulled my shirt off, tossing it into a dainty chair beside the door. "I wear a bikini in public kind of modest?"

He nodded. "I can work with that."

"Nick? You want to explain a little of this?" I gestured to the marble table. "Or are you just going to keep me guessing?"

"Weaving aether generates heat," Nick reminded me. "It has to do with molecular vibrations. Stone doesn't transfer it. That means we can do workings on the table without burning down the house."

That sounded like an awful lot of heat, I thought as I kicked off my shoes. Tucking them under the chair, I fumbled with the button on my jeans next, feeling like I was undressing for a doctor's exam. "Ok. And you do this often?"

He leaned back to look around the closet door. "Yeah, um. Sometimes we need to alter or repair a skin, or craft weapons, bring over some of our technology like the map... You know, things like that."

"I really don't know, Nick. That's why I'm asking."

"Right." He pulled out a stack of grey material. The weave was coarse, almost like burlap. "Fire retardant blanket," he said, lifting it up. "Mostly wool and fiberglass."

I was almost naked by this time – and feeling very self-conscious. "Ok. Now walk me through this plan again?"

He tossed the fabric over his shoulder and returned to the table, patting it. "You lay up here, Luke and I do some stuff, you get branded." He grinned. "You trying to dawdle long enough to give Luke a show?"

I hurried over to the table's edge, my arms wrapped around my chest. Nick spread a layer of the blanket over the cold stone then grabbed my waist, easily lifting my rump to the top as if I weighed nothing. Before I could open my mouth, he flipped the rest over my lap.

"Thanks."

"Welcome. Now, we're going to need to see your chest," he

pressed his finger over my heart. "I don't care if you want to cocoon yourself in the blanket, but it gets a little warm. If it were me, I'd just cover the sexy parts."

"Planning on giving me a hand with that?"

His eyes glinted deviously. "Sure. Lie down."

I gasped when my back was on the blanket. "It's still cold!"

His eyes flicked to my chest. "Yeah. Just a nice bonus." He pressed my shoulder back, encouraging me to relax, and began adjusting the cloth so it covered my breasts and hips but nothing else. After tucking the ends under my body, he made his way around the table to look at me from all sides. "Ok. You're safe from angelic eyes."

"Is this going to suck?" I was starting to get very nervous.

He sighed, but a tap came at the door before he could answer. "She decent?" Luke called through the wood.

"Yeah," Nick replied, turning to me. "It's not fun, but it doesn't hurt for long."

Luke barely opened the door to slip inside. "Nice. Fire blanket. Forgot about that."

"I feel like I'm about to be sacrificed by Satanists," I grumbled.

Luke chuckled, moving to stand beside the table. "Nah, we'd never let flunkies do something this fun. You get the real deal." He gently touched my bare shoulder. "This is easy, Sia. Just lay there, don't break contact with us, and try not to freak out the neighbors when you scream?"

"I'm gonna scream?"

Luke nodded. "*Everyone* screams."

"Fuck," I groaned. Here I was, lying on a sacrificial altar, surrounded by beautiful men, basically naked, being told this was going to hurt. "Aren't y'all supposed to, you know, tell me it's just a pinch?"

"I'll tell you it's quick," Nick said. "But I'm not going to lie to you. Ten minutes of nothing, ten seconds of searing pain, then it's done. Just don't pull away from us or we have to start over."

"Right. Hot guys groping my body while causing extreme pain. Maybe we should YouTube this?"

Luke laughed and reached for the hem of his shirt, pulling it over his head. "That would probably end up banned, so let's skip it and say we did."

I couldn't help it. I'd never seen Luke without a shirt, and Nick's comment made me wonder about wards. As the cloth slid over his head, trim abs were revealed below smooth lean pectorals, but no runes. I looked to my right, where Nick stood, and realized he was watching.

"Why doesn't he have runes?"

"Because he's an angel." His jaw clenched for a moment, then he sighed and yanked off his own shirt.

"Think of demons as engineers," Luke said. "They work with patterns and external forces. Angels work with hypnotism and internal forces like biochemists." He chuckled. "I'm marked, but you won't see it. Nick's way works better but is a lot more obvious." He leaned closer. "He's also jealous."

"I'm the one naked on a table."

"Looking at Luke," Nick muttered.

"And spending every night with you." I giggled. "Although you're cute when you're jealous."

"Not really," Luke said. "He's gotten better, but he's not fun to be around when he's in a rage."

"Aw damn," I teased, twisting to see Nick. "And here I was hoping this would end up being more kink and less pain. I mean, those leather wings and his little feathery ones..."

"Not funny," Nick said, but the corner of his lip betrayed him. "Those feathers get everywhere, and you don't want that, missy."

"Hmm, guess we'll just have to have an orgy with Sam then." Nick and Luke looked at each other quickly, as if hiding something. I groaned. "What?"

"The seal," Nick said.

Luke chuckled. "You aren't going to tell her that little piece of demonic history?"

"No."

"What?" I asked, trying to sit up.

Luke pressed me back. "Took a few million years to get the other races, Sia. Didn't take that long for men to figure out that touching certain things felt good."

"Right. So you masturbate. Not really news."

"We going to do this?" Nick asked.

Luke chuckled. "Sure. You know, she's not disgusted by Sam at all. I'm not sure why you haven't crawled out of the fifteen hundreds."

I looked at Nick, then back to Luke, realizing what they were talking about. "Hey, Nick? If you screwed some demon, I'm ok with that. Just promise you'll tell me some hot stories later?"

"No stories," he grumbled, reaching down to take my hand. "Ready?"

Luke grabbed my other hand, weaving his fingers through mine, then held his open palm across the table. "Let's make this the best one yet, Satanael."

Nick slapped his palm into Luke's, his eyes never leaving my face. "Definitely. Lucifer, you start."

*L*uke closed his eyes and began to speak. The words were soft, silky, and unnatural, like no language I'd heard before. When he took a breath, Nick joined in, forming a countermelody. Unlike Luke's, his words were harsh, filled with consonants and primitive syllables that my ears did not want to acknowledge. The sounds blended, forming a dissonance that was somehow soothing, calling to something deep inside me.

I could hear the chant. It reminded me of ancient monks. Their words wove around each other, building on the meaning, but the only comprehension was the tone, the melody, and the rhythm of it all. Like a dance, it urged my body to sway and drift and writhe. I gave into it, knowing this was magic. Not superstition or illusion, but a type of science so advanced that humans couldn't hope to understand. To me, that made it magic. Pure, lyrical, soothing magic.

I found myself humming softly to the melody and let my eyes slip closed, relaxing into it. Nick said this would take a while, like ten minutes or something, so I might as well enjoy the sound of their native languages. On and on it went, playing with my mind like some narcotic, leaving me feeling satiated but dizzy, pleased but anxious, and then I began to feel warm.

At first, it was like someone turned up the heater. It wasn't much, just a flush to my skin, a little less chill on my bare toes, but it grew. Soon, it felt like the Oklahoma summers from my youth, hot and dry. My skin started to sweat. The thick wool blanket clung in all the wrong places. I opened my eyes, hoping they'd finish soon so I could get rid of the thick fabric, and saw aether. Swirls of pale blue and gold, with vermillion streaks burning in contrast, the colors danced to their voices, twining around each other like lovers. All three shades intertwined perfectly in some beautiful representation of harmony. I felt Nick squeeze my fingers, then Luke, as more began to appear. Yellows, greens, purples, pinks, and shades I couldn't even describe. Some were translucent, others metallic, but they all swirled like fog in a breeze, centered around me.

Then the burning started. It felt like I'd leaned too close to the stove – and it would not subside. When I glanced down, the flesh over my left breast had turned angry and red, growing steadily redder. Before my eyes, the skin blistered and peeled, popped and bubbled, the cracked edges searing to charred black crisps.

I screamed.

I screamed so hard I thought my lungs would pour through my throat, so hard my tongue felt swollen in my mouth. My back arched from the hot, damp stone, seeking a breath of air, some breeze that would stop the pain. My tears leaked out, streaming down my face as the wound grew steadily over my heart. No matter what I did, it burned, from the center of my soul right through my skin, marking me for who I was, clear for all the world to see. It hurt in ways that words just couldn't describe.

And Nick held my hand.

So beautiful and perfect, his voice sounded like peace. The words were harsh enough to cut through the pain. The rhythm stayed steady, rocking me slowly to ease the torture. His eyes were closed, his body as strong as a mountain, completely unmoving, except for his fingers in mine reminding me I was not alone. It hurt. Like those words from my youth, convincing me I didn't matter, the aether hammered at something so deep inside that no one else could see, pulling it to the surface, revealing it to any eye that turned in my direction.

And Luke squeezed my fingers.

The silky words that came from his mouth were spoken with a velvet voice. Every syllable worked to ease my suffering while forging me into something so much better. Deep in my bones, I could feel the changes claiming me, but Luke was there to keep me stable. The eerie green of his eyes was no longer cold. It was burning with power, shifting to the same gold as his aether, and begging me to look a little deeper. I couldn't. My mind couldn't settle on anything except the searing hot pain racing in tiny swirls across my chest. It hurt. It hurt so badly, I felt blackness clawing at me.

It hurt more than anything else in my life.

The hot edges seared a line from my spine to my chest, like burning metal cutting through everything inside me, and no matter how hard I tried to close my mouth, bite my tongue, or clench my jaw, I screamed. I didn't remember breathing, or begging, or trying to pull away, but the force of that scream tore at my vocal chords like a feeling that would stay with me forever. I knew it as it happened. A part of my mind, locked away from the ritual, observed, ashamed of my weakness but knowing there was nothing I could do to change it.

Then it just stopped.

Nick's hand pressed the mark on my chest as he pulled the other free from Luke's. Exhausted, he leaned over my waist, resting his head on my stomach. Luke took great gulps of air as he gently caressed my sweat-soaked hair. I cried, soundlessly, but I couldn't stop the tears as I tried to breathe slowly, begging my body to relax, promising that it was over.

"You ok, Sia?" Luke asked.

"Let's not do that again?" I croaked.

He chuckled softly and pressed his palm against my scalding scalp. "I can agree to that. At least you only have to do it once."

"Nick?"

Luke petted my hair again. "Give him a second. He's healing the burns."

"Thank you, Nick," I whispered, looking down my body for his face.

The corner of his lip curled, but he didn't look up. Luke squatted beside me, resting one hand on my head, the other on my shoulder. While Nick worked, Luke's touch convinced me to just relax until, finally, Nick was done. The sigh could mean nothing else. With a gentle pat on my arm, Luke pushed to his feet, grabbed his shirt, and left without a word. The door closed softly behind him.

"Hey?" I asked Nick, his head still pressed against my stomach. "You alive down there?" My throat was raw and hoarse.

"Yeah, a little tired, but we nailed it." He smiled and slowly lifted his hand. "Your seal is perfect, and Luke locked in the wards to protect you from just about everything."

"Except you?" I didn't know how to key my seal to him, and I wasn't ready to try.

"Except us," Nick corrected. "Luke and I sealed you. If you want to lock us out, you'll have to do it later."

I nodded, accepting that. "Is there any reason I'd want to lock Luke out?"

He shook his head. "No. Not after the deal he made you. I mean, he's not perfect, dove, but he's all heart."

"Why didn't you ever unlock to him, then?" I licked at my lips, wishing I had a drink.

Nick saw, pulled himself back to his feet, and headed to the bathroom, talking while he went. "Never had a reason to. Our abilities tend to be in opposition in a lot of ways. Think of it like earth, fire, and water. Luke and I are fire and water."

"So you two cancel each other out?"

"Yeah, and both work well with you." He walked back into the room carrying a tall, clear glass, filled full. "Can you sit up, or do you need help?"

I tried to do it on my own, but Nick hurried over to wrap his arm around my shoulders. His other hand held out the glass like an offering. I took it gratefully, sucking back gulp after gulp of cool relief. For a second, I paused to breathe, then drank again until the glass was empty. Only then did Nick take it from my hands and place it out of sight behind him.

"Shower?" he asked.

"A cool one," I agreed.

He nodded and swept me into his arms, pressing my chest tight against his. The blanket tangled between us. I could have walked, but he never gave me the chance. Instead, he carried me into the bathroom before gently easing my feet to the floor.

"See if you like that." He gestured to the mirror as he turned to adjust the shower temperature to be soothing.

My reflection looked like a wreck, so it was no wonder he was worried. My hair hung damp and limp against my shoulders. My skin was pallid and pasty, except across my chest. There, a large gilded circle had been branded into my skin. The molten gold looked like it was meant to be there, but surreal. The seal was made of two rings, words in a language I'd never seen written between them in copper on an icy blue background. Inside it all was a pattern of iridescent rainbow spirals that twined around each other. It was elegant, dainty, feminine, and oddly beautiful.

"What if I hate it?" I looked up to see Nick watching my reflection.

His eyes met mine in the glass, aware of the smile on my lips. "Then you'd be shit out of luck, wouldn't ya?"

I laughed, turning gently to see him pulling off his own clothes.

"I guess so. It's lovely, but why is mine gold and yours is just a brand?"

He shoved his pants down his hips, obviously planning to share the shower with me. "Luke's aether is gold. Mine is a very pale blue. If you look at his seal, you'll see it's tinted, just like Sam's is pinkish. Because we all worked together on yours, and because you're a damned Muse, well, you get the pretty one." He gestured to the space between the circles. "See how that's pale? That's my aether. Luke locked the edges, so he got that."

"And mine is in the writing?"

Nick smiled. "You organized all the colors, little dove. Your aether is that color because you want it to be, not because you don't have a choice."

"Oh."

He pulled open the door to the shower and guided me in. The cool water felt amazing on my parched skin. I rinsed the sweat and salt away, worried for only a moment that the raw flesh would sting with water, but it was healed. Nick had seen to that as soon as the sealing was done.

"So, when will we get the stones you talked about?" I moved out from under the water, looking for shampoo.

He passed me the bottle, then lifted his hair to rinse his own body. "Next week. Right now, you need food and sleep."

"You cooking?" I looked up at him with the best pouty face I could manage.

Nick laughed. "No, Sam is." He took a step closer and wrapped his arms around me, guiding me back under the water.

I grabbed conditioner. "Well at least I won't starve, since I can't cook to save my own life. It's not something I've ever had the chance to learn."

He growled playfully and spun me around, reaching for my hair to work the cream through my locks. "Maybe I need to keep you in the kitchen then?"

"Next you'll start adding pregnant to that list."

"Nope." Nick kissed my shoulder and eased me back under the water. "What would you do with little winged children?"

"Make their daddy deal with it." I knew full well he wasn't serious.

"I have no interest in seeing my children die, Sia."

"Me either," I assured him. "And since you said I can manipulate my aging, well, I think we'll just let someone else do the breeding. Deal?"

"Deal." He pressed against me, kissing my face as the water ran over us both, soaking the hair he'd been trying to keep dry. "But you need to eat. You shouldn't be up and about."

I wiped the water from my eyes. "Why not?"

"Because that's about as serious of a working as you've ever done. Well, in theory. At some point, you're going to feel exhausted."

"I do feel a bit tired, but not exhausted."

He chuckled once. "At least we know you're not unstoppable."

Clean, and feeling a lot less sticky, I turned off the shower and found one of those super soft towels, gold this time, to wrap myself in. Nick followed, always staying within reach like he expected me to collapse any moment or something. My clothes were still in the other room, but Nick had left most of his on the floor. I watched, enjoying the view while he pulled his pants on, damp hair clinging to his broad chest.

"So, what's that bit about ancient demon history and masturbation?" I asked as I made my way back into the gold room.

Nick groaned. "You were supposed to forget about that."

"I didn't. Now, you can tell me, or you can say you don't want to talk about it." I shrugged. "Either is an acceptable option, Mr. I-Walked-With-Dinosaurs."

With a deep sigh, he leaned against the table, waiting while I pulled on my clothes. "So," he said slowly, dragging the word out. "When we began – because we weren't born, we simply were. One day nothing, the next day completely grown and formed. Well, we didn't know anything."

"That's a little freakish."

He shrugged. "It's what happened. The first few weeks of life were the same for most demons. We managed to injure ourselves a lot, we tried to figure out how to fly, usually catastrophically, and, um, we were amazed at our own bodies."

"They are pretty magnificent bodies."

He laughed. "Well, we agreed, and like most young boys, we experimented. Since we had no women, a pair of demons meeting up usually went one of two ways, either we fought, or we showed off."

I nodded, seeing where he was going. "And sex happened."

His eyes flicked to the far wall. "We didn't even know women were an option."

I got the impression that bothered him, so I decided to change the subject. "So, how long before demons started forming societies?"

His shoulders relaxed as I took the conversation in a less awkward direction. "About two hundred years. There aren't many of us, so we first gathered in groups of two to ten, which we called legions. Then we staked out claims, and eventually ran into others, and, well, one day we started making homes. From there, we just kept going."

"What's it like, now?"

Nick smiled, letting his eyes close. "Organized. There's a few on the other side of the world that do their own thing, but most of the unconscious demons are brought to us, cared for, and when we can, revived." He smiled. "In some ways, it's more primitive, but in others more advanced."

"Ok?"

"Well, like our technology. We're far ahead of you on that, but limited by fuel – aether. The place is amazing, though. The entrance is marked with a massive statue, probably thirty stories tall. Inside that, we live in a commune-like society. It keeps the guys social, forming friendships, and gives us the closest thing to a family that demons can know."

His pride hinted at something, and I could tell he was choosing his words carefully.

"So what aren't you saying?"

"Our city is run by a council."

"And?"

"Leader of the aethersmiths, leader of the warriors, and leader of the people. We have a word for that. It means something like citizens but with responsibilities. Anyway, um, Samyaza and I are two of the leaders."

"And the third?"

"Azrael. He doesn't leave Daemin much."

"So, is he like a king or something?"

Nick shook his head. "Think of us more like elected officials. One is not higher than the other, even if he does speak for more people."

"So I'm fucking a demon prince?"

Nick laughed. "No, you're fucking the Master of Hell, or something – get it right. C'mon, let's feed you."

I turned to the door and paused. "Thanks for the seal, Nick. Thanks for doing it yourself, for healing me, for taking care of me, and for answering all of my annoying questions."

"You're welcome." He pulled the door open and pressed his hand gently against my back, but his smile was proud, as if I'd just told him he'd saved the world.

Walking down the stairs, I felt weary but not any worse than after a long shift at Mac's. Every muscle in my body hurt – but that wasn't surprising considering the writhing I'd just done. My chest felt fine, the mark of the seal barely noticeable unless I thought about it. The skin seemed a bit heavier, like I'd painted on it, but it wasn't uncomfortable. Nick led me to the small table in the kitchen and motioned for me to sit.

As soon as the chair screeched against the tile floor, Sam appeared, looking worried. "You ok, Sia?" he asked.

"Yeah. A little tired, but that's it. Starving."

He nodded. "So, do I get to see it?"

I yanked at the neck of my t-shirt, pulling it over to reveal the side of my new seal. Sam leaned closer, hooking his finger under the cloth to pull a bit more. "Elegant. Very nice. Damn, looks good when you combine angelic and demonic weavings."

"They did good," I agreed.

"Holy shit," Beelzebub said, walking in.

"What?" I asked, shocked.

He chuckled. "Such a strange phrase, you know? Holy and shit, back to back? Doesn't really make sense."

"Also means something's a big deal," Sam told him.

"Oh." Beelzebub shrugged. "Well, she's standing, Satan isn't suffering, and Lucifer's ok. That's a big deal, right?"

"It is?" I looked from Sam to Nick, wanting verification.

"It was like sealing pure aether," Nick told the big guy. "She's oozing with it, and didn't fight us, not even when the burning started." He smiled at me. "She helped."

"Sure." I chuckled. "If you say so."

"The humming – before you started screaming," Luke explained, standing by the door. "Kitchen's a little crowded, guys. Nick, make her a coffee. Sam, get dinner going before she uses the last of what she has left." He pushed further into the room, his leaner body weaving between the other guys. "And I get to steal the Muse long enough to get her comfy."

"When did you become the savior?" I asked, my eyes widening over his offered hand.

Luke winked. "The day an angel grabbed you, and you reached for my help without thinking."

Nick tapped his chest. "Aether transfer. The gold is from Luke. It's a little different for angels than it is for demons."

"You in love with me now or something?" I teased Luke.

"You wish," he shot back. "Nah. Just weird to have someone walking around with a stabilized bit of my life in them. It fades eventually, but, I dunno."

I understood. "Feels all warm and fuzzy, huh?"

"Something like that," he agreed, pulling me to my feet. "Pillows are on the sofa. I have a real soft blanket in there too, since I know how much you like those. You're staying off your feet until you eat. If you aren't out by then, you can..." He paused. "...finish your lessons."

"I almost feel like the outsider," Beelzebub said, nudging Sam's arm. "Damn smiths, always acting like their shit is such a big deal."

"Kinda is," Sam said. "Bel, they just sealed the most powerful Muse in history with angelic, demonic, and human aether."

Beelzebub chuckled, following Luke and me into the sitting room. The sound of Sam digging for pans clanked behind us. I assumed Nick was helping because he didn't come with us.

"You gonna learn to fight too?" Beelzebub asked when we reached the living room.

Luke was pointing to the couch facing the door, pillows and a blanket laid out, just like he'd promised, and I cuddled into them without shame. "Do I need to?"

Beelzebub huffed as he dropped onto the opposite couch. "You going to fight angels?"

"She's got weapons," Luke said. "She's a Muse."

"Yeah? And what happens when she's like this? You guys going to hover around her constantly? What do you think will happen to her if Michael catches her alone?"

"She'll drain him," Luke almost growled.

Beelzebub laughed. "He's too smart for that. Isn't a thing she can try that he hasn't already seen at least once."

"So, y'all have aether guns or something?" I asked, turning over so I could see Bel.

"No, we call those smiths. Gunpowder doesn't really do much

to us. It's all about the level of aether. The point is to drain or be drained."

I dropped my head onto the pillow, thinking about that. "But unlike y'all, I can die."

He shrugged. "We tend not to think about that in the rush of the moment. I mean, sure, ripping you apart will kill you, and it might happen if someone gets excited and all, but mostly, they'll want your aether. It's too tempting to risk releasing. They'll drain you dry if they can. That means I'll have to teach you how to keep their hands off you."

"Like self-defense courses?"

He shrugged. "Don't know that one."

"Yes," Luke told me. "Hand-to-hand combat. Most of us learn it while flying as well."

"Well, flying is going to take me a bit. Nick said it's like ten years to make a skin."

Luke leaned back and tossed his legs over the arm of the chair. "For a demon, Sia. Things are a little different for a Muse. Just paint it."

"Seriously?"

He nodded, green eyes gleaming. "Very. You'll have to be on the world you want to use it, but yes. Just like that pencil. Make art, then make it live. I weave, Nick smiths, you create. Don't try to follow our rules, because they don't apply to you."

I groaned and rolled onto my back. "Do all of y'all know about the pencil?"

"Yep," Luke said.

"No," Beelzebub admitted. "Sleeping for a while. Missed that."

Luke explained easily. "Her art falls off the page, real."

"Oh, damn. Holy shit. Fuck yeah." He chuckled. "I'm sure there's more I haven't learned yet, but that's nice. Little Muse, I am so glad you're on our side."

I smiled, snuggling into the blankets. "Me too. Y'all are a lot more fun than the angels. And nice." I yawned. "I like having real friends, even if y'all do want me for my supernatural talents." I blinked, and my eyes didn't want to open again.

"She's out," I heard Luke say softly.

Nick's voice trickled into my mind before sleep took control. "It's about time. Never seen anyone that resilient. Kept waiting for her to pass out on her feet."

"Not her," Beelzebub assured him. "No, that one's tough. She's not the kind that's going to let anything stop her once she sets her mind to it."

*a*fter that, Nick sequestered me in the office, putting me through a crash course of aethersmithing. It made me finally understand why they'd chosen such a massive house. Being locked inside for days at a time? Yeah, a few extra rooms kept me from wanting to kill someone. Even worse, no one around me could die, which took all the fun out of my threats. Thankfully, Nick found something to help me vent my frustrations. He taught me how to create weapons, tiny little things that looked alive and acted sentient. They called them sprites, and they were a lot like the drawings I'd had turn real.

Trusting the wards to prevent any of my creations from leaking out, I made many. We found most of my sprites could only last two hours before they simply dissipated on their own. My mind preferred the fanciful and pretty while Nick's minions were efficient and often horrifying. When we set them on each other, mine were stronger, but not by much. Unfortunately, his were smarter.

It wasn't only life I learned to create, but also objects and patterns. Lots of patterns. He taught me how to ward against unwanted power by creating a shield of aether that would bind where I placed it – a room, my skin, or even a bubble around us – and how to destroy someone else's wards. He didn't instruct like the teachers I was used to. Instead of giving me a step-by-step tutorial, he explained the idea then encouraged my mind to run wild. I learned through trial and error instead of repetition - supposedly, so nothing would inhibit my creativity.

After five long days of creating things, destroying them, and reabsorbing the aether, I was as ready for the next step as I could be. There was only one thing left to do before I could start learning how to cross between worlds. We had to make the binding stones he'd talked about. That way, if I screwed this up, he'd be able to save me.

Opening the top drawer of his desk, Nick turned serious as he pulled out something. His large hands blocked my view, but I saw a chain dangle between his fingers before he gathered it to his palm. Without a word, I lifted my hand. When he finally opened his fingers, a knot of jewelry slipped into my palm.

Two necklaces. Both were large, circular gems mounted plainly on chains made like dense cables. They weren't extravagant, but the stones looked real. One pale blue on a gold chain, the other a deep, vibrant orangey-red hanging from silver. Their surface was cut flat and smooth.

"Where did you get these?" I asked.

"Ordered them. Poppy topaz for you, blue diamond for me. The color is a near-perfect match to our aether." He moved to sit beside me. "There's one last thing to do before I can teach you to walk in the corridor," Nick said.

"Bind the necklaces. And then you can show me how to gather more aether, right?"

His jaw clenched. "That will not happen until you are perfectly stable between worlds. After you can prove that to me, our deal still holds. Just one soul, and then you will wait."

I nodded, excited to be doing something new. "So my first task is learning to walk again. I can do that."

"Yeah." He passed across the large, reddish topaz. "Which means you finally get to seal that."

I took the stone, in awe of not just its beauty but also the price tag I was pretty sure it had come with. "Just imagine my seal and push aether deep into the gem?"

"Into the pattern of the gem," he clarified. "Crystals are a lattice that can be organized. Watch."

He closed his eyes and gripped his pendant tight between two fingers. It took concentration. Nick's mind was locked on the stone, his breathing slow and steady. Tendrils of aether wove through his fingers, centered around the gem in his hand. The colors swirled from almost white to a dark midnight blue. He didn't need to explain. I could tell exactly what he was doing. With the strength of his will, he pushed his life force into the stone, reorganizing the crystals to match his own pattern. The gem had just become a separate part of himself, like DNA left behind at a crime scene. It was him, but not tied to his body, like he'd sculpted it with his mind.

When he was done, he opened his eyes and met mine. "Now make that one match your vision of yourself."

My vision of myself. That sounded so nice and simple, but it wasn't. All my life, my vision of myself had been layered with responsibilities, impressions others had of me, and a litany of things I'd never quite measured up to. But that wasn't what he meant. He meant the way it felt to be me. The knowledge of my space, my form, and my crazy way of thinking. That silence we have when we aren't quite asleep and aren't yet awake. That was what I felt like, and with everything I'd learned so far, I pushed it toward the gem, keeping the swirling pattern of my seal ever at the front of my mind.

In my hand, I felt the stone warm as the molecules shivered to realign. It was still a topaz, but deep in the heart of it, I could feel the space where my symbol was growing and the trickle of my own life surged to fill the gap left behind. Smiling, I leaned back and opened my eyes.

"I think I did it."

"Yes," Nick agreed in a soft purr. "You did it beautifully."

I pushed my topaz toward him on the desk. "So now, I get yours and you get mine?"

"If you're still ok with that?" Catching my hand, he dropped the pale blue diamond into my palm. "This is the key to my aether, Sia."

Something in his voice made it clear this wasn't a casual gift from him. I ran my thumb across the jewel. It was larger than a quarter, the seal of Satanael visible under the surface. I knew how protective he was of letting anyone have access to his wards, but he'd already given me that ability. Strangely, my gut said that wasn't all.

"So not something you give easily?" I asked.

"To you, yes."

"But to others?"

"I've never given a binding stone to anyone," he admitted.

"Why?" I tilted my head. "I'm not being belligerent, Nick. I can see this is a big deal, and I don't want to make more of it than I should, or less."

He smiled and nodded, relaxing a bit. "I forget how little you know of us sometimes. Binding stones are only given to those you trust completely, without any reservations. It's the one thing that can compel an outworlder to obey. I can only assume the same will be true for a Muse."

"But it means more than that, doesn't it?" I could tell from his tone.

He nodded slowly. "Demons do not make relationships like humans. We have the ability to protect our friends and lovers, even provide for them beyond anything your society can imagine simply because we are not tied to a single world. Our promises are fleeting because your lives are so short."

"Ok?"

He looked into my eyes for a moment, then turned his gaze to the stone in my hand. "That? There's no bigger commitment I can offer you than to give you that. It's a promise that I simply cannot break, not while you have that stone. For as much weight as humans put on marriage, that is more. It's trust made corporeal and given freely. If there's anything in all the worlds that can force me to obey, it's that diamond."

I closed my fingers around the pendant as my stomach flipped and a wave of butterflies exploded inside it. "What are you saying, Nick?"

He blew out his tension in a quick breath. "For the first time in my very long life, I have nothing to hide, Sia. You do not judge me for things I did thousands of years ago. You don't even flinch away from the knowledge that I'm the Angel of Death or the supposed Lord of Hell." He wrapped his strong hand around mine. "You even like my horns." He smiled at that, daring to look up into my face. "You make me feel like a man, a very perfect, desirable, wonderful man, not a monster. And you are beautiful, intelligent, filled with a life that most humans could only wish to embrace. You are everything I have ever wanted, all wrapped up into one small, vivacious, and very powerful package." He licked his lips quickly, like his mouth had suddenly gone dry. "I'm giving you that stone because I have no reason to ever lie to you."

I'd heard men make romantic speeches before. Most had wanted to talk me into bed, some had believed it at the time, not realizing what love was, but none had said it with as much feeling and understanding as Nick did. I also heard very clearly the three words he didn't say, but could have, and it made my heart pound hard and heavy. All I could do was clasp his diamond close to my heart.

"Really?" I whispered.

He nodded, a hint of worry in his eyes.

I let my thumb swipe across the gem that proved he was falling for me even if he wasn't ready to say it. "So this is a really big deal?"

"It is." He flicked his eyes to mine. "Will you wear it?"

"Of course!" I twisted, simultaneously lifting the hair off my neck. "Put it on me?"

"Gladly." He took the chain and reached around my neck to carefully secure the clasp, then kissed the side of my throat. "You do know that both demons and angels will act as if I own you now, right?"

"Am I not yours?" I leaned over to the desk, grabbing my topaz. "You found me, protected me, have been training me, and showed this whole new world to me. I'm yours, *Satanael*, completely and totally, and I wouldn't want it any other way. Let them think of me as whatever they want. I know you don't." I let the pendant dangle from my hand. "You even designed my stone to look perfect on a man, so will you wear it?"

He nodded. "Until you ask for it back."

I giggled as I leaned around his neck, securing it to him. "Not for a million years, at least."

He reached up and caught my wrist. "Will you live that long with me?" he begged.

I shrugged, unable to wipe the girlish grin from my face. "I'm gonna try. There are a few angels who have other plans, but yeah, Nick. I plan to see the sun grow large and red, find a way to another planet that is perfect for life, and figure out if all these crazy rules apply there as well. And when I get bored? I'll just change the world, right?"

"Exactly, but first, you need to learn to walk the corridors."

I nodded, the thought making me nervous yet excited while the thrill of Nick's declaration still bounced in my chest. "What happens if I, I dunno, fall or something?"

Nick touched the necklace he wore. "Then I'll save you. We'll start slow." He stood, holding out a hand to me. "And we *will* stay inside the house. The wards on this place extend into the corridor.

I removed the ones for the winds so you could learn to do this without fear of angels, but you're only safe inside these walls."

"Ok." I took a deep, nervous breath then pulled myself up, my fingers touching his. "So how do I slip across?"

"That's the last lesson. First," he tugged, shifting us both between worlds, his hand firmly on mine, "you need to understand what this is."

"The corridor?"

"Yeah." Death's mouth smiled from beneath the cowl. "It still shocks me that you never flinch from the change of my skin." He reached up with one hand and pushed the hood back, revealing his demonic blue face, crowned in horns, with the stars of his eyes gleaming. "Now do you see why I wouldn't show you?"

"No." I bit my lip to hold in a giggle. "Could have saved us a whole lot of explaining. I still think you're lovely. Even better blue than all flesh-colored."

He chuckled, the sound so pure and perfect, and stepped closer. "Focus, my little dove. This is where the atoms of one realm mix with those from another and the strings change pitch. Matter leaches through the walls, tumbles against the material from the world beside us, and it all tries to stabilize. The feeling when you pass through is your body shedding everything from Earth, replacing it with the material from here. It is nearly instantaneous and painless. One carbon atom from Earth for one aether filled carbon from the corridor, and if you moved into Vesdar, it would change again to a carbon from Vesdar with the altered pitch native to that plane complete with aether-dense molecular components."

"Atoms are different too?"

His lips split wide enough to show that perfect line of teeth. "Yes, everything changes. Chemically speaking, Earth is the more simple world. The outer realms are complex, with isotopes and extra particles to balance the changes. Water acts one way on Earth, but behaves just a bit differently on Daemin."

"How?"

The stars swirled in his eyes each time he blinked. "It doesn't expand when frozen, as a start. The variables we live in – like gravity or the speed of light – are just slightly different in each universe, and that means the nature of reality has to change to compensate."

I nodded, trying to comprehend the altered physics. "So, why are there winds in the corridors, and why can't I really feel it now?"

With his free hand, he gestured around us. "The wind is a current caused by the influx of particles. Now, look at what *isn't* there."

Where his hand pointed, I saw it. At first, it was subtle, but once I noticed the difference, it got easier to see. Like those prints that had three-dimensional images hidden when your eyes were unfocused, the shield around us was the same. Pieces of the world had been asked to stand still, bracketed by hair-thin lines of nothing, giving the structure form.

"You made a pattern out of the lack of aether?"

"Perfect. Now, do you know why?"

"Not a clue!"

He laughed and spun me to face the world around us without letting go. "Look at the pattern, little dove. Don't memorize. Conceptualize."

I looked. It was complex and interlocking, buffering the wind like a screen would, letting some through, but not enough to knock him from his feet. I couldn't understand why it would only serve him, and then I saw what he meant. Over and over, the pattern was made of tiles. They locked together, twisted and angled in such a way as to make a whole, but each tile was the same. It was the symbol on the innermost circle of his seal.

"It only recognizes you?"

He made an affirmative sound. "Because it *is* me. Now, we need to teach you to do the same thing."

"How?"

He wrapped his arms around me. Each of his hands held one of my wrists and his chest pressed close to my back. When I turned to look at him, he laughed, tilting his head quickly to prevent his horn from catching the side of my face.

"Big, blue, and still very solid," he teased.

"I'll figure it out eventually."

"I know." He kissed my cheek. "Now, think of your seal and the symbol inside it. Yours is easier since it's so well balanced. Just lock the spirals of that symbol together so it makes links." His fingers guided my hands, one making a curve, the other drawing an imaginary swirl into the hook. "Imagine it in your mind, just like with the shields we worked on earlier, then relax and release it. Make it only large enough for your fingertips to touch."

It took a few tries before I managed to make gaps in the world around me, like glass blocks to buffer the current. The first time I succeeded, Nick waved it away almost immediately, telling me I had it backwards before forcing me to do it again. So I did it again, then one more time, and yet again, until he said it was finally good enough.

"Ok," he breathed, his voice tight. "That's good, dove. You ready to try it?"

I turned to look at him, careful not to hit his horns this time. "How many people fall their first time?"

"Most." His voice dripped with warning.

"And they were immortal, right?" When he nodded, my throat tightened. "So, what happens if I get blown away?"

"Then I will catch you," he swore. "It will take a few minutes, so do *not* panic, but I will catch you, Sia. Just keep that image in the back of your mind, like a buffer for the winds, and you'll be ok. I won't let anything happen to you."

I nodded, looking at the gaps I'd made. "How many people die from this?"

"Demons can't die, nor angels."

"K." I pulled my arm to my face, his hand still twined around my wrist, and kissed the back of his forearm. "Nick, you'd better not let me fall too far."

"You'll be fine. You can't do amazing things if you can't do this. Think of it as Muse puberty."

I laughed, feeling some of the tension drain out, and checked the pattern again. "Ok. So, do I just let go?"

"Yes." He turned me to face him, looking at the space around me, shifting his hand to rest inside mine. "Baby steps, my little Muse."

I let go with my right hand first, but the world felt no different. My heart pounded from the warnings they'd repeated. Over and over, they told me to never let go in the corridor, that it was too dangerous, and that humans couldn't stand in the winds between worlds. I swallowed away my fears and loosened my fingers, focusing on the pattern, then gently lifted my hand free.

Once my contact with Nick was broken, I could feel the currents myself. They teased the symbols of my aether, my identity, but it held, flexing in the flow like a net. Slowly, I smiled, realizing I was doing it. I was standing on my own, touching nothing but the ground.

"Take one step," Nick said. "Just one, and keep the pattern with you."

I nodded, my mind fixed on the interlocked swirls, and stepped. When my foot left the ground, the world swayed, like someone had rippled the sheet of reality. The rules of the corridor were so different from that of time and space. I staggered, and Nick reached out, but I caught my balance before we touched. I heard him sigh in relief as I tried to walk again, feeling like a child trying out her legs for the first time.

First one foot, then the other, I took a pace forward, finding the ground and meeting it without the world floating away. Secure in my balance, I looked up and grinned, gesturing around me. "I just walked the corridor! It's like a spacewalk, but cooler."

"That it is," he agreed, offering his hand.

Feeling very proud of something that sounded so simple, I took it, not shocked at all when he tugged me back to Earth's reality. His blue skin tanned and his horns faded away, the cloak blending to a simple t-shirt, but I was excited enough not to care. Nick was beautiful regardless of his form, and I had just taken my first steps between worlds all on my own!

"So that's good, right?" I asked.

He sank into the chair and sighed deeply. "That's fucking amazing, Sia." He looked up, a twisted smile on his lips. "I just forgot to mention one little thing."

"What?"

"Never, in the history of humanity, has any human managed to walk in the corridor without being lost."

"What?!"

He nodded. "Luke and I talked about it a lot. We can think of three Muses who probably tried. All three knew about the other worlds and simply vanished one day." He paused, glancing up at my face. "The winds will tear a human apart if you don't have someone able to catch you. Without that stone, *finding* you to catch you would take a miracle. Distance doesn't work the same in the corridor as what you're used to."

"But..." I couldn't find the words. I didn't know if I was pissed, shocked, or horrified. "You..."

He tapped the necklace. "I could have found you. It's not that fast of a thing, and they didn't have a mentor. Humans last for months between the worlds, slowly wasting away. With this, I would have been able to catch you in minutes."

"Why didn't you tell me?" Shocked. That was the emotion I decided to go with.

He rubbed a shaking hand across his mouth. "Because you do better when you aren't afraid."

"And has that little theory of catching someone been proven?"

He nodded. "A few times. Any human can be caught in the currents. Luke slipped through the veil and saw a man tumbling toward him, so reached out and snagged his arm. It was a freak thing, and if he hadn't caught the poor soul, his body would have tumbled across the mirror of the world. So, he pushed back to his home, tugged him back to Earth, and started these crazy myths about zombies or some shit."

"How'd the guy end up in the corridor?" I was horrifically fascinated.

Nick lifted his eyebrow and looked up at me. "Do you have to ask?"

"Angels." I nodded. "Probably some punishment?"

"I'd guess. That, or he was just foolish enough to pull away when they tried to gather slaves."

I took a long, deep breath, feeling elated and worried all at the same time, probably like someone who'd just finished her first skydive. With a nervous chuckle, I claimed a spot in Nick's lap, wrapping my arms around his neck as I pressed my head to his shoulder.

"Ok. So I lived through that. No one's really done that before?"

A laugh barked out before he could stop it. "Human, you imp. I'm pretty sure I'm still someone!"

"You know what I meant."

"None that we know of."

"So why'd you let me try?" I leaned back to see his face, not surprised at all to find him smiling.

"Because you're stronger than any demon or angel I know. There's no reason you couldn't do it." He shrugged. "That, and you said you wanted to reap the dead. It's kind of an important part of that unless you want me holding your hand the whole time."

"I might." I cocked my head to the side. "I mean, since you're so worried about me killing off sick, old, and dying people."

"Then I'll hold your hand." He reached up to trace the line of my face. "But I hope you can do this. I don't ever want to see you hurt, but if you can reap?" He sighed, his lips lifting at the thought. "You can pull so much aether, my little dove, that you could raise a legion. *All* the legions. You could secure the veils. You could stop the atrocities the angels are doing."

"Why me?"

His eyes looked between each of mine. "I don't know. All I know is that you're like a Muse, an angel, and a demon, all at the same time. You do things I can't even fathom, and you do it unconsciously. You are the answer to every prayer we demons have dared for the last million years."

"But no pressure or anything," I teased.

"No pressure," he promised.

32

*S*ince I'd managed to stand on my own two feet in the corridor, Nick insisted I also learn to step through without assistance. Thankfully, that was easier. I'd already come close a few times on my own – and managed at least once. Granted, it took a few hours of practice, but each time I tried, walking became easier. At first, Nick was right there, ready to grab me if I stumbled, but he eventually realized I had this figured out. The sun was setting outside when he declared me good enough to do it on my own, but only between the corridor and Earth.

"So, does that mean I can make it to the living room?" I begged.

He chuckled, well aware That was where the rest of the guys were hanging out. "You've done enough for one day. The guys will be just as excited tomorrow."

"Nick!" I whined. "I've been busting my ass to learn all of this as fast as I can so you'll let me out of Muse jail. C'mon, *please?*"

"Dove, no matter what, you still have a big arrow in the veils pointing out your every move. Being able to walk in the corridor isn't the only thing you need to learn. Unless we can get you into

Daemin, you aren't safe outside the wards." His voice was sympathetic, but the set of his jaw said he wasn't about to budge on this.

"So how do we stop that? The veil bending?"

"We figure out why you're bending them." Then he shook his head as if clearing his thoughts. "But it's still not safe."

"I am *not* made of glass!" I snapped. "I get it, you want to protect and pamper me. It's sweet. Honestly, it really is. It's also going to make my puny little unevolved brain snap into a billion pieces, and your superweapon will be nothing more than a drooling moron. I can't sit here studying for years at a time!"

"Oh."

"Oh?" I had no idea what he meant. "Nick?"

With a groan, he leaned back in his chair. "You work so hard to learn everything I show you. Sometimes, it's hard to remember that you live faster than I do and a week is a big deal."

"It's almost been two. Half a month since I've stepped outside this house!"

He huffed around a wry smile. "Exactly my point. How about if we mix up your training a bit, and give you something besides aethersmithing all day, every day?"

"I still want to go out, see people, enjoy the sunshine, and do all those normal things that crazy artists kinda *like*."

"I can get Luke to help me shield the yard. I'd planned to teach you how to do it, but you're not quite that adept at working systematic patterns yet. If you're that desperate to just get outside, I'm sure he'll help. It won't be as safe as the house, and I don't want you out there alone, but at least it's a *little* more freedom."

I looked at him pointedly. "I hear Daemin's nice this time of year. If I can stand in the corridor..."

Nick lifted a hand in surrender. "That's the plan. The problem is that every spare second I've had has gone to teaching you. It hasn't given me the time to prepare the weaving that will key you in. Never mind that the second you step outside these wards, every angel in five realms will know and come running. Sia, not everything can be solved by simply bending aether. Sometimes we have to do a little more complicated stuff like find a way to trick the veils long enough to key you in or plan for a serious battle. Just a bit longer, little dove. I promise."

I knew he was trying, and I honestly felt a little guilty about pushing. Every day since Luke had flown me back from Angelis, Nick had worked non-stop, aware the angels wouldn't be kept out of this house forever. Not only did he need to train me, but he also had to manage the protections on the property. The confinement might be driving me crazy, but Nick was working twice as hard, and it showed. Between the constant worry and the lack of sleep, he had to be exhausted. And all of it was to keep me safe. If he was willing to give me a little longer leash, I'd take it and be grateful.

"I guess this means I should take Beelzebub up on his offer, huh?" I asked, showing I wasn't going to push anymore.

Nick's brow creased. "What offer?"

"He said he could teach me to fight."

For the first time in my life, I saw Satan himself truly and completely surprised. His eyes widened just a bit and his mouth softened. "Beelzebub said that?"

I nodded. "After you sealed me, he said I should learn because angels won't fight back like I'm used to."

"Beelzebub?"

"Yeah. Big guy, dark-skinned, bit of a pig, but not the fun type like Sam? Pretty sure you know him. He lives in the green room?"

Nick blinked a few times. "Yeah, no. Um, it's just that he doesn't train anyone. Not unless they have a lot of potential."

"So, is this combat training a big deal?"

Nick made a gesture, but I couldn't figure out if it meant yes or no. "Deflecting aether, avoiding physical touches, and quick defensive spells. Beelzebub trained me, and I'm pretty sure he trained Sam. He was formed beside a Chajin – big nasty beast with lots of teeth. It chewed on him a bit, he healed, it chewed, he healed, until he figured out how to stop it long enough to get away." Nick chuckled at that. "See, on Daemin, you can't just kill something. Everything regenerates and, well, we all heal pretty damned fast."

I tapped Nick's nose. "Then we need to figure out something to keep me from dying too soon. I mean, another car accident and your little Muse is toast."

"Bel and Sam can help with that." He reached out and caught my hand, holding it gently. "How to slip at the last minute is a big part of what they do. And if showing off will make you feel a little less trapped -" He smiled at me. "- then you can use the corridor to get to the living room. Ok?"

"Really?" I gasped, trying to imagine the surprise on the faces of my friends. "Thank you, Nick!" I wrapped my arms around his neck and kissed him soundly.

He chuckled and eased me back so he could stand. "Give me thirty seconds, then step through. If you're not there in five minutes, I'm hunting you down. If you get blown away, just grab that necklace and scream my real name – and I *will* find you." Then he walked out the door.

I couldn't believe he was really going to let me do this. Waiting, I counted down the seconds in my head. This would be my first spacewalk – well, corridor walk – without a babysitter hovering over me. I was a little nervous, but it was the excitement kind, not fear. After living with three demons and an angel, my priorities had already started to shift. Everything I'd spent my life working for didn't matter. Now, walking between worlds was something to brag about.

I didn't push. That was what they called it when they traveled quickly across space. I just walked, looking at the grey of dead materials along the walls as I made my way toward the brilliant colors of the live bodies. Going for the most impact, I moved right in front of the TV then stepped back across to Earth, seeming to appear right in front of them.

Beelzebub wrinkled his forehead briefly, then his face lit into a massive grin. Sam just stared. Nick leaned over the back of the sofa, a beer in his hand, looking very proud of me, but Luke? He surged to his feet, his mouth open, then looked at Nick before whipping his head back to me.

"Sia?" he gasped. "How far?"

"Just from the study." I shrugged it away.

That didn't seem to dim Luke's shock at all. He looked back to Nick. "You just let a human walk from one end of the house to the other *in the corridor?*"

"Yeah," Nick said, letting the smile show. "She's been at it all afternoon. I even pushed her once – lightly – and she didn't fall."

Luke whooped excitedly and took the two steps between us, wrapping me in a tight embrace. "I'm so proud of you!" He lifted my feet off the ground, rocking me back and forth. "Do you know what this means? I finally get to buy you a drink!"

Nick let out a long grunt. "Not quite. She's still got a target pointing at her from the heavens, so can't leave the house."

"But..."

Nick shook his head. "Sorry, Luke. On the upside, I'm going to let her start working with Sam and Bel in the yard. If you want, you can take over her aether lessons while I try to find a way to shield her?"

Luke tossed a proud smile my way. "Definitely. I want to see if we can teach our little Muse how to mind-fuck people."

"Yeah?" I asked, thrilled to have something new and different to look forward to. "Does it work on demons?"

"I'll volunteer," Sam said. "Angels can't compel us like they can inworlders, but we're not completely immune to them either."

"And you're helping me teach her to block," Bel told Sam, then jerked his chin at me. "Go put on something you can move in. I believe they are called yoga pants?"

"I like yoga pants," Sam agreed.

Nick groaned. "Everyone likes yoga pants. Dove, Bel just wants to check out your ass."

"Wait." I looked at each of them, one after the other. "You mean now? I can actually go outside?"

"Yes!" Nick agreed. "Don't rush, but go change. It'll give Luke and me time to throw an aether net over the yard."

With a squeal of excitement, I turned, scurrying for the stairs, intending to jog up them. The guys grinned at me, but they didn't understand. They'd all made at least one trip out of the house since I'd been locked in – even Beelzebub – and I was so ready for a change of pace. Even if that meant getting tossed around for self-defense.

I wasn't even halfway up the stairs before I heard Bel speak up, but it wasn't to me. "Nice necklace," he said.

Luke chuckled right after. "Hers too. Strong bindings."

"Happy for ya, man. About time you found a girl like that." That was Sam, and it sounded like someone was slapping someone else's shoulder.

Damned demons noticed everything, but this time, I honestly didn't mind.

───────────

WEARING YOGA PANTS – AS REQUESTED – AND A TIGHT-FITTING shirt, I made my way back downstairs to find the house empty. The silence was a bit eerie after the constant bustle of people for so long, but I wasn't worried. The guys were outside. I turned for the front door they always used but didn't make it more than a handful of steps before I heard someone's voice. It was coming from the opposite direction.

The problem with living in a gorgeous Victorian mansion was

that it did not have an open layout. Nope, every room had been designed for a purpose and organized for privacy. In other words, I had to weave through half the house before I made it to the back door. The one that was standing wide open to reveal a lush green yard surrounded by a very tall cedar privacy fence. In the waning light, it looked like my own personal utopia.

"My kennel?" I asked, leaning against the door frame.

Sam waved for me to come closer. "It is safe to cross the threshold," he announced proudly.

Or it was about to be, at any rate. The moment I was on the back porch, I saw Luke and Nick standing in the middle of the yard, hands clasped, with their foreheads touching. The translucent wafts of aether moving around them proved they were still working. It also meant I got a chance to just enjoy the view.

Nick was the taller of the two, but not by much. Mostly, he just looked bigger because of his bulk. He probably had a good thirty pounds on Luke, and it was nothing but muscle. That didn't mean Luke was a weakling. Not by any stretch of the imagination. In all honesty, they looked like the kind of perfect couple that belonged on the front of some gay or ménage romance novel. Nick's dark against Luke's light, and both were sexy as hell.

Literally.

"You're drooling," Sam said softly as he moved to stand beside me.

I smacked at his arm. "Do you blame me?"

"Nope. They're both rather impressive specimens."

I scoffed. "All of y'all are. It's kinda not fair. We humans spend all our lives trying to eat right, stay in shape, choose the right clothes, and everything else to impress the opposite sex, but you?" I let my eyes rake over him, trying not to show how much I enjoyed the view. "You eat anything you want and play video games all day."

He leaned back so I could get a better look. In his workout clothes, it wasn't hard to imagine each and every muscle on his body. Not even the baggy pants could hide the lean lines of his hips or the flatness of his waist. Reminding myself that he'd invented the idea of seduction, I blinked my eyes away.

"And burn it all weaving magic, fighting off angels, and flying." He grinned and mimicked me, letting his eyes roam down my body. "I mean, doesn't look like it's been hurting *you* any, either."

"Quit," I hissed.

He ducked his head a little to see my face. "Are you blushing?"

"Sam!" I pressed both hands to my cheeks and turned my back on him. "I said quit."

The problem was that my great evasion technique pointed me right at Beelzebub. He took one look at me, bobbed his head, and glanced over my shoulder at Sam. "She's blushing."

From the middle of the yard, Nick called over, "She doesn't like it when you point it out."

Evidently, they were done with whatever protections they'd put up because both Nick and Luke were making their way back to the porch. Naturally, that just made my face turn even warmer. Yep, the joys of being fair-skinned. It didn't take much and everyone could see my face light up.

"You done?" Bel asked.

Nick nodded. "It's not impenetrable, but there's a layer of aether netting about twenty feet up and all the way around. Should be enough to keep them from grabbing her."

"And low enough they won't look," Sam added, smiling like he approved. "So if one tries to slip in from above, he'll get a real nasty surprise."

"Exactly," Luke agreed. "Put a few confusion wards and distractions on it as well."

"Sia," Nick said, climbing the stairs to stand before me. "If the guys say to get inside, don't ask. Do it. Questions can always come later, do you understand?"

"Promise," I swore. "Inside, right to the study, then wait."

"That's my girl." He bent and kissed me. When he pulled back, he looked at Sam. "Don't let Bel hurt her. She won't complain, but she's still human. If one of you breaks her, even a little, I will tear your wings off myself."

Sam lifted his hands. "Can't promise she won't bruise, but nothing bad."

"No bruises," Nick insisted.

Sam thrust a hand toward me. "Redhead. Hello? I look at her wrong and she might."

"Bruises are fine," I insisted.

Nick sighed. "No hurting. I will not debate semantics before leaving you flightless."

"Understood," Sam mumbled.

Then Nick turned his attention to Beelzebub. "And you?"

"I understand, Satan."

"Good. Have fun, little dove."

I watched him head inside and close the door with my mouth hanging open. "He just threatened you two?"

"Uh, yeah." Sam gestured for me to head onto the grass. "Sia, he's kinda a big deal. I mean, he's a great guy and all, but there's a reason Nick calls the shots."

"He's the strongest of all the demons," Bel added, sounding awed. "Satan is the only one of us that has never been defeated by the angels."

"Never taken a nap," Sam clarified. "And it's Nick, Bel. Can't use the other name in this day and age. It fell out of favor."

"He hates Nick."

I shook my head. "He said he likes it."

"He used to hate it," the big guy insisted.

"Until *she* liked it," Sam pointed out. "Trust me, man. He'd prefer you called him Nick."

"I'll try. I'm just used to the other." Then Beelzebub gestured for me to come closer. "Why does he use an angel phrase to adore you, Muse?"

I stepped before him as directed. "Huh?"

He used his foot to kick mine apart, correcting my stance. "He calls you his dove. It's from the Song of Songs. The Bible. Why did he pick that?"

"I don't know," I admitted as Bel made his way around me. "Luke wanted me to look it up, but I refused to take his deal."

"Hips back and bend your knees slightly." Then he looked at Sam. "Why does he use it?"

"*Do not hand over your dove to beasts. Do not forget the life of the afflicted,*" Sam quoted. "Not quite right, but Nick saw her and thought it fit. If the angels are the beasts and we're the afflicted? He's called her that since he first saw her because he didn't know her name."

I turned. "Really?"

Bel groaned in frustration. "I almost had you ready. Back the way you were!"

"Sorry," I yelped, trying to return to how he'd been posing me. "Like this?"

"Bent knees!"

Sam just chuckled under his breath. "Really, Sia. Now focus, or Bel will send you back inside."

He chuckled. "I prefer spankings."

"Uh..."

Sam cleared his throat, but I could tell he was struggling not to laugh. "At her age, it's not typically used for punishment, you know."

Bel just grinned, white teeth hard to miss against his dark skin. "Yeah. I know."

Yep, that was a very good way to get me to pay attention. For the next half hour, I learned exactly how I was supposed to stand to defend myself properly. That was it, but it wasn't exactly easy. Bel insisted I pose the exact same way, then he pushed me off balance, growling when I stepped back to keep from staggering. Each time my foot moved, he told me I'd just been pulled into the corridor and was lost. Then he made me do it all over again.

I complained. Of course, I did, but I didn't honestly mind. For the first time in almost two weeks, I was finally getting to do something besides pull out my life and push it around. My brain needed the break, my body needed the exercise, and my spirit needed the challenge. By the time we were done, I could feel it in every muscle I still had left.

Even better, Bel wanted to make this a regular thing.

33

The next morning, I woke up late. Nick was still asleep beside me. For a moment, I laid there looking at him, trying to wrap my mind around the changes that had come so fast. The hot guy in Calculus was the Grim Reaper. The Grim Reaper was Satan. Satan was a mostly normal guy, all things considered. Even so, that meant my drug-induced hallucinations were actually real. Then there was the big one. Someone thought I was beautiful enough to spend the next million years with.

It was surreal.

Day to day, those things all seemed normal. When the next task needed to be done, there wasn't any spare time to think about the fantastical nature of all this, but here I was, lying in bed with the man of my dreams – and he was supposedly a nightmare. Talk about the ultimate bad boy. But while I knew that, I also knew better. This was Nick. Not once had I seen a cruel bone in his body. At least not toward me.

Yet with the sunlight illuminating his face, it was hard to believe this was real. It felt like any moment I'd wake up and realize I wasn't really special. That no one cared about my struggles. I was just the crazy orange-haired girl with a sordid past. The one people laughed at behind their hands. The confused child no one had wanted – except my demons.

That was when Nick opened his eyes, smiling when he caught me looking. "Hey, beautiful," he whispered.

"Morning."

"Mm." He snuggled closer. "Those look like deep thoughts. Wanna share?"

I ducked my head back into the pillow. "Was just trying to decide if I was lucky or insane."

"Yeah?" He pulled himself higher. The blankets slid down in the process, revealing the deep V along the inside of his hip. "So what's the verdict?"

"Lucky," I whispered as I reached for those hard ridges across his stomach. "Even if I'm insane, if this is the way my mind broke, then I'm one very lucky girl."

Chuckling, he rolled over me, pushing me onto my back. "And here I thought I was the lucky one." His mouth slid along the side of my neck, leaving dampness from his kisses.

"Maybe it's a mutual lucky," I teased, pulling his hips closer.

The demon obeyed, sliding himself along the side of my leg so his mouth could reach mine. He kissed me quickly. "Nope. I'm the one who found not only a miracle, but also a woman he can't keep his hands off." Another quick kiss as his palm slid across my belly to clasp my waist, proving his point. "I think this was your devious plan all along. Get close enough that I'd be pulled in by your womanly magnetism."

"Well, then I hope you think magnets are sexy." I reached for his mouth, but Nick pulled back.

"A magnet..." he mumbled. A second later, his eyes snapped to mine. "That's it! You're brilliant. A brilliant, amazing, inescapable magnet!"

Before I knew what was happening, he rolled off me and kicked his legs over the side. Almost in a daze, he shoved himself out of bed, snagged a pair of pants from his dresser and headed to the door while he tried to find which way was up. Clearly, he was a man on a mission.

"Nick?"

"A magnet," he said, glancing back. "I know how to fix this."

"Damn it, Nick!" I sat up, holding the covers to my chest. "I don't care what is going on in your head, or if you happen to think that a four hundred year dry spell is no big deal, but if you walk out of this room right now, I'm *going* to be pissed."

He paused with his hand on the door and chuckled. "Saying you want something?" When he looked back, his smile was devilish.

"I thought I was being pretty clear about that, yeah."

He tossed his pants onto the floor and turned to me. "And what would that be, little dove?"

I gestured in the vicinity of his quickly rising interest. "Dick. Right here. Right now. Whatever devious plot you're about to concoct can wait long enough for you to wake me up the right way."

Two steps brought him back to the foot of the bed, and from the gleam in his eye, I knew we were back on the same page. Without a word, Nick grabbed my leg and flipped me onto my stomach. The same time his weight dented the mattress, his other arm pushed under my belly, pulling me to my knees. Then I felt the fist in my hair.

"Grab the headboard, Sia," he whispered into my ear. "And hold on."

Oh, I obeyed. As my hand closed around the ornate wood frame, he tugged my head to the side and kissed my neck, hard. I was completely at his mercy and loving every second of it. Before now, Nick had always been so gentle and careful, but I wouldn't break. Over and over, I'd done my best to prove it to him. It seemed he finally believed me.

The tip of his tongue traced the edge of my earlobe. His breath was heavy against my skin, but it was the other hand, the one pressed a lot lower, that had my complete attention. Thick and strong, it slid down the center of my body until it met dampness. Then he pressed against the knot of nerves, sending sparks straight through my body. I gasped but couldn't writhe, pinned perfectly between his hands and his hard body.

"I like it when you moan," he growled in my ear. "I like it more when you buck."

So he pressed again. I couldn't have stopped it if I wanted to. My pelvis pressed into the wonderful pressure, seeking more. He gave it. Shifting his hand, he thrust two fingers into me, leaving his thumb to tease my clit. The whole time, his mouth worshiped the back of my neck, moving slowly down to my shoulder. When I tried to look at him, to press my lips to his, that fist in my hair stopped me, holding me prisoner. This time, Death would have things his way.

"Nick," I begged.

"Mm." He stroked my core again, making a deep, pleased noise when I sighed. "Moan, dove. Tell me what you want, or show me, but you don't get to start this and expect me to do all the work."

I couldn't bring myself to beg. Even thinking about saying what I wanted was just too much. A million thoughts flashed through my mind while his hand continued to tease me higher, but none of them sounded sexy, and the idea of saying it was terrifying. Nope, that was a line I couldn't quite cross, but he'd given me options. Pressing my hips back, I made his arm follow until my ass felt something long, thick, and so very solid. Then I tilted my pelvis, sliding along his length. If that wasn't showing, I sure as hell didn't know what was.

"Is that what you want?" he breathed against my shoulder. "Tell me, Sia. Do you want me to fuck you like this?"

"Yes."

He chuckled. "No, my sweet little dove. That's not good enough. You don't get to demand my attention and then turn shy.

Pick a side. Are you a bad girl who wants the demon, or are you a quiet, well-mannered little lady? You can't have it both ways."

I pulled against my hair to see his face. "You know what I want."

"Mhm. You're so wet in my hand. The problem is that I'm not sure you know how to tell me." Sliding his fingers out, he found that knot again and swirled his fingertips around it. I moaned, making him press just a little harder. "That's my girl. I can make you happy just like this. Wake you up just fine, exactly like you told me. Is that what you want?"

"I want you to fuck me," I snapped.

That damp hand withdrew to grab my hip and, before I knew what was happening, I felt him pressing at my opening. "Now *that* I can do."

Then he thrust. There was no gentle tease, no slowly filling me. Nick slammed his hard dick deep into my body, and I gasped in pleasure, arching my back to take him. When his balls rested against my flesh, he paused, letting my body adjust, then he slowly withdrew. I moaned, trying to follow, to keep him with me.

"Hold the headboard," he reminded me, using that fistful of hair to push me closer. "Both hands, Sia, and don't you dare move them."

The moment I returned my grip to the wood, he released my hair, but I didn't get the chance to think about it. His hips moved. Sometimes slowly, sometimes fast, always just right. And his hands? They roamed across my skin, teasing my lower back, pressing me deeper onto him, or caressing my belly. I couldn't think, only feel, and I didn't want anything else.

My breasts swayed with the pounding, my core pulsed from the friction. Beneath us, the bed protested in soft squeaks, but I didn't care. Let the guys hear. Hell, let the world hear for all I cared. My sweet, gentle man had just become something so much more, and I liked it. Oh, I liked this side of him a lot. It was as if he'd finally started to believe that I wasn't scared of him. Now, I just had to prove I could take it.

He gave me more than any man ever had before. It wasn't just the size or the tempo of our lovemaking, but the attention. Every moan told him what I liked. Every thrust explored my body. He brought me so close, then backed off, only to show me something better. His hips slapped against my rump, the sound of our human flesh too normal for the sensations he was creating, but I loved it. I loved that all I had to do was just hold on and take what he had to give.

"Nick," I panted, feeling the tension in my body growing. "I'm gonna..."

"Say it," he growled.

"I'm gonna cum."

"Yes," he promised, tilting his hips to hit something even more sweet. "Oh, yes, you are."

Then his hand returned to my clit, and I couldn't stop myself. I tensed. I bucked. And, yeah, I came with a grunt that was anything but sexy, but I was too far gone to worry about that. All I could do was hang onto the headboard as my body spasmed in response to his touch, and Nick rode me through it, teasing the waves of pleasure as he swelled and tensed inside me. His groan a moment later proved I wasn't the only one who'd found release.

Then his lips kissed my spine, right between my shoulder blades. "Sia?"

"My knees are rubber."

He chuckled. "And that's a good thing?"

"Mhm." I leaned forward, removing him from my body, then dropped back onto the mattress. "Please tell me I have aethersmithing lessons and not Bel's defensive training?"

"Aetherweaving," he corrected. "Angels weave instead of smith, but yes. I'll tell Sam you need a little break."

I grabbed a pillow and flung it at him. "There's easier ways to brag, Satan."

He caught it and flopped down beside me. "Say it again?"

"What?"

"My name. With a laugh."

"Satan," I teased, rolling into his amazing chest. "With a laugh."

"Imp!" He shoved his fingers into my ribs and wiggled them, sending me into squeals of laughter.

I rolled, trying to get away from the tickling, but it was in vain. When a man twice my size wanted to hang on, there wasn't much I could do but squeal. Not even tickling him back worked. It was like he was impervious.

"Say it now!" he demanded, grinning like a little boy.

"Satan!"

And he stopped. "That's my girl." With a contented sigh, he pulled me against his chest. "We should start the day like this more often."

"Oh yeah. I'm down for that."

"Yeah?"

I nodded against his skin. "Slow and gentle, fast and hard. Yep, either one works." Then I looked up at his face. "And you were on a mission about a magnet."

His brow furrowed then shot up. "Right! I think I know how to block the veils from showing where you are." He kissed the top of my head. "Get dressed and meet Luke in the study whenever you're ready. I'll be locked in the gold room. I think I know how to get you out of the house, dove."

That made me smile. It wasn't that I minded being with him or any of the rest of the guys. Mostly it was just being told I couldn't go out that bothered me. Knowing it was off-limits made me unable to think of anything else and brought the walls of this monstrosity of a home that much closer. I knew it was all mental, but I still wanted to be free, not trapped until I completely mastered my strange abilities.

"I need a shower first," I decided. "Get a little demon off me."

Nick paused with one leg in his pants. "Not quite that easy to get rid of me. I'll just keep coming back."

"So long as you're coming, right?" Giggling at my own bad joke, I headed into the bathroom.

By the time I got out, he was gone. I went to the dresser I'd claimed as mine, found a clean set of yoga pants and matching shirt, then headed downstairs. I didn't even need to worry about coffee. That was one thing that seemed to always be going in this house. So were the roommates.

Beelzebub sat at the table when I walked past, nibbling on a doughnut. Yes, nibbling. He had a tablet sitting before him, one finger hovering as he read through what I could only guess was news. The moment I entered the room, his dark eyes flicked up.

"I left you coffee. Sam said not to ask questions until after you've been given some. Should I make you a cup?"

"Thanks, Bel. I got it." I kept going, but his voice followed me into the kitchen.

"Why do you never let me make you coffee, but you do all of them?"

I placed the cup beside the pot and began pouring. "I don't let them half the time. They just do it."

"Oh."

Something about the way he said that sounded sad. I quickly mixed in my cream and sugar then made my way back to the dining room. "Why?" I asked.

He swiped at the screen. "It says women find small gestures like making her coffee to be endearing. This says that men need to open up. I do neither, so I am trying."

Ok, I had to know. Walking around the table, I looked over his shoulder to see a self-help slide show. One of those top ten things meant to get more clicks. The title at the top? *How to Make Her Like You.*

"Bel? You know this is garbage, right? It's just clickbait."

"Sam said it's good information."

"Sure, if you want a shallow and thoughtless type of girl. I mean, it has a few good points, but it's too simple. Making someone like you is more about being yourself and letting them get to know you. There's no simple recipe for fitting in except to try it." Then I patted his shoulder. "Besides, why would you worry about it? If you want to impress a girl, just go to a bar, buy her a drink, and talk to her. Typically works better than this crap."

"I don't want to impress a girl," he grumbled, swiping to the next page. "I want to make our Muse like me."

"What?" I stepped back to see his face better. "You don't think I like you?"

His head never lifted from the tablet as he mumbled, "You don't let me make you coffee."

I had to bite my lips together to keep from laughing. Beelzebub was a big guy. He made Nick look like nothing more than an athletic college boy. Seeing him pouting was adorable, and a little sad. On impulse, I wrapped my arms around his shoulders and hugged him from the side.

"I don't want to put you out since you're already babysitting me and keeping me safe. But if it means that much to you, then sure, you can make my next coffee."

"And then you'll kiss me, too?"

I jerked back. "What?"

"You kiss Nick. Sam got a kiss, once. He told me. I want to learn how to make a modern woman want to kiss me. It's not as easy as it used to be."

"Bel..." I paused, trying to find the right words. "Hun, I'm dating Nick. Women don't just kiss every guy they're friends with."

"I know, but you're *our* Muse, and I don't want to be the only one you don't like."

"No, it doesn't work like that. Nick is my boyfriend. Sam is just a friend. I only kissed him because Raphael was there and we didn't want him to know I had a clue what was going on. I mean, I've never kissed Luke."

He blew that off. "Don't blame you. No one wants to kiss an

angel. They get excited and their feathers fall out everywhere. Not the same with demons."

"Ok." Unable to think of anything else – and struggling to ignore the visions of Luke as a bad cartoon character with explosive molting – I leaned over to steal his tablet and opened a Google search. Typing in "monogamy," I waited for the screen to load then pushed it back in front of him. "I want you to research this, Bel. It might explain the difference between a girlfriend and a friend that is a girl. I know you've missed a lot, but it's ok to treat us just like everyone else and just hang out without needing to worry about weddings and all of that nonsense, ok?"

"But I liked my wives. I took very good care of them, too." He looked up at me with the biggest brown puppy-dog eyes. "Why does only Nick get to snuggle with you?"

"Because I'm dating him." Clearly, this was only going to go in circles. I decided it was time to seek out a little expert help. "Just read that, Bel. I have lessons."

"Ok." He smiled at me as he reached for the doughnut, and I took the chance to escape.

Nick said Luke would be in the study. I wasn't sure if he could help me, but I had a funny feeling he'd know where Sam was. One of them would be able to convince Bel that I couldn't just date all of them. I had no idea what had happened back in Jesus's time, but whatever it was, that crap wouldn't fly now. We needed to get the big guy up to speed before my protectors decided that having one girl in the house was going to make problems.

"*L*uke?" I asked as I stepped into the room. "How well do you know Bel?"

He didn't look up from the desk. "Well enough. Why?"

That wasn't exactly the response I'd been hoping for. "Um, because I'm not sure he understands what it means that I'm Nick's girlfriend."

"Nope." His mouth struggled not to smile. "Not a term that existed back in his day. Women were girls, available, promised, or married. Those were the only options. Terms like sweetheart and girlfriend imply control of your own dating choices, and when Bel was last awake, women didn't get that option." Then he finally looked up. "Well, unless she ended up catching the attention of a demon."

"Ok?" I could tell there was a story there.

He pushed away whatever he'd been working on and turned to face me. "For as long as I can remember – and that's a very long time – demons have always moved in groups. Legions, they call them. Angels have choirs." He waved that off. "Anyway, while the members of a legion aren't inseparable or anything, as you've seen with us, we do tend to stick pretty close. It's the only way to keep from getting surprised by the enemy."

"And how does this apply to Bel's crush on me?"

He leaned back, looking a little too smug. "Most human mating ideas are based on religion, sexism, generations, and possessions – and the construct is passed down through society. Now, for those of us outside those boundaries, we've made different rules."

"Not helping."

Luke chuckled. "Back when Bel last walked the Earth, women were traded like a commodity. We brought them into *our* culture, not the other way around. Often, we were the wealthiest men around, so fathers were more than happy to sell us their daughters. We just made sure to keep the girls happy, even if that meant not just with us, hence the stories of our hedonistic societies. Well, technically theirs, but I've been with the demons long enough to count as one."

I thought back through all the history they'd shared so far. "Except Nick, right?"

"Uh..." He rubbed at his mouth. "He spent most of his time on Tyrnigg because it was on the front line. He didn't always bring his legion with him. They waited on Earth to lend support and handle the staging area here, building supplies of aether and such. Just like this place. They made a home that served as a safe spot and often got to know the locals while he was doing his thing."

"Luke." I sighed. "Stop trying to be nice. What the hell are you hemming and hawing around?"

"When a woman's husband is gone for years at a time, she gets lonely. A man spending weeks locked away with her might do the same, and who knows if she'll live long enough for one of us to make it back? We don't see a reason to put unrealistic expectations on ourselves or our lovers, so we never have. One man, one woman – that's a societal construct made to secure property inheritance in a species that dies quickly. In case you forgot, we don't die."

"And you think Nick would be just fine with me jumping on, I dunno, you?"

Luke smiled. "Has he ever complained? Look, this is one of those things that if you want to know, you should ask *him*, not me. As for dealing with Beelzebub? Talk to Sam. If anyone can read Bel's mind, he's the one."

He didn't let me push the issue anymore. Instead, Luke moved right into aetherweaving, explaining the theory and asking hard enough questions that I had to let it go. That was how I learned that aetherweaving was a lot like aethersmithing. Mostly.

The main difference was that weaving required a container. Didn't matter if that was a plant, bacteria, or a sentient creature like an angel. So long as there was aether inside it, I could alter things about it. Aethersmithing took the aether from one thing and used it to make something outside the container. Smithing was what I'd been doing so far. Weaving was more subtle and insidious - and often didn't require the container's cooperation. Naturally, I practiced by changing Luke's eyes.

The eerie green had always bothered me. It wasn't the same color most people had. This was closer to spring green, just a little too vivid to come across as anything but colored contacts. Then there was that ring of yellow meant to hypnotize. Sure, it made mind-fucking people easier for him, but Luke seemed a lot more charming with ocean blue eyes. They matched the pretty-boy blonde hair thing he had going on. I debated making them brown to match the other demons, but the blue just looked too good.

And changing his Earth skin wasn't the only thing I could do. According to Luke, altering thoughts was harder with outworlders, but for me, it was impossible. Changing the inner resonance wasn't. Every plane – and the corridors in between – had its own speed of atomic vibration and tone. In other words, I could shift him into the corridor with a thought. Oh, it wasn't easy, and according to Luke, I'd also be able to send him back to other planes once I knew the worlds better, but he was *very* impressed.

Mostly, though, we just worked on shielding. That meant forcing my own aether into a hard shell that couldn't be bent or twisted. Over and over, Luke had me shield myself, then he'd try to make me do something stupid. Yeah, after walking around the study pretending to be a chicken – complete with crowing at the top of my lungs, I got better. Nothing like a little shame between friends to drive the point home.

But this was how Mike had mind-fucked my ex-boyfriend. It was how angels had set some devout country boy up to die as a gas station robber. It was how outworlders had twisted the worldview so everyone ended up hating someone else. I wanted to master not only my defense against it, but also the ability to use it on the people who'd made my life a living hell. Sadly, it seemed I wasn't good at everything.

Then he brought in Sam. Working with a demon was very different from trying to twist an angel. For the first hour, I strained, pushed, and tried everything I could think of to change one thing about Sam. Anything. I got nowhere, and the smug little smile was starting to get on my nerves.

"Sia," Luke finally sighed, "how are you trying to move his aether?"

"The same way I did yours."

He nodded, sucking at an incisor. "Ok, but how did you do that? Nick said I'm not allowed to give you directions, just concepts so you don't learn hard limits. Talk me through this."

"I..." I looked at Sam where he sat on the stool before me. "I think of him as being filled with smoke and I want to push it around. To sculpt with it. Like blowing away a cloud of cigarette smoke."

"Ah." Luke crossed his arms and leaned back. "But he's warded. Maybe that's why you're having so much trouble?"

I paused, immediately seeing a problem. "You are too, but I was at least able to touch you enough for you to feel it."

Sam chuckled. "Because you two are already linked." He

pointed at where my seal was hidden behind my shirt. "That aether in your skin is no different than a pinhole in a Ziploc bag. Not a whole lot can get through it, but some can." Then he tapped his head. "Waterproof, baby."

"Ok..." I let out a deep breath, trying not to be annoyed at this. "So how do I get in?"

As calm as ever, Luke asked, "How would you get into a sealed Ziploc?"

"Smash it?"

Sam quickly lifted a hand, holding me back. "Easy there. Those are my wards we're talking about, sweetheart. Maybe try the zipper, first?"

"Great. Sounds like a plan. Just one problem. I have no clue what would even correlate to the zipper sealing thing. Anyone wanna explain to me how demon wards even work?"

They tried. Both of them did their best to find an analogy that would settle in my mind, but it didn't help. Wards were like insect repellent. They were traffic signs that directed the aether. Oh, and they were even razor wire on the edge of a battlefield. All I got from that was that their fancy magic symbols worked like a wall, keeping things out and other things in.

But aether worked on resonance. It was all about the pitch, or song. So, closing my eyes, I decided to try again. This time, I didn't force my way in. My goal was to leave what was already inside there but make it work for me. To tell it a story or sing to it, and let it spread the word. It was slower and more subtle, but if it worked?

Sam began to hum softly. When I looked, his eyes had grown heavy. My goal was to make him sleepy, maybe even drunk. To remove his attention so I could do a little more – and it seemed it was working! Struggling not to squeal in excitement, I pushed a little harder...

And something cracked. It wasn't anything tangible, but I could still feel it, like a change in the air pressure but between Sam and me. The wall that had been holding me out was no longer quite as solid. I had control of both sides. Complete control, and Sam had just become my puppet.

"Stand up," I whispered softly.

A smile touched his woozy face, but he did.

"Sia?" Luke asked, sitting straighter.

"Go open the door, Sam." I was going to keep my commands simple.

Luke didn't care. He reached over and caught my arm, demanding my attention. "How'd you get in?"

His voice didn't bother Sam at all. Just like Aaron had when Mike mind-fucked him at my old house, Sam obediently walked to the exit and pulled the door open. Then he did nothing. Absolutely nothing, just stared into the hall like he'd forgotten he was there.

"Put him back," Luke insisted.

"Shut up and I will!" The problem was that putting him back wasn't as easy as getting inside. I had to change his resonance back to the way it had been before I started, but I didn't remember how that was. Desperate to fix him, I decided to go another way. I told his aether to be free. To listen to Sam. To do whatever it wanted.

The demon of seduction dropped like a rock.

"Shit," I hissed, rushing to his side. "Sam?" When he said nothing, I looked back at Luke. "Can you see what I did?"

"No," he insisted. "And I couldn't before."

"Then go get Nick!"

Before Luke could even rush out of the hall, Beelzebub walked up, chuckling at our panic. "Muse? You broke Sam?"

"I don't know! I didn't mean to, I just figured out how to do aetherweaving so I told him to open the door, but I don't know how to put him back. Bel, go get Nick?"

He ignored me. The jerk completely acted like I wasn't in a full-blown panic attack as he knelt at Sam's side. Sliding one hand up his shirt, his palm found Sam's chest and paused over the seal. "Samyaza," Bel said softly. "Be still. Be whole. Be here, Samyaza."

Immediately, Sam sucked in a breath and sat up. "Fuck," he grunted.

"Sam?" I grabbed his arm, trying to help stabilize him. "Are you ok, sweetie?"

"Just..." He groaned and rubbed at his face. "Someone check my wards? See if there's a leak?"

Both Luke and Bel closed their eyes, evidently doing exactly that. I figured I'd already messed up enough I'd just keep my aetherweaving to myself for a little bit. While we waited to hear the verdict, I smoothed Sam's magenta hair out of his eyes and back along the top of his head.

"Are you ok?" I asked.

"I'm fine, sweetheart," he insisted. "Can't feel a leak, but the last thing we need is an angel having a direct line into your inner circle. I'm just so tired. Feel like you gave me a sleeping pill."

"I don't know what I did."

He flashed me one of those seductive smiles he was known for. "Gathered that. Whatever it was, don't forget it, because damn. It worked."

"I'm sorry."

He caught my hand, pulling my attention back to him. "Sia, it *worked*. Angels can't do much to us. You slipped right between my wards and took over. I don't have a clue how, but I didn't feel it and couldn't stop it. That's a good thing, sweetheart. A *good* thing."

"I managed to change Luke's eyes color, too."

His smile turned into a grin. "Gonna make my hair grow in this color, then?"

"Oh, Sam. I don't want to mess you up anymore. In case you missed it, I don't have a clue what I'm doing."

"Aw, c'mon."

Luke made a pleased noise as he opened his eyes. "She somehow managed to manipulate his aether without blowing apart his wards. Sam, I can't find any vulnerabilities."

"He's good," Bel said a second later. "What happened?"

Sam tipped his head to me. "I just got mind-fucked by a Muse. That's what happened."

The strangest part was that the guys were all smiling like they'd just won the lottery. I couldn't even begin to imagine what they thought this was good for, but I had a funny feeling it meant I'd be practicing this for a while. Next time, I'd make sure I remembered what he felt like *before* I started making changes. I was not going to mess up my boys - but I did end up fixing Sam's hair.

LUKE LOCKED ME IN THE STUDY ALONE WITH HIM FOR THE REST OF the day. Bel grumbled that he wanted to work on my defensive moves, but Luke was having none of it. He insisted I needed to master my inner shields first. Second, I had to figure out how to slip between wards faster. Fast enough to make it into a weapon. The problem was that it didn't work that way.

I finally broke free when Nick announced dinner. Unfortunately, Sam wasn't there. Bel said he'd passed out, which had me worried. It didn't help at all that Nick was distracted by whatever idea he had about magnets. Bel and I traded eye rolls while they yammered on about polar attraction, anti-aetheric properties, and repelling resonances. As soon as the meal was done, Nick gave me a kiss, apologized, then vanished back inside the gold room.

I went to find Sam.

His room was across the hall from Nick's. Standing outside the door, I tapped softly and listened for any hint of life inside. I was expecting a snore, or maybe the sound of blankets as he rolled over. Instead, the response came back fast enough to make me flinch in place.

"Come in!"

Well, ok then. I twisted the knob and opened the door a crack. "Sam?"

"Hey," he said. "Come on in. I'm decent."

I opened the door a little more and poked my head inside. "You feeling ok?"

"Good as new," he assured me. "Had a hardcore nap, but I'm trying to find anything on Muses working with aether. Come see."

Ok, that was an offer I couldn't refuse. Without even thinking about it, I stepped the rest of the way in and paused. Not only was Sam sitting there on his bed, bare-chested, wearing only a thin pair of pajama pants, but I couldn't miss the painting of fire hanging right above him. The one I'd given him. Then there was the thing he was looking at, which wasn't exactly a laptop. Oh, it looked enough like one to pass a casual glance. But the three-dimensional projection gave it away as demon tech.

"So does that thing need to recharge?"

He shook his head. "Not on Earth. There's enough free aether that the conductor never drains. Back home, it's only good for about a day."

"Cool. And Muses working aether?"

He pushed his hand through his fancy new hair, revealing the black lowlights I'd added at his insistence. "Merlin was a master of it, but he had chants and symbols to channel his intentions. There are a few others, but they cast it, Sia. They didn't weave or smith."

"And that's a big deal?" I asked.

He rocked his hand from side to side. "It's unique, but they all seem to be unique. You also seem to have a whole different set of rules than outworlders. The theme is always that a Muse can inspire. Doesn't matter if that's inspire people to fight back, invent marvelous things, or start an artistic revolution. Muses are the catalyst, not the weapon." He paused, wrinkling his forehead like he was thinking. "They're the crack in the dam that starts the flood. That's why they're so powerful, because once the population is in motion, it's unstoppable and a new era is upon us."

"But –"

He smiled before I could even form a real sentence. "But not you," he agreed. "From what we can tell, you have no influence over the masses. Your childhood stories make it sound almost the opposite. Yet you have *complete* control of aether. I'm trying to see if there's a reason why."

"Maybe I'm just not human?" They'd compared me to a demon often enough, maybe that had something to do with it?

He just shook his head. "Twenty-four years old? Trust me, you're human. A fairy or satyr at your age would still be a child, similar to a ten-year-old human." Then he ran his eyes over me. "Not all grown up. Trust me, you're human."

"But what if one of my ancestors was a demon?"

He shrugged. "Offspring always take the lifespan of the mortal parent. It's not a half and half thing. Not exactly."

"Oh." But that gave me the chance to ask what I'd come up here to find out. "So, you've had a few kids, right?"

"Yeah." His tone was flat. "Why?"

"Well, Luke said Demons didn't necessarily worry about their children being theirs, and that, um..." With a groan, I gave in. "And it was the best segue I could think of. See, Bel wants me to like him. When I tried to explain I'm Nick's girlfriend he didn't get it, and Luke told me it's because that concept is foreign to demonic culture."

The frozen expression on his face began to thaw. "And you want to know if our immoral habits are really true, huh?"

I let out a sound that said he was just missing the mark. "Mostly, I don't want to hurt Bel's feelings, but I definitely don't want to screw up things between Nick and me."

"Mm." Sam patted the bed beside him, encouraging me to come sit. "I'll talk to the big lug, but you gotta understand, he's not going to expect you to jump into his bed. He just wants you to show more affection. Hug him, hang out with him, and treat him the same way you would me."

"Sam, I don't just go randomly hugging guys!"

He chuckled. "Maybe you should try? Pretty sure none of us would mind."

"Yeah, but -"

"Nick," he said, cutting me off, "won't care. If that's what was about to come out of your mouth, then just stop. Don't refuse to do something because of what some *guy* might think, Sia. Just don't. Figure it out for yourself but stop worrying about fitting in with us. After a few million years of screwing things up, we're still friends. Not just working together, but actually friends. I think we've been around long enough to talk before anyone overreacts."

A little sigh managed to slip out of my mouth. "The truth is I suck at dating. Getting a boyfriend is easy enough. It's keeping them around that's the problem." I chuckled and glanced down, hoping he wouldn't care that I was telling him this. "It's like after we start sleeping together, the new is all worn off and they move on, you know? I guess I'm just a little scared that if Nick gets jealous because I do something stupid, I'll be left to fend off the angels on my own."

"Hey." He reached over and wrapped an arm around my shoulders. "Not gonna happen. You're already slipping into the corridor on your own. You can do some pretty kick-ass stuff with your little Muse skills, and while I may not be able to teach you how to manipulate the force of life, I swear I will be right there if any angel tries to put his hands on you. Nick or no Nick, ok?"

"But I'd kinda rather there's a Nick. Sam, I really do like him."

He gave me a side hug. "I know you do, but I also know that he's really into you, too. Look, Nick's not going to freak out. He's just not like that. In all honesty, he's more likely to let you walk all over him because he'd rather forgive you than lose you. This paranoia about you 'cheating' on him is all in *your* head, not his. In all the years he's been watching you, I can't remember him ever being upset because you were happy. Not even when he showed up here and found you were dating some dick."

"Uh..."

Sam smiled slyly. "Aaron. Granted, Nick checked him out pretty good, which is how we figured out that Delta Phi had some green-eyed hooligans running the show over there, but yeah. He was honestly ok with just being a friend and seeing you happy. It's pretty much his thing when it comes to women he cares about – and that isn't a very long list, Sia."

"Wait. Angels were joining Delta Phi?"

Sam waved that away. "Yeah. We're pretty sure angels were using the frat guys to hunt down some perfect redhead, among other things. The guys just didn't realize that they weren't looking for a girl with massive boobs, but one with massive multiverse skills. After they mind-fucked those kids to run into your car, we started putting the pieces together. And we may have made the decision not to tell you about it for a bit because we still aren't quite sure what their end goal is. Anyway, that has nothing to do with Nick. My point is that you're fine with him. He's not worried, so you shouldn't be."

"Ok." I had to pause to let some of that sink in, then decided to just not worry about it for a minute and stay on track. "Sam, I'm living with nothing but good-looking demons, and the line between dating and not is kinda a thin one that I sure don't want to cross."

He slowly looked up at me with those pretty plum-colored eyes. "Good-looking, huh?" Then he smiled. "Seriously, though, we've screwed up your life in so many ways, and we all feel bad about it. The last thing we want to do is stress you out about your relationship. You do you, Sia. Let us worry about who is getting pissed, who is up to something nefarious, and how we're going to get you back home so you can become a badass. Right now, that's all Nick wants – to get you safe."

Again, I said, "Ok." Then I took a deep breath. "So, you want to fill me in on the stuff that pre-Muse Sia should've been told."

The tip of his tongue jutted out between his teeth, but it didn't stop the smile. "Nope, because I'm pretty sure that *would* piss you off, and you're supposed to be focused on learning. How about we go back to how I'm good-looking?"

I gasped and shoved him hard enough to make him flop back on the bed. "Sam!"

He just folded his arms behind his head. "And here I thought you weren't the kind of girl to roll around in bed with another man."

Yep. That was my cue to leave, because this demon looked a little too good like that, and I didn't dare forget that he was the master of seduction. Sometimes, retreat really was the wisest choice.

For the next few days, I barely saw Nick. Sam, on the other hand, became my constant companion. Bel had him working with me on defensive moves, and I was finally showing improvement. I could actually slip between the corridor and Earth when and where I wanted. That was pretty much it, but I was calling it a win. Thankfully, I did a lot better with the aetherweaving lessons where Sam let me try to mind-fuck him over and over. Most times, it worked. Sometimes, he figured out how to block me, and I had to come up with something new.

In only a few weeks, the guys said I'd become one hell of a force to be reckoned with. I figured that was a compliment. Seriously, who wouldn't want to be the super-special badass paranormal heroine? I was definitely enjoying this. From Luke's sexy blue eyes to Sam's magenta and black punk hair, these skills clearly had a few tangible benefits. Then there were the other things, like learning how to manipulate the systems. I couldn't create money out of thin air – nor cyberspace. There wasn't any aether to manipulate. What I could do was call my bank and speak to an aether-filled human.

That was how Luke worked his miracles. The trick was in the voice, to be soft and soothing, almost hypnotic. Once I had them drawn in, even over great distances, I could alter their inner aether enough to make things start happening. It was almost like I could hear the resonance and just had to change it a little. After I did that, I could convince people to do almost anything I wanted. I practiced by getting myself a wonderful black credit card – which wasn't black – and VIP access to a famous museum in New York. Not that I could use either while under house arrest, but Luke said I'd earned an A for that lesson.

Then, five days after Nick had locked himself away in the gold room, he casually trotted down the stairs to join us at lunch. All conversation paused as the four of us looked up at him in shock. Without saying a word, he marched to the end of the table and leaned on it. Only then did the smile touch his lips.

"I got it."

That was it. He didn't say what he had or how he'd done it, but we all knew. Somehow, Nick had finally figured out what it would take to keep the veils from pointing at me. If he was right, then this meant I'd no longer be restricted to the confines of his house. I could finally be free – without needing to worry about angels showing up to steal me away.

"How?" Luke asked, keeping it just as simple.

Nick's smile grew a little more. "The veils point to her because she's a magnet. She's drawing aether in faster than it can balance out. Like water going down a drain, the suction causes a funnel from the void, so all we have to do is block her pull on the world around her."

I was nodding enthusiastically, thrilled to hear it was something so simple. Right up until I looked at the guys on either side of me, that was. Bel's mouth was parted in shock, Sam's eyes were bulging, and Luke was slowly shaking his head. With a heavy sigh, I realized that a simple answer did not mean a simple *solution*.

"So how do we fix me?" I asked.

Nick waggled a finger in my direction. "We shield that hot little body."

"Won't work," Luke said. "Our shields aren't airtight. We have to let oxygen and aether leak through or we'd be powerless."

"Right. But put a few layers around her and the amount able to pass through will be normal. No more than water through multiple layers of cloth," he shrugged. "- or such. We just need to *slow* her pull on the world."

Finally, Sam found his tongue. "But she's pulling that much aether in? What the hell is she?"

"A Muse," Nick told him. "And like all Muses before her, she's unique. We just happened to get the one that's a walking, talking aether vacuum. I don't know how – or exactly what – she's doing yet, but it seems that something about Sia draws free aether to her. Look at how Gabriel's clung to her across multiple veils. It's like she's the magnet and the force of life is made of iron filings."

"No." Bel didn't move or throw a fit. He just dumped that word into the room so hard everyone else shut up immediately. "For all you know, sealing her off could kill her. If that much aether is running to her, who's to say she doesn't *need* it. You're not killing our Muse."

"We'll test it first," Nick assured him.

Bel just shook his head once. "Too much of a risk. We all know Sia's powerful. The things she can do? No human has managed half of what she's learned in her first month. Maybe she's like the kid in that movie and made of special force stuff."

"Midichlorians," Sam explained to the rest of us. "I let him watch Star Wars – and Bel, she's not Anakin. This isn't a movie, and she's not exactly made of aether. If we try the shields and she feels anything at all, we'll pull them off."

He thrust one dark arm toward me. "And what happens to her, huh?"

"Bel?" I asked. "If I need aether to live, and there's no free aether on Daemin..." I shrugged, unable to figure out how to ask my question but hoping he understood. "Isn't it better to test this here?"

His jaw clenched hard, the muscles bulging to prove it. "What if it's like suffocating? What if it hurts when they do that to you?"

"I'm pretty tough, big guy." I looked over to Nick. "If all it takes are a few shields, then can't we layer them up one by one, checking to see if I feel weak or weird in between?"

"That's basically what I was thinking," he agreed. "Put yours on the inner layer, then add mine over it, then Luke's."

"I can shield, too," Sam offered.

Nick just lifted a hand. "If three isn't enough, then we'll add you and Beelzebub. I just don't like the idea of you two having anything draining your defenses."

I pushed back from the table. "So let's do this. I'm so ready to get out of this house."

Nick dropped his head, but I could still hear his chuckle. "Dove, setting a shield on something, especially something that moves, is going to take a little work – on your part. This is probably going to take all day."

I just shrugged. "The sooner we start, the sooner we're done, right?"

Stepping back, Nick gestured toward the hall that led into the office. "I'm ready when you are. I figure we know your shield doesn't cause problems, so we'll put mine over it and see if the veils react. Then we can give it a few hours before putting Luke's on."

As I passed around the back of the guys, I patted Bel's shoulder. "And if there are any problems, I'll scream 'pineapple,' ok?"

It was supposed to have been a joke, a reference to using a safe word for dangerous play. I just didn't think about the fact that Bel still wasn't quite caught up on modern culture. Most days, he did pretty good, but the nuances often passed him by. This was one of those times.

He caught my wrist. "I don't like this, Sia. I don't like the idea of you hurting. Satan brought me here to keep you safe."

"I know," I assured him, patting his hand with my free one. "But Nick won't hurt me, either. He's already promised to keep me safe."

"If not, I will rip *his* wings off. I swear it."

He was so adamant that I wanted to laugh in his face. I also didn't want to hurt his feelings, so I quickly bent and planted a kiss on his cheek to keep control of my smiling mouth. "You're a good hero, Bel, but I'm going to be just fine. I have no intention of being babysat for the rest of my life. Think of this like losing my Muse virginity. Just a little pinch, then it's all over."

With a wink, I hurried out of the room, hearing the others chuckle softly at my analogy. Even Bel. Clearly, there were some types of pain they didn't mind a woman suffering through. In my opinion, this was definitely in that category, because if I couldn't leave the house, I'd never be able to protect my friends.

THE SHIELD I'D BEEN USING IN THE CORRIDOR AND AS DEFENSE IN Bel's lessons wasn't the same thing Nick had me make this time. Unlike that one, this shield was more dense and required less conscious thought. In many ways, building it was more like making a sprite. I had to imagine the form, believe in it completely, and then will it to live.

The whole point was to create something that would survive on its own without me needing to constantly direct it. The trick was tying it back to me so it didn't simply expire after a few hours. My first attempt was a tragic failure.

The second was better. The seventeenth was finally determined to be good enough. Then, Nick had me remove it and remake it at least ten more times until little more than a thought had me encased in a layer of microscopic little Sia symbols. These, however, spun on themselves like millions of little gears, making my shield into a truly resilient barrier that was nearly invisible.

After a few minutes inside it, the thing was no more bothersome than trying to look around my own nose.

Then Nick put his on top. That was a little strange. The moment it closed around me, my ears popped, and it felt like the pressure changed. Sitting behind Nick's desk, Luke was staring intently at the map, leaned over to get the best view of the veil bubbles. For a moment he tensed, but it didn't last long. With a sigh, he leaned closer and shook his head.

"It's better, but there's still a peak pointing at the house. About half as big as it used to be, though."

Nick waved that off. "Not really surprised. She's been increasing in power for a while now, and I assumed two layers wouldn't be enough. At least the second shield is making a difference."

"Yeah, but..." Luke glanced over to me. "How are you feeling, Sia?"

Lifting my arms, I let them flop back down. "Fine. I mean, I can see Nick's shield in front of my eyes, and that's going to take a bit to get used to, but that's my only complaint."

"Can you still make sprites?"

I immediately conjured one up, a pretty little blue butterfly. I half expected the thing to stick to the transparent layer clinging to my skin, but after flapping for a few seconds, it made its way out without any hesitation. When it reached the other side of the room, I unmade it and pulled the aether back. That was where we found the first problem.

The aether didn't just return like it always had. The moment it reached me, it began to waft, hesitating in the microscopic gap between Nick's shield and mine. I wasn't the only one who noticed. Nick and Luke both sighed.

"It's fine," I assured them. "I'll just make sure I'm charged up before I go anywhere an angel could be. That way, if refueling takes longer, I'll have plenty of extra stockpiled and available. We can do this, guys."

"Yeah," Luke grumbled, "but how much slower will it be with a third or even fourth shield on you?"

"I'll learn. I haven't had this crazy ability long enough to take it for granted, so it won't even be hard. Besides, if there's ever a need, we probably won't have to worry about the shields, right? If I need that much aether that fast, then the angels will already know where I am."

Luke cocked his head at Nick. "She has a point. We should probably build in an emergency escape hatch for her, so she can remove our shields herself."

"Sure, we can do that, but she just wants out of the house," Nick reminded him, mostly joking. "I'm pretty sure she'd agree to just about anything if we'd let her do something normal for a few hours."

"Maybe if this works, we should." Leaning back, Luke kicked his feet up on the desk. "Maybe take her out and spoil her? Find someplace where there are enough people around that no angel would start anything, and, well... I bet she's a cute drunk."

Nick's smile was slowly growing. "Would also help to see if she can hold her shield while she's a little tipsy."

"I am so down with that," I agreed. "And y'all have all been so busy watching over me, you've missed out on the zillions of easy college girls. Kinda like a win for everyone." I paused. "Except you, Nick. You're all mine."

"I am," he agreed. "But I'm not sure the guys will have time to do much besides keep an eye on you. Some of us are working here, dove."

"I'm trying to say you don't have to! Nick, it's been weeks and all four of y'all have done nothing but take care of *me*. I'm starting to feel a little guilty here."

Slyly, Luke looked over. "We were hoping it felt more like pampered."

"Definitely pampered." I waved toward the kitchen. "I can't remember the last time I had to make coffee. I figure the only way y'all could spoil me any more would be to give me foot rubs after a hard day of doing, um, nothing."

"Learning to control aether," Nick corrected. "And for your information, most people struggle a bit more than you have."

"Muses, you mean?"

"And demons." He grabbed both arms of the chair and leaned in toward me. "Believe it or not, we have to actually learn this stuff, too. Every time someone comes up with a new way to do anything, the rest of us go back to school." Then he pressed a quick peck on my lips.

I couldn't help but smile. It was a natural reaction to him – and to knowing I wasn't doing as bad as I'd feared. "So do y'all live in shields like this all the time?"

Both of them shook their heads, but Nick answered, "Typically, we only throw on shields like these when we expect the worst. Even if you can't feel it, you'll start to itch after a while. Not literally, but no different than the urge to kick your shoes off when you get home. Your body will get tired of even the most comfortable constraints eventually."

"But it's like a second skin, right?" I looked down at my bare arm, which looked the exact same as it always had unless I focused really hard to see the magical shapes shimmering just over it. "I mean, I can take a piss in this thing and not make a mess, right?"

That made both of them laugh. "Yes," Luke groaned. "And eat, and pick your nose, and anything else disgusting you want to do..." He flashed me a devious little smile. "Like, Nick, for example."

He meant sex. "Really?" I asked. "So it's not like a full-body condom or something?"

"It is not," Nick told me. "The only thing that shield blocks you from is aether or an aether-generated attack. Granted, if Michael decides to start throwing fancy magic bolts at you, you won't need to worry, but that's pretty much all it will keep out."

"Gotcha. And have I proven I'm stable enough for the next layer yet?"

They shared a look. For a moment, I half expected Nick to give me some remark about patience and making sure things were working the way they wanted, but then Luke shrugged. Nick tilted his head a bit, and in whatever silent conversation they were having, it clearly looked like I was winning. Nick's next words confirmed it.

"We might as well. I can't think of anything that would happen to her *now* that she wouldn't have felt when we first sealed her off. Beelzebub's just being paranoid."

"Ok, then I'll add a few extra protections and see if that does anything," Luke said as he tilted his head back and closed his eyes.

Luke's shield felt nothing like Nick's. It was lighter, for one thing. I hadn't realized that binding aether had a weight, just like I didn't really notice my shirt did, until I experienced something new to compare it to, and Luke's shield was definitely new. It clung to me, pushing the inner two shields a little closer, and for a brief moment, there was a feeling of shivering all across my body. The only thing I could think was that the shields inside were contracting to fit beneath it. Then it sealed, and like before, my ears popped.

Immediately, both guys jerked their heads up. The feel of the atmosphere around me was different. Subtle, but not the same as it had been before, and it seemed I wasn't the only one who'd noticed. Then, Luke bent to check the aether map on Nick's desk. The problem was he didn't say anything.

"Well?" I asked.

"It's gone," Luke breathed. "At least I think it's gone, and if it's not, it's so small I can't really see it. Nick, come look."

But before Nick even made it across the room, the study's door burst open and Bel was there. His eyes immediately went to me. "Sia? Are you ok?"

"I'm fine," I assured him. "Completely ok, even if I'm encased in strange demon magic. Why?"

His lips curled slightly. "Because we felt that."

Nick chuckled, sounding almost relieved. "Well, come tell me if you can *see* it." And he gestured to the map.

Bel moved that way, bent, and just stared for a little while too long. "It's like she's gone," he finally breathed.

"Yeah..." Nick agreed. "Like she just vanished off the face of the map." He tossed a smile over his shoulder at me. "Evidently, three really is the magic number for you."

"So I can leave the house?" I asked.

Luke was nodding. Bel looked confused. Nick? He just looked at me for way too long before he couldn't keep his face calm anymore. A grin took over his face.

"Yes, dove. Give it a little time, but if you're still fine and not devouring the shields for their aether, then yes, we'll take you to Mac's tonight. How's that?"

"Yes!" I hissed, jumping up from the chair. "I love y'all to death, but I'm so sick of this house. I just want to put on some makeup, find something cute to wear, and go somewhere that other girls will be checking out my man, so I can hang all over him in public without needing to worry about seeing those nasty fairy trees again."

"Nothing wrong with fairy trees," Nick assured me.

I just lifted a finger up between us. "I'm sure that's true for you, but I can still die, and I'm not really interested in something that wants to eat me, thank you very much."

Sam chuckled from the doorway. "And that sounds like it's working. So she's off the map?"

"Yep," Luke said.

"Good because..." Sam jerked his thumb toward the back door. "Seems we have some angels sitting in the corridor watching the yard."

I groaned – and it wasn't playful. Hearing that hit me harder than it should've. If there were angels watching the house, then I wasn't really free. I was trapped, and so long as those green-eyed creeps kept me locked away, I couldn't fight back. I couldn't really do *anything* until I learned how to control these abilities more, and to do that, I needed to figure out a way around them.

"Let them look," Nick said. "Luke's protections prevent them from looking inside the house – even on that side of the corridor – and we can just slip from here. They'll never even know we're gone."

Wait. Did that mean what I think it did? "So we're still going out? Even with angels so close?"

"Angels are always close," Nick told me. "The trick is to take a path they don't expect."

"Besides," Luke added, "if they're here watching for you, then they won't be there watching us."

Sam flashed me a devious smile. "Which means we all need to fill up, because it sounds like Sia's finally being released from jail."

3 6

It didn't take me too long to get dressed. I managed to shower, shave, put on makeup, dry my hair, and style it, all in less than an hour. Deciding what to wear, that was harder. First, because I'd never lived with the man I wanted to pick up before, and second, my perfect outfit exposed the top of the seal. Pulling that off, I went for option number two, a cute little white dress. It showed off my assets, made my hair look that much brighter, yet was still comfortable. With the massive diamond at my throat, even my eyes stood out. From the way Nick kept smiling at me, he clearly approved.

Once we were all dressed to impress – which took the guys a lot less time than me – we gathered in the living room. The moment I walked in, all four of them shot to their feet. Nick looked proud, Sam's eyes went right to my cleavage, Luke refused to look at anything but my face, and then there was Bel. His lips were parted slightly, and his eyes kept moving up and down, over and over like he couldn't believe my transformation. I took that as a sign I really did clean up well, which was exactly what I'd been going for.

"All right," Nick said. "Sam, Bel, you two go first. If there's a problem, one comes back and the other deals with it. If we don't see you in sixty seconds, we'll meet you there."

"Deal," Sam agreed, then they both stepped out of sight.

Sixty seconds later, we followed. Nick held my hand, but he let me direct the trip – and I almost got it. We showed up about four feet away from my intended "landing spot," so to speak. Not bad for my first try. As a group, we walked around to the entrance just like any other cluster of typical college kids, but I felt on top of the world.

Inside, it was early enough that some of the chairs were still empty, as were two of the pool tables. Beelzebub grabbed one and begged Nick to teach him the rules. That, of course, was right up Nick's alley, since it involved so much math. Sam and I headed to the bar to grab drinks. By the time we made it back, they'd already started drawing a crowd.

Two pretty girls leaned against the wall. Cocktails in hand, their faces were pressed close to hide their words, but their eyes were on the two demons. Sam noticed too. Tapping my arm, he tilted his head at the pair.

"Didn't I hear something about you wanting to show off a bit? Looks like the perfect time to go hang on your man."

"Oh yeah," I agreed.

Holding both my glass and Nick's bottle of beer, I made my way over and set them on the edge of the pool table beside Nick. One on either side, which gave me an excuse to wrap my arms around him. With a deep chuckle, he stole his drink from my hand and turned to face me.

"Well hello, beautiful."

"Hey, yourself. You trying to draw a crowd?" I flicked my eyes toward the girls.

Nick didn't bother looking. "I was trying to catch the eye of the most beautiful woman in all five realms." His free hand pressed against my back, encouraging me to come just a little closer. "Because that dress is perfectly sinful."

"Punny," I teased. "But I guess that means you approve, huh?"

"Mhm. Trust me, I can't wait to take you out of it." He leaned closer and kissed my neck. "So are you enjoying being let off your leash for a bit?"

"Yeah." I giggled when he kissed me again. "And you are not going to convince me to rush home, as tempting as it may be right now."

"Busted," he admitted, pulling back. "Just promise me that if anything goes wrong, you'll jump there. No waiting for the rest of us, ok?"

"I promise!" To prove my point, I poked my finger into his side. "Now stop being paranoid and enjoy yourself. Hell, if nothing else, show Bel some of the more exciting changes he missed over the last few years."

"Like miniskirts?" Nick teased. "Yep, he's already noticed. He likes bras, too, it seems."

"What?" Bel asked. "I heard that."

Which he clearly hadn't if he was asking what we'd said, so I called back, "Nick was just saying that you're an embarrassment at pool!"

"Then you play him. It's not exactly a fair match."

I flapped a hand at him then turned back to Nick. "So I think Sam's on the prowl. Where'd Luke take off to?"

He tilted his head toward the other side of the bar. "Looking around. He doesn't tend to draw as much attention from Mike's friends. And Sam's asking about Delta Phi."

"Gotcha. In other words, they're still working, huh?"

"Always. But *you*, my dear, are here to have fun." Stepping around me, he gestured at the balls scattered across the table. "How do you feel about pool?"

The next thing I knew, Nick had talked me into playing against

Bel. I was horrible, but so was the newly awoken demon, so it worked out. The guys returned only to vanish again when something caught their eye. More people showed up, pushing us all closer together, but none of them set off my angel alarm bells. Then again, my glass was never empty, although the drink often changed, and I probably wouldn't have noticed if an angel bumped right into me. By the second game, I was definitely smiling way too much. That was when Luke appeared, handing me yet one more.

"Drunk yet?" he asked.

"Tipsy!" I giggled, passing him my pool cue. "But, I need the one room you boys can't use. Can you win this game for me? I'm solids."

"Sure." Luke lined up a shot, and I somehow managed to stagger to the ladies room.

Like all bars, inside the women's restroom was a social club, and a line. Dozens of single women vied for space at the mirrors, all trying to make sure they looked good enough to find a friend before the end of the night. Most of them were giggling about guys. I'd finally gotten my turn in one of the stalls when I heard a pair talking about my friends.

"Oh my god, there's four of them, and each one is better than the last!" one squealed. "And did you see the guy with the pink hair? He's so hot!"

"I am *definitely* going home with one of them," the other girl declared.

"First, you have to actually talk to them."

I stepped out in time to see a pair of backs retreating. I knew exactly how I'd felt the first time I saw Nick, so couldn't blame them at all. That didn't mean I was honestly thrilled about it. Sure, I knew the guys deserved a little attention, but I'd kinda gotten used to it just being the five of us against the world. Unconsciously, my mind tried to make those girls into villains, dreaming up ways the angels could've mind-fucked them just to cause problems, but I knew better. The feeling twisting my gut was a whole lot more mundane.

And the boys really were hotties. Of *course,* women were going to hit on them. Trying to remind myself they deserved this, I washed my hands, thinking about Bel's possible reactions. If I hurried, I might even get to see him blush. If I didn't, I wouldn't have to see them kissing someone.

Ugh! Taking a deep breath, I forced my stupid jealousy back down and left the bathroom. Tonight was going to be *fun.* I finally had the chance to seduce Nick properly, and I'd been dreaming about making Death drool for far too long. I was almost over it when I wove my way through the last line of people and reached my friends. The first thing I saw was Sam's magenta hair. The second? Well, she was tall, curvy, and bent over to give him a perfect view right down her dress.

Just as I forced my eyes away, a breath tickled the side of my neck. "You should go save him." It was Nick, and he sounded amused.

"Oh?" I glanced back to see his eyes sparkling. "And how would I do that?"

His gaze dropped to my lips. "I wouldn't want to pressure you, but I'm sure if his 'girlfriend' appeared, he'd be appreciative."

"Nick," I hissed. "Maybe he's into her?"

"Nope." He smiled. "Trust me, Sia. She's not his type. Just go bail him out so this doesn't get ugly. We're trying to blend in, remember?"

"Then *you* remember," I told him, "that this was *your* idea."

"Mm, and it's not like you haven't made out with him before. This time, I get to watch." With his smile growing even bigger, he grabbed my shoulders and turned me toward the demon of seduction, then gave a little push.

I staggered forward, mostly because that was the very last thing I'd ever expected to come out of Nick's mouth. Granted, he had a point, but still! It also made it clear exactly how he expected me to make this happen. So, doing my best to make the stagger look intoxicated instead of just stupefied, I brushed past the girl and threw my arms around Sam's neck.

"Hey, baby!" I drawled, aware that my drunk impersonation was a little too good. I wasn't wasted, but it wouldn't take much more before I was.

Sam's hands immediately closed on my waist. "Whoa, there. You ok, sweetie?"

"Mhm." I leaned closer, pressing my mouth beside his ear. "Nick said you might need your girlfriend for a few minutes."

He ducked his head and chuckled. "You have no idea." Then he pulled away just enough to gesture to the girl beside us. "Sia, this is Alison. And this is my girlfriend, Sia."

"Your..." Alison's mouth paused, still open. "Oh." Then she looked at me. "Sorry."

"All good. He is pretty cute, so I don't blame you at all."

She sighed. "That obvious, huh? So, any of your friends single?"

"Nope," Sam answered before I could offer a name. "Sorry."

She slowly nodded her head, clearly trying to come up with a good excuse to get out of there. "Yeah. I'll, um, go try my luck elsewhere, I guess. Nice to meet you, Sam and Sia."

The moment she was far enough away, both Bel and Luke snorted out their laughter like they'd only barely held it in. Sam, however, just groaned and shot Nick a dirty look. Me? I was a little confused. Clearly, there was a joke I'd missed.

"Someone wanna fill me in?"

"Nope," Luke said, suddenly a little too interested in his pool game. The one that used to be mine.

"But I thought..." I let that trail off when Nick tried to smother a laugh. "Ok, what's so damned funny?"

"You," Bel said. Leaning on his pool cue, he looked over at me. "They think it's cute how you keep treating us like normal men."

"And how the hell am I supposed to treat you guys?"

Sam's hands reclaimed their spot on my waist, and he pressed in behind me. "Like demons," he whispered. "Now go kiss your boyfriend and stop worrying about it."

This time, Sam was the one nudging me to make my way around the table. Nick didn't move, just lifted his beer to his lips and splashed back a drink. That didn't hide the little smile playing on his lips. I decided Sam was right, and with as many drinks as I'd had, worrying was far beyond my capabilities. Nick didn't look mad, so I was still in his good graces. I'd also just saved Sam without having to resort to any public displays of affection.

"I think you set me up," I accused as I slid my arm around his waist.

He made a face but shook his head. "No setting up, dove. Just helping out a friend." Then he turned to face me and leaned closer. "And proving that you can stop worrying all the time about upsetting me. I heard about your talk the other day."

"Uh..."

"Bad at keeping boyfriends, worried we'll ditch you and leave you to deal with angels alone. Any of this sound familiar?" He lifted a brow.

It did, and he knew it. "So you talked to Sam, huh?"

"Sam talked to me. He said this has been eating at you for a while, so why didn't you say something?"

I flailed an arm toward him. "Suck at dating. Hello! What am I going to say? Hey, Nick, your best friend is hot and smells good, but don't take that the wrong way?"

He nodded. "Yeah, basically. Or how about Luke's great abs? Maybe Bel's cute dimples?" Then he hooked a finger under my chin and made me look at him. "I told you. For the first time in four and a half billion years, Sia, I don't feel the need to lie about who I am. You shouldn't either."

That was a very long time. Just hearing him say it like that made it sound even more impressive. "I didn't lie, Nick. I just don't want you to think I'm not thrilled with us – because I am!"

"I know that. Just like I now know that the reason you looked so scared when I caught Sam sitting beside you wasn't because you thought he'd force you to do something you weren't interested in, but because you thought I'd assume the worst. Right?"

Biting at my lip, I managed to both hang my head and nod it. "Pretty much. He was helping me with a drawing of you, I mean, the blue you, and I didn't think you'd approve."

"Ah. So why did you avoid him for days after?"

"Because I was pretty sure I'd crossed a line and wanted to put some distance between us. I mean, I didn't want Sam to get the wrong idea – or you!"

"Mm." He stepped a little closer. "Would it help if I said I won't dump you because I get jealous?"

All I could do was shrug. "But I don't want to make you jealous. That's kinda the point. I mean, we're together, and I'm perfectly happy with you – but checking out guys is... I dunno... a habit?"

"Natural," he corrected. "Big secret of the universe, Sia – dating someone doesn't make you either blind or stupid."

"Ha. Ha," I mock laughed. "You know exactly what I'm saying."

"Uh-huh." He paused, leaning back to look at me. "But I don't think you understand what I'm trying to tell you. We've been chasing each other for years, and you didn't spend that time just waiting for me. And I don't care. You were happy, and that makes me happy. Whether you were dating that plump kid from the grocery store or the asshole frat boy, you still thought about me. You still painted me."

"But I thought you were a hallucination."

He shrugged. "And you still *wanted* me. Nothing else matters. I can't promise I won't get jealous, but I can promise I will never try to turn you into a possession."

To buy a little time for that to sink in, I lifted my drink and finished it off. When that was done, I pulled away from him to find a trash can, holding up a finger to show I'd be back. So far as I could tell, Nick was trying to say he didn't want to be exclusive. Was that honestly what he meant? Had this thing between us already run its course? I tossed the plastic cup away with a little more force than necessary and turned back. I guess if I wanted to know, the easiest way would be to just ask.

If only that was as easy as it sounded. Asking meant I might get an answer I didn't like. It also meant I could make a complete fool of myself. While I wanted to be all tough and sure of myself, it seemed there were certain simple things that scared the hell out of me. Like laying it all out there, and I was about to do exactly that.

"Ok," I said when I returned. "So you want us to date other people?"

Nick's head twitched slightly. "No. Not really where I was going with that." He huffed out a heavy breath and glanced away.

I couldn't tell if he was annoyed, hurt, or confused. Either way, his eyes landed right on Sam, the person who'd started all of this. While I watched, a smile slowly pulled one corner of Nick's lip higher.

"Do you remember what Luke mentioned at your sealing? About me not telling you a piece of demonic history?" he asked.

"Yeah..."

Nick nodded. "And do you remember your response about wanting some hot stories?"

I felt my face growing warmer. "You mean about some hot demon on demon –" Before I could finish, Nick just walked away.

I stood there in complete shock. I knew he was listening, and I knew he was trying to make a serious point, but he hadn't even let me finish? Then I realized where he was going. Without pausing, Nick slipped around behind Bel, ignored the group of coeds sitting at a table watching our game, and marched straight up to Sam. The magenta-haired demon looked up but Nick didn't hesitate. His hand cupped the side of Sam's face, the other closing on the shorter guy's ribs, and without even bothering to ask permission, Satan kissed the shit out of the demon of seduction.

I slapped both of my hands over my mouth, but I didn't dare blink.

It was hot. It was probably the sexiest thing I'd ever seen in my life. As their mouths met, Sam caught Nick's neck, pulling him closer. I could see their tongues through the gaps in their lips, but there wasn't space between their bodies. Muscles bulged and hands grasped. They kissed like lovers who knew each other well, with the kind of passion I'd only found in Nick, and all I could think was that it was the most amazing thing I'd ever seen in my life.

And that I probably needed a new set of panties after watching that.

With one last brush of lips, Nick pulled away. For a moment, the two demons locked eyes, then Sam's head jerked to the side, toward me. Nick's eyes followed. I swear I was breathing as hard as either one of them. To prove it, I fanned myself, making a show of it. I watched as Sam's shoulders relaxed and he laughed.

"Jealous?" Nick asked, raising his voice to carry.

I just shook my head, torn between smiling stupidly and gaping at them like they were a spectacle. Thankfully, Nick didn't expect a retort across the bar. After saying something to Sam, he made his way back over and pulled me up against him.

"That's what I'm trying to tell you," he said softly. "Sometimes, there's nothing to be worried about."

I tilted my head across the pool table. "You and Sam have a thing?"

"Had. A long time ago. Like before the fairy kind of long ago." He ducked his head to meet my eyes. "Am I in shit for that?"

"Nope. Oh, no. Not at all. That was..."

"Hot?" he offered with a smile.

I nodded emphatically. "Yep, very."

"But aren't you jealous and going to dump me? Clearly, kissing someone else is a big no-no according to your rules."

"Yeah, but, no..." I groaned and shoved a hand across my face, wishing my words would return. "Sam's cool. He's my friend. I mean, if you were ditching me to pick up guys – or girls – it'd be different but –" Again, I just stopped. This time, it was because I realized I was saying almost exactly what he had.

"Yeah, I think you finally get it. The five of us share something that no one else will ever be able to understand, and that changes all the rules. When I see you practicing with Bel, drawing with Sam, or hanging out with Luke, I like it. I'm never going to put rules on you that can't withstand a few million years, Sia. You shouldn't try to put them on yourself either. Sure, I want you to like me most, but we are a legion, and you're a part of that now."

"You know," I said softly, sliding a little closer to him. "I think that little display may have gotten your wish, because I'm suddenly very ready to go home and show you which demon I like most."

"Yeah?" He palmed the back of my neck. "And here I was thinking that since your shields are working so well, this would be the perfect chance to see what you thought of that demon in real life."

"Vesdar?" I asked.

Nick nodded. "I did make you a promise, after all." Then he raised his voice. "Hey, Luke?"

"Yeah?"

"I'm taking Sia to the beach. If anything happens, I'll call."

Luke laughed. "I'm pretty sure *something* will happen, but I'll be listening. Go have fun, you two. The water should be nice this time of year."

37

*N*ick laced his fingers through mine and started pulling me toward the front door. "Ever been skinny dipping in the purple sea? Want to?"

"Seriously?"

He lifted a brow and smiled seductively. "Well, it's supposed to be a celebration, right? It's also summer there. The water gets wonderfully warm."

We left the bar just like everyone else, but instead of heading home, Nick guided me around the back of the building, behind a tree that blocked the view from the street. He paused only long enough to check for anyone watching, then tugged me into the corridor with him. Thankfully, there wasn't an angel in sight.

"Since you've never been there before, this time I get to drive," he said, wrapping his arms around my back. His hood was still down, and those galactic eyes were warm and mesmerizing. "I'm going to show you my favorite place in the five worlds."

I nodded, but didn't even have time to answer before he tugged again and we fell across the next veil into Vesdar. I could only assume it was a planet like Earth, round and filled with many climates and time zones. Where we stepped out was at the tail end of sunset. Blues, pinks, golds, and greens tinted the lilac sky. Verdant sands lay soft underfoot, but this wasn't the same beach I'd been to the last time. That one had been an open expanse. This one was isolated, and before us spread a royal purple ocean. The cove was circular, a wall of green cliffs to the left, and a powder-soft beach spread off to the right, making the view impossibly gorgeous.

"Why is the water purple?" I asked, trying to take it all in.

"Violet sky." He pulled my hair back, his demonic nails teasing my neck. "The planar densities are just different enough to shift the light refraction toward red, and the sea reflects it. Want to go swimming?"

Biting my lip, I turned back to him with the best pouty face I could manage. "Flying?"

He laughed but grabbed my arm and looped it over his neck. "That's what I was hoping you'd say. Hold on, little dove. The takeoff might be bumpy."

I hugged his shoulders, my arms high enough to stay away from the reach of his wings but low enough to avoid the horns, and Nick lifted me against his chest. He looked up, checking the sky, then pushed. His wings cracked as they caught the first rush of air, wider than I'd realized. Each thrust lifted us higher, and I pressed against him, partly scared of falling, partly wanting to see everything. Being with Nick was like a mixture of exhilaration and terror as everything I'd ever known was proven wrong and the world became a much more interesting place.

The ground fell away, the wind whipped through our hair, but I was secure. There was nowhere to go but down, and he'd be able to catch me easily. When the cliffs looked like grains of sand, his body tilted slowly, and we moved more forward than up. My eyes watered but I wouldn't look away, trying to take it all in. On the horizon, the sun was a brilliant pink. Behind us, the sky was a rich indigo, and in between, I held my demon, feeling like any minute I'd wake up from this perfect dream.

"Look to my left," Nick called, trying to be heard over the wind.

I did, seeing a pack of what I first thought were birds. As we angled toward them, I realized they also had leather wings and were a lot farther away than I first thought. Seconds ticked past, and I tried to make out exactly what they were, expecting something from a myth. Then they finally got close enough. Dragons. At least a dozen of them flew right at us. I squealed, gripping his neck, but Nick laughed and shook his head.

"We're too small, not worth the effort in flight. I'll show you."

His wings pushed hard, gaining speed, each flap rocking us closer together. It was amazing and magical, and then I looked into the wind one more time to find the dragons bearing down on us. Huge did not begin to describe them. Every law of physics I'd believed existed broke in my head. Four legs, long tails, and bodies the size of a whale, their wings were even bigger. I could imagine only one fitting on a football field, and I wasn't even sure of that.

Nick wove between them, twisting and turning. His arms held tight around me, but he was laughing as my head turned to take it all in. They were like flying mountains, but in the most amazing colors. Blues, yellows, and the same verdant green as the sands below, I couldn't even see them all in the fading light, but I loved it. The group passed and Nick banked, following them back to the circular cove so far below.

"What do they eat?" I asked, almost screaming into his ear.

"Fish." He banked again, giving me a view of the ocean below. "Really big ones."

I could see them. Under the dark water, even darker shadows moved in schools. I wondered if they were like whales, but didn't want to know. I just made a mental note that we'd have to come back when it was daylight so I could see everything. That was when I realized this was all worth it. Losing my independence, giving up on my life goals, and stepping into a world of insanity, I wouldn't trade it for anything. I'd always thought I was a pragmatist, but I was wrong. Everyone wishes there's something more, something fantastic just beneath the surface, but I'd thought that was nothing more than the dreams of a foolish orphan wanting to believe she was a fairy princess.

It wasn't. I was a Muse, and that was so much better. With the wind twining my copper locks into Nick's midnight blue, his strong arms held me tight as we soared into the sunset. If this was what I could expect in life, I didn't want to be a fairy princess anymore. I wanted to be a demon.

Slowly, he landed, the process being easier than I'd expected, but his wings threw sand into the air around us. He set me down, making sure I had my legs under me, then shook out his arms and stretched his wings. I couldn't help myself. I hugged him.

"Thank you," I whispered into his chest. "I love this, I love your wings, and dragons, and the green sand. Thank you for finding me, Nick. Thank you for making me something special."

He pressed his palm against my face as his wings folded behind him. "You made yourself special, not me." His starry eyes searched my face. "But thank you for not running away from it, Sienna."

With a giggle, I stepped back and thrust my arms out wide as I spun in place. "This has been the best day of my *life!*"

He chuckled at me. "Well, it definitely ranks at the top of mine. I love seeing you so happy like this."

"Oh? Know what would make me even happier?" I stopped, staggering a little from dizziness, then sighed. "We should've brought a blanket."

He lifted a brow as he tugged at the old-fashioned laces of his pants. "Why? The water's warm."

"But sand gets in the worst places."

He just shook his head, then tugged off a boot with the toe of the opposite foot. "That's why you don't fuck on the beach, Muse. Do I have to teach you everything?" In one quick motion, he stepped out of his pants, leaving them there in the sand, then started backing toward the water. "C'mon. I might get lonely."

For a moment, I just stared. Satanael the demon was *hot!* Here on Vesdar, his skin looked almost iridescent, those rune wards a half shade darker. Then there was the trail of dark blue hair running from his belly button to... wow. Yep, *that* had a rune on it, too.

"I promise touching is better than staring," he teased.

Yes, I had a feeling it would be. I tugged my dress over my head, kicked off my shoes, and wiggled free of my bra and panties as fast as I could, watching him slowly step backwards. He made it no more than twenty feet before I ran to beat him into the water, but Nick was devious. He lunged at me as I passed, catching my waist, and flapped, just lifting us off the ground to propel us forward.

I squealed.

That one beat of his wings was enough to take us to knee-deep water, but I staggered as we landed – if you could call the end of a glide landing. Thankfully, the sea was there to catch me, and Nick wasn't any better. We both splashed down, completely soaked but laughing. The water ran over my lips, just as salty as any other ocean, but pure, like ours must have been before pollution. I loved it.

He caught my back up against his chest, more than happy to haul me around with his demonic strength, and pushed us deeper into the sea. What I didn't expect was how he used his wings as an efficient set of swimming arms. Giving in, I leaned my head back on his shoulder and relaxed, letting him take us out farther. Nick stopped with the waves lapping around his chest, deep enough that I could barely touch. I had to cling to him to keep my head above water.

"This is perfect," I said softly, looking up at the strange stars above. "The only thing better would be to have my own skin so I could fly with you."

"Soon," he promised. "Although I think your first lesson as a demon might not be flying."

Turning to face him, I shifted my arms around his neck. "Oh?"

Dripping water, his hand reached up to push a lock of hair behind my ear. "There's never been a female demon, little dove. I might have to sample the wares, but I don't even know how all the limbs would fit together."

"How does it work with the men?"

He looked away. "We tended to use different positions."

I grabbed his face and turned it back to mine. "Talk to me, Nick. What is it?"

"I've never actually talked about this before. I mean, not with a woman." He ran his fingers through my hair again. "Back then, we were all foolish children. Sometimes, friends messed around, but," he shook his head, "mostly it was groping and fondling."

"Handjobs and tail jobs, huh?" I pulled myself high enough to kiss his strong cheekbone. "And it doesn't sound like it was that good."

"No." From the tone of his voice, I had it all wrong. "I won't tell you that I haven't," a smile flashed across his mouth, "you know, gotten myself off, but I mean it wasn't normally emotional between demons. It felt good, so we did it – and I mean actual sex – but I'm not like Sam."

He was trying to tell me something, and he thought it mattered, but I just wasn't quite getting it. I just wanted to make sure he knew I didn't care what he'd done or who he'd been with over a few billion years. "So you weren't easy, is that what you mean?"

"I've been easy, I've been a prude, and everything in between. It's been a long time, dove. Jesus was only two *thousand* years ago, and I remember millions. No, what I'm saying is that I had demon lovers before women existed. I didn't know there was an option, but now that I do? I'm not repulsed by men, but that doesn't mean I'm bisexual, either. There's only a few I'm honestly attracted to. The rest? It was nothing more than playing to most of us."

"Then why did you kiss Sam tonight?"

The tip of his tongue flicked across his lips. "When we're young and foolish, it's easy to convince ourselves that lust is love." The stars in his eyes were dim. "It feels so immediate and persistent."

I could see the pain in his memories. "Did someone break your heart?"

Nick laughed softly, looking away. "No. We met in our first century and spent a few hundred thousand years together, convinced it had to be possible to cross the veils." Gently, he shifted back, putting space between us as he bared his soul. "It started as a way to stay safe, then stay warm, then to hold back the loneliness. Somewhere in there, those hours alone got boring, and, well, we learned how to keep ourselves entertained."

"There's nothing wrong with that," I assured him.

He shrugged. "We couldn't even imagine women, Sia. Not even our animals have females. We never thought to wonder why we're built like we are. We just figured out that our parts fit together, and it felt good, so we did it more and more, until it turned into something else."

"Love?"

He licked his lips, his eyes barely flicking to my face. "Yeah. For him."

"Did you feel anything for him?" For a moment, a surge of jealousy raced through me.

He saw it and smiled, relaxing. "Yes and no. He was my friend, and someone I trusted with all things – even when I realized I preferred women. He tried to understand, but jealousy almost destroyed the friendship we had. I left him for many years, hoping space would repair the damage, but when the woman I was with died, he found me again and was there for me." He shrugged weakly. "I do love him, but as a dear friend, not enough to be what he needs. But if there's any man in the world that can turn me on, it's him."

"Nick," I said, meeting his eyes. "I don't care if you still like men, or if you changed your mind when you realized women were an option, or whatever. It doesn't change who you are, ok? Just tell me you didn't sleep with any angels?"

"Uh..." He laughed. "No angels. Never had sex with Luke or Bel."

I heard what he didn't say. "Sam?"

A sad smile touched his lips. "I broke his heart, Sia. He's the one I spent so many centuries with."

"Oh."

He nodded. "Now you know why I didn't want to laugh and joke about it. The guys know, don't get me wrong, but Sam's feelings aren't a joke to me."

"God, I'm so sorry! I never meant -"

"No," he breathed. "You didn't do anything wrong. It's just hard to talk about at home, but I want you to know."

I nodded, but he hadn't answered my question. "So why *did* you kiss him tonight?"

"Because you don't care." He paused to take a deep breath, then kept going. "Because I sometimes miss what we had and how he made me feel about myself, even if I can't help myself from liking women more. Because you're so open and accepting of us that..." A breathy laugh slipped out. "There are some things a demon can do that a woman will never be able to match. I guess, after you said you thought it was hot, I wondered just how open-minded you really are."

"You mean you'd like to have sex with Sam again, and hope I'm ok with that?"

"No," he almost purred. "I mean that one day, I hope you'd be willing to try both of us. I can see the way you look at him. I know how he feels about you. For the first time since I broke his heart, Samyaza has found someone he honestly cares about, and that someone is you. I may not love him the way he loved me, but I love him enough that I want to see him happy, just like I want you to be."

My heart was pounding way too fast. The problem was that my gut was also twisting into knots. "And us?"

"Oh, my sweet little dove, I will never give you up." Closing his eyes, he tilted his head back to the stars. "This sounds so wrong, but I'm trying to give you permission. It's not something you should need, but when Sam told me why you were avoiding him? Well, there's no reason for you to feel that way. Sam, Luke, or even Beelzebub, it doesn't matter. Throughout history, we have lived and fought together, and we've shared our loves. This time, it's different. Better. We are legion, and you're a part of us. Whether that's as a friend, lover, family, or whatever part you think works best for you, I don't ever want being with us to make you feel bad in any way."

"Just so long as I'm still doing you, huh?"

"Oh yeah." He pulled me closer, and I felt his tail slowly twining up my leg. "Because no matter what, you are my Muse, my girlfriend, and I can't stop thinking about how perfectly you fit with all of us. How natural being with you feels. And I have every intention of *proving* to you that you can't live without your demons."

"My Satan." I wrapped my legs around his waist, feeling the base of his tail brush against my calf. "Nick, you'd better find someplace very soft," I pressed my body closer to his, "or you will never get me out of this water."

His arms wrapped around my back, and he surged upward, water flying as his wings cracked open, carrying us to a smooth, soft ledge tucked in one of those impossibly green cliffs. His feet barely touched down before his mouth was on mine, hard and insistent while he eased my feet back to the ground. With my arm around his back, I felt it when his wings closed. Then I felt when his tail flicked across my hips, pulling me into him as his hands slid down my wet skin.

So many sensations. From the new smells to the feel of his skin, it was overwhelming, but I loved this. I loved him. My tongue danced with his and my hands tangled in his hair, but this wasn't just about feeling good. It was about a man who'd just bared his soul, and who had stolen mine. It was about trust and new experiences, and finding someone who cared enough to set me free instead of trying to force me into a cage.

I loved him. It was hard to separate that from how much I loved this new life, but I did. I really did. I loved how he treated me as an equal, how he didn't judge me for what I didn't know, and how he wanted nothing more than to make me happy – even when it wasn't always what made him happy. And I loved how he touched me. How his wings gently wrapped around my ass and his thumbs teased my nipples. I even loved how he growled like a beast when I gasped in pleasure.

"Sia," he whispered, "turn around, dove. Hold the rocks so I can touch all of you."

I spun, grabbing at the cliff wall. Soft moss cushioned my hands, but I barely had time to think about that before his tail curled across my belly, the tip moving lower. Spreading my legs, I gave him access. The smooth skin taunted me, slipping through my folds as hands grabbed my hips. No, those were his wings, I realized when his real hands found my breasts. The moan that came out was loud in the darkness descending on us, but I didn't care. I couldn't stop. There was too many sensations to focus on, and his tail was pressing hard into my clit.

"Nick," I panted. "If you keep that up, I'll finish without you."

He flicked my nipples again, but I felt his breath on my neck. "Like that, do you?"

"God, yes."

"Nuh-uh. Not God."

"Satan," I growled, "if you start worrying about what the hell I say when you're driving me insane –" His tail pressed harder, sliding back the other way. "Oh, God," I mumbled.

"Close enough," he chuckled, then his wings pulled my hips back.

And I committed the most amazing sin imaginable. The devil himself entered me, thick and hard, and I didn't care at all about religion, sins, or anything except the feel of my man loving me like no one else could. I bucked. I mewled in pleasure. I also didn't last very long at all. With every inch of my body stimulated, all I could do was gasp, scream, and take it, over and over. When my orgasm hit, it never wanted to end, flowing through me like magic.

I screamed out a primal yell as my knees went weak, and one pale, moonlight blue hand shoved over my shoulder and against the wall. The other was wrapped around my waist, holding me up as he groaned and pulsed inside me, savoring his own climax.

"Are you ok?" he eventually managed to ask.

I grabbed his arm for support but nodded. "Oh, yeah. Wow."

That got a weary chuckle. "Can you stand?"

"Oh, no. I'm nothing but rubber."

Slowly, he withdrew, then turned me to face him. "I had no idea it would be that good. Come here, dove."

Carefully, he knelt, easing me down with him. Those wings reached down to support our collapse, his hands cradled me, and somehow we ended up on the softest natural bed I could imagine. With a pleased little moan in the back of my throat, I curled into him and pillowed my head on his shoulder.

"Nick?"

"Mhm?"

"I love you. I just want you to know that."

"Mm." His tail flicked over my leg and gently wrapped around it. "I love you too, Sienna. I have for a very long time."

"Good," I whispered as my exhausted eyes slipped closed. "I'm just going to rest for a minute before we have to go home. It's so nice here, I want to enjoy it just a little longer."

His fingers tightened on my shoulder. "Yeah, me too."

38

---

*S*omething thumped down hard beside me, jolting me awake. Cracking open my eyes, I reached out and felt cloth. Familiar cloth. My dress! I'd left that on the beach.

I was immediately awake, but Nick moved faster. Surging to his feet, he stood naked over me, those wings spread for protection. I rolled to the side, grabbing my dress as I made it to my knees, searching for some hint of what was going on as I frantically pulled my clothes on. Screw the bra and panties. I just wanted to be covered.

Just as I saw the angel, Nick acted. Slapping his right hand down on his left forearm, he growled, "Samyaza, Beelzebub, Lucifer."

Marks glowed, flaring to life even while clothes began to materialize on his body.

And Michael laughed.

The bastard was flying just out of reach, hovering even with the ledge we were on, in all of his natural glory. His white gold hair had become truly metallic, his wings were the typical pearly white, but those green eyes were a sick and putrid flame, all too visible in the darkness. He also wasn't alone.

I had no idea how, but the angels had found us. "Nick, we have to go," I whispered.

He shook his head. "He brought them all, Sia. I count at least twenty on this plane. I'm willing to bet there's more in either corridor."

"Of course there are," Michael said. "You have the worst habit of getting away from us, and I really want that Muse."

"Yeah? So why didn't you just grab her when she was asleep?" Nick asked smugly.

The archangel snarled something I couldn't understand, then, "Because I can see Lucifer's shield on her, and I'm well aware of those little tricks he likes to weave into such things."

Nick lifted his chin and crossed those strong arms over his chest. "Then I guess that means you can't have her. Go find your own Muse, Michael. We're not about to give up ours."

Like an exclamation point, something whooshed into existence beside me. I flinched away, seeing nothing but gold and feathers, then there was a soft pop on my other side. Taloned hands caught me as my head whipped around. I'd never seen him like this before, but it was Sam in all his stormy dawn brilliance – and his horns were just as impressive as I'd imagined. In the darkness, I couldn't quite make out the color of his skin, but he blended perfectly in this purplish world.

Then a third pop came right behind us. I didn't need to look to know it was Bel, but I'd wanted to see him as a demon. When I did, I was glad Sam held me, because I flinched again, stepping into my friend for protection.

Beelzebub was big, completely black, and probably the scariest looking thing I could imagine. Even the short, thick horns on his head were meant to cause nightmares. As a human, I'd gotten used to his charming smiles and teddy bear personality, but as a demon? That was one scary-ass mother fucker.

Michael made a point of sighing dramatically. "Really? Do you idiots want to feed us aether so badly that you'll bring your whole legion for us to drain?" He lifted his hands like he just couldn't imagine such a thing. "If you insist."

"Nick," Luke said, "drop her shields."

"What the fuck happened?" Nick asked.

Luke moved to guard the edge. "Her peak appeared on the map a few minutes ago. Sia's shield is gone. I think she lost control of it. You need to drop yours."

And without a word, he did, the nearly invisible Satanael symbols dissipating from around me. I'd woken up so fast I felt like I was barely keeping up, but I still understood what that meant. I had full access to all aether, and we were about to throw down with the enemy. I just hoped those idiots had no idea what I could do.

"Plans?" I asked Sam, keeping my voice low.

"You," he said, "are going to hide behind Bel. Do not cross the veil. We came straight through from Earth, but I'll bet they have a few choirs waiting to grab you."

"And you," Michael said, pointing at Sam, "and you, and you, and you!" He moved his finger to each of the guys. "And there's not a damned thing you can do to stop us. We're going to do horrible things to your little Muse."

Sam leaned closer. "He's trying to taunt us into the air. It would make things easier for them since this is a defensible position. Whatever you do, sweetie, don't let his words make you do something stupid."

I shrugged that off. "He's an idiot. Just like most guys. I'm kinda used to it."

Mike heard me, and from the furrow of his brow, he was not impressed. "Like most *guys*? Like humans? You stupid little –"

"Now!" Nick yelled.

Sam shoved, pushing me toward Bel. The scary black demon was already in motion. Grabbing me by the waist, he spun, damned near slinging me against the wall before planting his bulk between me and the flock of angels hovering over the sea. From here, I couldn't see much, but I didn't need to. I could hear it.

Someone screamed. Something hummed like electricity. Bel opened his wings, but I could still make out an eerie purple glow from whatever he held. And they were all moving. Fighting, I was pretty sure, but demon wings were huge. They worked better than any curtain I could imagine.

"Can you call a shield?" Bel asked.

Days of training made it easy. I wrapped myself in one as I answered, "Yep. Covered."

"Good, because we're about to be swarmed. Do *not* let them touch you, Muse. I taught you better than that."

So he thought, but my self-defense lessons had been something I wasn't very good at. However, if all bets were off, there were a few things I did excel at. Draining aether was one. It might even be the biggest one.

From directly above us, something moved. I ducked, reaching one arm up as defense but Bel was faster. He turned, swinging what looked to me like a lightning bolt, and I watched as a white, feathered wing separated from the tin looking man it had been attached to. With a scream, the angel plummeted down, landing hard only feet away. What I didn't expect was the blood. Bright red and more than I'd ever seen before, it drained from the severed limb and spurted from the remaining stump. A part of me was grossed out, but I couldn't stop to think. While he was trying to grab at the remnants of his wing, I darted in and slapped my hand against him. Then I pulled, refusing to stop until the asshole was unconscious.

Aether. This war was about the resource they needed most, and I was a magnet for it. Doing my best to stay low, out of Bel's way, I kept to the cliff wall and searched the skies. Angels were everywhere, each one trying to find an opening, but Sam was right. This ledge was small enough that four demons could hold it, and positioned so they couldn't come directly at us except for from the front.

That didn't mean I couldn't come at them. Spotting an angel at the top of the cliff, I reached, straining to call the life force inside him. I had no idea how to do it, or if it was even possible. All I knew was that I'd pulled out the robber's life without touching him. I'd drawn Gabe's after I let go. That meant there was a chance I could do it from here. I just had to try a little harder.

When the man began to scream, I knew it was working. This time, the aether was chrome, beautiful in its own way, but it was about to be mine. Trusting Beelzebub to keep me safe, I dared to close my eyes and pull as hard as I could. Completely focused on the power rushing into me, I never stopped to think about what would happen if it worked. Not until Bel suddenly jerked me out of the way and a dazed Angel crashed onto the ledge where I'd been only seconds before.

Without remorse, Bel cleaved the creep's body in half and turned back for more. Me? I sucked up the last of the aether then thrust my palm against Bel's back. "Refill incoming," I warned, then relaxed. Just like I had with Sam, the trick to get through Bel's wards was to convince them that this aether already belonged to the big lug. I just had to make his protections believe it was one and the same. It wasn't even hard.

"Luke next," Bel growled over his shoulder. "He's throwing too much."

I nodded even though he couldn't see and kept pushing. That didn't mean Bel stopped fighting, he just kept his feet planted while he did it. Clinging to his back, I twisted and turned with him, but I kept pushing, encouraging the life to flow from me to him until it felt too thick and sluggish. Only then did I let go and scramble away from the demon's wild thrusts.

Avoiding the body against the cliff, I searched for a way to Luke. Where humans would have stood shoulder to shoulder, demons needed more room. Their wings were massive, and Luke's were no smaller. Each one had to be at least twelve feet long, which meant about twenty-five to the next man, if I had to guess, and that was a lot of distance to run when angels were trying to kill me.

But I did it. Running bent at the waist, I covered my head with my hands and just went. A wing flared over my head. A bolt of something crashed onto the moss to my right, and Luke was making a lot of sparks. Sparks I could only assume cost him aether – but I still had more to give.

"Luke," I called as I reached his back. "Refuel incoming!"

Then I grabbed his wing with one hand and palmed his back with the other. Holding on kept me out of his way. It also made me aware of the vibrations coursing through him. They said aether was life, but it was also music, made up of the microscopic vibrations of particles, all humming together in symphony. It wasn't loud, but it was still hard to miss, and getting harder. Like grabbing a jackhammer, I could feel the tremors in my bones, and I realized something. I'd been doing this wrong the whole time. I'd been trying to play by their rules, but those limitations didn't apply to me.

No, I created and destroyed. I painted and erased. I didn't need to work in patterns or suggestions. I was an artist, and the only thing inhibiting me was my own lack of imagination. As the last of my excess aether flowed into Luke, I was feeling a little too inspired. I was a god damned magnet, and their power was nothing more than *my* iron filings. They had it, my friends needed it, and I could make this happen.

"I gotta get more," I told Luke as I let go. "Just give me a second."

He thrust out an arm, forming a small shield between us and the open beach then looked back at me. "You need to stay by Bel, Sia."

"Nope." I glanced around, quickly counting the number of angels still in the air. "There's more of them than us. Hold the ledge. I'll be right back."

"Sia!" he hissed, but I was already stepping back to the gap between this place and Earth.

I hit the corridor and saw too many glowing specks. Some were close, more were farther away, but the army assaulting my friends on Vesdar was nothing compared to the numbers here. Good. That was exactly what I'd hoped for. If there were six hundred and some odd angels available to take me down, then that was a shit ton of power for me. I just had to catch it before any of them could touch me.

And hold it.

Without bursting.

But I was a vacuum. A funnel. A magnet that pulled so hard I could bend the veils, and if that was going to be my bane, then I'd make it my strongest power. I'd do this through sheer willpower, if nothing else.

A wave of my hand changed the protective screen beside me into a wall. A thought made a chain spring up from the billowy ground to clamp around my leg. A really *big* chain, attached to an even bigger bolt that went so far through the center of this plane that nothing would be able to drag me out of here without permission.

Just as the first angel reached for me, I dropped the last of my protections, threw my head back, and just pulled. In my mind, I saw myself as a drain, sucking all the life force into me. It didn't matter where it started, in an angel or flowing on the current, I needed it so it would come. I believed it with every cell in my body, and I pulled as hard as I could possibly imagine anyone having pulled before.

It worked.

Angels began to scream, their voices echoing through the corridor like banshee wails. Slapping my hands to my ears, I tried to ignore it. That was all I could do. That, or give up, but my friends needed me right now. They needed this power, and I was going to make it happen. If nothing else, this would be my legacy, downing more angels than even Beelzebub, but by doing it my own way. As I felt the aether flow into my body, stretching the limitations I hadn't even known existed before now, I just hoped that history would remember me as theirs. As the Demons' Muse, not just some stupid girl who couldn't get anything right – so I pulled harder.

Filling with too much aether felt strange. It was like being stuffed after Thanksgiving, but all over. My mind, my heart, my fingers, and even my hair felt bloated and stretched, as if the cells themselves were about to burst, but I couldn't stop. If I ruptured whatever aether bladder a person had, I knew someone would fix it. Luke or Nick, probably. Those guys always took care of me, and I had to do this. There was no other way to –

Suddenly, the corridor fell silent. The sound of the wind rushing past was the only thing I could hear because the voices were all gone. Forcing my aether-puffed eyes open, I looked, shocked to see grey silhouettes of angels scattered around, lit by a glow pulsing out of me. The aether. I had too much, but I knew exactly how to relieve just a bit of it.

Tossing my hand out, I imagined painting those bodies as dust flying on the breeze. In my mind, I could see them lifted, dissolving, and dissipating in the winds until they'd be impossible to collect. Molecule by molecule, the angels would tumble between worlds preventing anyone from putting them back together. Before me, it happened. At least fifty angels dissolved right in front of my eyes, making the balance of power just a little more equal. But I couldn't stay to enjoy this. I still had friends to save.

I tried to step back, but my leg jerked to a halt. Sucking in a little breath, I remembered the chain. A thought dispelled it, and I tried again, this time stepping easily through the veil and into a world of chaos. The skies of Vesdar were filled with lightning, energy balls, glowing swords, and the screams of men. I paused for a split second to find my bearings, then shoved both hands down, painting the biggest protection I could imagine with the force of my will.

A gigantic bubble appeared, mimicking the gesture. It formed at the top and grew, using the aether inside me to make a shield from raw power. Like an oil slick, it shimmered in a myriad of colors, but I could see through it enough to watch every angel on the other side pause in shock. Nothing would be able to get through that.

"What did you do?" Nick asked, turning to look at me.

"We're shielded and I cleared the corridor. Guy's, let's go!"

But Nick was shaking his head. "Sia, there's no pattern." He turned back and my eyes followed his.

"Oh, shit," I breathed, realizing my mistake.

There was no pattern to my shield, just pure, raw aether, there for the taking, and the angels hadn't hesitated for long. All of them pulled, sucking at it, but the way I'd built it had only made things worse. I couldn't pull it back. I couldn't stop them. No, instead of helping my friends, I'd just given aid to the enemy, and the beautiful swirls of life were getting thinner and thinner right before my eyes.

"Sam," Nick snapped. "Get her home. Luke, make sure she learns *something* this time." Then he sucked in a deep breath. "Bel, you're with me."

"Always, Satan," the big guy promised as he moved to stand beside Nick.

"No," I gasped, holding up my hands. "I can fix this."

"Get her *safe!*" Nick ordered.

But Sam and Luke looked like they dreaded leaving as much as I did. "Just..." I thrust my hand out, banishing the shield to swirl away in the atmosphere. "Give me back my aether, Mike."

"Come to Angelis with me, Muse," he countered, dropping lower to see me better. "Come with me, and I'll even let your friends go back to their forsaken little home."

"Damn it," Nick snarled. "Sam!"

Beside me, Sam took a deep breath and braced. "I'm not leaving you, Nick. We are legion."

"You need to protect Sia," Nick growled while Michael's hands were starting to glow brighter and brighter. "She can wake me up, you idiot, but she can *die*." He turned to meet Sam's eyes, nothing but determination on Nick's face.

"Let's go," Luke hissed, daring to grab my arm, but it was already too late.

Mike thrust both palms out, and behind him, the other angels did the same. My one mistake had just become even bigger as the wrath of at least a dozen angels rained down on us in the form of sprites. Big ones, little ones, and all sizes in between, the angels cast them at us, knowing we could either defend against the beasties or defend against their masters, but not both. The one thing they didn't count on... was me.

That was my aether. This was my mistake. For my entire life, I'd had to learn how to fix it when I screwed up, and I was damned good at it. So I pulled. I pushed. I waved them away while beside me, my friends hacked and slashed at them. Luke threw something white – I didn't get the chance to see what, but it flashed like a strobe. There was just one problem.

Mike wasn't stupid.

He must've been able to feel the drain, because his only target was me. Beelzebub did his best to block and deflect, but I was busy. I had to get that stupid archangel out of play or we'd all end up regretting this. Changing my focus, I ignored the rest and reached up, calling to only the life inside that one arrogant asshole, just as he threw something big.

"No," Nick yelled, launching into the sky.

The something was hideous, green, and about the size of a big dog. Nick grabbed it, but the blob was still forming, growing teeth as I watched, then arms, legs, and wings. All of them had claws, and every single one found a home in Nick's flesh. A leg slashed at his wing, tearing through the flight membrane. A hand hacked at his chest, marring one of the wards. That wasn't the worst. I watched in shock as long, sharp teeth buried themselves in the uppermost bone of Nick's other wing and pulled.

Then Sam vanished from beside me, just to reappear in the air by Nick. An ethereal dagger in his hand plunged into the sprite as he wrenched it away, but he was only one man. He'd removed the beast, but Nick's wing was useless and gravity was more powerful than wishes. Nick fell, crashing into the plush moss that had been an amazing bed only hours before – and didn't move.

"Nick!" Sam screamed, dropping down at his side.

Me? I didn't bother screaming. I couldn't quite find any tears to cry. All I had was rage, and it was fueling something deep inside me. Something that rumbled, begging for release and all it needed was a form. Nick had asked me once if I could kill a butterfly and I'd said yes, to save the rest. Well, right now, I couldn't think of anything more perfect to extract my revenge.

If a sprite had just killed the man I loved, then I wanted a million sprites to make them pay. Every drop of aether I'd stolen from those angels went to fuel it, burning when it rushed out as a mass of delicate blue and black wings. Perfect, beautiful little monsters to make those assholes pay, I made them in droves with no other desire than to consume the flesh of angels. Not demons, not dragons, and certainly not of humans. They only wanted the sweet metallic skin of angels, and I ordered them to continue until they couldn't find any more.

"What the –" Luke gasped as he ducked under my surge of blue to rush for Nick.

Bel's response was even better. "Damn," he breathed.

But Mike couldn't see the threat. Butterfly after butterfly appeared, some bursting from my body while others materialized in the air beneath our ledge, and the idiot laughed. He dared to *laugh* at the most beautiful and harmless looking weapon he'd probably ever seen. That is, until the first one reached him, because my butterflies weren't like any others.

Those tiny little bodies and harmless little heads opened to be nothing but teeth. Having read too many dark fantasies, I'd made the proportions impossible, the fangs extra sharp, and their appetite unstoppable. Like a lazily flapping school of piranha, my sprites fell on them, clinging with their six sticky little legs, and they began to bite off hunks of metallic angel flesh to keep them going.

"Send them back," Bel yelled over the screams of pain. "Sia, send it all to Angelis!"

Perfect, and all it took was a wave of my arm and the last of that power inside me. I'd been to Angelis. I knew the resonance, and Luke had taught me how to move people to other realms, but never before had I sent so many. I didn't bother to think about it, I just did it, forcing every angel on this entire planet to cross the dimensions whether they liked it or not. The bloating inside me vanished as bodies disappeared right in front of my eyes like candles blown out on a cake. My head felt light, my heart began to race, and my knees crumpled out from under me. Just as I fell into the moss, I realized that the world had gotten a whole lot quieter.

The only sound I could still hear was Sam calling Nick's name over and over. "Satan. C'mon, Satan, take it! Take my damned aether, *please*."

"*N*ick?" I gasped, struggling to get back to my feet. Unfortunately, I didn't have the energy left to do more than crawl. I finally understood what Gabe had felt like when I'd sucked his life out, and it wasn't a good feeling. I also didn't have time to worry about it. Nick was lying unconscious, his head limp in Sam's arms. I didn't even care that my guys only barely looked familiar, all I could see was my boyfriend's lifeless form.

"Is he..."

Feathers rustled as Luke bent to wrap his arms around me. "He can't die, Sia." Without asking, he pulled me against his chest. "You can't say the same. I don't have much, but..."

His hand cupped the side of my face, and I felt it. My own protections were made from Luke's life and they wouldn't keep him out. Oh no, they welcomed his gift of life, and I felt the rush inside me like kisses up my spine, all too personal and so very sweet. I sucked in a breath, but I simply could not ignore that feeling.

"Luke, stop," I breathed.

He bent, pressing his head to my brow. "It's ok, hun. I know it feels weird, but you need this."

"No," I grumbled as he began to push again. "Luke, I'm human. I'm fine. I don't need as... Oh!"

I swear every cell on my skin flushed and reacted when my body reached a sustainable level. There were no words to describe the sensation, but it was sweet, erotic, and so very sensual all at the same time, but my gasp was the sign Luke had been waiting for. With a chuckle, he cut off the flow of life between us and smiled.

"Nick's out, Sam's running on fumes, and I don't have a lot left. You're going to have to pull from Bel, Sia. He's the only one with enough to spare to get Nick awake long enough to key you into Daemin."

I glanced over at the terrifying monster my friend had become. "This isn't enough, Luke. There's no extra aether on Daemin."

"I know, but let's get you in there and then worry about it. The angels won't stay gone for long."

I pulled out of his grasp and stumbled to my feet. "Longer than you'd guess. I sent the butterflies with them and told them to use their meals as fuel to keep going as long as they could."

"Then you may have bought us enough time to fix this. We still need our wounded to be someplace safe."

Ok, he had a point. The problem was that if getting a refill from Luke was that exciting, I wasn't quite sure how this transfer from Bel to me to Nick would go. Talk about making things awkward, but I could handle this. I always did. I was a pro at awkward.

Besides, these were my guys.

"Sam?" I asked as I knelt beside him.

He looked up to reveal beautiful magenta nebulas in his eyes. "I can't get through his wards. He never let me in."

"I know," I whispered, pressing my hand over his on Nick's cheek. "And he told me about long ago, but you can't do this. You don't have enough left."

He nodded. "Sia, he's never been drained before. Not once, and with all these wounds, it's going to take a lot to get him fixed. He's vulnerable out here."

"Yeah." Then I glanced back to Bel. "So let's get him home and safe, first. I swear, Sam, I'm going to take care of the rest, ok?"

He shifted his hand to catch my fingers between his. "I know you will, sweetie. I'm so glad he has you."

I didn't know what to say to that, but I knew how to do something that would help. "Yeah. Bel?"

The big guy knelt down beside me. "Take all you need, Muse."

"No. I'm taking enough for him to get us in, but we need one of y'all to guard our backs, ok? Nick said they'd come at us in the corridor." I looked back to Sam. "When he's safe, I'll get more. He won't sleep more than a few days, I swear."

"Just do it," Bel grumbled, thrusting out his hand.

I took it, pressing my other over Nick's seal, and then I let the life just flow through me. I'd expected it to be awkward, to feel the seductive rush from Bel and the desire of giving to Nick, but it wasn't like that. It was different, maybe better.

This time, I began to understand what they meant about nurturing. It felt like that warm glow in my stomach when I'd saved a kitten, or the contentment found with my head pillowed on my demon's shoulder. This magic I was playing with was life and love, and everything in between. It was responsibility and seduction, care and temptation, all wrapped into one. It felt like what I'd imagined it would be like to have a family.

Nick hadn't been empty, but the damage from the fall had used its own share of his life. He was hurting, drained, and a complete mess, but this was Satan, the one man who had never succumbed before. The moment his body reached the minimum threshold, he gasped, sucking in a deep breath as those starry eyes flew open.

I kept pushing.

"Enough," he croaked, having to force the word out.

"Shut up, Nick," I said and kept pushing. "You have to get me into Daemin. That means you need a little to burn keying the veil to me."

He paused, taking that in, then asked, "Where are the angels?"

"Angelis, along with about a million sprites. I bought us enough time to get through."

Then he looked over my shoulder at Beelzebub. "Don't let her do anything stupid. Her heart's too big for her own good, and not everyone will be happy to know there's a new Muse."

"Then they can come through me," Bel swore.

Nick smiled and grabbed my hand, lifting it from his chest. "That's enough, dove." He groaned at the movement. "Sam? I'm going to need you to help me."

"Always," Sam promised.

Nick gave him a smile then looked the other way. "Luke?"

"I know," Luke said softly, proving he was just behind me. "If things get out of hand, I have the key to the house on Tyrnigg. We'll keep her safe."

He nodded once then finally turned his eyes back to mine. "I love you, Sia. Please don't forget me, and don't trust anyone but your legion. As soon as they know what you are, people will want to use you. I don't want to lose you before I wake up."

"Nick, I'm not going to let you sleep very long."

He tried to smile, but it was weak. "You know as well as I do how plans tend to work out. Just in case, I wanted you to know that." Then, with a grunt, he forced himself to sit up. "Let's take our girl home. Sam, you're driving."

"Arm over my neck," Sam said, carefully ducking his long, antelope-like horns under Nick's shoulder before heaving the guy up.

Nick groaned. I wanted to wince in sympathy when I saw his wing hanging limp behind him. Gashes and scratches covered his body, but most had already stopped bleeding. That didn't mean the flesh had returned to his wing. The mangled bicep, to my eye, appeared damaged beyond repair. It had to be excruciating.

"I got Sia," Luke said as he slipped a hand around me. "Bel, watch our back."

"Can do, boss."

Just as he said that, Sam and Nick disappeared into the corridor. Luke tugged me with him a second later. Unlike the corridor I was used to between Earth and Vesdar, this version lined the veils between Vesdar and Daemin – and it felt different. The light was more purple, where the one I was used to was closer to blue. The winds were less constant but just as strong, making it even harder to balance on the precarious footing. Then there was the silhouette of the world. I'd gotten so used to the impression of Earth on the other side of the veil that seeing Vesdar's cliffs and plains drawn out in greys and muted colors was a bit disconcerting.

Even worse was the color of my friends. Part of that was from the robes that shielded the demons' bodies, but I also knew it showed how drained they'd become. Normally, in the corridor, life glowed in neon colors. This time, my friends weren't nearly as vibrant. We were all spent and tired, and this was the one place it showed more than any of us wanted.

We looked like a motley mess. Luke was the same as he'd been on Vesdar, a weary golden angel. I still had on the filthy dress without any underwear beneath it. Talk about awkward. But the rest of my guys? I was shocked that any of us were standing. We all needed aether, and badly.

Clutching at Sam for support, Nick reached out and pressed his hand against what looked like nothing – until it rippled. Only then did I realize he was touching the Daeminside veil. In here, it was hard to have any perspective on location, but the shimmer of wards, patterns, and symbols that rushed along the membrane allowed me to see just how close the border always was. Just one step inside or outside wherever I was.

"Sia?" Nick asked, his voice sounding strained. "Touch the veil."

Like he had, I pressed my palm to thin air – reaching for the symbols he'd made visible – and felt it. The best description I could think of was Jell-O. The surface was solid but gelatinous, and it shouldn't take much to push through it. Unlike Jell-O, it wasn't cold. No, like a window on a hot summer day, I could feel the heat of the world beyond leaching through. It was nice and comfortable, but made me wonder just how hot Hell really was while Nick mumbled softly beside me in his own language.

It took a moment before anything happened, just like it had with my sealing. First, the power built, aether flowing from Nick into the veil. More symbols lit up and dimmed out. The pattern changed, shifting slightly as I watched. Then his voice grew more insistent. Looking over, I could see Sam straining to hold him up as Nick put everything he had into making his world accept me.

"We got friends," Bel announced, pulling a lightning bolt out of thin air with an ominous electric buzz.

They'd told me about aether weapons, but I'd never had the chance to actually stop and look at one before. Stuck standing against the veil, I couldn't help, so I tried to take it all in, learning enough that I wouldn't screw things up if this ever happened again. It seemed Bel's lightning bolt was really a sword, but not one shaped like anything I'd seen before. If anything, it looked more like something I'd expect a Klingon to have on Star Trek, but I had a feeling he did more with it than just sling it around.

Then Luke moved behind me, shielding me from the newcomers, his arms braced like he was ready to throw. "We've got four incoming."

"He's almost done," Sam said.

Nick, however, was still chanting. The veil was slowly sucking my hand deeper inside, oozing its way over my fingers. If I had to guess, I would say it was accepting me, but we hadn't exactly covered this in Muse lessons.

Then, one of the approaching angels lifted his hand and called out in a foreign language. Luke huffed in surprise and yelled back, "English!"

So the angel changed languages. "We're not here to fight!"

"No?" Sam shot back. "Then what do you want?"

"Amnesty." The man lifted his other hand and kept walking forward like he was approaching the police. "We're from Vesdar, not Angelis. We refuse to fight for Michael."

"So why are you here?" Luke asked.

The guy chuckled. "Um, Lucifer, I just got swept to Angelis, and I want to know if returning home is going to bring down demonic wrath on my family."

All eyes turned to me.

"What?" I asked. "I just pushed *all* angels back to their world."

"Whoa," one of the other angels breathed. "A Muse? Is she Satyr?"

"Human," Beelzebub corrected.

"But she looks Satyr. She has the eyes."

"She's human," Bel said again, but this time it wasn't nearly as nice.

"Ok," the first angel said, waving the other back. "Not that it matters. If she swept the world clear of our kind, then I certainly don't want to fight. We just wanted to make sure you know we have permanently moved to Vesdar and are just trying to take care of the wives, husbands, children, and homes we've made here. We don't want any problems."

Luke leaned back, closer to me. "You ok with that, Sia?"

"Yep." I dropped my voice so only Luke could hear. "And I'd really prefer they go before Nick's done."

"Can do." He sucked in a breath and raised his voice. "The Muse says she'll do her best to keep you out of it, and if you don't come after her or her legion, then we will treat you like the natives of Vesdar."

"All we wanted," the man assured us. "And if you need a rest, your Muse is always welcome in Sayeptal. Just tell the people Phanuel sent you."

And with that, the group all stepped back, returning to their own world as a group. Luke sighed, Bel deactivated his sword-thing, and Nick started talking just a little faster. Now, I could really feel it, but I also saw Nick drooping, like he was struggling to make this happen. I wished I was a little closer so I could give him something but –

Between one thought and the next, the veil gave way. I fell through, stumbling to my knees in a desert straight out of nightmares. And yes, it was hot. The rocky ground was a slate grey color. The sky wasn't quite orange and not all the way red. Instead, it looked like a really intense and vibrant shade of salmon. Then there were the wisps of yellow-orange clouds that were almost the color of marigolds. In its own way, it was pretty, but it also fit the descriptions of Hell a little too well.

Before I could start to worry, Luke stepped through beside me. Then came Sam, holding up Nick on one side with Beelzebub helping on the other. What surprised me was that Nick was still conscious. Barely, but he was hanging on.

I rushed to his side. "Nick?"

"I..." He forced his eyes up. "I need a nap."

I palmed both sides of his face. "I'm sure. Let me –"

"No," he breathed. "Not here. You're going to need your aether to prove you belong here. I'll be fine, Sia."

"He will," Bel promised, shifting his grip to Nick's back. "Sam, you get the Muse, I'll get Satan."

I looked between them, confused. "What? Why?"

Luke thrust out one golden arm, pointing at the horizon. "Those hills? That's Hell, Sia, and the only way in is with wings. We need to get Nick someplace a chajin can't find him, and if we don't introduce you to the council, things are going to get really uncomfortable for us really fast."

Bel chuckled. "They don't like it when Nick goes rogue, but they always like it when he wins."

"Uh-huh," I mumbled. "So I'm dating a rebel. Of course, I am."

With a sigh, I looped my arm over Sam's shoulders, letting my finger trace along his skin. "Hey, I like the pink."

He smiled and I swear his cheeks turned a bit darker. "Thanks, um, just make sure you don't strangle me, ok?"

"Nick took me flying after we left the bar."

Sam's teeth clamped on his lower lip. "With the dragons?"

I bobbed my head. "Yeah. Sam? I'm sorry I screwed this up."

"You *didn't* screw it up, sweetie. You saved our asses back there. No matter what, that's all that matters, ok?"

"That, and getting Nick some aether. Yeah. I just have to figure out how to do that without committing mass murder. He's going to be ok, right?"

He scooped me into his arms and hugged me against his very solid chest. "We'll figure it out. Shame you can't just suck up another hoard of angels."

Then he pushed off. Bel followed, holding Nick to his chest like a sleeping baby with the broken wing cradled under Bel's arm. Behind that came Luke, standing out with his gold skin and white feathers. Under the scarlet light of this place, it was like a fantasy, as if the five of us were flying off into the sunset – which in itself was just crazy, the flying part – but I had a sinking feeling we weren't heading to a perfectly happy ending. From the way these guys were talking, I could see a fight coming, and I was so far out of my depths it wasn't funny.

But there was *one* thing I could handle. Sam had just given me the perfect idea. We needed aether, I didn't really want to kill a lot of people, and Nick hadn't taught me how to tell which were on their last breath or how to reap properly. But I could get into Angelis. I'd just proven I was an aether vacuum, and they'd been collecting slaves and growing trees to make their world more like mine. That meant there had to be a little extra out there I could suck up and bring back to get Nick up and walking again. And whole. Even if Nick couldn't fix himself, I was pretty sure I could do it. How much different could magical healing be than medical illustration, right?

Halfway there, making my big plans took a distant second to the view stretching out before me. The place I'd arrived was in the middle of a massive chasm. Where we were going was one of the walls, and I swear it had to be as tall as a skyscraper. But that wasn't the shocking part. Nope, it was the giant statues carved out of the rock to make two perfectly matched sentinels, complete with bas-relief wings. Each one stood with his mouth open, and I was pretty sure those things moving behind the teeth were men. Demons.

And they were waiting for us.

"Stay close to me," Sam yelled in my ear to be heard over the wind. "I don't know how they're going to take this, but there's never been a woman on Daemin that I know of."

"Never?"

He shook his head, keeping it slight so his horns didn't catch my arm. "Not that I've heard of."

"And a Muse?"

For a moment, Sam didn't say anything, just bit his lips together. "I need to talk to the guys, but I don't think we should tell them."

"So I'm just Nick's girlfriend, huh?"

Slowly, he turned to meet my eyes. "Nick's out, sweetie. He's not exactly able to chase off your suitors."

"Right. How about yours? I mean, you know..."

He looked back to where he was going to land. "I can do that." But the smile on his lips said he didn't mind at all.

Well, Nick said he was ok with this. Hell, he said he was more than ok with it, so for the extent of my stay on Daemin, I was going to make sure I didn't feel guilty at all about pretending to date someone else. At least not too much. Or not where anyone could tell.

But I also didn't plan to stay here that long. They just didn't know it yet. I'd screwed this up, and I already had an idea how to fix it. No matter what, I would not make Nick pay for my mistakes. Not this time, and not ever.

⟨W⟩ e landed on a giant, smoothly-carved tongue before a crowd of wildly colored men. No – demons. Each one had wings, most of them had horns, and just like the people on Earth, they came in all sizes and shapes. Granted, most of them were a little more fit than the average American, but if this was the only way in, then it seemed working out was mandatory.

The guys barely had their wings furled before a greyish colored demon stepped forward, glaring at each and every one of us. Unlike the rest of the demons who looked at my group with respect, this one glared. He snapped out something that sounded like the same language Nick used when sealing me, then braced up before us.

Sam ignored it. "Nick's been attacked, Mammon," he explained as he set me down. "Our home's been compromised."

"Who?" the demon asked.

Sam gestured to the limp form in Bel's arms. "Satan. He's been using Nick on Earth for a few hundred years to blend. Habits."

Mammon, as Sam had called him, shifted his gaze to me. "So you planned to just move your wench with you?" He stepped closer as a cruel smile took over his lips. "Welcome to Hell, my dear. I can only assume you're the reason we're using this disgusting language."

"English," Luke clarified from behind me, "and it is polite."

But Mammon didn't look away. "Fine. I'll give you four a room for your fallen leader, but I get the girl for the night."

"No," Bel said, dropping the word like it was made of stone.

"Come, she clearly likes to walk on the wild side. Let her enjoy a real demon."

I bit my lips together but wisely didn't say a thing. It was harder than I thought.

"No," Bel said again. "Earth has equality now, and she is not a prize. She is our partner, part of our legion."

"A human?" Mammon asked, laughing out the word. "She's your warm, wet hole. Clearly, a good one, if you've shown her your real bodies."

"And she's mine," Sam growled, reaching back to grab my hand with his. "Don't make me pull rank here, Mammon."

"And mine," Luke said, stepping up beside me. "And Satanael's."

Bel shifted Nick in his arms and stormed closer. "She is *our* woman, our friend, and anyone who touches her without her permission will forfeit their aether to Satan."

Mammon's jaw clenched, but before he could say another word, the sound of a deep, rich laugh broke the stalemate. At the back, the crowd began to move, and a form pushed through. People began to murmur in that demonic language, mostly sounding stunned. I couldn't see much, but the spiraling horns on this guy's head were tall enough to look like a pair of masts parting the sea of bodies. When he finally made it through the crush of onlookers, I understood where the myths about the devil's appearance came from.

This man was as red as blood, with hair so dark it was nearly black. The talons on his hands were long and ominous, matching the brick color tipping his wings and tail. He was also huge, and carried himself with an air of confidence, but the most disturbing thing was how he smiled when he looked at me.

"Hello, Sienna. I see you've made friends."

"Uh.." I glanced back to Luke, then over to Sam, hoping for some hint.

"Azrael," Luke told me. "Leader of the people. He rarely leaves this plane."

The red demon smiled at me. "Rarely, but when I heard about you, I couldn't help myself. You have your great-grandmother's eyes, my girl."

"I don't know my parents," I said, shaking my head. "So I have no idea what you're talking about."

"I know." He pushed Mammon to the side and came closer. "I *do* know, child, but I remember her eyes. Her son had them, too, like peacock feathers. I'm sure I told you that when you were little. I used to check on you often. I couldn't stay, but I made sure they treated you good."

"Who *are* you?" I paused. "I mean, I know your name, but we've never met."

He offered one terrifying hand. "Charles Hancock, my dear, when I'm pretending to be human. Your CPS advocate. Like I said, I pulled strings where I could, but your demonic nature seems to be very strong."

"Oh yeah," Luke grumbled.

Azrael chuckled. "Mammon, get my great-granddaughter and our other leaders a place to be comfortable. And so the rest of you know, this girl is *mine,* and I will be offended if she's forced to do anything she doesn't want."

"Your *what?!*" I snapped. Sure, he may know the name of the guy who helped me shuffle through foster homes, but it was going to take a lot more than that before I bought into his story. "Nuh-uh. It's not that easy. You don't get to just claim some relation and think that's going to wipe away all the shit I went through as a kid."

"Sia," Luke whispered as he clasped my shoulder. "We need to get Nick comfortable. He's still conscious."

Hearing that, Azrael's head whipped around to Mammon. "*Now!* I don't care how much you want his position, Mammon, *he* has earned it – so treat him like it! The first legion will go with him, to make sure Satan is cared for properly. Anything the rest of you want with the leaders of smiths and warriors can wait until they are rested." Then he offered me that hand again. "Sienna and I have things to talk about."

Again, I ignored it. "I go with Nick."

Azrael's eyes narrowed. "I see. So that's how things are, is it? Hmm." He took a breath. "Lucifer, would you care to join us? To make sure I don't do anything nefarious to my only living descendant?"

Luke leaned closer to my ear. "Sia, he runs the show inside these walls, and we don't need to make waves until Nick can fight his own battles."

"Fine, but I'm not going anywhere alone." I turned to Sam. "Please take care of him?"

"Always, sweetie." He glanced back, paused, then lowered his voice. "Az is ok. I don't know anything about him having a kid, but he's always respected our decision to work offworld. Just keep Luke close, ok?"

I grabbed the last two fingers on his hand and squeezed. "Promise. I also know how to go home."

"I'll make sure Bel knows." This time, he did the squeezing before he pulled away, gesturing for Bel to carry Nick wherever Mammon led.

I shifted closer to Luke. The two of us were the outsiders here, and it was impossible to miss that. His golden skin and feathered wings. My boring human appearance. Both of us stood out like sore thumbs, but Azrael didn't seem to mind at all. Instead, he offered me his arm like a polite gentleman. When Luke nodded, I finally accepted, letting the red demon lead me deeper into the mouth of this strange place. Unfortunately, we weren't going the same way they'd taken Nick.

I knew he'd be ok. They swore he couldn't die, so at worst he'd just lose consciousness and sleep for a really long time. That didn't mean I liked it. That was *my* man back there, who'd taken the hit meant for me. The sprite that had torn him apart had been thrown at *me*, but I'd given the angels raw power. No matter how hard I tried to push that aside and keep going, panic and worry kept twisting in my gut.

"This," Azrael said, oblivious to my inner turmoil, "is Hell, as I'm sure you've been told. Just like the angels have a city named Heaven, it's where most of our people congregate, but it's really just a city. Ours happens to be built into the side of a cliff."

Burrowed out of one was more accurate. The halls of this place were huge, rounded at the top, and completely solid. There were no windows, no doors that I could see, and only a strange illumination that leached from the stone. As the number of bodies around us thinned out, I tried to look closer, and Azrael noticed.

"It's a bioluminescent bacteria, or close enough for that word to work for you. What little aether makes it into the atmosphere is ingested by these things, so it serves two purposes. The first, of course, is light. Secondly, we're able to use it as a battery in the event we run out of other sources."

"Right." I filed that in the back of my head. "And where are we going?"

"My rooms... I suppose you'd call it a suite. Because of the weather, most of us prefer to live deep underground, so we all keep rooms here. Then there are those who live outside Daemin, like your friends. We have guest rooms for when they return, but many of those are taken with the unconscious. Have your friends explained that to you?"

"No aether, no wakey. Yeah. That's why we need to get Nick some help."

Azrael glanced down at me. "There is no extra aether here, and

I'd rather we talk about the rest in my room, child." With a smile, he patted my hand on his arm.

Yeah, that really was as creepy as it sounded. This demon acted like an elderly grandfather but he sure didn't look like one. To my eye, he appeared no older than Sam or Nick, maybe in his mid to late twenties, but I knew that didn't mean anything. He'd been around since the dawn of time, just like they had, yet my brain refused to accept the idea of someone so young as my father, let alone great-grandfather.

After a few more turns, I finally saw the doors that had been missing from the other hall. Azrael went to the first one on the left and pressed his hand to the center. I heard a click just before he nudged it open and gestured for me to go first. I did, half expecting some kind of trap.

Instead, I found a beautiful room filled with furniture I couldn't begin to describe. Nothing was quite like what we had on Earth, yet all of it was close enough to be recognizable. Then again, it made sense. Chairs with backs wouldn't work with wings like these guys had, nor would couches. The tables were taller, but so were the chairs. The one thing I didn't see was a bed. It actually made me feel better about being in here.

"Make yourselves comfortable," Azrael said, heading to a counter at the side. "I'm sure you won't find our water palatable, but maybe wine? Ale? Um..." He opened one of the doors and rummaged inside. "Pamplin juice?"

"She'd like that," Luke said.

I gave him a shocked look. "I will?"

"From Vesdar. Sorta like kiwi juice, if I had to describe it."

"Sure." I looked up and accepted the glass Azrael offered. It was chilled, as if the beverage inside had been refrigerated. Interesting.

Luke got something else that was a lot thicker and almost golden colored. "Wine?" I asked.

"No. It's made from rotten leaves. They call it tariklak." He took a sip and sighed like it tasted good. "We do things a little different when we can't grow the organisms to ferment our drinks."

"Oh." Well, ok. I guess that made sense, but it sure sounded disgusting. "And it's good?"

Luke offered the glass. I put mine on the table beside me and sniffed at his, then took the smallest sip. Surprised, both of my eyebrows shot up, and I took a bigger one before handing it back. The drink was very natural-flavored, almost like lemon water, being neither sweet nor sour. Curious now, I reclaimed mine and repeated the process. If anything, it tasted more like honeydew melon juice than kiwi, but yes, it was very good.

"So," Azrael finally said as he eased himself into a monstrosity of a chair. "Who thought it was a good idea to bring the Muse to Daemin?"

Talk about cutting through the bullshit. Damn. Evidently, behind closed doors, Azrael didn't mess around. "That was Nick," I explained. "It seems I'm in a little danger out there."

"And you might be in even more here." He gestured to the far wall. "Out there are almost two hundred desperate demons who know we're losing this war. You think they won't sell you off for a few centuries of peace?"

"You really think the angels will follow through with any of their promises?" I countered. "Because I don't."

We both looked to Luke. "Don't ask me," he hissed. "I fell out of favor over there a *long* time ago."

"Well, believable offer or not," Azrael told me, "some of these guys would risk it. Besides, it's not like they'd lose anything."

"Except the one person who can seal the angels on their own world," I pointed out.

Azrael paused, his eyes growing a little larger. "I'm sorry. What?"

"Sam – er, Samyaza – said that was a dream around here, to lock the angels away so this crap would stop."

"Yes, but how exactly would you do that?"

Luke gently touched my knee, halting what I was about to say. "I want to hear more about your connection to Sia before she answers that."

Azrael chuckled. "Of course. I'm afraid I won't be able to convince you completely, because what little I know only barely convinced me, but I'll tell you what I've been told." He leaned forward, letting his wings relax behind him, and flicked his tail into his lap. "About five thousand years ago, give or take, I used to vacation on Vesdar. It's a close hop from here, and having so much available water is amazing. Well, I met the most impressive woman." His starry gaze dropped to the ground, and he smiled at the memory. "Her hair was as dark as a shadow but her eyes were as brilliant as the tropics on Earth. It took me nearly seventy-five years to convince her I was serious."

"To sleep with her," Luke clarified. "Azrael's English is a bit antiquated, and I'm willing to guess he doesn't know most modern colloquialisms."

"Gotcha." I gestured for the demon to keep going.

"Lucifer is right, but the point is, my attentions eventually brought us a child. A little boy. We named him Therion, and he had a scarlet mane and his mother's blue-green eyes. Oh, he was the light of my life for many centuries, but about fifteen hundred years ago, the angels came. I thought he'd died and mourned him with the loss of his mother. That is, until I got a message."

"How?" Luke asked. "From who?"

"I don't know from whom, but it was left on Kacira's grave. Just a small bit of weaving that told me my line had continued on Angelis, and if I wanted to know more, to leave my mark."

"Mark?" I asked.

Luke tapped his chest. "The innermost symbol."

"It's a signature that can't be faked," Azrael explained. "Well, of course I did, and came back the very next day. This time, it gave me a location on Earth. Now, I have no idea how long that message had been waiting for me, since I don't leave Daemin often, but of course, I went to the spot. I expected to find an angel, or maybe another demon. What I did not expect was a common human house with a few dozen foster children running around the yard."

I sucked in a breath because I remembered that. "I was like eight!"

"Yes, and I recognized you immediately. That long, elegant neck of yours is proof that your ancestor was a satyr. Sadly, I don't know what came after my son was taken, but the message said Therion was your grandfather. Needless to say, I did what I could to make sure you were treated well and raised properly, but I'm not a skilled smith or a warrior to make anyone obey. I'm just a politician here, and that doesn't help much on Earth."

"So you just left me?" I asked.

Azrael shrugged. "What did you want me to do, child? Bring you to live in Hell? No, these demons would have been too tempted. Never mind that I saw your power. Even at that age, you were a natural with the type of physics humans don't even believe exist. No, I tried to wean you off it, showing you how to live without the aether you'd already grown to love like an addiction. What else did you think those meditation games were for?"

"My temper," I grumbled. "So why didn't you send a smith to train me?"

He tilted his head slightly. "And show the angels exactly what you are? Let some idiot crush your natural ability with the rules we use in our own workings? No, my plan was to wait a few more years, until after you had your degree, then bribe Ronwe to travel to Earth."

"Who?" I asked.

Luke chuckled. "He's a scholar. A master of aether theory."

"Mm." That sounded rather boring. "Is he as good as Nick?"

The two men beside me shared a look. Azrael shook his head slightly and Luke chuckled, shifting a bit in his chair. "He's got better theory but less practical application," Luke explained.

"Nick's made a name for himself with the things he can pull out of his ass when he needs to."

"Lucifer!" Azrael growled. "Language!"

"Not the Middle Ages," Luke shot back. "Trust me, Sia already knows all of those words and isn't afraid to use them."

"Right," I drawled, stopping them before these two could drag this discussion down a path I didn't care about at all. "So you honestly believe you're my great-grandpa? I mean, that would explain why the guys kept saying I was so much like a demon, but what good does it do me? I'm here, with my legion, and I have no intention of just sitting back and watching angels screw up everything I care about. Why does any of this matter?"

"Your legion?" Azrael countered. "Child, legions are for demons."

I lifted my chin and met his darkened eyes. "And you just said I'm part demon. Guess I'm right where I need to be." Then I gulped back another drink of the juice and pushed to my feet. "I need to check on my boyfriend, Gramps. Want to show me the way, or should I just assume Luke knows?"

"I know," Luke assured me, taking his time about standing. "Azrael, give her time to think about this. Sia may be young, but she's not foolish. From her perspective, everyone here is a stranger, and the last thing Nick told her was not to trust anyone."

"Ah," Azrael said as he also stood up. "Well, that makes a lot more sense." Then he paused. "Can I at least have a hug, Sienna? Just once, because your kind lives much too fast, and I don't want it to be something I regret."

"Your call," Luke said, "but he can't do anything."

Which meant there was no reason not to, so I opened my arms and made the offer. I swear I saw the tension drain from Azrael's body as he stepped into me, pulling me against his broad chest to wrap his arms around my back. Then he bent his head to press against the top of mine, but I didn't expect the wings or tail. It seemed that when a demon hugged someone, they did it completely, and the craziest thing was that it actually felt good. It felt right. Hell, it felt like something I'd spent my entire life wishing for, but I wasn't ready to start playing house with a complete stranger. Not yet.

"Thanks, Gramps," I muttered as I pulled away. "Even if you aren't really my distant relation, it's still nice to think you could be. Weird, but nice."

He chuckled. "Well, after talking with you, I'm more convinced than ever. Go check on your husband, child."

"Uh... boyfriend. We are *not* married." And I wanted to make it clear that I wasn't Nick's possession.

Azrael's brow furrowed. "But you made it sound as if..."

Luke caught my arm and guided me back. "They do things differently in modern times, Azrael. The first legion is her family, just go with that."

He nodded. "Well, I couldn't think of a finer group of men for her. You all have my blessing."

I opened my mouth to let him know I needed nothing of the sort, but Luke squeezed my arm. Hard. It hurt just enough to make my lips snap closed again as the angel turned me for the door. "I will be sure Satanael knows. Thank you for giving her protection."

"You're welcome, and I do expect you to do the same."

"Of course," Luke promised, but the moment we were through the door, he added under his breath, "Just try and stop me from doing anything else."

"*L*uke?" I asked when we were a few steps from the door.

He shook his head and pulled me along, stretching his legs just enough that I had to almost skip to keep up. The problem was we weren't going back the way we'd come. Nope, he was taking me deeper into this strange city, and I was pretty sure I'd never find my way out on my own.

"Where are we going?"

"Where the guests are kept. I want to see if they've done anything to Nick yet."

So I put on the breaks, forcing him to stop. "What the hell just happened in there?" I demanded.

He released my arm with a sigh and turned to face me. "You're sleeping with the leader of smiths, publicly claimed by the leader of warriors – Sam – and just got told you're related to the leader of people. Sia, you're basically demon royalty, and that makes you pretty fucking impressive in this place. Considering that you also have tits and a vagina? Every bat-winged hooligan is going to try to force himself on you because most of them haven't figured out how much things have changed in the last two hundred years."

"They'd try to rape me?"

"I sure wouldn't put it past them. Between trying to gain favor with one group or another, lower your defenses so they can whisk you off to trade for peace, or just being dumb enough to want to screw a woman, anything is possible. So can we please go find the rest and get a little backup? In case you missed it, I'm not a native, and most of these guys expect me to betray them."

"Great. So Hell is even more cliquish than high school. Why am I not surprised?"

Luke stepped closer, pulling his wings tight to his body. "They're good people, for the most part. That's why I joined them, but there's always someone willing to cause problems, and you're important enough that I'm not about to take any risks, ok?"

"Yeah, that's going to be a problem, because I need your help." I leaned back so he couldn't grab my arm again. "I told Nick I'd fix this. I'm the one that screwed this up, Luke, but you? You are the only person on this entire planet. Plane? Who can help me."

His head drooped. "What are you planning?"

I scrunched up my nose and looked into his green-flame eyes. "To get a little aether?"

His eyes closed slowly, and his chin dropped the rest of the way to land against his chest. "Angelis?"

"Yeah. I'd kinda like to go and come back before Sam and Bel even know we're gone."

"And if we don't come back?"

I stepped closer and grabbed his arms, shaking him slightly. "We're coming back, Luke. If we go now, my sprites will do half our work for us. They just lost a good chunk of angels in the corridor. At least fifty. Those will take a while to get back. My sprites should be making chaos in Heaven. We have to go *right now*."

"And your peak?" He gestured to my body. "We pulled down your shields, Sia. Anyone who looks at a map can see exactly where you are."

But I'd thought of that, too. "And they won't expect me to be in Angelis. And if I am? Won't they assume someone caught me? That's why I think Angelis is the only place I can get the aether. Right under their nose. Luke, we have to try."

He groaned. "Nick's going to break both of my wings for this."

"No, he won't."

"Yes, Sia, he will. He said you're only allowed to reap one soul, then you promised to wait. What you're talking about doing is a *lot* more than one soul."

I smiled. "Pretty sure trees don't have souls. We got this, Luke. I just need someone to show me around, and maybe watch my back a little. Please? Pretty please, Lucifer?"

The use of his real name worked. Luke sighed and shook his head, but it was with a smile on his lips. "Well," he finally said, offering his hand, "I guess it's a good thing Azrael decided to give us refreshments, because I have a funny feeling you're about to wear my ass out."

"Oh yeah." I slapped my palm against his and did my best to mimic Azrael's way of talking. "Would you please take me to the closest fairy orchard on Angelis, please, good Lucifer."

He tugged me against his chest and wrapped an arm around my back. "Only if you promise to never do that again."

"Swear."

And he stepped back across the veil.

FROM DAEMIN TO THE CORRIDOR WAS EASY. FROM THE CORRIDOR all the way to Angelis was a trip that took forever. The only reason I knew we weren't lost was because I could feel Luke's arms around my waist, holding me close. Around me, all I could see were swirls of color, shifting from nearly red all the way to a vibrant yellow, slowly, so I had enough time to enjoy each and every shade before it moved onto the next.

Then, without much warning at all, we stumbled onto the fuchsia grass of Angelis, smack between some giant blue trees. I shook my head, trying to regain my bearings, and looked around before pushing off the ground.

"Don't get close to the trees," Luke warned me. "No matter how much they're fed, they always prefer live meat."

"That's just not right," I muttered, but I didn't move closer. "Where is everyone?"

"This is how it is on the outer worlds. We're at a grove on Uriel's lands. He's the only person I know who won't turn us in on sight. Now you want to tell me what we're doing?"

With a devious smile, I pointed at the tree. "I don't want to kill anyone. I don't want to hurt any slaves. My butterflies have probably fucked up most of the angels around here, so I can only think of one viable power source I won't feel bad about killing."

"The trees?" he asked. "Sia, those things are thousands of years old, like giant redwoods."

"And not exactly native." I took a few steps down the middle of the very straight alley. "So no one can get close to them at all?"

"Supposedly, there's a front and a back side, but I've never been able to tell which is safe. Sia, you can't just kill hundreds of trees."

I spun back to face him. "Watch me, Luke. This world, in case you forgot, wasn't supposed to look like this. Everything here, from the trees to the grass, I'm betting, was pilfered from another plane to make yours better without a single care about what happened to wherever they came from, right?"

"Yeah..."

"And it's not like I can just uproot these things and move them, so guess what. A big ol' Sia vortex is going to wipe them out. Now, you can go back home and wait for me, or you can stay here and take some of this aether so we'll have more than enough to put Nick back together since I fucked him up."

His mouth slowly fell open. "Sia, you didn't fuck him up. Mike did that, not you."

"And why did Mike find us? You said it yourself. I dropped my shield. I told them exactly where we were, and Nick paid for it." I sucked in a breath and started walking again. "I just want to leave one standing so I can make a diversion."

"What are you even talking about?" he demanded, hurrying to catch up.

But I'd just found the exact tree I wanted to use. The thing was much bigger than all the rest, standing over them like a proud queen overlooking her subjects. In all honesty, I had no clue if the trees even had sexes, but this one just seemed like a queen to me, and if any of them could survive what I was about to do, I had a funny feeling it would be her.

The trunk was the color of a winter sky on Earth and its leaves were a deep royal blue. Variations in shading traveled up the bark, separating the new growth from the old. Then there were the flowers. Tiny orange blossoms were nestled in between the stalks that held each cluster of leaves, barely big enough to see if it wasn't for the color. The whole thing was warped and twisted like something I would expect to find in the middle of a desert, except for the size. This tree was big enough it would take at least four angels to reach around it, wingtip to wingtip.

It would make the perfect distraction.

"So do they bite?" I asked, taking one single step closer.

"Yes!" Luke snapped. "Somewhere in that trunk is a mouth, and the branches will herd you into it if you get in range."

"Efficient." I stepped back, making sure I was squarely in the middle of the aisle. "So let's get the aether first."

"Right. Sure." Luke sighed. "And please don't forget we're on a timer. If anyone bothers to look at a map right now, it's not exactly a long trip to come catch us."

"And they won't expect me to be dumb enough to come here. I have a feeling the confusion of seeing my peak pointing at Angelis will be enough for us to slip back home." I waggled my brows at him. "But fine. You keep the trees off me and an eye open for anyone passing by. I'm going to see how much aether a forest holds."

I closed my eyes just in time to hear Luke mumble, "One little victory over the angels and she thinks she's unstoppable. Nick's going to pull out all my feathers for this."

"Shut up, Luke."

He mimicked my tone. "Pull aether, Sia."

So I did. With no shields to block me from the world, it was easy. Out here on the angel homeworld, there wasn't a mass of life around every corner to identify and discard from my choices. Nope, the only aether I could "hear" was humming inside the trees around me, the grass at my feet, and the man beside me. The pitch was different from what I was used to, but the theory was still the same, all I had to do was want it bad enough and it should come.

Lifting my lids, I looked at one of the smaller trees beside me and pulled. For a moment, nothing happened, but when it did, I almost stopped. Suddenly, the placid tree writhed. Yes, writhed. Long branches began to thrash like something out of a horror movie and the mouth opened in a silent scream. I honestly felt bad, that was, until the tendril of power hit me. Feeling the emptiness inside me begin to fill, I realized that trees had more aether than I'd expected. At least as much as an angel, and Nick needed this.

But I wasn't used to killing things with my power. I hated the idea and, as the tree's reaction grew weaker, I decided that maybe I didn't have to. Breaking off the pull, I focused my attention on the next. Just like the one beside it, the tree tried to fight me off, but it couldn't reach me.

The first one, however, didn't look so good. Its leaves were wilted and a few had fallen during its panic. I felt bad, but that took a back seat to my guilt over what had happened to Nick. These were trees. Ones that ate people. I figured they owed it to us all to give a little of their bounty back, and if I kept thinking that, hopefully, the sinking feeling in my chest would go away.

Over and over, I drained the trees down halfway. The shocking thing was how fast I was filling up. As the influx of life began to grow sluggish and my body began to feel a bit bloated, I stopped and turned to Luke.

"Ready for a refill?"

He held out both hands. "How much can you hold, Sia?"

I wrapped my fingers around his. "A lot. I'm an aether magnet, remember?"

He nodded. "Then hit me."

I pushed, but it wasn't as easy to do in a quiet fantasy orchard. There was no desperation, only the smallest sense of urgency, and no pull from him using it as fast as I could offer. If I wanted to get this aether across, I had to relax like Nick had taught me. I had to give in and let it happen. But it wasn't.

"I suck at this," I grumbled.

"You're doing it wrong," Luke explained. "Relax, Sia. Don't try to force it. That would be an attack. You have to give, not force."

"Yeah but..." I sighed and released his hands. "We need this aether, and I need to get more. Can you pull it from the trees?"

"Nope. Angel, remember? That's why Mike used sprites to drain us, because we can't just yank it through the air." He smiled and caught my waist. "But I can pull it from you another way. Look in my eyes, Sia."

Without hesitation, I did. Here, in his natural form, they were even more mesmerizing. His pupils were like a portal into an inferno, the flames all emanating across his eyes from that dark center. Yellow at the base, green at the tips, and they danced, lulling me to look just a little harder.

"I can take that excess aether from you," Luke whispered softly. "You want to give it to me. I'll take it to make room for you to have more so we can help Nick. Do we have a deal, Sienna?"

"Mhm."

"Then relax, hun, because I don't want to hurt you."

His palm pressed against my cheek, and he leaned just a little closer. Then I felt it. Like a gentle caress, he coaxed the excess from deep inside me, carefully pulling it into him, and I gave. I did nothing to fight the loss because it felt good. I couldn't have stopped him if I wanted to, just like I couldn't shut up the first time he'd controlled my mind, but this was ok. My problem was that I was afraid of how good it felt, how easy it was to rely on these guys and trust them, and how much I wanted this to really mean more. That was the gate I hadn't been able to open, but with Luke's suggestion, my fears had become no more than a memory in the back of my head.

And I gave. A little sound came from the back of my throat as I pushed a little harder, and his fingers tightened on my jaw. Standing there, staring eye to eye, we kept leaning just a little closer, pressing more of our bodies together as he took what I offered until our lips were almost touching. Letting his eyes close, Luke tipped his head and pulled his mouth away, gently ending the transfer.

"I'm full," he said, but his voice was just a little too rough. "And I'm not going to kiss you when you're mind-fucked."

"Probably a good idea," I mumbled, hoping I didn't look as distracted as I felt. Then, "Wait. Are you saying you wanted to?"

"Yeah, uh..." Luke stepped back. "Aether, Sia. We need to get out of here. They may be distracted, but that won't last forever."

"Right. Um, is there any way you can disappear for a minute or two?" For some reason, I had to fight the urge to smooth my hair into place. "So I can just vacuum up all of this?"

"Not happening," he said, stepping back to raise a dense shield around himself. "Just do your thing. I'm full enough that even if you do rip at my shields, I'll be fine."

"Ok," I said softly to myself, "just the trees. No people, just aether from the world." Then I threw my head back and pulled.

I pulled from the air, from the trees, and even from the grass under my feet. Just like I had with those angels in the corridor, I pulled as hard as I could, trying to ignore the sounds of the branches thrashing much too close to me, but whoever had designed this orchard had done it well. No matter how hard they tried, the trees couldn't reach and the grass wasn't the kind to fight back.

I was almost done, but for every good thing that had happened in my life, something bad always tried to ruin it. This time, it was the sound of screams – and they were getting closer.

"Sia," Luke hissed. "We gotta go!"

Wrenching my eyes open, I stopped the drain and looked back to see the first person run into the orchard. She wasn't human, but I had no idea what race she was. All I knew was that no one had told her about the trees because she was weaving right through the middle of their trunks.

My drain had stunned the trees, but while I watched, one of them swiped a branch out and knocked her closer to the base. That was when I saw the butterfly. Flittering around as harmlessly as any other on Earth, it seemed to be the source of her panic.

"Oh, hell no," I growled, focusing my pull on the tree. "Luke, we have to help these people!"

"No, we need to get you safe."

He grabbed my arm, intending to pull me back, but I yanked free. If there were butterflies here, then the angels wouldn't come after us. They'd keep me safe for a second longer. Long enough to help these slaves.

"Damn it," Luke growled, trying to grab me again. "They aren't your problem."

I took off down the aisle, pointing at the trees. "They are now. Help me or I'll send your ass back to Earth."

That woman wasn't the only one, just the first. Dozens of people were headed right toward me, and most of them were yelling in a panic. If I wanted to keep them from becoming a meal, I had to pull the trees down far enough to make them comatose.

"It only eats angels," I yelled, hoping they understood me. "Don't be afraid of the butterflies, they only eat angels!"

Before I could say anything else, a man grabbed me and shoved me against the trunk of the closest tree, straight through all the branches. "Hush," he whispered, pressing a lavender hand over my lips. "It's not the flitters we're afraid of, it's the angels trying to refill faster than those things are draining them." Then he leaned back and looked at me again, blinking pastel pink eyes. "Kacira?"

"What?" In the background, I could hear Luke calling for me, but I ignored him.

His pointed brows shot up high then crashed down in confusion. "Never mind. You look just like her, except for the hair." The man leaned out and looked across the orchard. "Whoever you are, we need to stay in the trees. There are angels out there."

I jerked my thumb over my shoulder at the trunk I was leaning against. "Rumor has it these things like fresh meat."

The guy chuckled, revealing teeth that were a little sharper than I expected. "I asked them to hide us. They asked me to..." He stopped. "*You* are the one hurting them?"

"What?!"

"The tree says you are the pain."

Holy shit. So this guy talked to trees? "I had to," I insisted. "We need aether, and I didn't want to hurt the slaves, but I didn't kill them."

His eyes grew even bigger. "You're a Muse?"

"And I'm going to guess you're a fairy. Yeah. Can you get me to the big tree?" Hopefully, he wouldn't be too pissed about the draining them thing.

A million expressions flashed across his very expressive face and he tried to hide none of them. "Why? I won't let you keep hurting them."

"I WANT TO SHOW THAT BIG TREE HOW TO PULL HER OWN AETHER. I dunno, maybe it will help the rest?"

He followed where I pointed, then nodded. "Come, Muse."

Grabbing my wrist, I wasn't exactly given the option. This guy was willowy and lithe, but much stronger than me. As he towed me through the branches, across the aisle and right at the queen tree I'd picked out, I saw his wings. Tiny little things, clearly not big enough for flight, but they looked like something that belonged on a dragonfly. Kinda. Even more impressive was the way his shirt was cut low in the back to make room for them.

I also saw Luke grappling with another angel. He didn't say a word, and he was clearly winning, so I decided to just get this done. Then we'd leave, and I'd let him scream at me as much as he wanted to.

I was distracted enough by Luke's fight that I didn't even protest as the fairy led me right to what could possibly be my death. Thankfully, the trees seemed to like this guy, because they didn't move at all. Not even when we both thumped up against the side of the massive one and peered around it to check on the stampede of people still seeking cover.

Yep, I'd have nightmares about this place for a long time, but first thing first. This monster tree was about to get a real nice boost. Reaching down, I rubbed my fingers in some of the dirt at the base – refusing to think of what had made that compost – then used it to draw on the bark. Just a little tornado symbol. That was all I needed, but as I created it with loose dirt and my imagination, I envisioned it as a black hole for the aether in this world, sucking up any loose in the atmosphere but doing nothing to the people and plants around it.

If this worked, the queen tree would become as strong of a pull on the world as me. Hopefully, it would be enough to confuse the angels for a while. If not, then at least she'd be draining their resources. I figured it was a win-win, and worth the risk of staying here long enough to make it happen.

This tree would be stronger and more powerful than all the rest. A safety net for the people enslaved on this world. As I pushed my desires into the art, I felt it happen. The image began to move, slowly at first, and the tree shuddered. It was working!

"She likes that," the fairy said. "She –" He yelped before finishing the thought and ducked away just as a breeze hit me.

I turned to see white wings through the branches. "Luke?" I asked, stepping away from the trunk.

The man landing before me was definitely not Luke. This guy was very, very copper. Not the pretty green patina kind, but the brand new penny color, all shiny and sparkly. Something about him seemed a little too familiar, but he also looked pissed, and from the bites on his arms and shoulder, I had a funny feeling I knew why.

"Why are you *here?*" he demanded, storming closer.

"Get back," I warned, pointing to the tree. "She's my friend." Then I screamed out, "Luke!"

The angel before me didn't seem to care. "If that tree dares to touch me, I will uproot her and leave her to rot." He didn't bother slowing down. Even worse, the branches actually lifted to move out of his way. "Why in all of Heaven are you here?"

"Shit!" I yelped, ducking around the trunk and preparing to slip back to Earth.

Just then, a voice I did recognize called out, "Uriel!" Luke was running to my rescue, his hands engulfed in aether glow. My hero was about to save me.

The copper man didn't stop. He just changed direction and grabbed my arm, jerking me to stand before him. I slapped my other hand over his and braced to pull but didn't get the chance. "Don't ever come back here again, you stupid little girl." Then *he* pushed, and I felt the veil wash over me.

42

The colors moved backwards, but a lot faster than they had on the trip here. The problem was I couldn't stop. I couldn't change direction. For all I knew, I was lost in a corridor somewhere, tumbling around until I was torn apart. Even worse, Nick wasn't exactly in the right shape to come save me, but maybe he'd tell Sam.

I managed to grab the necklace just as I crashed into something very solid, bright, and completely normal. With a gasp, I looked up at blue sky and the front of a lovely green Victorian home. Nick's place. Shit, I was on Earth!

Rolling to my feet, I hurried up the stairs to the porch. I tried the door but it was locked. Luckily, I knew where they kept a spare key. Just as I grabbed it from under the fake stone, I realized I probably could have magicked it open, but this was easier. Either way, I wanted to be inside, and then I had to figure out how to get in touch with Luke. Maybe once he knew I was gone, he'd check here? It was our arranged meeting place.

Out of habit, I locked the door behind me and raced upstairs.

Everything looked exactly like we'd left it, right down to my dirty shirt on the floor. I'd give Luke ten minutes to come back. If he wasn't here, I would go face down that copper-colored freak and find out what had happened to my friend. Worst case, he'd been drained, but I had enough aether pumping through my body to fix that and still make Nick better.

I hoped.

It wasn't like I'd done this before, but if I had to guess, I thought I'd managed to get enough before my stupid-ass butterflies chased everyone into the orchard. Talk about Murphy's Law. My distraction ended up getting me caught. Regardless, right now, I needed to pack a few things for a long stay on a world that wasn't used to women. Most importantly, I needed some god-damned underwear, because mine was still on a beach somewhere on Vesdar.

Yanking the filthy dress over my head, I rushed around the room. First, I found a ponytail holder and tied my copper hair back while I headed to the dresser. I'd just pulled the drawer open when I heard the front door.

"Luke?" I yelled, pulling on a pair of panties at light speed.

Feet thundered on the stairs. "Thank god, you're..." He stopped in the open doorway while I was still clasping the bra, my bare back facing him. "Sorry."

"Are you ok?" I asked, quickly putting everything into place before turning around.

His eyes were on the ground. "I'm fine. Uriel's a friend. He's been saying he's neutral for a long time, but he helps us when he can. He didn't try to stop me from leaving."

"He kinda shoved me through the veils and onto the front yard!"

"Yeah." Luke took a step into the room. "Can you *please* get dressed?"

"Right. You talk, I'll find clothes." Comfortable ones, like my yoga pants, I decided, remembering the weather on Daemin.

Luke dragged a hand down his face as he turned to look at the far wall. "He pulled a few feathers from my wing to leave evidence. The plan is to make it look like I was the one who trashed their forest, and there's at least one malakim who will confirm it. It will make the other archangels think Uriel and I are at each other's throats, which will give him more reasons to seek me out without raising suspicions."

"So why doesn't he just come help the demons?"

"He is. How do you think we know what the enemy's doing? Someone has to be the spy, and Uriel has enough reasons to enjoy his life on Angelis." He paused. "Sia, he threw you out because he was trying to protect you. Uriel's the one who contacted Azrael. He says the story is true."

I pulled a babydoll strap tank on and turned to face Luke. "How would he know?" When he kept staring at the wall, I added, "I'm dressed, Luke."

"Right." Slowly, he turned, letting his eyes move from my feet up to my face. "Sia, Uriel knows your mom. She's not dead."

Not what I expected. Not at all. "She's alive?"

He nodded. "And on Angelis. He said her name is Kacira, after her father's mother, and her eyes are as blue as tropical water."

"Kacira," I breathed, thinking about the fairy. "The guy who helped me with the tree thought I was her. He said I looked just like her except for my hair."

"Uriel said the same. He said you got your father's hair, but I didn't get the chance to ask more. Cherubs were moving in, trying to hide from your sprites. He said he sent you back to Earth, so I came here first."

"So why did he tell Azrael? Why didn't he tell me?"

"I don't know," Luke insisted. "Sweetheart, we need to get back to Daemin before those angels find a reason for us to spend all this aether. Pack what you need, and let's get Nick back on his feet."

"Right."

In the closet, I still had my backpacks for school. I dumped one on the floor and started to walk away but saw my sketchpad. On impulse, I put it and a collection of colored pencils back in my bag, then went back to pile underwear, socks, and more comfortable clothes on top of it. There wasn't room for much, so I didn't bother with makeup. I did, however, toss in a handful of hair bands.

"You want to drive?" I asked, offering Luke my hand. "I've only been there once."

"Sure."

He clasped my fingers and pulled, tugging us both into the corridor I knew so well. Interestingly, we weren't on the second floor. It seemed this almost-plane of existence didn't care about things like that. Before I could ask, Luke shifted his arm around my waist and stepped back.

Twelve seconds. I counted this time. It took twelve seconds before we appeared under a dark crimson sky on the rocks of the Daemin ravine. It was night, but a large red-violet moon in the sky proved that wherever this place was, it was definitely a planet, just like Earth, and yet nothing at all like Earth. I'd have to ask about that later. Right now, I just wanted to know one thing.

"Why did we come back out here?" I pointed up to the faint glow in the distance where the demon statues should be. "And not inside there?"

"Warded," Luke explained. "They set it up that way a long time ago, and I will never be given the keys to just step through the veils and into their house. We have to fly."

I tightened the straps on my backpack so it fit snugly. "Think you can carry me?"

He laughed. "Sweetheart, you're still from Earth. I promise you're not heavy at all." Grinning, he scooped me into his arms to prove it. "Hang on."

Unlike the demons, Luke's takeoff was smoother. Still jarring, and I still squeezed my arms tight around his neck and shoulders, but I think it was the feathers. Where Nick and Sam caught all the air against their leather wings, Luke's had a little give, like a shock absorber. I kinda liked it. Just like I really enjoyed the view from way up here.

"You think we'll get another welcome party?" I asked, yelling over the wind.

"Probably," he called back. "The veil will alert them that someone came through. The problem is going to be your glow."

I glanced at my arm. "I'm not glowing!"

"Yeah, sweetheart, you are. Your aura's a lot more vibrant than normal, and it doesn't take much to guess why. Mine's the same. Outworlders can all see it."

"Is that a problem?"

He shook his head. "I'll make sure it's not, but it pretty much announces that you're a Muse. Hope this is worth it."

"Fixing Nick will be," I assured him. "And Sam, he's not much better."

"Well, the trick will be, once we're inside, not stopping until we make it to their rooms. Time to hang on again."

The words were barely out of his mouth before he tilted his body and changed the angle of his wings to prepare for landing. I was actually starting to get used to this. Tucking my face against his neck, I closed my eyes, shielding them from the dust. Then we were down. As if we'd practiced it a million times, Luke eased me to the ground and stepped around me, catching my fingers in his hand.

Without a word, he started walking farther into the mouth of Hell. People had arrived, just like I'd expected, but they were all staring in shock at the pair of us. Not a single one tried to stop us, some ducked their heads in an almost nod of respect, but I wasn't sure I liked the look in their eyes. Granted, I could just be projecting, because the swirls of space they looked out of weren't exactly the most expressive things in the world.

Just when I was sure we wouldn't have a problem, my least

favorite demon came jogging up from one of the side halls in the throat. "What have you done?" Mammon demanded.

"Get out of my way," Luke snarled at him.

That only made Mammon more belligerent. He shifted to be directly in Luke's path and held up a hand. "Stop, angel. You're only here at our invitation, and it won't take much to rescind that."

A chuckle came from the shadows. "Do not touch my friends, Mammon." It was Bel's voice. "I may have passed my title, but you've never managed to earn one. Back away from my Muse."

"Bel!" I gasped, releasing Luke to rush to him. "Where's Nick?"

The big guy bent enough that I could wrap my arms around his neck. "With Sam. You stupid girl, going to Angelis like that. What were you thinking?"

"Shut up and hug me, Bel."

With a deep rumble, he did. His arms went around my back, his wings around my shoulders, his tail across my legs, and his lips pressed hard on the top of my head. For a moment, he just held me, then, with a heavy sigh, he carefully set me back on the ground.

"When you didn't come, Nick had to check. He saw you on Angelis and nearly crawled out of the bed. I told him I would wait at the mouth for your return, and that our Muse was too strong to be stopped by angels, but he's not happy."

"He will be." I tilted my head up the hall. "Show us where?"

"And the rest of us?" Mammon demanded. "You cannot bring that much aether here and keep it for yourselves!"

I held up a finger to Bel, then turned and stormed toward the grey asshole who'd become a serious pain in my ass. "Let me make this real clear," I warned him. "Those who hide far behind the battle lines in deep dark holes are the least of my concern. There's a war going on out there. I came back to raise a legion. *My* legion, and if you think you're going to stop me, then just know that Angelis is in chaos right now because they pissed me off. If there's any aether left, I'll raise as many demons as I can. Now, do you really want to keep me waiting?"

"Angelis is..." He looked over at Luke. "You went home?"

"That is not my home," Luke corrected. "This is. Now, move."

Bel chuckled when the other guy hurried out of the way, then he pushed himself off the wall. "Follow me, Lucifer."

Without asking – then again, he didn't need to – Bel picked me up like a toy and took off. He didn't get a lot of height, but there wasn't that much space in here to do so. The hallway was just tall enough to let a demon soar over the heads of anyone walking, and only wide enough for one set of wings at a time. When we reached an intersection and he turned, I winced, expecting his wingtip to collide with the wall, but I should have known better. He'd been doing this for a few million years, I reminded myself.

Luke followed behind us as Bel picked every road to take us lower and deeper inside this place. Down, always down, our path was almost spiraling. One block lower, turn left, at the next intersection make another left. Over and over until I lost count and swore I could feel the air pressure changing, but the light never did. Soft and yellowish, whatever microscopic thing grew on these rocks made it all too easy to see how fast we were going.

Then Beelzebub clutched me tighter and put on the brakes. The air rushed from my lungs, my world tilted, and once we were back on the ground, my head was spinning at the sudden change. I grabbed Bel's arm to keep me from staggering.

"Sia?" Sam asked, his voice coming from an open doorway.

I hurried to him. "Where's Nick?"

He pointed to the far wall where a bed was cut in like an alcove. "He slipped under when he used the necklace. It was too much for what he had left."

"Does anyone know?" I asked, moving to kneel at Nick's side.

"No," Bel said from the doorway. "I tried to tell Sam we should take him back to Earth. That's the only way he's going to refill, but it will take years. He said we had to wait for you to come back. That we couldn't leave you unprotected here."

Right. We'd kept my access to Nick's wards a secret, and Bel hadn't been awake when that happened. "Close the door, guys."

Luke did, then leaned against the strange stone-like portal. "You want me to fill up Sam?" he asked.

I shook my head. "I want you full just in case we have problems. Mammon isn't making me feel very welcome. Bel, don't let anyone in until I'm done."

"Sia, he's..."

Before he could finish the sentence, I pressed my palm over Nick's seal and relaxed. This time, I knew why this had been so difficult for me, and I ignored all those stupid worries that ran circles in my brain. It didn't matter if I hated asking for help. These guys were always there for me. I'd done the most ignorant things in front of them, and they still respected me. And when it came to someone to rely on, I knew that all four of them would have my back, but most of all, I could trust Nick.

As I thought it, I began to feel the transfer. My demon. My Death. My lover. The man lying before me was everything I'd ever wanted and so much more. He'd always treated me as a friend and an equal, and all he wanted was my happiness. All I wanted was his, and I'd give anything to make that happen. Even my life.

Nick's chest began to rise and fall, then I felt his pulse pounding against my hand. I kept going until he sucked in a breath and opened his eyes, turning to look at me. A weary smile found his mouth, and he reached up for my hand.

"Sia?"

"I was on Angelis getting aether and causing problems. Just take this, Nick. I have plenty."

"Mhm," he said softly, but he tugged again. "It works better when you kiss me, Muse."

Pinning my hand between our bodies, I did exactly that, not surprised at all when he palmed the back of my head. The kiss was slow, sweet, and lazy, but he was awake to give it, and growing stronger with each brush of our lips. I smiled against his mouth, just happy to know this had actually worked.

"That's enough," he whispered. "Fill up Sam while Luke fixes my wing."

"I can -"

"No," he chuckled. "I'd prefer Luke does this. No offense, flightless one."

"Ok." I pressed another quick kiss on him then leaned back. "But you're ok?"

"Will be." He pointed to Sam. "It works better if you kiss her. Makes her relax."

"Nick," Sam said, lifting his hands. "We've already talked about this."

"And I was wrong, ok? She likes you, you like her, and we think it's hot, so shut up and kiss the Muse. You need the aether."

I couldn't help but think about our conversation at the bar. Seeing Nick kiss Sam was hot. Clearly, that worked both ways. So, before I could chicken out, I stepped forward, cupped the side of Sam's face, and pressed my lips to his.

For a split second, he froze, then his hands found my back and he pulled my hips against his. The moment I gasped, I also pressed my hand on his seal and just gave in. Behind me, I couldn't help but hear Beelzebub chuckle.

"Seems we have the sex Muse, huh?"

"I wouldn't say that," Luke countered. "I think it's more that she's making up her own rules. I, for one, am not going to complain if I ever need a little aether."

"Me, either," Bel agreed. "Almost want to burn what I have so I get my turn."

Sam, feeling a lot more vibrant against me, broke our kiss so he could turn his head and laugh. "Guys? According to her, you have to try flirting first. She told me so."

"I need to learn about flirting," Bel grumbled. "I don't want to be the only one she doesn't kiss."

Luke slapped his arm. "In case you missed it, Beelzebub, those two are the only ones getting any."

"Yeah, but you have feathers. That shit's just gross."

I jerked my chin at Luke. "I like his feathers."

"Right," Nick drawled, sitting up. "Luke, fix my wing. Bel, open the door. Sam?" He paused, turning those starry eyes to the ground. "Thanks for taking care of me."

"Always," Sam promised.

Nick glanced up, then turned his eyes to me. "What comes next, dove?"

I leaned against the strong chest beside me, letting Sam's body hold my exhausted ass up. "We wake up an army. As soon as you're feeling better, I'll give you as much of this as you can hold, and you can teach me how to do it without kissing all of them."

"How about you just kiss us and we'll handle the waking?"

"Sounds good to me," I agreed. "Because when we're all out of the good stuff, I know a few hospitals, and someone said he'd show me how to reap the dead. We need an army, Nick. I just pissed off a whole lot of angels, and I'll be damned if I'm going to give away that advantage."

"I hear being damned isn't a bad place to be," he pointed out.

I nodded in agreement. "Y'all know I spent my whole life wishing I could just be normal? Dreaming of the day I would be able to take care of myself?"

"Sia..." Nick said.

"No," I assured him. "Nick, I was wrong. I don't want to be normal. I want this. I want to be something magical and special. I want to change the world – or five. Most of all..." I paused, looking from one guy to the next. "More than anything else, I just don't want to mess this up."

Sam slid his wing around my back. "You can't, sweetie."

"No way am I letting that happen," Luke promised.

"We won't let you," Nick assured me. "We're your family – *your* demons – and I've worked hard to teach you that the only limits that matter are the ones you make yourself."

But it was Bel who said it best. "You're our Muse, baby. *Ours.* No matter what happens, we aren't ever going to let you dump us. Not even if I'm bad at flirting."

"Not for millions of years, at least," Nick added. "Sorry, dove. Welcome to the first legion of daemoni. Membership is for life."

EPILOGUE

*L*iving with demons was weird. After two weeks in Hell – which still made me pause when I thought of it like that – I'd finally learned my way around, but I still didn't quite understand the men on this plane. Probably because I was the only girl on the entire planet. I'd learned that tidbit last week in my theory lessons; each world really was a planet. Some were bigger, others smaller, but they all had the same gravity because of the physics variances across the planes.

Speaking of lessons, I rapped at the door. "Ronwe?"

"Come in," he called through the stone. "It's unlocked."

I used my shoulder to nudge it open and my foot to ease it closed behind me because my arms were full of paper and pencils. "Where can I put this?"

Ronwe looked up, revealing the mangled side of his face. "Take the table, Sia. Nothing on there is important, and you're early. Any special reason?"

"The guys are flying." I could hear the pout in my own voice. "Working out combat moves with the ones we woke up. I can't play until I figure out how to get wings."

He chuckled. Of all the people on this world, he was the only one who understood how much it sucked to be flightless. His entire right side was deformed. He said that was how he'd come to be, but he was as stuck to the ground as I was. It also kept him from actually using the theories he'd spent his very long life perfecting. Not only was his body mangled, but also his ability to manipulate aether in quantities large enough to matter.

"Soon, little one," he assured me, just like he always did, "you will get to enjoy that as well."

I nudged his papers to the edge and let mine drop onto the tabletop. "You know I'm starting to get sick of hearing 'soon' all the time, right? How can I reap the dead if I can't even get out of this city?"

"Then learn faster, Muse." He smiled. It was crooked because of the scarring on his face, but still sweet. "Relying on your emotions may have worked to get you here, but if you want to be a master aethersculptor, you're going to need skill as well."

"Right now," I pointed out, "I'm a little more worried about being stuck in a city where the only exit is a hundred feet above the ground! Wings, Ronwe, are my top priority."

"And that means you need skill to get them, Muse" he countered. "So far, all you have done is panic and react. Not all worlds have an abundance of life available for you to waste it frivolously. Before you can create your skin, you must learn the limitations of your abilities. I'm sure none of your lovers would want to kiss that visage you made yesterday."

"They aren't *all* my lovers. Just Satan," I grumbled to myself, because he knew that. He just liked picking on me about it.

And the visage he was talking about was my self-portrait. Faces had always been hard for me to draw, except Death, but I'd mostly concentrated on his mouth. When I tried to make my own portrait, I'd ended up with two different sized eyes and a warped nose. From what Ronwe said, the lack of aether here meant I had to actually draw like most normal people on Earth, not just imagine what I wanted, because my super-special powers didn't have any oomph to make it better.

And this sucked.

When Nick had offered to strip my powers, I'd made the right choice by saying no. It seemed half my artistic talent really did come from aethersculpting, as Ronwe called it, and that was built from my emotions. I saw what I wanted something to feel like in my mind, and my powers made it happen from my hand. It was also why my art had a tendency to fall off the page, because it had never really been *on* it to start with.

"Ok," I reluctantly agreed. "I know you're right, but I really want to learn how to fly."

"Then maybe you need to stop always doing what you're told and start looking for answers that fit *you* better. Sia, why are you drawing your face if all you need are wings?"

"What?"

"And a tail." He winked. "Hard to steer without one of those, unless you plan to have feathers like Luke?"

I adamantly shook my head. "No feathers. That crap gets everywhere! I found fluff in my pajamas this morning."

"And what was Luke doing in your pajamas?"

"He wasn't! That's kinda my point."

"Mm." Ronwe leaned a little closer. "And what would Satan think if he was?"

I groaned. "Don't tell me you have the hots for him, too?"

"Satan?" Ronwe asked. "No. Lucifer, on the other hand..."

"Seriously?"

"Unlike you," he said, lowering his voice, "I happen to like feathers just fine."

Catching his eye, I flipped a few pages back in my sketchbook. "Ever seen Raphael in the nude?"

"No, how did you..." He sucked in a breath when I reached the picture from my Drawing class. "Angels always have the most beautiful bodies. I don't know why they have to be our enemy."

"Me, either. Might be because they all seem to be dicks." With a sigh, I moved back to the outline of my ideal demonic form that I kept trying to perfect. "So how do most demons make their skins anyway?"

He eased himself down onto the bench across from me. "They build it layer by layer, from the inside out. It takes many years to complete, and if they stop for too long, it will begin to degrade before they can slip it on."

"Like a shell?"

"Like a skin," he corrected. "The final part of crafting is to convince the body's molecules to trade places, using the skin as a framework to organize around."

I nodded, seeing how that would make sense. "So how do angels do it? Luke said they can't build things like demons, but they all seem to have skins?"

"Ah." He braced his left arm on the table and leaned against it. "They work from the outside in, starting just under the skin and forcing the molecules to change as they go. I can only assume it would be a very painful process, but no one has ever wanted to talk to me about it."

"Right," I mumbled. "So where *does* it go when we change worlds?"

He chuckled. "The same place the rest of you goes. Every atom is exchanged. That means you have a whole new body in every single world. A skin is just directions for the molecules to follow."

"So, on Earth, Demons really *don't* have wings?" I asked.

He nodded, smiling like I was a very good child. "Exactly! They've been amputated from the body's blueprint. You can imagine the bravery it took for the first demon to do that." He shook his head in wonder. "He risked being flightless forever, but it worked."

"Uh..."

Ronwe waved that away. "For your human mind, just imagine

that you're making a body on each world and transferring your consciousness into it. Probably easier that way."

"But is it true?"

"True enough." He sighed and rubbed at the bridge of his nose. "The manipulation of aether alters the patterns of life. To you, it's magic. To us, it's science, but either way, there are still rules that we *will* teach you. You just have be patient enough to learn each step, and not try to rush right to the end."

"Ok," I mumbled. "So you're saying I need to learn more before I can get a set of wings, huh?"

He shrugged, using all four of his upper limbs to do it. "I'm saying that you're more than an aether vortex, Sienna. That trick may have worked once, but if you want to be a force of change, then you need to *create*, not just imitate. Be an artist. Your power is tied to your feelings. Photorealism isn't the only style. Try stipple, impressionistic, or even postmodernism. A style based on *emotion*. Create what you feel, and trust that it will work. *That* is how your talent works. Once you wrap your mind around that, you might be able to finally fly."

I chewed on my lower lip around a growing smile. He was right. That bird on my notes that Nick had stopped me from finishing? I hadn't drawn the lines. I'd just felt like I was soaring because of his attention. The infamous pencil? I'd been trying to convince myself to be studious, not distracted by guys.

Now, when it came to the body I'd probably be wearing in this world for thousands of years, I knew exactly what I wanted. Beauty. I wanted to make sure that my legion had eyes for only me. I also wanted to be strong enough to handle everything that would come at us. Most of all, I wanted to just be me.

"Ronwe?" I asked. "Do you have a mirror?"

"Mm." Pushing himself up, he gestured for me to follow. "In here."

Here was his bedroom, and it was a complete mess. Along the far wall, however, was the one thing I needed. The mirror was bigger than what I was used to. This one was a large square, at least six feet on both sides, with plenty of room for a demon to check out not just his body, but also his wings.

"Here goes nothing," I said softly.

"Wait," Ronwe gasped, holding up a hand. "You will need to disrobe first. Your clothing is not made for a tail, let alone the wings."

I looked at him in the reflection, lifting an eyebrow. "Uh-huh. And if this works, what the hell am I supposed to wear? Not like you all bother with shirts!"

He stepped back, easing his way out of the room. "I know where to get a fae shirt. Please do not break yourself while I am gone, Muse? Satan would never forgive me."

I chuckled as he closed the door, then listened to him limp across his main room and out into the hall. Only then did I strip off my workout clothes and look in the mirror again. I could do this.

I also needed slightly bigger boobs, and I wished my nose was a little – No. I wouldn't do that. Wings and a tail. I wanted to be me, and I wanted to fly. Staring at my own image long enough to burn it into my mind, I closed my eyes, repeating that over and over. Just wings and a tail. I wanted to be me, but able to fly. My guys didn't care about my pale skin and orange hair, they just…

Fire seared my back, and my ass hurt. A lot! Biting back a scream, I crumpled to my knees, but I wouldn't stop. *I wanted to fly!* Nothing would take that from me. Not a little – or a lot – of pain, and certainly not a lack of willpower. Trying to ignore the feeling of my body being pulled out from my spine and tailbone, I concentrated on the fantastical image of myself as a demon.

When the pain stopped, I was lying on the floor of Ronwe's room. The first thing I saw when I opened my eyes was a copper tipped tail, complete with the metallic shimmer like Luke's skin had. I smiled and flopped back, then sat right back up when I landed on an extra set of *something.*

Trying to look sent a wing out to my side, clearing the top of Ronwe's bed. The pale ivory skin and copper edging proved it belonged to me. Even worse, the shock made my tail lash. I paused for a moment, mostly in confusion, then realized the one very big problem in my grand idea: I had no clue how to operate this many limbs.

But I knew someone who would.

Grabbing the comforter off the bed with one hand, I pulled it across my naked body while my other clasped the blue diamond hanging from my neck. *Satanael,* I thought. *Gonna need a little help here, so I need you, Satanael.*

Less than ten seconds later, the outer door to Ronwe's suite burst open and feet stormed in. Lots of them. Clearly, he'd brought some backup.

"Sia?" Nick yelled.

"In here. I'm fine, just need some help getting up."

He shoved open the door and rushed in, stopping at the end of the bed. Behind him, Luke, Sam, and Bel spread out to get a better look at the pathetic thing lying helpless on the floor. All I could do was cock my head in a fake shrug.

"Um, I got wings, and I have no clue how to get up without breaking everything."

"Damn," Sam breathed, moving a step closer. "Our Sia just made herself into a succubus."

I rolled my eyes. "Just a demon, guys."

"Nope," Bel chuckled. "Succubus. She even has the sexy wings."

Luke reached up and patted Nick's back. "So is she all you hoped for?"

"Yeah," Nick breathed, nodding his head as if dumbfounded. "Our Muse is perfect. Now we just have to teach her to fly."

I lifted a hand. "Can we start with walking? Maybe standing without breaking one of my new limbs?"

"We can start with anything you want," Nick promised. "So long as that includes some clothes."

BOOKS BY AURYN HADLEY

Contemporary Romance: *Standalone Book*

One More Day

End of Days - Auryn Hadley & Kitty Cox writing as Cerise Cole (Paranormal Reverse Harem):

Still of the Night

Tainted Love

Enter Sandman

Highway to Hell

Gamer Girls - cowritten w/ Kitty Cox

(Contemporary Romance): *Completed Series*

Flawed

Challenge Accepted

Virtual Reality

Fragged

Collateral Damage

For The Win

Game Over

Rise of the Iliri (Epic Science Fantasy):

Completed Series

BloodLust

Instinctual

Defiance

Inseparable

Tenacity

Resilience

Dissent

Upheaval

Havoc

Risen

Hope

The Dark Orchid (Fantasy Reverse Harem):

Completed Series

Power of Lies

Magic of Lust

Spell of Love

The Demons' Muse (Paranormal Reverse Harem):

Completed Series

The Kiss of Death

For Love of Evil

The Sins of Desire

The Lure of the Devil

The Wrath of Angels

The Mimics (Contemporary Science Fiction

Reverse Harem): *On Hold*

Bioluminescent

Iridescent

Opalescent

Phosphorescent

Incandescent

Fluorescent

The Path of Temptation (Fantasy Reverse Harem):

Completed Series

The Price We Pay

The Paths We Lay

The Games We Play

The Ways We Betray

The Prayers We Pray

The Wolf of Oberhame (Fantasy):

Completed Series

When We Were Kings

When We Were Dancing

When We Were Crowned

Wolves Next Door (Paranormal Reverse Harem):

Completed Series

Wolf's Bane

Wolf's Call

Wolf's Pack

ABOUT THE AUTHOR

Auryn Hadley is happily married with three canine children and a herd of feral cats that her husband keeps feeding. Between her love for animals, video games, and a good book, she has enough ideas to spend the rest of her life trying to get them out. They all live in Texas, land of the blistering sun, where she spends her days feeding her addictions – including drinking way too much coffee.

For a complete list of books by Auryn Hadley, visit:

My website -
aurynhadley.com

Amazon Author Page -
amazon.com/author/aurynhadley

Books2Read Reading List -
books2read.com/rl/AurynHadley

Merchandise is available from -
Etsy Shop - The Book Muse - www.etsy.com/shop/TheBookMuse

Threadless - The Book Muse -
https://thebookmuse.threadless.com/

You can also join my Facebook readers group -
The Literary Army
www.facebook.com/groups/TheLiteraryArmy/

Also visit any of the sites below:

- facebook.com/AurynHadleyAuthor
- twitter.com/AurynHadley
- amazon.com/author/aurynhadley
- goodreads.com/AurynHadley
- bookbub.com/profile/auryn-hadley

Manufactured by Amazon.ca
Bolton, ON

19045861R00282